I0525724

CARRY YOU HOME

a novel by

K. Ryan

Copyright © 2016 K. Ryan

All rights reserved.

Cover Design by Paper and Sage

This is a work of fiction. All of the characters, organizations, places, and events portrayed in this novel are fictitious in every regard. Any similarities to actual events and persons, living or dead, are purely coincidental.

No part of this book may be reproduced in any form, including Internet usage, without permission in writing from the author. The only exception is by a reviewer, who may quote short excerpts in a review.

Any trademarks, product names, or named features are only used in reference and are assumed to be property of their respective owners.

Printed in the United States of America.

IBSN:978-0692634479

For my first readers. You know who you are. Thank you so much.

PROLOGUE

Hey Iz,

I honestly have no idea if you've been getting my letters. I think I just want to believe you're reading them, so I just keeping writing. It's weird being in here, where time pretty much stands still, and knowing that life just keeps going on without you. Honestly, writing these letters to you is the only thing that keeps me sane. The only thing that makes me feel normal. The only thing that makes me feel close to you.

If you're not reading this, I guess I can't blame you. If I were you, I don't know if I'd be reading this either. I'm such an idiot, Iz. I know I'll never be able to say that enough. I don't deserve you and I deserve to be exactly where I am. Hell, I'm not even worth this piece of paper I'm writing on right now. I'm kinda surprised they even gave me a pencil.

I miss you, Iz. I miss your smile. I miss your laugh. I miss the way you always bite down on your bottom lip when you get nervous. I miss how soft your hair is when I touch it. I miss your lips. I miss your eyes. I miss the way you used to look at me. I miss everything, Iz.

I wish you would visit, but I get why you won't. I wouldn't want to visit me either. I think if we could see each other face to face, maybe we'd be able to talk this through, and I'd be able to explain better than I've been able to in my letters. You know I'm shit with words, but this is all I've got right now. I wish there was another way I could reach out to you, to talk to you, but since you won't take my calls and you won't visit, you're just going to have to get used to me sending you these letters.

I know what I did. I know how much I hurt you, but I'm not going to give up.

Love you always,

Caleb

Part One

"Wisely and slow,/They stumble that run fast."
—*Romeo and Juliet,* II iii

CHAPTER ONE
Positive

Isabelle

Swirl. Tap. Pull. Twirl. Repeat.

Why was that so hard?

It wasn't.

Not really, at least. The process was simple. The technique was something I'd practiced a thousand times, but the longer I sat here on this stool and stared at the blank canvas in front of me, the less I found myself actually able to concentrate.

I woke up this morning feeling like I'd drank a whole bottle of vodka and swallowed eight fistfuls of sand. All the symptoms of the worst hangover ever were currently conspiring against my body: brutal headache, churning stomach, aching muscles.

Resigning myself to the most unproductive studio practice hour ever, I tossed my paintbrush into the little water-filled mason jar at my side and stretched my arms over my head. Part of me was a little worried that if I moved too fast, I'd be running for the closest garbage faster than you can say morning sickness.

This routine of nausea, puke, and repeat had been going on for a little over a week now and here I was, sitting on my hands and trying to pretend this wasn't actually happening. It wasn't just because Caleb had been in Pittsburgh on a run for the last week, although admittedly, that was sort of why I'd held off on making that fateful journey to my nearest pharmacy.

If this was real, life as I knew it would be over. Life as *we* knew it would be over.

Everything had a time and a place. A house, a wedding, a family, a happily ever after—all that would come when the time was right and we just weren't quite there yet. What was wrong with enjoying the moment and just savoring how good things were now?

What I really wanted to focus on was starting the empty project in front of me and getting my ass back to my apartment so I could prep dinner for tonight when we got back from the clubhouse. Even though, to be fair, my dinners needed to come with an *eat at your own risk* disclaimer.

The last time I made chicken, right before Caleb left for Pittsburgh, the thigh was so rock-hard, he could barely cut through it with a steak knife. It wasn't burned or anything. It was...just the thought of it, the smell of it, and my body suddenly jerked like I'd just been slapped and my throat felt watery and dry at the same time, like something terrible was trying to force its way out of my body. I squeezed my eyes shut as my stomach quivered and groaned and churned and my body swayed backward on the tiny stool. Before I knew it, I shot off the stool, flung open the door of my studio space, and sprinted down the hall.

I didn't make it to the bathroom.

Unfortunately, my head was currently ducked into the first garbage can I could find as I heaved up the little bit of egg sandwich I'd managed to choke down this morning. Everything was a little hazy and I had to crouch down just to keep myself from tumbling right over the garbage can. It felt like someone shoved burning coals down my throat. Everything burned. Everything was shaky. My hands. My stomach. My knees.

Breathe in. Breathe out. Deep breaths. That's all I could focus on right now and I somehow shifted my weight just enough to lean back against the cold wall behind me.

Breathe in. Breathe out. Deep breaths. Breathe—

"Isabelle?"

My eyes squeezed shut at the sound of that all-too-familiar voice, the same one that haunted my dreams, and then, with a wince, I opened one eye and then the other to find my academic adviser staring back at me like I'd just told her Monet was trash.

"Oh hey, Dr. Jacobs," I threw back weakly. "How's it going?"

Dr. Jacobs arched a critical eyebrow my way, but it was nothing I'd never seen before. That woman had a way of twisting my insides around and pulling them out through my nostrils. Every time she entered my university-issued studio space, I had trouble swallowing the vomit that threatened to spew all over my latest project.

Despite her willowy stature, Dr. Jacobs never failed to intimidate me with her eerily silent, detached, and cold appraisal of each stroke. Given the fact that I'd only really tried painting seriously at the start of the semester and with no real professional training, I lived in fear every day that Dr. Jacobs would tell me I wasn't cutting it. Somehow, I'd also let her to talk me into summer classes and studio work to hurry along through the program, as Dr. Jacobs said and right about now, with the semester showcase breathing down my neck in about two months, I really wished I'd opted for the time off instead.

Dr. Jacobs tucked a long strand of salt and pepper hair behind her ear and now, both eyebrows lifted high into her forehead as she appraised me.

"Oh, I don't know, Isabelle," she told me, that faint French lilt floating out with each syllable. "It's not very often that I find one of my students hunched over a garbage can. Care to explain?"

I had no idea what to say. And in between wringing my hands anxiously in front of me and groping for some words, my stomach took charge of the situation and I flung my head, once again, right into the center of the garbage can and puked what was left of my guts out.

A hand gently rubbed my back and swept some hair away from my face. Even in this shitty state, I still couldn't reconcile that this woman, who intimidated me just as much as Skyler initially had, was *comforting* me. Did the whole world decide to go crazy and forget to tell me?

"Come on," Dr. Jacobs murmured to me now. "Let's get out of the hallway, shall we?"

I nodded mutely, allowing her to lead me into the bathroom where I rinsed my mouth out and splashed some water on my face, acutely aware that Dr. Jacobs was watching me underneath furrowed eyebrows even as she handed me some paper towels.

"Are you feeling better, Isabelle?"

I swallowed hard and winced before the words even left my mouth, "No. I'm not. I think I might be..."

Oh God, the words just wouldn't come. Whether it was lucky or not, Dr. Jacobs was already nodding like she'd known what I wanted to say, but just couldn't muster the strength to actually follow through with it.

"Why don't you head on home?" Dr. Jacobs suggested as she handed me another paper towel. "Get some rest. Take care of your business," she paused to give me a pointed look from her reflection in the mirror, "and then email me as soon as you know when you'll be back."

"But I have—"

"I'm aware of your schedule, Isabelle. I made it, remember?" she pointed out, rare amusement playing on her lips and I almost fell over from shock. "If you're unable to come in for your studio hours tomorrow, you'll just have to make them up some other time. You're allowed to be, uh, under the weather from time to time, especially since you're not the type of student to shirk your responsibilities. Go on then," she waved me out the door.

I blinked back at her.

"You heard me," Dr. Jacobs shooed me out the door again, her lips curving up and paralyzing me right into the bathroom's tiled flooring.

Finally, my brain caught up with the rest of my body and took the out she was giving me, speed-walking back to my studio space to grab my bag so I could get the hell out of there.

. . .

Reality caught up to me about two hours later.

I'd been in a staring match with that little purple box perched on my bathroom counter for about a half hour now. Against my better judgment, I hadn't been able to stop myself from taking a detour to a pharmacy on my way home from campus, even though I'd spent the whole 45-minute drive trying to talk myself out of it.

On impulse, I snatched the box off the counter and tore the thing open. I could sit here and drive myself crazy or I could get my answer.

My eyes skimmed over the instructions. Nothing too complicated. One line meant I was in the clear. Two lines meant I was in the shit. No time like the present to find out if life as I knew it was basically over. And with that, I got down to the business of peeing on that stick, set a timer on my phone, and waited.

When the timer on my phone chirped at me in my hand, everything went a little numb as I stood on shaky legs and shuffled over to the counter. I blew out a deep breath, that watery feeling thickening my throat again as I peered over the counter.

Two lines.

Diagnosis? Knocked up.

I shuffled aimlessly backward until my back hit the wall, my heart pounding like a jackhammer in my chest.

Oh shit.

Holy mother of ever-loving shit.

Panic crept up through my throat and squeezed it tight. We were only 22-years-old. We had no business being parents right now, at least not by choice. Not to mention the fact that I could barely scrape together enough money for rent and my tuition. God, I didn't even have my own health insurance to pay for having a baby, let alone actually raising one.

My hands shakily groped for my phone and skimmed to my favorites with my finger hovering over Caleb's number. No. I wasn't ready for that yet. Besides, he was on the road right now and wouldn't be able to talk to me even if I wanted him to. So I hit Skyler's number instead.

The phone rang twice and then Skyler's deep, husky voice answered, "Hey, sweetie. What's up?"

I gulped. "Hey, Skyler. Um, have you heard from Caleb yet?"

Of course she hadn't heard from Caleb yet today. *I* hadn't heard from Caleb yet today. I just needed to kill some time.

"Uh, no," Skyler replied slowly and I could already hear the suspicion in her voice. Great. "Have you? Is everything okay?"

"Yeah. Everything's fine. I mean, at least I think it is. We would've heard something by now if it wasn't, right? I was just trying to figure out what time I should plan on getting dinner going since I know we're going to meet up at the clubhouse first and—"

"Isabelle, I'm gonna stop you right there," Skyler cut in abruptly. "What is this really about? Are you okay? You're scaring me here, sweetie."

I pushed out a deep breath. I had to say it out loud now and then there would be no taking it back.

"I'm pregnant."

It all came out in one whoosh, so fast that I wasn't sure Skyler would even be able to understand me. I glanced at my screen to make sure the call hadn't dropped or something. Nope, Grandma was still there. Oh God. *Grandma.*

"Oh," Skyler finally whispered through the phone. "*Oh!* This is...I can't believe it! This is the best news I've heard in a long time!"

If only the feeling was mutual.

As if she could sense my thoughts, Skyler abruptly changed her tune. "Wait a minute. You don't sound okay. But it's gonna be, Isabelle. I promise you that. This is all gonna be okay, sweetie."

"I don't think I'm ready for this," I choked out and shook my head furiously.

"Honey, first of all, where are you right now?"

"I'm at my apartment."

"Okay," she told me in probably the most reassuring tone she could muster right now. "Good. When did you find out?"

"Just now," I managed to croak out.

"That's what I figured. Now, I understand what you're feeling," Skyler reassured me. "Trust me, I really do. I couldn't even walk I was so shocked when I found out I was pregnant with Caleb. I wasn't even 18 yet and I was an idiot and I thought my life was over and that I'd stolen Connor's right along with it. But he just took everything in stride. He was there for me. He married me. He built a life with me that we lived together until the day he died. So trust me when I say that Caleb is cut from the exact same cloth his father was and after the initial shock wears off, he's gonna do the same thing Connor did."

She paused just for a moment, probably to make sure I was listening.

"Caleb is gonna be all in, Isabelle," Skyler went on softly. "I know my son and I know he's more serious about you than he's ever been about anything in his life. Maybe it's happening sooner than you thought it would, but it's happening now whether you're ready for it or not. You two will figure everything out. You just have to give it a little time to settle."

I nodded slowly and found myself laughing shakily, in spite of the situation. All the tension in the room quickly evaporated and for the first time in about a week, I felt like I could finally breathe.

"You feeling better now, Isabelle?"

"Yeah," I pushed out roughly, but a slow smile still crept across my face. "I'm feeling better. I'm sorry. I just freaked out there for a little while."

"I think that's a completely normal reaction," Skyler chuckled. "And I think that as soon as you get a chance to bring Caleb in on this tonight, you'll be feeling a lot better too. You're just freakin' out now 'cuz you're all alone in your apartment right now, but you're not really alone, sweetheart. You know that, right?"

I exhaled one more time just for good measure. "I know."

"I just can't believe it. I'm gonna be a grandma! Thank you for telling me! So, I'm the first one to know even before Daddy then? Aw, I can't wait, Isabelle. I just can't wait!"

A laugh somehow strangled itself from my throat and despite my initial panic attack, I could feel all my anxiety slowly slip away. And the craziest thing of all? I could feel myself smiling at the word *daddy*.

"Oh, I can't wait to order a little Horsemen onesie for my grand-baby...and stuffed animals. Caleb's favorite was always this ratty little teddy bear that he used to carry with him everywhere. I wonder where that thing went. I bet if I could find it and wash it about a million times, I—"

"Sky," I laughed. "Slow down. There's gonna be plenty of time for all that."

"You're right. I'm sorry. I'm so just excited. I don't know how I'm gonna be able to keep quiet about this when I see him at the clubhouse today."

"You're going to have to," I instructed warily. "So what do I do now?"

It was the first of many questions swirling around, but for now, it seemed like the most imperative one.

"Well," Skyler laughed. "I think you need to just rest. You still sound so tired and worn-out, honey, and I don't want you stressing yourself out. Just lay down. Get some rest. We'll schedule you a doctor's appointment tomorrow and when Caleb gets to the clubhouse, I'll tell him you weren't feeling well and send him your way after he's out of church."

"He's going to be kinda upset if he doesn't see me at the clubhouse right away, you know."

"Yeah, well, he'll get over it as soon as you bring him up to speed on everything. He'll have his undies in a bunch anyway because of tonight..."

"Wait a minute, what?"

There was a long pause on the other end before I finally heard, "Oops."

"Oops, what?"

"Oops, I can't tell you," Skyler told me pointedly. "I'd really like to live long enough to at least hold my first grand-baby, you know?"

"Okay..."

"Don't worry about anything, Isabelle. Like I said, this will all work itself out."

Even if Skyler obviously knew something I didn't, my best bet was just to focus on resting and feeling better. So after I hung up and settled into my bed, I pulled the covers around me and hugged Caleb's pillow, inhaling deeply to try to get a little whiff of that musky, citrusy scent that lingered in his pillow.

He would be home in just a few more hours and then, when I mustered up the courage, I'd give him the news that would completely alter the course of our lives from here on out.

I was having a baby...Caleb's baby. A soft smile spread across my face as a hand drifted down to cover my stomach.

Okay, so maybe I wasn't as completely at peace with it as I wanted to be, but like Skyler said, everything would work itself out.

And besides, finally having a good, peaceful night's sleep next to the father of my baby sounded really good right about now.

CHAPTER TWO
Timing Is Everything

Caleb

With the shop's parking lot in sight, I blew out the breath I felt like I'd been holding since I pulled out of this place a week ago.

Finally.

Home honestly never looked so good. This last run had been a rough one for a couple reasons, but being away from home was easily the hardest part. The entire ride back from Pittsburgh to Claremont just dragged and dragged with each mile feeling longer than the one before it and I hadn't been able to keep the grin off my face since we passed city limits.

The second my bike came to a stop in the parking lot was the second nerves slammed right through me. Tonight was about a month in the making, with some meticulous planning on my part and a lot of help from my mom and now that it was finally within reach, any hint of cold feet just needed to be shoved away. I'd already come this far and all I had to do now was follow through.

But as I swung my leg over the side of my bike and scanned the parking lot for that shiny blonde hair and those long, tanned legs, I just couldn't find her. Immediately, my instincts shot into overdrive as my mind worked through all the possible scenarios to explain why she wasn't here in the crowd of people who'd gathered in the parking lot to greet us. Wouldn't I have a text message on my phone already telling me what was up? It wasn't like her to just not communicate like this and now all the scenarios running through my head took a turn for the worse. My phone was in my hand before I could stop myself and I'd already flipped it open with my finger poised over Isabelle's number when some waving to my left caught my eye.

"Caleb!" my mom called out to me, still waving to me even as she approached me. "I think I know where you're heading, but everything's fine."

She pulled me into a quick hug and pecked me on the cheek. That didn't do anything to calm my nerves.

"Isabelle called me about two hours ago and said she wasn't feelin' well."

All the air in my lungs whooshed out in relief. I knew it was stupid to automatically assume the worst, but what else was I supposed to think?

"I told her to just get some rest," my mom went on with a smirk that made me a little nervous. "The best thing for her right now is just to sleep and she sounded pretty worn-out."

"Yeah," I nodded slowly. "She mentioned she hasn't been sleeping too good."

Now, all my worries shifted and my mind sifted through the conversations we'd had this last week. Even though I hadn't been able to see her, she'd still sounded dead on her feet. The fatigue in her voice...she'd mentioned being stressed about getting ready for the semester showcase. She'd taken on way too much over these last few months and I could only imagine that me being gone this last week hadn't helped.

"She's fine," my mom put her hand on my cheek to my attention again. "Just head over to her apartment once church is done. Besides, this way you can make sure everything's ready for tonight without her getting any hints, right?"

I blew out a breath. Knowing that she was sick, maybe I should just—

"I know what you're thinking, Caleb," my mom told me pointedly. "And I think you should go ahead with your plans. Trust me, you won't be sorry."

"What do you mean?" I frowned.

She just shook her head and wrapped an arm around me. "I'm so proud of you. I really am. Everything is starting to work out, isn't it?" She must've seen the way my mouth dipped down and jumped to change the subject. "So, everything all set then?"

"I just gotta run to the safe in my dorm," I shrugged. "That's all I gotta do. I got the keys and the paperwork in my bike. After church, I'll be all set."

"That's what I figured," she grinned back at me. "Just as a heads up, she's makin' you dinner tonight too."

My lips pulled apart in a wince. I figured she'd planned something like that and my stomach churned a little.

"She really is a horrible cook, isn't she?" she mused.

"I don't know what you're talkin' about, Ma," I shot my hands up in the air in defense. "My ol' lady's cooking is the bomb."

Better to be safe than sorry, you know? I'd have to be hog-tied and dragged for a few miles before I'd ever admit out loud that Isabelle's cooking was the worst food I'd ever had in my life.

My mom just arched an amused eyebrow my way, clearly knowing my game, and shook her head. "Whatever you say. Just let her rest until you get to her apartment, okay? I know you probably wanna call to check on her, but she's fine."

Huh. That was different. And weird as hell. She was trying a little bit too hard to keep from smiling and a little too hard to keep me from calling Isabelle. Luckily for her, I needed to get my ass to church more than I needed to find out what she was up to.

Besides, even though I just wanted to hop back on my bike and speed over to Isabelle's apartment, I needed to get paid first. In light of all these monumental steps I'd taken in my life recently, picking up that money-filled envelope was as important now as ever.

. . .

"Alright, alright," Marcus pounded the gavel to call church to start. "Let's make this quick, huh? It's Friday. We all got places to be. First of all, we gotta talk about what happened on this last run," his eyes settled on me as he spoke, "Caleb, why don't you give us the run-down."

I stared back at my club prez for a split second, acutely aware of the way both Casey and Tiny straightened up a little in their seats across from me. None of us had really expected Marcus to put me on the spot like this, but this was just yet another test and another way to prove myself.

Knowing I needed to get down to business, I cleared my throat and tapped my cigarette into the ashtray in front of me.

"We got all the way through Charleston with no problems, but when we stopped at a gas station right outside of town, it was pretty obvious we had a tail. Definitely ATF. They weren't even trying to downplay it all—it was like they wanted us to know they were right behind us, watching our every move."

"Shit," Dom exhaled next to me. "The re-route went okay though, right?"

"Yeah," I nodded. "No problems. We hopped on a backroad and changed course to Cincinnati and doubled down there for a few days. Once we got back on the road, we didn't have any other issues."

It was exactly what had turned a three-day run into a seven-day run and it had also royally pissed me off. These assholes had been in town for at least a few months now and they were always hanging around, like they were daring us to make a wrong move. They acted like we hadn't been an operational club for decades and that we'd be stupid enough to put ourselves in a position to get caught.

"Pricks," Heath huffed from his seat next to Marcus. "I'm real sick of seein' them in my town."

"Gotta say though," I mused and took a long drag from my cigarette. "I'm kinda surprised they haven't done more than they have. I mean, they've tailed us around town, tailed us all the way up to Charleston this last run, but that's really it. They've obviously got nothing, but I have a hard time figuring out why they haven't even stepped foot on Horsemen property yet."

"You'd think that would've been their first move," Casey nodded to me, his eyes crinkled up in thought.

"Well, after them following us on this last run, I have a feeling we're gonna be hearin' from them sooner rather than later," Marcus called out from the head of the table. "But, that being said, they're not gonna find shit. And until those assholes get outta our backyard, we gotta lay low. No more runs. No more transfers. Meetings only."

"They keep tailin' us and eventually they'll get what they need," Heath nodded to his prez. "After awhile, they'll either get reassigned or just move on. We've seen it before and this time ain't gonna be any different if we play it the same as every other time."

"Yeah, but we're also gutting our income by playing it that way," Dom reasoned and I could practically see the wheels in his head turning.

I was thinking the exact same thing: that income paid the bills. We needed that money. Shit.

"Yeah, well," Heath shot his son a pointed look from across the table. "If you've got a handle on your money the way you should, holdin' off on runs and other club business for a few more months should be no problem."

When Dom's hands clenched into white-knuckled fists underneath the table, that was pretty much my cue to step in and diffuse.

"If we've gotta back down on runs and other business like that for awhile, which I think we can all agree is a good idea, maybe it's time we start looking into other ways to earn and see if—"

"We're not hard-up for cash, Caleb," Marcus cut in abruptly. "We just keep our shit together for a few months and all this'll blow over before we know it."

Now it was my turn to fist my hands underneath the table. Everything with him was just one giant battle. One step forward, two steps back. One test after another. I was beginning to wonder if I'd ever have a shot at actually passing all these tests, especially if Marcus could so easily dismiss me like that at the table when all I was trying to do was help for shit's sake. It just wasn't up for discussion.

His way or the fucking highway.

Given that I'd just spent a shit-ton of money all in the span of about 30 days, I didn't think it was so unreasonable to talk about other ways the club could earn other than guns. All Marcus saw were dollar signs and a quick, easy way out.

"Let's wrap this up now, huh?" Marcus went on, as if he hadn't just disrespected me in front of the whole club and produced four stuffed envelopes from inside his cut, promptly tossing one to me, Tiny, Casey, and Doc. "Happy payday, boys. Don't spend it all at one strip joint, alright? You gotta spread the love a little. Make sure all the girls know who their daddy is."

I just shook my head and opted not to comment. What my mom saw in that guy...nah, not going there. Not worth it. Besides, what I needed to do now was swap my earnings for this week with that little velvet box I'd had in my safe for a month.

. . .

I let myself into Isabelle's apartment, using the key she'd given me the day she moved in, and tossed my keys on the kitchen counter. It was a pretty small space, but she'd somehow managed to make this tiny one-bedroom apartment feel a little like home even on an equally tiny budget. Her influence in this apartment was everywhere, from the kitchen table and its mismatched chairs we'd found at a consignment shop to the evidence of her blood, sweat, and tears hanging on every wall.

Man, it was good to be home.

And, hopefully, if everything went as planned, we'd be calling somewhere else home soon, too.

I turned the corner and headed right for the hallway, pausing just a moment to smile at the painting hanging right in the center of the wall. The whole canvas was covered in swirls of different shades of blue and sometimes, if I stopped and stared at it for too long, I could get completely lost in the movements of her paintbrush.

I grinned at the painting one last time before gingerly opening the bedroom door and sneaking inside. Now that grin slipped back up my face again, but this time, it was because my eyes hungrily settled on Isabelle for the first time in seven days. Talk about a sight for sore eyes. She was all curled up onto my side of the bed, hugging my pillow with her hair fanning out all over her face, and I had to take a moment to drink all this in.

Beautiful. Peaceful. Mine.

That was all the time I needed before I kicked off my shoes and slid into the bed right behind her so I could pull her against my chest and wrap my arms around her. She stirred a little and yawned before finally opening those beautiful blue eyes I'd missed so much.

"Hey," I murmured into her hair.

"Hi," she whispered back, her lips curving up into a sweet, tired smile. "I'm glad you're home. I missed you."

"I missed you, too," I leaned in to kiss her as I spoke, but she crinkled up her nose and quickly turned her head so my lips found her cheek instead.

"Maybe you shouldn't kiss me," she grimaced.

"Hey now, I don't care about that. I'm gonna be sleepin' next to you tonight anyway, so I don't think it really matters."

She laughed a little and shifted in my arms. "I'm pretty sure you can't catch it, but I threw up before I laid down and haven't gotten a chance to brush my teeth yet."

I frowned at her. "Threw up? My mom said you weren't feeling too hot, but she didn't say anything about that."

"Yeah," she laughed again and I just didn't see what was so funny about puking. "I feel like I've been throwing up all day."

The words flew out of my mouth before I could stop them. "Did you cook last night?"

Isabelle whipped around, her eyes darkening with a scary mix of playful animosity and she smacked me in the chest. "Shut up, ya jerk! Yes, I cooked last night and I did *not* make myself sick."

Right. Just like I didn't get sick the last time she served me spaghetti with meat sauce that was so raw she might as well have just unwrapped the ground beef and dumped it into the sauce. At least I was smart enough to plaster a smile on my face, swallow down a few bites, and thank her for cooking for me.

"Okay, okay," I held my hands up in defense. "Sorry. Seriously, though, are you feeling okay?"

She shrugged a little and leaned into my chest. "My stomach's still a little queasy, but I'll be fine."

Jesus, if she was this sick—and was she really puking all day or was she exaggerating?—maybe I needed to postpone my plans until she was feeling a little better. But then again, I heard my mom's words in my head: *trust me, you won't be sorry.*

I guessed this was just one of those times in my life where I was going to have to trust my mother. Shit. That didn't feel too good.

Might as well get on with it before those cold feet snuck up on me again.

"Hey, I know you've been feeling shitty lately, but do you think you're up for a ride tonight? I gotta show you something."

She eyed me carefully, like she was trying to figure me out. If she just gave me an hour or so...

"Well, I was gonna make dinner and—"

Ah. That probably wasn't a good idea, especially if she was already sick. Didn't need to add her cooking into the mix, too.

"Let me take you out," I suggested, careful to keep my tone as far away from critical as possible. "We're gonna have to make a stop first, but I'll take you wherever you wanna go. You pick, I'll pay."

Her eyes narrowed. "You're just trying to get out of eating my spaghetti, aren't you?"

She was planning on making spaghetti? I threw up a little in my mouth just thinking about it.

"Uh," I winced a little and she buried her face in my chest, her whole body shaking with laughter. "Maybe?"

"Since it's a special occasion and all, I think maybe we should go out."

Yeah, definitely dodged a bullet there.

"But," she went on, chewing on her bottom lip a little as spoke. "I have to talk to you about something first though."

I grinned down at her, but that quickly faded away when I found careful, hesitant blue eyes staring back up at me.

"Okay, well, us talking is kinda the point of going for that ride, Iz. Can we wait to have that talk until we get there?"

I had no idea what was up with her because something clearly was, but I needed to get her on my bike and where I needed her to be before anything else happened. Waiting a month was long enough.

"Um, okay. But do you think maybe we could take the truck instead of your bike? You know, with..."

Right. If she'd really been puking all day, taking my bike was probably a bad choice anyway. Whatever got her on the road with me.

"Yeah, that's no problem. Why don't you get that sweet ass out of bed so we can get on the road, huh?"

When she just laughed and smacked me on the chest again, all my worries and all the things making me trip up just slipped away.

She was *it* and I'd be a damned idiot if I did anything but spend the rest of my life proving it to her.

. . .

"Um, Caleb," Isabelle's voice floated through the silence in the cab. "What are you doing?"

I almost wanted to laugh. She was probably sitting here wondering why the hell we were parked in the driveway of some strange house.

"I, uh," I scratched the back of my head nervously as I spoke. "I just bought this house."

Her eyes just about fell out of her head and I wanted to kick myself in the balls. Was it too much to ask to say one thing eloquently? Jesus, there was no way I was going to survive the rest of this night if I couldn't get my shit together. Why the hell was I so nervous all of a sudden? This was Isabelle. I loved her and wanted her with me for as long as I could have her.

"You...bought it?" Her eyes glimmered with something I couldn't quite place and I almost wanted to roll my window down and vomit onto the pavement I'd just bought.

"Uh, yeah. You wanna go inside? I just got the keys last week."

A hesitant smile broke out across her face and that had to be a good sign. When we were finally inside, her feet stalled inside the main hallway to our little three-bedroom ranch house and that little bit of panic I'd batted down before suddenly fanned out, spreading through my chest and threatening to take over my lungs.

My throat tightened when she still didn't say anything. I figured I knew her well enough by now to know that she'd be more than a little annoyed, upset, disturbed, and everything in between that I'd gone ahead and made a decision like this without at least discussing it with her first. But to be fair, it was my money and it was time for me to grow up already. Besides, I figured as soon as she heard me out, she'd be on board too. At least I hoped.

But she still hadn't said a word. Her face was just blank, like she couldn't process all this at once. Now I felt like I'd just made a huge mistake.

"I know I should've said something, but I wanted to surprise you."

Her blue eyes sparkled and she moved into the kitchen, carefully stepping inside the empty space and taking everything in.

"The way I see it," I explained desperately, trailing after her as she traveled into the living room and then down the hall. "I've been living in the clubhouse since I was 18 and now that I've got you, I guess I figured it was time to move on. You know, be an adult and all that shit."

That didn't even get me a smile. I swallowed hard, feeling my Adam's apple bob up and down way too many times. I'd epically screwed this up. I should've brought her in on this sooner. I should've showed her the house before I put the offer down. I should've at least *talked* to her about this before just jumping in head first and before I knew how she'd feel about it and now I had to do some serious fast talking.

"Look, we practically live together already," she was padding down the hallway now toward the bedrooms and I started to wonder if she was even hearing me, but I just pushed on. "I can't remember the last time I slept at the clubhouse when you weren't with me and we're always at your apartment anyway. I figured if we're gonna live together, we should do it right. Do it for real, you know? I know you've still got the lease on your apartment, but we can figure all that out later. I just...I saw this house, Iz, and it was perfect. I knew I had to buy it for you."

Finally, her head turned to face me and those beautiful blue eyes were shining with tears, but they were the good kind of tears. The kind of tears I was hoping for with all this.

"So you just bought a house, huh?" she asked me quietly.

I leaned against the wall closest to the living room and shrugged.

She smiled, her eyes trained on the three bedroom doors in front of us. "I have to say though, I didn't realize you had enough money to afford something like this."

It was right on the tip of my tongue to tell her that the spoils of club business made this all possible, but I'd already stuck my foot in my mouth enough times when it came to her to last us both a lifetime. The last thing I wanted to do was ruin this moment.

"I've been saving for a while," I modified.

"Okay," she replied slowly as she took it all in. "So three bedrooms, huh?"

I nodded tightly, gesturing with my head for her to follow me down the hallway, my hand closing around her fingers to draw her closer to me. I pushed open the door to the master bedroom and waved her inside to check it out.

"This'll be our room. There's a bathroom connected to it right over..." I trailed off because her eyes had already found it.

I tugged on her hand a little to get her to follow me and nodded to the door right next to ours. "I figured this could be your studio. Every artist needs her own workspace, right?"

Her eyes snapped to me and now I knew I was finally back on the right track. Her eyes were swimming, but I saw nothing but happiness with a little shock mixed in, but that was okay, too.

"And, um," she gestured to the third bedroom. "What about that one?"

"Well," I started slowly, gingerly pushing open the door so we could step inside the doorway. "Someday, when we're ready and the time is right, I figured this'll be our nursery."

I watched her suck in a deep breath and she quickly brushed aside a stray tear. What did I do wrong? Everything was actually going okay there for a little while. I should've just said we could use this room for storage or something because this was obviously too much, too soon for her. And just as I was about to jump into damage control, Isabelle turned to me with soft, happy eyes.

"What if that time is now?"

I wasn't sure I'd heard her right her voice was so soft. "What?"

Her lips lifted softly. "You said when the time is right. What if that time is now?"

My head reared back a little as my brain worked overtime to compute those words and I frowned even when her fingers squeezed my hand.

"What? Are you..." I didn't even know how to say the words, let alone understand them.

Isabelle chewed on her bottom lip a little and nodded, her eyes still shining with unshed tears. "Yeah."

My eyebrows shot into my forehead and I rubbed the side of my head, my mouth slack-jawed and hanging on its hinges.

"I'm pregnant."

All my breath pushed out in one crazed, happy laugh. Now my hands closed around her face like they had a will of their own and she stood up on her tip-toes to kiss me.

"I just found out today," she murmured into my lips. "I threw up in the hallway on campus and Dr. Jacobs sent me home."

"No shit. I guess that explains why you've been sick, huh?"

"And then some. Look, I'm sorry I didn't wait for you to take the test, but

I just couldn't wait. I was driving myself crazy and—"

"Iz," I leaned forward and pressed a quick kiss into her lips. "It's okay. It's really okay. I just can't believe it. I mean...holy *shit,* we're having a baby."

"Yeah," she smiled. "We're having a baby."

I pulled her into my arms and buried my face in her hair, needing to sear this memory into my brain as deeply as possible. I never wanted to forget this feeling, even though part of me was scared shitless about what this meant for us now, and I felt like I could stand here, with this woman in my arms, kissing her, loving her, touching her, for the rest of my life and not need to do anything else.

And as the shock wore off, my overprotective tendencies reared back with full force.

"How are you feeling? I mean, you've been sick, right? Do you need—"

"I'm okay, Caleb," she laughed and gave me a quick kiss. "Like I said, I've been throwing up all week, but I think that's pretty normal. Taking a nap today definitely helped."

"Good," my hands closed around her face again and I kissed her again, unable to help myself. "We gotta call my mom now, right? She's gonna piss herself when she finds out, you know."

"Uh, about that...your mom actually already knows."

I huffed out a laugh and shook my head, grinning down at her. Of course.

"I called her right after I took the test," Isabelle explained, reaching out until both her hands rested on my chest so she could pull me in closer. "I knew you were on the road and I guess I just wasn't ready to tell you yet. I sorta freaked out. Well, not sort of. I *did* freak out. I totally freaked out."

I nodded, taking a second to kiss her forehead. She'd been all alone in her apartment, taking that on by herself...yeah, I probably would've had a freak out too. I think sooner or later, when all this finally caught up to me, I was probably due for one of those myself.

"This is just all happening really fast, Caleb," she went on and my hand flew back up to her cheek to remind her that I was still here, that I wasn't going anywhere. "It's not exactly the way I thought all this would happen."

"What do you mean, Iz?"

She smiled quickly. "I guess I just always pictured us already having a house, being married, being ready to try, and *wanting* to get pregnant, you know? It's not that I don't...ugh, you know what I mean?"

My thumb brushed across her cheek and I found myself digging into my pocket with my free hand to find that little velvet box I'd shoved in there right before leaving the clubhouse. Well, no time like the present.

"I hear you," I murmured, kissing her one last time before taking this last step. "Nothing's ever gonna be the same, but that's okay. And yeah, maybe this didn't happen the way we thought it would, but that's okay, too. But this, Iz, *this* is a good thing and I know you think things are happening too fast, but maybe it's not. We have a house now. We're gonna have a family now and I honestly couldn't have planned for better timing."

I pulled the black velvet box out of my pocket, watching as her eyebrows flew up into her forehead, and handed it to her. She sucked in a breath, her eyes watery and shimmering deep blue, and then she gingerly took the box from me. As she opened it, I grinned at the way her whole face seemed to light up from the inside.

While my mom had wisely encouraged me to stay a little more within my budget, especially since I was literally in the middle of buying a house at the time, I knew I had to either go big or go home. And I'd went big. Real big. Even I knew that two carats was a lot and that was really saying something. Set in platinum gold, the round diamond was surrounded by smaller ones that wrapped all the way around the band, it was beautiful and classy. Just like my old lady.

Now I just had one more thing I had to do before we could get this celebration started. I grinned down at the love of my life and reached out to tuck some hair behind her ear.

"I wanna marry you," I told her hoarsely, memorizing the way she looked right now, the way her eyes shone, giving me the answer to a question I hadn't even asked her yet. "But that only works if you wanna marry me too. So...marry me, Iz?"

Those beautiful lips I loved so much curved up into a smile and she was already nodding as I took the ring out of the box so I could slid it onto her left hand.

"Yeah," she whispered.

"Yeah?" I exhaled, finally sliding the ring all the way up her finger and squeezing her hand.

Barely giving her enough time to nod, I wrapped my arms around her to pull her in close and kissed her, feeling her melt into me and giving me back everything I'd just given her.

"I love you," I murmured against her lips.

"I love you, too," she whispered back and I reached up to brush a tear off her face. She laughed a little and shook her head. "You're really lucky, you know that?"

"What do you mean?"

"You're lucky I love this house. Can you imagine if I didn't?"

Shit. I hadn't thought of that.

I guessed I was lucky in more ways than one.

CHAPTER THREE
Sit Down, Part One

Caleb

There was honestly nothing better than waking up in your own bed, in your own house, with your old lady burrowed against your chest. I slipped a hand protectively over her stomach and smiled into her hair, letting my fingers lightly trace over her skin.

It was crazy to think our kid had already been cooking in there for nine weeks. We'd already been to our first appointment, heard the heartbeat, and seen the little guy on those monitors. He didn't really look like a baby, at least not what I thought he was supposed to look like. It had taken me a few moments to even see what the doctor was pointing at on the screen. He just looked like a little dot. A blip. A kidney bean. But he was in there and now that reality had finally set in, now that I'd gotten a little time to wrap my head around what was happening, I couldn't wait.

Isabelle stirred a little in my arms and buried her face into my bare chest.

"This is nice," she murmured, nuzzling me a little more as she spoke. "I like waking up like this in our house, in our bed."

"My thoughts exactly," I mumbled into her hair. "You know, I've been thinking and I think it's gonna be a boy."

She laughed into my chest and hoisted herself up by her elbow. "Oh, sure. Of course you do."

"Hey, what's that supposed to mean, huh? What's wrong with wanting a little mini-me running around?"

"What about me?"

"Oh, no. No, no, no," I exhaled, shuddering playfully as I wrapped my arms around her. "I'm not ready for that yet."

"Come on, Caleb," she shot back and threw a leg around my waist just for good measure.

"Well, someday when we do have a girl, I know she's gonna look just like you and then I'll be a complete psycho for the rest of my life while I bat all the guys off her. I'll be completely grey by the time I'm 30 if it's a girl. So, I'm sure you can see why I'd like to put *that* off for as long as possible. Besides, do you know how much fun I'd have with a boy? Think of all the trouble we'd get into..."

I had so many things to teach him: how to fix up an engine, how to ride my bike, how to aim a fire cracker just right for maximum impact, how far to push Grandma before she snapped. Yeah, my kid had a lot to learn.

"Alright," she grinned. "I guess I can see why you'd think that, but that being said, *I* think it's going to be a girl."

"Ugh," I winced and scrubbed a hand over my face. "We'll see, Iz. How long do we have to wait again?"

"At least another nine weeks or so. They won't be able to tell the sex before then."

That was a hell of a long time to wait to see how much longer I'd have all my hair. With that disturbing thought, I dared a glance at the digital clock on our nightstand and groaned.

"Shit, I gotta get going soon."

"No," she moaned, jutting out her bottom lip in a cute pout just to sink the knife in even deeper. "Stay in bed."

"Can't, babe," I laughed and kissed her hair. "If I don't get my ass in the shower, I probably won't have enough time to make you breakfast."

Her nose crinkled up at that and I could see her mentally weighing her options. Finally, she must've decided breakfast trumped keeping me in bed a little bit longer and relented, rolling off me and curling into her pillow.

"Alright," she allowed with a sly grin. "But only because you said you'd make me breakfast."

I slid out of bed and got my ass in the shower. Reaching for the one bottle I had in the shower, next to the 20 others Isabelle needed for some reason, I finally let the spray settle over my shoulders and squeezed my eyes shut.

Part of me really wasn't looking forward to this sit-down with Theo Wallace and the Warlords mainly because I had a sinking feeling that the Warlords' problem had more to do with Padilla and less to do with the Horsemen than anything. Marcus had just gotten the call yesterday from Wallace saying he wanted to meet face-to-face and were willing to meet us halfway in Memphis instead of forcing us to make the trip all the way up to their clubhouse in Pittsburgh. If this meeting was what I thought it was, I had a feeling Wallace was only calling this sit-down as a formality to give us some bad news.

All signs pointed to Padilla, who'd been just as inconsistent in his productivity as he'd been during our first disastrous drop-off, and it wasn't like Ortega was even giving him tasks that were all that difficult. The excuses ran from anywhere to his mom was in the hospital to they'd been up all night partying. At this point, the asshole was better off just not making excuses anymore.

One of these days, Padilla was going to cross the wrong person and then it would be all over for him—I couldn't wait for that day. Still, I knew I'd be lying if I said I didn't enjoy every second of getting to report all the ineptitude that Ortega had hitched his wagon to. Jesus, the man was nuts if he didn't regret patching Padilla and his boys into the Lobos. If we didn't need the Lobos' business, there was no way we'd put up with this bullshit.

Taking a trip up to Memphis wasn't exactly how I wanted to spend a Sunday afternoon, but at least I could chalk all this up to one more reason why I wanted to see Padilla squirm. Maybe, if I was lucky, this sit-down would finally be the straw that broke the camel's back, so to speak.

By the time I stepped out of the shower, Isabelle was already holding a towel out to me from her perch on the counter. I took the towel from her, wiping myself off as I approached her, and wound it around my waist.

She pulled me in between her legs and ran her fingertips on the skin over my left pectoral where her full name was written in ink. A dreamy smile ghosted over her lips and I wound my fingers around hers so I could pull them up and brush my lips over her knuckles. Her tank top had ridden up a little, exposing the delicate angel wings on her lower back and I slipped my other hand around her waist so I could watch myself trace over the skin that held my initials through our reflection in the mirror.

"I wish you didn't have to go," Isabelle was telling me now, her ocean-blue eyes shining up at me and tugging at my insides.

"I'd rather be home with you, but duty calls, Iz. This'll be quick. Just business as usual and then I'll be back in time to make you dinner, okay?"

She cocked an eyebrow at me. "You're making me breakfast and dinner all in one day? Boy, you must really love me or you just really hate my cooking."

It was pretty much both.

"I just wanna take care of you, Iz," I told her instead. "Is that so terrible?"

"No," she replied as she leaned against my chest and wrapped her arms around my waist. "It's not. Please be safe today."

"I always am."

"I know, but you—"

She didn't get a chance to finish because her eyes were practically bugging out of her face and she pushed frantically against my chest to scramble off the counter. Her head was in the toilet before I could even reach for her and all I could do was pull her ponytail away from her face and rub her back as her stomach emptied itself. When her body was finally done, Isabelle straightened up and wiped her mouth, casting me a weak smile over her shoulder.

She didn't need to do anything to show me how strong she was. I already knew.

"Feeling a little better now?" I asked her, my hand still rubbing gently across her back.

"Ugh, I don't know. I mean, I know this is normal, but this just *sucks*. This is all your fault, you know."

My hands shot up in defense. "Guilty as charged. I guess this is what I get for not being able to keep it in my pants when it comes to you, huh?"

"I guess I could be saying the same thing to you," Isabelle allowed as she reached for her toothbrush.

I took that opening to finish up getting ready for this little road trip, threw on the first T-shirt and jeans I could find along with my cut, and then headed into the kitchen to put together a quick breakfast for Isabelle before I hit the road. By the time I set her breakfast down on the table, she was already settling into her chair with a weak smile on her face.

"Thanks."

"No problem, Iz," I grinned down at her and pointed to her oatmeal bowl, "Eat this," I pointed to her cup of orange juice, "Drink that," and then pointed to her massive prenatal vitamin, "And swallow that bastard down."

I bent down to kiss the side of her head, smirking as she eyed the vitamin warily, "Love you."

"Love you too."

"Have fun with Lex and my mom today," I called back to her as I headed for our front door. "Don't spend too much of my money, alright?"

Her light chuckle followed me out the door. "Oh, I don't know about that..."

. . .

We arrived at the Warlords-owned and operated bar right on the dot and as Marcus stepped inside, I practically stopped right in my tracks when Heath gestured for me to follow after the Prez. That was normally the VP's place and the only way I could reconcile this new development was the fact that all the club's dealings with Padilla had virtually been through me. So, it was only fair, I guessed, that I act as second-in-command in this meeting.

Right in the back corner of the bar, Theo Wallace and three other Warlord members sat waiting patiently for us and when Wallace caught sight of our entrance, he waved us over with the flick of his wrist.

On almost every level, Theo Wallace was living my dream, at least where the MC was concerned. Son of Conrad Wallace, the Warlords' prez, and the current VP, he had the status, the pull, and the legacy behind him now to back up the air of superiority wafting around him. We'd known each other off and on through these last few years—Wallace had about five years on me, which gave him the advantage in his own club that I was still waiting for in mine.

Every time I saw him, there was something harder about him, a little colder, a little more ruthless, and I figured that change in his demeanor just came with the job title, too. I'd never admit it out loud, especially not where anyone in my club could hear, or any other club for that matter, but I admired Theo Wallace. Looked up to him. Wanted to be him. Wanted the respect and the stability that came with his position. I'd heard he'd settled down with his long-time old lady not too long ago, had a kid with her and another one on the way, so I guess I was slowly but surely catching up to him.

When we sat down at the booth where they waited for us, Wallace's eyes took careful stock of our seating arrangement, and with the seasoned intuition that only comes with years spent in this kind of life, he focused only on me.

"Sawyer," he nodded to me respectfully as he pushed an ashtray toward me.

"Wallace," I dipped my chin down in greeting.

"Heard you got a kid on the way now with your girl," Wallace shot me a genuine grin. "Congrats."

An easy smile spread across my face, something that just came naturally whenever Isabelle and our new family were the topic of conversation. "Thanks, man."

He cocked an eyebrow at me. "You know, I never thought I'd see the day when Caleb Sawyer finally settled down with one girl. She must have a magic pussy or somethin', huh?"

I knew this was all supposed to be easy, good-natured small talk before the real conversation started, and even though he was treading on thin ice now, I rolled with it.

"Hey, man," I jabbed a finger at him with a smirk. "That's my future wife you're talkin' about."

Wallace's ringed hands shot up in defense and he laughed heartily. "Alright, alright. My bad. You're having a pretty good year, you know. Knocked up a girl, movin' up in the world and in the club...you're on a roll."

Marcus bristled a little next to me and Wallace's eyes flicked to him for just a moment before shifting his attention back to me.

"I guess," I shrugged. "How 'bout you? Family good?"

Wallace's eyes darkened for just a moment and he hesitated, lighting up a cigarette instead of answering me directly. "They're fine. My kid was in the hospital again. Some kinda lung infection."

Shit. I'd heard his kid had been pretty much been in and out of the hospital since he was born—cystic fibrosis, I think—and suddenly, any lightness in the room dimmed to black.

"I'm sorry to hear that, man."

"Don't worry about it," Wallace batted a hand my way and leaned forward on his elbows as he spoke. "I didn't call you down here to catch up, Sawyer. We got a problem and since you and I have never had any problems before, I figured we should talk it out first before we move forward on this."

My eyebrows lifted and I glanced at Marcus out of the corner of my eye. "What's the problem?"

"Ortega's boy is dealing and his shit is cutting into my shit."

I cursed under my breath and cast a glance at Marcus to my left, who was a running a hand wearily over his grizzled face. If the Warlords were pissed enough, they could cut off their business dealings with us altogether. The problem was that we were in too deep with the Lobos and their cronies to pull all our deals completely. We depended way too much on the income from our long-standing business with Ortega to bail altogether. Still, losing our relationship with the Warlords could stand to be just as detrimental. After all, they were our business contacts in the North. We needed them just as much as they needed us.

Talk about being between a rock and a hard place.

"So," Marcus bit out gruffly. "What are we doin' here, then?"

"I just wanted to give you a heads up," Wallace shrugged and ran a hand over his bald head. "But that doesn't mean I can afford to just let this go if your business deals interfere with mine, too."

"We can't control what Padilla does or doesn't do," I interjected quickly, hoping to diffuse the situation with as little heat as possible. I could already feel the steam pouring off Marcus in waves and I knew I needed to salvage what was left of our relationship with the Warlords quickly and efficiently.

"That's why I'm givin' you a heads up," Wallace turned to me now and seemed visibly grateful to not have to deal with Marcus, whose lips had curled up into a dangerous snarl. "I know all this business with the Lobos isn't your fault. If you cut ties with Ortega, we don't have a problem anymore."

I shook my head and lit up a cigarette before speaking again, mulling over what to do next. He was being pretty reasonable and logical about all this, but we just couldn't give him what he wanted.

"You know we can't do that, man. I'm just as pissed about this as you are. That dumbshit has caused too many problems as it is, but we gotta keep the cash flow goin'. We're in the same position as you're in right now and if there was a way we could stay afloat without the Lobos, we'd do it. But right now, it's just not possible."

Wallace's eyes darkened and he leaned back into the booth, creaking the plastic cushions to cut in through the silence that had taken over the meeting. "Then I guess we've got nothing more to say."

"What if we handle Padilla? Then there's no problem anymore."

Wallace eyed me carefully, searching for some sign of dishonesty for a few painfully silent moments. "How're you gonna do that?"

I looked briefly to Marcus, who just nodded in response, and then to Heath, who followed Marcus's lead. So, it looked like this was going to be on me then. Go big or go home, right?

"I doubt Ortega is going to be happy when he finds out his lap dog has really gone off the rails this time. Even if he doesn't care too much about the fact that Padilla's dealin', he definitely won't like that he did it behind his back to make a profit."

"So," Wallace stared back at me incredulously. "You're just gonna bring it to Ortega?"

"Look, man," I shot back quickly. "Ortega is just as smart as the rest of us. He knows when shit's worth hangin' onto and when it's not. He'll cut ties with Padilla so fast the asshole won't know what hit him. If the Cobras lose their patch, they can't afford to stay anywhere near here and it'll be business as usual then."

Wallace leaned back against the booth in thought and then nodded. "Alright. Fair enough."

With that, the meeting was over almost as quickly as it'd started. Marcus was on the phone with Ortega the second we stepped foot out of the bar to set up the next sit-down of the day. With a quick nod from my prez, I knew the arrangements had been made and then we were on our way to the Lobos' clubhouse in Raleigh. The entire ride over, I felt myself sweating bullets. Although it was logical and smart, the plan I'd devised literally from the seat of my pants could easily blow up in my face. And if it did, the repercussions, both seen and unforeseen, wouldn't be pretty.

"You sure this is gonna work?" Marcus clapped a hand on my shoulder as we closed in on the Lobos' doorway.

"They can't afford to lose our business either," I reasoned. "I don't think Ortega is stupid enough to hang on, do you?"

Marcus just grinned and clamped down on his cigarette.

Over all, the sit-down with Ortega went better than I could've hoped for. It didn't take much rationalizing for the Lobos' leader to clearly understand the long-reaching effects a continued relationship with Padilla could mean for his club.

The real fun began, though, when Ortega called Padilla to get his ass over to their clubhouse. Like the good little lapdog he was, Padilla came to heel in less than 15 minutes.

Padilla swung through the clubhouse doors and headed right for the table where his charter president was sitting. This had been a long time coming and I just hoped I'd get back to the table in time to snag a front row seat.

As Padilla passed us with a cigarette dangling from his lips, his smug, slightly dilated beady eyes froze on me for a little too long. Even though I didn't want to give the surprise away, I couldn't stop the knowing, evil smirk that tugged across my lips. Padilla's expression darkened with confusion, but he just pressed forward until he dropped in the chair across from Ortega.

"What's this about?" Padilla huffed as he took a long drag from his cigarette.

Ortega only hesitated to cast a sideways glance at Marcus, who nodded with approval. Padilla didn't seem to miss this nonverbal communication and his black eyes darted back and forth between them.

"You been dealin' behind my back?" Ortega bit out in Padilla's direction.

I had to fight the urge to rub my hands together in glee. This was just too damn good. Where the hell was the popcorn when you needed it?

Padilla swallowed tightly once. And then again. And then again. At some point, he must have realized he needed to supply an answer and he rubbed the back of his neck nervously.

"I...uh..."

"That's not the answer I'm lookin' for, *ese*," Ortega shot back, his thick accent enunciating every syllable. "I'll ask you again: you been dealin' behind my back?"

Padilla squeezed his eyes shut tightly and blew out a deep breath. At least the dipshit had enough sense to know it was over.

"You don't understand. I was waitin' 'til the deal was all settled to make sure it was all good. I didn't wanna take the chance that—"

"That what?" Ortega cut in sharply. "That I'd find out what you were doin' behind my back?"

With that, Ortega lunged forward until his hands were closing around the edges of his former mentee's cut. He abruptly loosened his grip with one hand to snap his fingers above his head. When someone handed him a knife, Ortega leaned closer with the blade extended dangerously close to Padilla's eye.

"Get the hell out of my clubhouse," the Lobos Prez exhaled venomously before slicing through the patch in the upper left-hand side of Padilla's cut. Then he flung the patch onto the floor below them and roughly shoved Padilla back against his chair.

Silence permeated the air for a few long moments, save for Padilla's heavy, stunted breathing. A beat later, he knocked his chair back as he furiously rose to his feet. With his chest heaving violently, Padilla's black eyes rounded the length of the table until they rested firmly on my victoriously smug smirk. Bottles smashed in his wake and chairs upended as Padilla lunged for me with both hands reared for attack.

My back slammed into the floor before I had time to even register what was happening as Padilla's fist smashed square in my jaw. Shattering pain splintered through the left side of my face and then instinct took over as both my hands shot up to block the next attack. With Dom yanking Padilla back, I took the opportunity to wind up and finally hit that prick right in the face.

Padilla spit out a tooth, narrowly missing the front of my shoes. "Fuck you, Sawyer."

"You think this is my fault?" I shot back hotly and jammed a pointed finger back at him, even though I was being tightly restrained by both Doc and Eli. "You did this. Not me. This is on all you, *ese*."

Padilla's eyes narrowed into menacingly dark slits. "You been waitin' for this since day one. You better watch your back if you know what's good for you, *bro*."

"Oh really?" I laughed bitterly, shoving myself free so I could inch up right in front of Padilla's face. "Bring it, asshole. You got nothin' to threaten me with and you know it."

Padilla just snarled and before he had a chance to reply, his ass was unceremoniously tossed out of the clubhouse and into the dirt where he belonged.

Good riddance, I thought bitterly as I rubbed my throbbing jaw. At least all this shit had essentially resolved itself and now Padilla was officially out of our hair. I'd been waiting for this moment for more than six months and now that it was finally here, the vindication was sweeter than I'd anticipated.

Buzzing in my back pocket jerked me from those thoughts and my first thought was that it must be Isabelle calling to check in. But when I saw my mom's name on the caller ID, I frowned at the screen.

"Yeah, Ma?" I answered quickly, catching Dom's gaze as I spoke.

"Where're you guys right now?" My mom's haggard voice sounded over the phone and I had to blow out a deep breath in preparation for whatever was coming next.

"Dealin' with some club shit. Why?"

"If you guys can get back anytime soon," my mom told me anxiously. "You'd better head over to the precinct because the ATF picked up Isabelle and Lex about 20 minutes ago."

For a second, I thought I hadn't heard her correctly.

All I could sputter in response was: "What?"

Dom was suddenly standing right next to me as my mom continued.

"They showed up at your house right after we got back from shopping, flashed their badges, and said they wanted to talk to the girls at the precinct. I think their angle's pretty obvious considering I'm still sitting here in your kitchen."

It wasn't a coincidence that the first time we had any sort of trouble with another club, the ATF swooped in and grabbed two old ladies, especially ones who'd never been in this position before. I knew exactly how these self-righteous pricks operated and the thought of Isabelle trapped in a room with just a bright light and an overzealous, aggressive agent was enough to make my blood boil.

Isabelle was smart, but federal agents were trained, ruthless interrogators who would play on any angle they could to get what they wanted. They could talk circles around her for hours if they really felt like it.

Jesus Christ, what else was going to happen today?

CHAPTER FOUR
Sit Down, Part Two

Isabelle

It wasn't until I found myself alone in a cramped interrogation room with Agent Jordan staring back at me that I started to get really pissed. I'd been sitting here for about 10 minutes already and I'd heard murmurings through the door that Becca had been brought in as well. Jesus, they were really pulling out all the stops here.

Standing just over six feet tall with cropped dark hair, Agent Jordan was clearly well-built underneath his suit jacket. Clean shaven and put together, he couldn't have been more than 30. And he might have been attractive if his dark, hooded gaze didn't feel so threatening and smug.

Under no circumstances did I want to be alone with this man any longer than necessary and I suddenly envied Lexie, who was more than likely being questioned by Agent Summers at that very moment. At least I might have been able to go toe to toe with Agent Summers a little easier because she didn't inherently intimidate me the way the agent currently sitting across from me did.

"Isabelle..." Agent Jordan started carefully. "Is it alright if I call you Isabelle?"

I nodded slowly, hesitant to speak to him unless absolutely necessary.

"Thank you," he grinned back at me gratefully and I felt myself frowning back at him. "Please, call me Matt. Agent Jordan is way too formal, don't you think?"

When I just stared impassively in his general direction, he frowned and leaned forward on his elbows. "So, it looks like you're almost finished with your first semester at UNC in Winston-Salem. And you've got a showcase coming up too. That's quite an accomplishment. You must be really proud."

I'd had enough of this already.

"Can we just cut to the chase, huh?" I snapped back at him. "I'm not stupid and I know that since you didn't arrest me, you can't keep me here against my will. Ask your questions so I can leave, please."

I hadn't meant for my tone to betray all the swirling emotions running through me, but there was nothing I could do about it now. When Agent

Jordan's lips tightened into a thin line, I wondered which part of what I'd just said had set him off more. If he'd really done his research, he would've known what I'd studied at Duke and so, my basic knowledge of the law couldn't have been a surprise. Still, the longer he stared back at me with that unfathomable expression, the more I wanted to squirm in my chair.

"Alright," Agent Jordan replied simply. "I'm sure you have a pretty good idea what I need to ask you."

"Yep," I nodded.

"You and Caleb Sawyer have been together for..." he flipped through a few pages of the file in front of him as he spoke. "About seven or eight months, right?"

He glanced up at me with inquisitive eyes while I nodded. "Something like that."

"And in that time, have you seen or heard anything related to illegal activity? Anything related to the illegal purchase and transfer of firearms?"

I frowned at the direct question. Didn't seasoned interrogators spend more time working up to those questions? I'd been expecting a little more resistance on his part, maybe even sly interrogation tactics to get me to trust him, but he hadn't wasted any time with that. What was really going on here?

"No, Agent Jordan, I haven't."

His eyes darkened slightly and it probably had something to do with the fact that I'd ignored his request to call him by his first name. That was too personal, too intimate, and I didn't want to have anything to do with him.

"Nothing that comes to mind?" he pressed again.

"Nope."

He abruptly slapped the file closed and leaned forward on his elbows. "You know why we're here, right? You know we're here to investigate the Iron Horsemen? And by extension, Caleb, too?" He waited for me to nod before continuing. "It's only a matter of time before we find what we're looking for, Isabelle."

I froze in my seat, knowing exactly where he was going with this, but I didn't want to hear it.

"Sooner or later," he went on softly and it felt like the temperature in this room had free-fallen. "He's going to end up in prison and then where will you be? Have you ever thought about that?"

I couldn't even conjure a reply and all I could do was sit quietly in my chair, willing this all to be over.

"He's already been arrested three times. The fourth could happen at anytime. You know that, don't you? At any given moment, we could find something or he could make a mistake and get caught and then he'll be gone, just like that."

My blood ran cold that this latest piece of information. I knew he'd been arrested once, but three times? Why didn't I know that? Why hadn't he told me? My head was barely above water as it was and if this went on for too much longer, it might drown me altogether.

Agent Jordan's head cocked to the side as he silently observed me. "He never told you that, did he? I can only imagine what else he hasn't told you, what else he's done that he doesn't want you to know."

I now understood what was really going on here: Agent Jordan had set out to twist my head around until I couldn't see straight. And goddammit, it was working.

"I don't even want to talk about what must go on at their clubhouse when you're not there—how many women he must have behind your back, especially now that you're living together. And he still has his room in the clubhouse, doesn't he? You'd never know, never have any idea what he was doing in that room whenever you're not around. They all do it, Isabelle, and trust me, Caleb isn't any different."

My eyes narrowed suspiciously at his current line of questioning and he seemed to realize his error. There was a line and he'd just crossed that invisible line. I didn't even want to know how he knew Caleb and I were living together and now, I was done with this conversation.

"I'm sorry," Agent Jordan backpedalled quickly, holding his hands up in the air in defense. "I'm just trying to help you. That's all this. I'm sure you don't believe me, but I really want to help you."

"How are you planning on doing that?" I shot back hotly.

Agent Jordan shrugged simply. "You may not have been around them long enough to see it yet, but their lives are just an endless cycle. They commit crimes, get caught, go to jail, get out, and then do it all over again. Sometimes there are months in between, sometimes years, but it always happens. The cycle never ends and Caleb is just getting in deeper with the Horsemen. Sooner or later, that's going to catch up to him."

My breath caught in my throat as his words sank deep.

"If you stay with him, Isabelle, you're just going to get caught up in it too. And the longer you stay, the more responsibility you have. Look at your friend Lexie—what would happen to her and her baby if Dominic went to prison? What would she do? How would she make ends meet?"

"We would help her. I would help her. I know she'd do the same for me," I shook my head furiously, trying to block out everything he was telling me.

"Maybe. But that's not the kind of life anyone aspires to. And someday, Isabelle, you might have kids with Caleb and even if he marries you, even if you have some help around you, you'll still be alone at the end of the day."

It was like he'd just taken everything Caleb and I had planned and twisted it into something evil and ugly. There was no way he could know how close all that hit home, but still...I hated myself for even giving his words a moment's thought.

My eyes burned from the impact and all I wanted to do was get out of this room. In that instant, I hated Agent Jordan. The fear and intimidation he'd instilled in me crept away, leaving only frustration and disbelief in their wake. I had the sudden urge to leap to my feet and punch that slimy smile off Agent Jordan's face, or at the very least, use the pepper spray on him that Caleb had given me a long time ago. It was just too bad something like that would get me arrested because then I'd have to actually stay here in this precinct.

"Why do you care so much?" I glared back at him.

"I told you," he shrugged again. "I just want to help you. You've got a wonderful future ahead of you. One you won't be able to realize if you stay in this environment. I've seen it happen plenty of times before with women who get caught up in a whirlwind relationship, completely in over their heads, with no information and no experience in these kinds of organization. You know what always happens to those women, Isabelle? They get eaten alive."

"That's not going to happen to me," I told him defiantly.

"Sure," he shrugged. "But when they suspect you now, when they wonder what you told me in this room today, you might think differently. You might be scared enough to realize you don't have any other safe way out other than the protection my partner and I could offer you should you choose to cooperate."

He paused, as if to make sure his point was made, as if to make sure I knew how serious this was. That overwhelming sense of foreboding, that raw instinct that slipped down my spine told me that Agent Jordan wouldn't stop until he got what he wanted: Caleb and anyone else connected to the club behind bars. He wouldn't be able to use me to do it. His words and this doubt he'd planted in me wouldn't be enough to help him get what he wanted, but his words had hit their target all the same.

"And when that happens, Isabelle," he told me darkly. "You know where to find me."

. . .

It wasn't until Caleb ushered me inside the clubhouse, with Skyler right on our heels, that I finally felt myself relax a little more. At least now the heaviness Agent Asshole had set on my shoulders felt a little lighter, even if I still had some sorting out to do. Once we were alone in Caleb's dorm, then I could release some of this pent-up frustration. Until then, I had to keep up the appearance that everything was fine.

Marcus was already seated at a table near the bar and gestured with his head for us to get closer as Lexie and Becca took a seat across from him. For probably the tenth time today, a cold shiver crawled down my spine and I forced myself to fall into the empty seat next to Lexie in spite of my urge to cut and run.

Marcus was watching all three of us with sober, weary eyes and while there was no suspicion on the surface, there was only one reason why we were all currently seated at this table. And even though Caleb moved to stand protectively behind my chair, I felt totally and completely alone.

"First of all, ladies," Marcus began gruffly and took a swig from the beer bottle in his hand just for good measure. "I have to apologize for everything you must've went through today at the precinct. These ATF assholes think they have something here in our town and even though we all know they don't, they seem to be pretty persistent, don't you think?"

He grinned back at us, like he actually expected us to see the humor in the situation and I could only stare back as Agent Jordan's last words to me replayed in my head.

"Now, nobody here actually believes that any of you ladies had anything to say to those pricks and you don't need to tell me what they said, 'cuz I've got a pretty good idea," Marcus told us carefully and I sensed some serious manipulation was headed our way. "But it's been awhile since any old ladies have been brought in the way you were today. I just wanted to make sure that you all understand our policies about loyalty and discretion. You're family and I know none of you would ever do anything that could jeopardize your family."

Both Lexie and Becca nodded quickly and I immediately followed suit, not wanting to look even slightly suspicious by hesitating. Marcus's dark eyes appraised the three of us for a moment, taking plenty of time to study each of our expressions before moving on to the next one as he nonchalantly slicked a hand over his salt and pepper ponytail. It felt like he was readying himself to strike, like a coiled snake, and waiting for one of us to give ourselves away. This wasn't simply a friendly conversation or even a sincere apology. This was a thinly-veiled threat.

Marcus nodded his dismissal of us, emptying his beer bottle as he leaned back in his chair. Someone to his left handed him another frosty beer and I watched uneasily as Caleb's club president lounged around like he hadn't just not-so-discreetly threatened me and my two best friends three seconds earlier.

Like it was just any regular old day. Business as usual at the Horsemen clubhouse.

Marcus had always carried an air of superiority and I'd always understood it was necessary, given his position in the club, but today was the first time I saw the violence and danger in him as well. The possibility that, should the need arise, he wouldn't hesitate to act on the threats he'd just made.

I squeezed my eyes shut again and jumped a little when Caleb's hands ghosted over the top of my shoulders.

"We're gonna sit down for church quick to go over all this shit," he murmured in my ear. "Why don't you go lie down in my dorm? Rest a little bit until I'm done?"

"I'm fine," I snapped at him. I didn't mean to let my frustration bleed into hostility, but that was the only emotion I could come up with right now that made any sense to me.

Caleb blinked back at me in surprise for a moment before swallowing hard. "Okay, Iz. Whatever you want...just sit tight until I'm done. Then you'll tell me what happened, right?"

The best I could give him right now was a tight nod. He waited patiently for more, but when he realized he wouldn't be getting much else from me, opted to press a quick kiss into the side of my head before heading to church.

Yeah.

We were going to talk, alright.

CHAPTER FIVE
Baby Momma Drama

Caleb

I needed to get my head in the game and focus on getting through church, but as I sank down into my chair at the table, all I could see were Isabelle's eyes. Cold shards of blue glaring at me like *I* was the one who'd done something wrong, pissed at me for...I didn't know what.

"Let's get this shit straightened out," Marcus was saying now as he pounded the gavel and yanking me out of this current haze. "We all knew they would make a move, but I gotta say, I didn't really expect it would be like this. They're gonna play on every angle they can—money problems, safety concerns, any skeletons in their closets, whatever they can wrap their hands around."

"Lex doesn't have any skeletons in her closet," Dom chimed in and I could tell just from the wary glint in his dark eyes that he was feeling just on edge about all this shit as I was.

"Neither does Iz," I threw in and cast a tight nod in Dom's direction to let him know I was with him all the way on this one.

If there were any dark, dirty secrets in Isabelle's life, I would've already known about them. We wouldn't have come this far together if we kept secrets from each other. Lex wasn't an issue either, but...

"I think the real problem here is that we don't know what these girls know and what they don't," Heath was saying gruffly now.

"Nah," I shook my head and tapped my cigarette into the ashtray in front of me. "What matters is which one might talk. It's not gonna be Iz. And it's not gonna be Lex either."

Out of the corner of my eye, I could see Eli shifting anxiously in his seat and I couldn't blame him. If I were him, I figured a whole slew of nasty emotions would be running through me right now: anger at my brothers for not trusting my girl, fear of what would happen if everyone was right and I think, right about now, my mind would be working overtime to sift through everything I knew about her. Where she went when I wasn't around, who she spent her time with when she wasn't with me, what secrets she'd buried deep that I didn't know about.

"That's a pretty damn big assumption to make about my girl," Eli tossed out. His tone was calm and even, but everyone in the room and their mother could sense the undercurrent of malice there too.

"How well do you really know her?" I asked with a frown. I wanted to keep the peace, but I wanted this resolved more.

Eli shifted again and clamped his hands together in front of him. "How well do you really know yours, huh? She's only been hangin' around the clubhouse for, what, not even a year? The only reason she even showed up here in the first place was because of *my* girl and come on, am I really the only one at this table who doesn't see how outta place Caleb's girl is here in our clubhouse? She's not one of us. I'm sorry, bro, but she's more of an outsider than Becca is and we all know it."

I loved Eli Harris like a brother. I really did. But he was treading some serious fucking thin ice right now. My elbow rested on the table now and I rubbed my mouth with my free hand to mask the animosity rolling off me.

"I don't appreciate you pointing fingers at my pregnant old lady," I told him and did nothing to hide the darkness curling around each word.

"Alright, alright," Marcus called out, clearly wanting to diffuse the growing tension in the room. "What *I* don't appreciate is that all it took was them bringin' in three old ladies and now, you two," he gestured toward me and Eli, "are starin' each other down like you got an itchy trigger-finger. That's exactly what they wanted and you're givin' it to them. This bullshit stops *now*."

He paused to make sure his point hit its target and waited until a round of nods passed around the table.

"Fact of the matter is," Marcus pushed on, "I think we can all agree none of these girls gets a free pass. I don't care how long they've been around or whether or not they're knocked up because we need to do a little recon of our own because they sure as shit have been diggin'. We need to know what their weak spots are and we need to know if those weak spots are anything we need to be concerned about."

"Cut 'em loose tonight and see where they land," Heath suggested heavily. That was his own daughter-in-law he was casting suspicion over, too, and the weariness attached to the act wore deep into the lines already etched into the old man's grizzled face. "If they've got anything to hide, anything that needs coverin' up, they're gonna take care of their business as soon as possible to keep us from catchin' wind of it."

Dom shot him a livid glare. "That sounds like you're sayin' you wanna set-up my wife."

Heath just shrugged. "It ain't a set-up if she's got nothin' to hide. You know I love Lex like a daughter, but that don't mean she wouldn't crack if they put pressure on her in all the right places."

"So, you three talk to your women as soon as we're done here, find out exactly what the ATF said to them, send them home with an escort, and then their escort will stick around, if you will," Marcus waved a hand like he was discussing just regular old business, "when and if there's anything that needs reporting. Eli, I think you should run a scan on the girls, see what pops up. Heath'll keep an eye on ya to make sure you don't decide to leave anything out. Casey, you stay on Becca. ZZ take Isabelle. And Doc, you stay with Lex. Everyone else parks it here for the rest of the night until we get a report. Is that clear?"

His eyes swept to me in a hard glare and I nodded tightly. Then he shifted that glare to Dom and Eli, waiting until he got the same reaction from them before calling church to an end.

I didn't like this at all. I didn't like the idea of anyone, myself included, casting any sort of shadow of doubt over the person I'd never been more sure of in my life. I didn't doubt for one second all ZZ would report tonight was that Isabelle went home, worked on a project or watched some TV, and then went to bed. My club putting a tail on my old lady was as unsettling as it was infuriating. Part of me just couldn't believe we were actually in this position, that we were investigating our own women like none of the commitments Dom and I had made to our respective old ladies mattered. Like *we* couldn't be trusted enough to attach ourselves to women who were loyal and trustworthy every step of the way.

The idiocy of the whole thing was unnerving. Being part of something that could cast this kind of suspicion on Isabelle, with what the repercussions of that suspicion could mean...the rest of that thought just couldn't take shape in my mind.

Marcus' words at Dom and Lex's wedding filled my mind now: *you gotta figure out if she's gonna be an asset or a weakness because she can't be both.*

She was absolutely an asset, but I'd just be lying to myself if I said my trigger-finger didn't get a little itchy, as Marcus had so aptly put it, when it came to her either. I had a very short, very thin fuse where Isabelle was concerned. Brandon Davis could attest to that.

Still, I was positive that by the time this night was over, all the club's doubt and all the club's suspicion would lie right where it belonged: squarely on Becca's shoulders. My mom's intuition rarely missed the mark and she'd said Becca was shifty. She'd said she didn't trust Becca as far as she could throw her. That was good enough for me.

It was that thought that carried me out of church and onto the clubhouse's main floor to find Isabelle, who still sat stiffly at one of the tables in the middle of the floor right where I'd left her. Judging by the firm, thin line pressed across her lips as she appraised my approach, she wasn't any happier now than she was before church started.

But she had something to prove to my club now, even if she didn't know it yet. She'd pull it out. I knew she would because I couldn't think about the alternative right now if she didn't.

I settled my hands over her shoulders and leaned down to murmur in her ear, "You wanna head back to my dorm, Iz?"

She just nodded silently, allowing me to pull her out of her chair and down the hallway to my dorm room. As soon as she was close enough to my bed, she sank down into the mattress and ran her hands through her hair. She glanced up at me with hard, albeit tired eyes and that only spiked my anxiety about this upcoming conversation.

"Iz," I started slowly, resting my hands on my knees to bring myself down to her level. "What happened back there? What the hell did they say to you?"

Those simple, hushed words must've broken through the wall she'd built up around herself and a tear slipped down her cheek. Now, everything else shoved aside for me. All I cared about was this girl in front of me and I sank to my knees, bringing both hands around her face to gently wipe away her tears.

"What happened?" I pressed again and moved my hands around her face to force her to look at me.

She roughly pushed my hands off her and spat out: "I was ambushed, Caleb. That's what happened."

I sat back on my heels again to give her some space, but staying close enough that I could get to her again easily if she needed me to. I'd expected confusion. I'd even expected anger, but what I hadn't expected was the anguish, the frustration, and the disappointment all directed right at me.

"God, I really wish I could have a drink right now," she muttered under her breath and abruptly leaned back to put some more space between us.

It was probably for the best I just ignore that. "You said you felt ambushed. What do you mean, Iz?"

"That agent...Agent Jordan, he made me feel like such an idiot," she shook her head furiously and wiped a stray tear away with the back of her hand. "He knew so many things I hadn't thought about, things I didn't know."

My hands rested gently on the top of her knees and I hoped she needed that physical contact just as much as I did right now. "Like what?"

"Have you really been arrested three times?"

I sucked in a harsh breath and then hung my head down in between us, scrubbing a hand over my face. We needed to be on the same page here, but our lines of communication had gotten crossed somehow.

Yeah. Definitely hadn't expected this shit. This was my fault. Her feeling ambushed. Her looking at me like I was a liar and a damned fraud. All my fault.

"Why didn't I know that?" she demanded. "I mean, I knew about that time when we were in high school, but the other two...why didn't you tell me?"

One arrest, especially for something like idiotic, teenage antics, might not have mattered so much to her, but two others she had no knowledge of? I should've told her at the Lobos-Cobra patch-over. That was my chance and I didn't take it.

And now I was paying for it.

I sighed and tugged a hand through my hair. "I really screwed up, didn't I?"

"Yeah," she replied simply. "You did. How are we supposed to have a life together if you don't trust me enough to tell me something like that? And the problem is now, I'm sitting here wondering what else you haven't told me. What else you've decided I'm not important enough to know."

I exhaled one more time before rocking back on my heels again so I could get a better look at her. This was on me. This was my fault. My issues. My insecurities.

Well, I guess it was time for me to man-up and face those issues and insecurities head-on.

"Iz," I started slowly to gauge her reaction and calm her down a little. "Whatever went down this morning is because of me, not you. Him ambushing you like that is my fault. I just never found the right time to sit you down and tell you. I should've told you at that patch-over party, but you didn't ask and so I didn't tell you."

Her eyes flared blue fire at me and I almost ducked to get out of the way. "So you're saying you didn't tell me you were arrested three times because I didn't *ask?*"

My hands shot up in defense. "I'm not sayin' that makes it okay because it's not. And it's not that I don't trust you. What can I do, Iz? What do I need to do to make this right?"

"You can start by telling me why you were arrested."

I nodded and swallowed tightly. "Alright. You already know about the first one, so, I got the second one for petty theft when I was 18 and stupid because I got caught lifting some shit outta some asshole's crotch rocket at a gas station. I really shouldn't have done it, but the jerk was just askin' for it. I got two weeks in County, so I guess the joke was on me, right?"

I laughed stiffly and my eyebrows lifted, watching her closely for some reaction, but she gave me nothing. Yeah, I guess I could see why she'd have a hard time finding humor in a situation where I was sitting here, joking about my arrest history. So in an effort to save face, I cleared my throat and fisted my palm on her knee.

"I got the third about two years ago for assault," her eyes widened in alarm and I immediately jumped into damage control. "Pretty much half the club all got brought in too. Some shit went down with the Warlords and someone called the cops. We all got our asses thrown in County for a month while the Warlords licked their wounds and thought they'd made their point."

She was silent for a few long moments until her eyes finally lifted up to find me. "Is that supposed to make me feel better? You went to jail for a month for assault and I'm supposed to just be okay with that because other guys from the club went in too?"

"No," I pushed out roughly and I just wished she'd let me touch her more than she was letting me now. "You're not, but that's what happened."

She blew out a deep breath, her eyes trained on a spot in the carpet right in front of my feet. "Why didn't you tell me?"

"You and the baby are the most important things in my life, Iz. Please tell me you know that," I leaned forward to get her to look at me as both my hands rested on her knees. She still wouldn't look at me, but I had to keep going. "I should've told you right away when we first got together. I guess I just wanted to avoid the way you're lookin' at me right now. Not that I don't deserve it."

Isabelle's eyes snapped up and I knew I wasn't going to like what she said next. "Okay. Tell me what else I don't know. There's gotta be more than just that."

There was one other thing she didn't know. One other thing I'd never wanted to tell her. One other thing I never thought I'd even be able to say out loud. I didn't want to have to look her in the eye and say it to her face. So like the coward I was, I needed her to help me get there first.

"Ask me what you need me to tell you," I didn't even try to hide the desperation in my voice, "and I'll do it."

Isabelle studied me carefully, like she was sorting out whether or not both of us could handle what was coming next, but when she finally spoke, it wasn't the question I was expecting.

"Have there been...have you..." she stuttered helplessly and looked down at our feet again. "Do you still take girls back to your dorm when I'm not around?"

A hard laugh erupted from my throat and then that hard laugh died right where it landed when the seriousness of her question finally slapped me in the face. She was serious. Dead serious.

"Where is this coming from, Iz?"

Isabelle's eyes snapped to mine and there was an accusation in her eyes now that had me jumping to explain.

"You told me once there couldn't be any other girls. You told me you just needed to hear me say the words and you would trust me and I told you I didn't want anyone but you. What's changed since then?"

She paled almost instantly and for the first time since we'd come into my dorm, she reached for me. "I'm sorry. I'm not trying to accuse you of anything. I know that's probably not how it sounded, but I just don't know what to think here, you know? Since the night we talked about all that, I've honestly never even thought about it again, at least not before that agent basically told me you were cheating on me every chance you got."

The air in the room suddenly ran cold and now I was imagining myself wrapping my hands around that bastard agent's throat for having the balls to even suggest something like that to her.

"I'm not cheating on you," I told her slowly. "I would never do that to you. I asked you to marry me. I bought you a house. We're having a kid. Why would I do all those things and then turn around and..."

I couldn't even finish that sentence. Couldn't stomach even thinking the words. When my gaze found Isabelle again, the hard, judgmental, suspicious glint was gone from her eyes and had replaced all that with a softer expression I was more accustomed to as she anxiously spun her engagement ring around her finger.

"I'm sorry."

Those words shoved away the darkness that had just surrounded us, but unfortunately, I had a feeling things were just about to get a little darker. She'd have more questions and I'd have to give her more answers. I squeezed my eyes shut and when they shot open again, I reached out to tuck some stray hair behind her ear and pulled her knuckles up to my mouth so I could brush my lips against them.

That was for me just as much as it was for her.

"Don't be sorry, Iz," my voice, so quiet and hoarse, was almost unrecognizable at this point. "You and the baby are the only good things in my life. I wish we didn't have to talk about this, but I've been in the clubhouse too, you know? I know what you see, I know what it looks like...I know how I used to be. But I need you to understand there is nowhere I wanna be than right next to you and there's nothing I wouldn't do for you or the baby. Please tell me you understand that."

Her watery eyes widened a little and suddenly, she was leaning forward to wrap her arms around my neck to hold me close.

"I do understand," she murmured in my ear. "I guess I just needed to hear you say it one more time."

My lips curled up into a smile and I sealed them over her mouth, finally feeling some of that darkness slip away completely.

"I'm sorry I've been such a basket case today," she whispered. "My head just got so twisted around. I didn't know which way was up, you know? He said so many things that just *hurt*."

My head shot up at her words. "What else did that agent—what's his name? What else did he say to you?"

With a heavy sigh, she lifted a shoulder and I knew this was going to be yet another mood killer.

"He basically said it was only a matter of time before you get arrested again and end up in jail. He said it'll be a cycle: you'll commit crimes, get caught, go to jail, get out, and then do it all over again."

Dark fury clouded my vision and now she looked a little afraid to continue. I felt like I was going to tear the carpet off the floorboards.

"What else..." I fumed, my nostrils flaring and my chest heaving furiously.

"What else did he say?"

She gulped and probably against her better judgment, delivered the last blow: "He told me that someday, you'll just be in prison and I'll be all alone with our kids."

My lips twitched and then I was up on my feet, barely aware of what I was even reaching for until I heard the crash. The best I could come up with in close quarters was the nearby ashtray I'd sent hurtling to the wall, but it didn't make me feel better. Putting my fist through the wall wouldn't have made me feel any better at this point.

Isabelle jumped at the sound of shattering glass and sat frozen on the bed, watching helplessly while I staggered a few feet away from her, clenching and unclenching my fists with my back to her. I just couldn't face her, just couldn't let her see me like this right now, and my shoulders hunched dangerously until I could get a handle on my shit so I didn't erupt again in front of her.

There was a truth in what that agent said to her today that I just couldn't reconcile.

When a soft hand rested gently on my shoulder, I jumped at the contact and just that little bit of connection sent the fury slipping away as I turned to face her. Just as I felt her arms wrapping around my neck, my head fell to the crook of her neck as I drew her in deeper into my chest.

"I'm so sorry, Iz," I whispered into her skin. "That shouldn't have happened to you today. I should've been there with you."

"It's okay, Caleb—"

"No," I cut in sharply, bringing my head up to look at her. "It's not okay that he blindsided you like that. These goddamned assholes think they know everything and they don't care who they run over to get what they want."

"It's not just that, Caleb," she started unevenly. "He scared me."

I frowned at her words. "What do you mean?"

"I know I shouldn't have let him get to me. I know I shouldn't have let anything he said mean anything," she blew out a deep breath as she tried to conjure the right words to accurately describe this. "But I've never felt this scared before, Caleb. They're not going to stop, are they?"

"You don't have anything to worry about," I promised her quietly and ran a thumb over her cheek. "We're gonna take it easy, lay low, and ride it out. This will all be over before you know it."

She nodded into my hands and I pulled her into my arms, holding her as tightly as I could, hoping this was enough.

"Is there anything else I need to know, Caleb?" Isabelle whispered into my chest and I knew what she was really asking.

"You know I'd never say anything, right?" she pressed anxiously, needing me to understand that all of my secrets were safe with her. "Everything you've ever told me—I'd never say a word to anyone, not even if the person was holding a gun to my head."

I winced and scrubbed a hand over my face to wipe that image from my mind. "Don't say that, Iz."

"It's true though," she shrugged a little too easily. "It doesn't matter what you've done for the club or what you might do. If you tell me about it and honestly, I hope you do because we need to trust each other, but if you tell me, I don't care what it is. Drugs or—"

"We don't run drugs, Iz," I told her. "The club gets into enough bad shit as it is and we don't need that extra pressure. Besides, something like that could carry a life sentence, depending on how much you've got on you, and none of us are stupid enough to go down that road just for a paycheck."

She nodded slowly, but there was no relief on her face. I think I knew why as she opened her mouth again to speak.

"Have you ever—"

"Yes," I cut in quietly. I didn't want her to have to say it out loud anymore than I did, but if someone had to say it, I was going to be the one to do it. "I've killed for the club before."

At this point, all the blood drained out of her beautiful face and tears welled up in her eyes, but I had to keep going.

"If you wanna know who and when and why, I'll tell you."

I waited for something from her, but she just shook her head. All those faces flashed across my mind now—all six of them. Six lives I'd taken to save my brothers, to help my club. Six lives who would've shot Dom, who would've slit Tiny's throat, who would've beaten Casey into a coma, who would've stolen thousands of dollars from the club, who would've ratted on the club and sent us to prison if I hadn't stepped in and put them down first. It wasn't an excuse and it didn't justify my actions. All I'd done was my job.

"I can't apologize for protecting my club, Iz," I murmured and dared a step closer to see if she'd move away. She didn't. "I wouldn't hesitate to do it again if I had to. I'll always protect my family. The club, my mom, Lex and Chloe...you and our baby. *Especially* you and our baby. I wouldn't hesitate. You know that, right?"

Isabelle frowned back at me, even as my hand slid over her fingertips and squeezed. For someone like her, who'd never known what being connected to the club really meant on this most basic level, who'd never had to draw a gun to protect someone she cared about, I knew how hearing all this must feel for her. The shock. The disbelief. The disgust. It was all there, written across her pale face. I couldn't blame her.

"I didn't want to talk to you about all of this," I whispered hoarsely. "Because I knew I wouldn't be able to handle the way you're lookin' at me. I didn't want you to know, even though you deserved to."

She deserved to know who she was about to marry, have a kid with, and have a life with. And if it was really too much, if she really couldn't take it, maybe it was better that I just knew it now.

But instead of running away, instead of looking at me with the disgust I probably deserved, Isabelle just nodded soberly and reached out to touch my face. "I get it. I really do. I can't believe I'm saying this right now, but at the end of the day, I don't think I care what you've done as long as you're safe and you're coming home to me."

That acceptance, even if there was resignation attached to it too, was exactly what I needed from her. While all of this had shed new light on everything Isabelle probably thought she knew about the club, she wasn't running out the door screaming her head off and taking our kid with her.

But now, with the weight of the club's orders settling on my shoulders, I knew it was pretty much time for her to leave the clubhouse so she could prove to Marcus, for once and for all, that she was an old lady who could be trusted.

"Hey, Iz," I rested both hands around her face and brushed some hair out of her eyes. "I gotta ask you a question now and I'm sorry I have to ask it, but if there's anything I need to know, anything they might try to use against us, you need to tell me now."

That wasn't really a question, but it was mainly because I already knew the answer anyway. I just needed to be sure and cover all my bases before Eli and ZZ came back with their report.

"Right," Isabelle sighed and stepped out of my hands so she could settle back on the mattress. "You know what else that agent told me? He said that if the club ever had a reason to doubt me, if they were suspected I had said anything to him today I would need protection."

I crouched down so I could fold my arms over her knees and tilted her chin up with my thumb. "Look at me, Iz. Nothing is gonna happen to you. I swear on my life. Nobody will come anywhere near you while I'm standing next to you, okay?"

The thought of her scared of the club and what they could do did nothing but twist the churning in my stomach.

"It's just these shitty circumstances," I told her. She didn't need to see that I was almost as terrified as she was. "And it's no different than how the club's looking at Lex and Becca right now either."

"Fair enough," she nodded and a small smile crept up her lips. God, I hoped she was going to change the subject. "So if we're talking skeletons in the closet, do you mean that time I smoked weed, for the first and only time in my life, mind you, and went streaking through campus?"

My mouth dropped open.

"Wha...no," I laughed because that was the only reaction I could come up with. "That's not—you're messing with me, right?"

"Nope," she grinned as she leaned forward to kiss me. I was too stunned to really kiss her back. "Campus security chased me all the way from the library to the plaza, but they never caught me. Bet you didn't think I had it in me, did you?"

My eyebrows shot to my forehead. "Jesus, Iz. I had no idea you were such a wild child. Why the hell is this the first time I'm hearing about this?"

"You never asked," she shrugged, playfully throwing this whole messed-up situation back in my face. "So I never told you."

"Alright, smartass," I relented. "You know, I take back what I said this morning about me going grey before I'm 30 if our kid is a girl. I'm gonna be grey before I'm 25 'cuz both you ladies are gonna make me lose my mind."

"Oh," she laughed. "I see how it is. So you're finally admitting I'm right?"

"I ain't admittin' shit, Iz," I grinned back at her. "Man, now all I can see is you running bare-ass naked through Duke. I know exactly why campus security couldn't catch you—they were too busy drooling over the view."

She just laughed and gripped the front of my cut to pull me in between her legs. "Shut it. But all joking aside, I'm pretty sure that's the wildest thing I've ever done. I mean, besides that little show we put on at the patch-over party, but that's it. They're not gonna find anything in my past that could put us at risk."

"That's what I thought," I smirked as I leaned down until her back planted into the mattress and her legs wrapped around my waist. "Everything's gonna be okay. You don't have anything to worry about. They'll probably bring you in again at least a couple more times just to put some pressure on us, but that's it."

"Okay," she nodded tightly.

I wished I hadn't had to bring all that shit up again, especially now that we'd moved past it, but she needed to understand I was always going to do whatever she needed me to do, whatever kept her safe, and whatever kept her happy.

"Can you do something for me, Caleb?"

"Whatever you want."

"Can we finally sit down with my dad and tell him?"

I blew out a hard breath and scrubbed a hand over my face. Shit. The thought of being anywhere near that asshole, let alone have that asshole anywhere near Isabelle...rehab and some counseling sessions with his daughter did not mean he was suddenly a reformed man.

"I know you don't want anything to do with him," Isabelle told me quietly and I just huffed out a laugh. "But he's still my dad and whether you like it or not, he's gonna be our baby's grandpa, too. He's been trying and I don't think it's right for him to find out from anyone but us."

When I just exhaled again and tugged a hand through my hair, Isabelle pulled me a little closer.

"I'm not saying it has to be tomorrow or even this week, but I think we should talk to him soon before you know..." she gestured to her flat stomach, "she decides to make her presence a little more obvious."

My lips twitched a little and I just lifted my eyes to the ceiling, fighting that grin for as long as I could. I'd never be able to deny her, but that didn't mean I was happy about this particular development either.

"Ah, alright. I guess we have to tell him eventually," I allowed, even though I was pretty sure I was going to hate this upcoming sit-down more than that time Isabelle forced me to sit through two whole episodes of *Project Runway*. Sure, I'd gotten laid after it, but still...

"On that note," I leaned down to kiss her quick before murmuring against her lips, "I gotta stay here 'cuz of club bullshit, so Z's gonna take you home."

Her blue eyes went wide. "They don't even trust—"

"It's just protocol, Iz," I told her gently, not wanting to upset her any more than she already had been today. "It's nothin' personal and it's nothin' against either of us. It's just the way we do things when this kinda thing comes up."

"Okay. You're gonna come home later, right?"

"Of course. Don't wait up for me though. I don't know how long all this club shit is gonna take."

Tomorrow, when everything was in the clear and when Marcus choked on his words about Isabelle's trustworthiness and loyalty, I'd be able to tell her what was really going on. Until then, I just had to sit on my hands and wait.

It was going to be a long night.

CHAPTER SIX
Haunted

Isabelle

I sighed heavily as I tossed my keys on the kitchen table and ducked down a little to peer through the blinds.

Yep, ZZ was still there.

He wasn't doing a very good job of hiding that he'd only moved down the street about four house-lengths. The truck was just sitting there in the darkness, waiting and watching with a diligence that was a little nerve-wracking, if not sort of impressive too.

ZZ would probably sit there all night, staring at my front door, if that's what the club wanted him to do. There was something about the whole thing that was honorable and completely idiotic at the same time. The kind of blind faith it took to just take orders like that, to literally do whatever the president said without question and without hesitation...it was hard to reconcile the dedication it took to live your life that way.

Everything they had to do from the runs, the meetings, the *killings*, all for the sake of the brotherhood, as Caleb would say, I wasn't sure I would ever completely understand. The average person just doesn't have a conversation with their fiancé like that every day and I needed some time not only to sift through everything I'd learned, but how I felt about it all too.

Before now, I'd turned a blind eye, unwilling to even consider what else the club did beyond the shop and running guns because I'd been too afraid of the answers to those lingering questions, but I couldn't afford to be ignorant anymore.

And while there were some things I knew I'd never be completely on board with, at the end of the day, none of that mattered. Could I live with myself, and Caleb, knowing what he might have done before coming home to me at night? Could I still look at him and feel the same way? Could I still marry him and have a family with him? God help me, but the answer to all those questions was an unequivocal yes.

I didn't know whether to feel happy or sad about that, especially since I was sitting here in my own home with a watchdog staring at my door and waiting for me to make a wrong move.

And with that unsettling thought, a distraction was in order. With my sketchbook and pencil in hand, I slid down the wall inside our nursery and settled in. In my mind's eye, I could already picture where everything would go and my pencil skimmed across the page to keep pace with my imagination.

My mind flew back to the sketch I'd done so long ago, the one I'd shown Caleb, the one that represented the ripped-out page from an ee cummings' poetry book that was framed on our nightstand.

Soon, the intertwined trees stretching out over the wall began to take shape with their branches reaching for each other. Each leaf took on the outline of an over-sized heart with some buds peppering the branches and the roots sweeping out underneath where the crib would sit on the carpet. I added a few birds and a cute little owl just for good measure and held the page up to the wall to survey my work.

Nodding to myself, I stepped up to the wall to begin the process of outlining my sketch onto the wall. It wasn't that different than a tattoo artist using tracing paper over their subject's skin and I didn't want to mess this up.

I was just finishing up the last strokes when a knock on the door jerked me out of work-mode. On instinct, I pulled my phone out of my back pocket and saw three missed calls from Becca that I'd been completely oblivious to as I worked.

When I opened the door, she didn't even wait to be invited in. She just barreled right through, almost knocking me over, and tossed her purse down on my couch.

"Hey, Becs," I started warily. "Nice to see you too. Come on in. Make yourself at home."

But when Becca finally turned to face me, I didn't see the friend I'd known all my life. I didn't see the girl who'd always made sure I wasn't picked last for dodgeball at recess. I didn't see the girl who'd gotten in Melissa Sullivan's face when she made fun of my Hello Kitty T-shirt in seventh grade. I didn't see the girl who'd held my hand through every second of my mom's funeral.

I didn't recognize this girl staring back at me and that scared the hell out of me.

"How can you be joking around at a time like this?" Becca demanded, hitching a hand on her hip as she spoke. "Do you think he's—can you look, Belle? Can you look to see if he's still following me?"

I frowned back at her. While the dramatics weren't necessarily anything new for her, this downright, no-holds-barred panic definitely was.

"Who's following you?"

Becca just shook her head furiously, her eyes darting around the room.

Someone had written once—was it Shakespeare maybe?—that suspicion haunted the mind of the guilty. I had nothing to feel guilty about and I had nothing to hide. Becca, with her wild dark eyes and her trembling hands, looked like suspicion trailed after her like a demonic ghost.

Alarm bells were already going off in my head.

Still, I obliged her and glanced out the tiny window in my front door. There was another truck parked right behind where ZZ sat and I figured that could only be Becca's club escort/tail, whether she was aware of it or not. I didn't know why I felt the need to do it, maybe it was just the stress of the day or my own annoyance at being treated like a second-class citizen by the club, but I decided to just run with this and see where it went.

"No," I told her carefully. "I don't see anything."

Relief washed over her face and she took off through the living room to head right for the kitchen. She had the refrigerator open before I could even offer her something from it and she threw me a glance over her shoulder.

"Do you have anything harder than beer?" she asked.

I figured Caleb wouldn't necessarily be happy to share his beer with her, so I offered up the Jack he'd kept hidden away in our pantry for when he had 'shit days', as he'd so eloquently put it.

Becca didn't even hesitate. She just grabbed the glass from me and downed it. With her eyes squeezed shut to cut the after-effects of the alcohol, she held the glass out to me for a refill, which I reluctantly did. This wasn't normal for her. This wasn't normal for *anyone*. Not after the day we'd had and not for someone who had nothing to hide.

"Becca," I started slowly. "Are you alright?"

She wiped her mouth and set her glass down on the counter. "I think so. I'm just scared, Belle. Aren't you?"

"Well, yeah. Of course I am. The ATF aren't messing around and if they find something, Caleb could end up in prison. That's scary as shit to me, Becs."

Becca nodded like that wasn't really what she'd wanted to hear and then she was leaning in a little closer. "Aren't you scared of the club? Of what they could do?"

I frowned back at her. "What do you mean?"

"Don't you know?" her eyes blazed back at me and it was then, with her leaning in so close I could smell her breath, that I finally saw the dilated eyes, the manic, almost crazed glint staring back at me.

"What would they do?"

"They'd kill us, Belle. Maybe they wouldn't kill you right away because of, you know," she gestured to my stomach, "but they'd do it eventually. They wouldn't hesitate."

Caleb's words from earlier tonight swirled around me and a slow chill ran down my spine.

"No, they wouldn't do that," I told her, unable to hide the desperation in my voice.

Becca just huffed out a laugh and ran a shaking hand through her hair. "Bullshit they wouldn't. I don't believe that for a second. They'd put a bullet right between my eyes and they wouldn't think twice about it. Eli would probably do it himself if it came down to it."

Why was she so goddamn paranoid? Why had she even risked coming over here in the first place when she had to have known she was being followed by either the ATF or the club?

"The only reason anyone would even consider doing that is if one of us gave something up. We're never going to do that, so we don't have anything to worry about. Right?"

Suddenly, Becca's eyes darkened and she took an aggressive step forward. "If you had to choose, you'd choose your baby daddy over me, wouldn't you? You'd let them kill me, wouldn't you?"

I shook my head and just couldn't grasp what was happening here. At some point, this had devolved into a me-versus-them situation and Becca had suddenly shoved me right in the middle of some disaster I knew she wouldn't clue me in on anyway.

"What's going on, Becca?" I asked. "What happened today?"

Her eyes darted nervously from one end of the kitchen to the other, like she expected someone to walk in here at any second.

"Do you think they've been following you too?" she asked abruptly. "Have they been tailing you too?"

"I don't know," I shrugged. "Probably. I guess if they've been following you, they've been following me too."

She stared back at me like I'd just sprouted a second head. "How can you be so...cavalier about all this? Like it's no big deal? Like them showing up here today and asking all these scary questions is just nothing?"

"I never said that," I frowned again. "It's absolutely a big deal. I was mad as hell at Caleb for putting me in that position today, but there's nothing we can do about it now and there was nothing we could've done to stop it either. But I've got nothing to hide. I'm not scared of them. But you are..."

I trailed off and our eyes met from across the kitchen. She must've seen the awareness, the suspicion, and the disappointment in my expression because all the blood seemed to drain right out of her face. This was probably the moment I was always going to remember as the moment I lost my best friend—I just didn't know it yet.

"I have to..." she snapped her mouth shut and stared down at her feet.

"Have to what? What do you have to do?"

A sinking feeling, coupled by paralyzing dread, settled into my stomach and I swallowed hard when she just shook her head.

"I want to tell you, Belle. I really do. I wish I could tell you."

"Becca, I can't help you if you won't tell me what's going on."

"You can't help me," she whispered. "I wish you could, but you can't. I don't think you would even if you could."

After everything we'd been through, after all our history and all the years we'd spent together as best friends, it looked like it had all spiraled down to this. The father of my baby and my future husband over my oldest friend in the world.

"Are you asking me to choose, Becs?" I whispered. Tears stung my eyes because I knew where this was going. I knew how this was going to end. It was just a matter of time now.

"I shouldn't have to," she murmured back. "You're my best friend in the entire world. The only real friend I've ever had. I love you, Belle. You know that. But I guess if push comes to shove, I know where we stand now."

"Did you..." I didn't know if I could even bring myself to say the words out loud. "Did you tell them something today?"

Becca just stared back at me. Finally, she shook her head. Whether that meant she hadn't said anything or just wouldn't tell me, I had a feeling I might never get the chance to ask her.

With that, she slammed the glass on the counter, stalked out of the kitchen, and then slammed the front door behind her.

Nothing about this short argument, if that's what it really was, made sense to me.

Somewhere along the way, she'd changed and it hadn't been for the better. The hard-partying, the drinking, the way she'd gradually shown more skin every time I saw her, her involvement with the Horsemen and the clubhouse in the first place—I'd just chalked it up to her flirting with a little bit of recklessness.

Becca was a girl unhinged. Unstable. Someone I didn't recognize. Someone I didn't know.

She was also my oldest friend, someone who'd been there for me and been in my life since we were in kindergarten. If the club was Caleb's family, then Becca was my family too.

But at the end of the day, if Becca was going to do something reckless that could put my *new* family at risk, who would I choose?

I swept a tear from my eye and rubbed a hand over my face.

I knew what the right choice was. I just wished it didn't have to be so goddamned hard.

CHAPTER SEVEN
Invasion

Caleb

"Here ya go," I handed Dom a cold beer as I dropped down on the bench and leaned my elbows all the way back on the picnic table, kicking my feet out in front of me. "Thought you could use this."

"Yeah," Dom huffed out a laugh and took a healthy pull from the bottle. "I'll probably need a few more of these before I feel normal again."

I shook my head and took another swig from my beer. "Amen to that."

"You know, I kept thinking to myself today, *there's no way this could possibly get any worse,* until it did. And it did again. And again. It was like one giant snowball of shit barreling down the highway, you know?"

"So now we just sit here and wait," I nodded ruefully. "This is gonna be a fun night, huh?"

Dom huffed out a laugh and that was probably the best either of us was going to be able to muster in this ridiculous scenario. I took a grateful gulp of my beer and thanked God I wasn't alone in my dorm to be tempted with that bottle of Jack.

It wasn't just the way the ATF had stirred the pot today. It was everything else too. Because for the first time in my entire life, I felt conflicted about my involvement with the club. For Isabelle, who was so good and honest and decent, to look at me with such horror, there was no stopping the knee-jerk guilt that shot up through my conscience. And for her to be almost understanding about this whole mess was almost just as bad, if not worse.

The fact that it was somehow worse for her to innately understand my commitment to the club in light of everything I'd told her made me want to tear my hair out. I'd never felt guilt like this over club business. Never questioned why we had to run guns in the first place. Never felt remorse over killing anyone for the sake of the club. I'd always just turned on auto-pilot and shut everything else off because I always knew that if I slowed down long enough to actually think about what I was doing, the guilt would eat me alive.

And now I was sitting here, wondering why I was even doing any of it in the first place. If it could land me in prison, if it could get me killed, if it could take me away from the things I wanted more than anything in my life, I just didn't know anymore.

That was it. I just didn't know.

Now, it was too quiet and my thoughts were too disturbing to sit with on my own.

"So, everything alright with Lex?" I asked Dom quietly.

Dom just shrugged. "She's not very happy. She had to drag our kid to the precinct where they pretty much told her she'd be living out of our car with Chloe if I get arrested, but I guess I can see where she's coming from with that one."

"Shit," I exhaled.

I hadn't even thought about how terrifying that must've been for Lex. I'd been so focused on taking care of my own old lady that I'd completely bypassed anything else that had happened today.

"Lex handled it okay though."

"They both did," Dom nodded to me quietly. "I think given the shit situation today, they both did pretty good, don't you think?"

I huffed out a laugh and shifted in my chair so I could dig my cigarettes out of my back pocket. Dom eyed the pack hungrily, and I put one in between my lips before holding out the pack to my drooling best friend.

"Now," I told him with a smirk. "I know I gotta quit, you know with the kid and all. Iz hasn't been on my ass about it yet, but—"

"She will be," Dom cut in warily. "Trust me, you got maybe a month. Tops. Then it's all over with."

"And until that day comes, I gotta enjoy every last one of these beautiful things while I still can. And since we've both had a shit day, probably the shittiest in a long-ass time, I think we should indulge while we still can."

Dom chewed on his bottom lip before begrudgingly sliding a cigarette out from my outstretched hand. With a knowing grin, I held out my lighter to Dom and then lit up my own. For a few moments, the difficulty of the day was almost completely behind us as Rage Against the Machine echoed from the speakers.

"Those assholes sure didn't hold anything back," I shook my head and took another long pull from my cigarette, letting the nicotine do its job. "I can only imagine the shit they're gonna try next when those agents bring them in again."

"When, not if?"

I just shook my head sadly. "You know that's exactly how it's gonna be.

They're not gonna stop until they think they've found something," and then I let my thoughts get the better of me, "The worse part about all this shit is that they're kinda right, aren't they? I mean, if they ever got enough on us to put us away for awhile, everything they threatened Lex and Isabelle with isn't too far off from reality."

"I wouldn't say that to Isabelle if I were you," Dom shot back lightly, but it was hard to justify any humor in a situation like this.

"Yeah, well, I won't tell if you won't."

We grinned back at each other, but the sadness I saw in Dom's face had to have been mirrored in my own. Dom and I were pretty much in the exact same position now: if things went south with the club, it didn't just affect us anymore.

Just the thought of it, the idea of Isabelle alone in our house every single day, sleeping alone in our bed, raising our kid all by herself—I didn't know whether to vomit or put my fist through a wall. It was the most helpless feeling: knowing you had no control, no real say in anything because everything you did was dictated by someone else.

"Hey, Dom?"

"Yeah, brother?"

"Do you ever wonder if Lex would be better off without you? If she'd be happier?"

Dom's eyebrows rose deep into his forehead and he stared out into the slick grass for a few long moments. Then, exhaling through his nose, he turned back to face me with a grave expression.

"I think about that every day. Keeps me up at night sometimes," he murmured hoarsely.

"Me, too," I nodded slowly as we both stared out at the grass in front of us. The setting sun had cast shadows of purple and red splintering across the parking lot and it was easier to focus on the beauty of the scenery at our feet, rather than the ugliness of the truth in this conversation.

"Is this about what Eli said at the table? About Isabelle not being one of us?"

I shifted uncomfortably on the bench and stared at the pavement at our feet. "I guess a part of me has always wondered if maybe she'd be happier if she could've just gone to that school in Richmond and forgotten all about me."

Dom scratched his beard in thought and just shrugged. "I don't know. Lex loves me. I don't doubt that for a second, you know? So if she wants to stay, have kids and a life with me, then, I guess I'd be a jackass to try and push her away just because I'm a scared as shit asshole."

"You calling me a scared as shit asshole?" I grinned back at him half-heartedly.

"Nah," Dom laughed. "Maybe not. But you love Isabelle, right?"

I didn't even hesitate. "Absolutely."

"And you're gonna marry her. I mean, you already knocked her up, so I guess you might as well."

I huffed out a laugh and lit another cigarette, offering one to Dom, who wisely declined a second. "Yeah, bro, I'm gonna marry her."

"I figured," Dom laughed, but when he started speaking again, the seriousness seeped back into his voice. "Did you ever wonder if Isabelle thinks that maybe your life would be easier if you had an old lady who grew up in the life, like your mom or even Lex, for that matter? You wouldn't have had to explain anything to her and maybe she'd have handled things a little differently today. What if she's sitting at your house right now thinking all that, too, on top of everything else?"

Christ. This whole time I'd wondered if her life might be easier if I just disappeared from it. I'd never once considered that maybe she wondered the same. It was all so backward that I just wanted to laugh and maybe hang my head and cry like the scared as shit asshole I was.

Dom's gruff voice floated across the night air, pulling me from my depressing thoughts.

"We've got two of the best kind of woman there is: loyal, good, gorgeous, who are gonna be good mothers, and able to take on all the other shit that comes along with being with guys like us. Women like that are hard to find in this life and you know it. So I get to sleep at night thinkin' that Lex's life might be easier without me in it, but I don't really believe she would be happier. I guess that's the funny thing about being in a committed relationship. You can't be scared of it or it'll eat you alive. You have to actually let the good things happen every once and awhile. Otherwise, all you're left with is bad."

I was going to need a few days before I could even fully comprehend the weight of those words, let alone what they truly meant for me and Isabelle. I'd always felt like I was somehow on borrowed time with her. That a criminal like me had no business being with someone like her. Dom was right, to an extent, but how much would she really be able to put up with if she wasn't already pregnant?

And just when I thought we were finally on the other side of all this bullshit, my phone buzzed on top of the picnic table. With a frown, I snapped it open and skimmed the text Marcus just sent me.

"Shit," I exhaled.

Dom frowned back at me. "What?"

"Apparently, Becca's at my house right now."

"Shit," Dom exhaled. "But that doesn't necessarily mean—"

"Everything's good on my end," I quickly dismissed even the suggestion of what he was about to say. "Becca's the one we gotta watch."

"Yeah," Dom nodded solemnly. "I was thinkin' that too. I don't know why or how, but something has just always seemed off about her."

Now, the problem was that Becca showing up at my house cast a net of suspicion over Isabelle too. Every second that went by, every moment she spent in my house would just make the club wonder what, exactly, was so important that Becca had to speed over to talk to Isabelle within just hours of being interrogated.

"She'll do the right thing," Dom told me, as if he could read my thoughts. "As soon as Becca's out of your house, she'll do the right thing."

Part of me wondered who he was trying to convince more. If she did the right thing, her status as my old lady and as family in the MC would be solidified. Whether that was good or bad was still something I needed to work out. And if she didn't do the right thing, I couldn't think about that right now. Just the thought of what could happen, of what that could lead to, of what the club would expect me to do...

Luckily, one beer and ten minutes later, I got the call. With Dom hanging on every word next to me, I listened as Isabelle related the details of Becca's visit and all signs pointed to what I'd already known.

Now I had the proof. Now I could breathe. Now I could shove aside that tiny, nagging feeling that maybe I didn't know Isabelle as well as I thought I did. Thank fucking Christ.

And just as I was about to text Marcus back that I'd heard from Isabelle, another incoming text from him nearly sent the beer in my free hand plummeting right into the pavement.

"What?" Dom asked next to me.

All I had to do was show Dom the text and he swore under his breath.

"Yeah," I nodded grimly. "I think we'd better get our asses back inside the chapel."

. . . .

When I shut door from the garage behind me a couple hours later, I tiptoed through the kitchen and kicked off my shoes. It was well past two in the morning and hell, after the day she'd had, Isabelle had better be sleeping. I couldn't remember when a day had felt this long, like it had somehow compacted weeks, even months into a full 24 hours, but right about now, I wanted nothing more than to just curl up into my bed with Isabelle and pass out.

But as I shuffled into the living room, fully prepared to peel off my clothes with every step so I was that much closer to falling into our bed, I found Isabelle already passed out, but on the couch. Careful not to wake her, I gently set my cut down over the side of the couch and padded around to her. A smile tugged across my lips when I got a better look at the book sprawled out on her chest and gently pulled the baby name book out from under her hands.

I glanced at the page she'd had open and grinned. She'd only circled one name, but she'd circled it three times and put a few stars next to it, too.

Ava.

That kinda had a nice ring to it. Short. Sweet, yet sophisticated. Ava Sawyer. Yeah, I liked the sound of that.

"Hey," a sleepy voice grumbled. "Give that back, jerk. I wasn't done with it yet."

I grinned down at her and held up the page. "Ava, huh?"

She yawned and stretched her arms over her head. "Mmm hmm. I was trying to think of girl names, because it's gonna be a girl, but you already knew that. Anyway, I was trying to come up with some that would work for her when she's little and when she's older, too."

"I like it," I nodded and crouched down so I could kiss her. "It's pretty. But you know, *if* it's a boy—and I said if—I think we should name him Connor. Keep it in the family, you know?"

"Yeah," she smiled. "I think so too."

I reached out for her hand so I could gently pull her off the couch and walk her down the hallway. With one hand at her waist and the other splayed protectively over her stomach, I leaned in to brush my lips against her neck. She shivered a little and I felt her body relax under my touch.

She leaned into my chest and inhaled deeply. "You smell like smoke, Caleb."

Jesus, she really didn't waste any time. *One month, my ass.*

"Uh yeah, Dom and me might've blown off a little steam, so to speak, while we were waiting for all this shit to resolve itself."

She shifted around to face me, one eyebrow arched slyly and I knew my days as a smoker were now officially numbered. So in an effort to just get this over with already, I beat her to the punch.

"I'm gonna quit, Iz. I promise."

She didn't look any more convinced than I felt. "When?"

"I'll start tomorrow if that's what you want," I just shrugged. "I'm not gonna do cold turkey or anything because that would suck balls. Dom did the patch and the gum before Chloe was born, so I'll give that a try."

"That's good," Isabelle nodded warily and it was clear she still wasn't completely convinced. "Because you know you can't just step outside for a cigarette and then come back in the house and go anywhere near the baby."

"Wow," I laughed. "We're barely three months into this thing and you're already sharpening your mama bear claws."

Her eyebrows lifted in amusement and a grin tugged across her lips. "And that's a bad thing?"

"Absolutely not, Iz. And, just so we're clear, when you're at school tomorrow, I'll grab some patches and a box of that nicotine gum on my way to the clubhouse."

That seemed to be enough for her and she turned back around in my arms to lean back against my chest again. Even with the lights off, even with her nestled against my chest in our bed, it didn't feel like this was going to get any easier.

"You did the right thing," I started softly, tightening my arms around her as I murmured into her hair. "You know that, don't you?"

She nodded wordlessly and maybe it was for the best that I just did all the talking right now.

"If there was ever any doubt about where your loyalties lie, that's gone now. You took care of that. And Becca...I don't know how to tell you this, Iz, so I'm just gonna come out and say it. After she left our house, literally *right* after, Casey tailed her to The Sundown Saloon."

Isabelle's head shot off my chest and even in the darkness, I could still make out her wide, terrified blue eyes shining back at me.

"He followed her inside," I went on. "He didn't have to wait too long before she was in a back corner with some guy, buying an eight-ball from him."

"Eight-ball as in..."

I nodded into her hair. "Coke."

She fell back against her pillow and her hands immediately shot up to her head almost as if she was tearing at her hair in disbelief. All she could do was shake her head and run a hand over her face. I guess that was probably as good a reaction as any to finding out your best friend was a closet junkie.

"I knew it," Isabelle whispered. "When she came over here tonight, something was just *off* with her, you know? The shaking, the twitching, and her eyes were so dilated it was freaky. I just never thought about it. All those times I was pissed at her for ditching me at the clubhouse when she was holed up in the bathroom, it makes a lot of sense now."

I froze, my eyes going wide. "She's been doing that shit at the clubhouse? In our goddamn bathroom? How long has this been going on, Iz?"

She blew out a breath and lifted a shoulder against my chest. "To be completely honest with you, probably since the first time I came to the clubhouse back in September, I think."

"Jesus."

"I never thought anything of it, you know? I think I was more annoyed she was leaving me alone in the clubhouse than anything. Well, at least at the beginning. Everything else—all the weird things she's been doing, I never really put it all together until tonight."

Becca was either desperate as shit or had a goddamn death wish to do something that reckless and that careless tonight of all nights.

"What's gonna happen to her, Caleb?"

The fear in her voice made my chest twist a little, but there was nothing I could do to reassure her, nothing I could do to save her best friend, especially since it looked like her best friend didn't really want to be saved.

"We'll tail her, just like we did tonight. We'll watch her. She really hasn't done anything yet, at least not anything we know about. And let's face it, if you and Eli cut ties with her right now, all that's gonna do is freak her out and send her right to the ATF either out of fear or retaliation."

"Keep your friends close and your enemies closer, I guess, huh?"

I nodded into her hair. "Something like that, yeah."

"And if she talks to them, what happens then?"

She had to have already known the answer to that before she asked it. Maybe she just needed to hear the words. Maybe she was looking for hope where there was none.

"I don't think she'll get far enough to actually give them something, Iz. We won't let that happen. We'll be too close for her to get into a meeting with them without us getting to her first."

"And if she does get into a meeting with them?"

I sighed and ran my free hand over my face. I didn't like having to say it out loud, but she needed to hear it. "Then she'd better hope they get her into an airtight witness protection program."

She shuddered a little against my chest and I wrapped both arms around her to pull her in even tighter. We were lying here, basically discussing her best friend's imminent punishment in the middle of the night with our arms wrapped around each other and Isabelle wasn't running from me. She wasn't screaming at me either. It was almost as if she'd already known the truth and come to terms with it long before I ever got home tonight.

The weight of that settled into my chest and just about crushed me.

"I feel like she's already gone," Isabelle whispered and turned her head to bury her face into my chest. "She asked me who I would choose—you or her. The second that happened I just knew it was already over. All those years, everything we've been through together, it's just all gone now and I don't really understand why."

"If the ATF ever got wind of her problem, they'd exploit that every chance they got. They'd hold a maximum prison sentence for possession over her head just to get her to crack. She knows that probably more than anybody."

She turned her face again and then I felt the wetness spreading onto my skin, coating and saturating the space underneath her cheek with her tears. All I could do was tug her across my chest and hold her. There was nothing more to say. Nothing more that could be done.

Becca's days were numbered. Now it was just a matter of when and how.

Nobody put the club at risk and was shown mercy.

Nobody put my family at risk and lived to tell about it.

. . .

Isabelle

The next morning, as I stretched and yawned with the sun, everything felt different. Better. It was like the darkness that had shrouded the day before had blossomed into a beautiful morning. All of yesterday's ugliness was gone now. My not-so-fun encounter at the precinct. Becca. God, Becca.

Today was going to be a good day. I could feel it. Besides, how could today possibly be any worse than yesterday?

Caleb was still dozing next to me and sleepily slung an arm around my waist to tug me back under his arm.

I really didn't want to leave, but the sooner I got to the studio and took care of business, the sooner I could get back to Caleb. So, I made a quick dash into our second bedroom, which now doubled as my home studio, grabbed my current project off the easel, then I grabbed a banana and a granola bar for the road and was out the door.

A little over six hours later, I pulled Caleb's truck into our driveway and my heart tugged in my chest at the sight of all that empty concrete. No Harley in sight.

Separation anxiety. That's what this was.

Separation anxiety? More like codependency. You're a complete loser. And a goner. Totally a goner.

Just as I absentmindedly put my key in the front door, I froze. That little bit of force pushed the whole door open and a cold chill ran down my spine. Caleb always tripled-checked all the locks on our doors before he left the house. I was already backing up, my project dropping to the ground as terror spiked through me and my fingers flying into my purse for something I could use to defend myself, when a figure hovered in the doorway and stilled.

Everything seemed to happen in a blur.

I saw a black leather cut, dark eyes, dark hair, and when his face finally came into clearer view, it only took me a second to place where I'd seen him before.

The patch-over party.

Diego Padilla.

We both moved at the same time. He jerked forward, flinging the door open at the exact moment I found my can of pepper spray. He blinked, momentarily stunned into immobility by what was in my hand and that gave me the opening I needed to flick the safety guard and cover the bastard head to shoulders in that white, foamy spray.

"Ah!" he screamed in pain, both hands snapping up to his face, scrubbing and pawing at his eyes. "Fucking bitch!"

Diego stumbled around the doorway with one hand covering his face and the other groping aimlessly for anything that could help him, but I was already backpedalling, nearly tripping over the front step and hightailing it back the truck as fast as my feet could carry me.

When I was safely locked back inside Caleb's truck, my eyes shot to the front door and found Diego slouched down in the doorway, still scrubbing furiously at his eyes and screaming obscenities my way. Pure adrenaline was the only thing keeping me moving right now and I fumbled to back out of the driveway, screeching the tires and everything.

My chest was still heaving. My lungs felt like they were about to collapse I was coughing so violently, but the house was in my rearview mirror right now and that was what really mattered.

I hated that the sight of my house in my rearview mirror made me feel relieved.

I hated that I knew I was going to be afraid to be in my own home now.

I hated what I knew Caleb was going to have to do now.

I hated this fear. I hated this stress. And, somewhere in the deep recesses of my mind, I knew I hated this life.

There was just nothing I could do about it.

CHAPTER EIGHT
Outlaw Justice

Caleb

I sped through the parking lot, oblivious to any passers-by, pedestrians, or other vehicles in my way. As I skidded my bike right next to where my truck was parked, my heart skidded to a halt right along with it. Immediately, I was searching for one thing and one thing only.

She wasn't there. Not in the truck. Not in the parking lot.

That was all I needed to see before I sprinted through the clubhouse's main doors, barreling my way inside, and barely cognizant of anything less than two feet in front of me. Dom was in front of me now and pointing me toward the hallway. I knew what that meant. I just had to get there first. My mom paced in front of the bathroom and her eyes widened when she saw me, reaching for me without moving from her spot at the door.

"She won't let me in, Caleb," my mom told me in a hushed whisper, but it was the fear in her dark eyes that scared me the most. "Told us what happened and then she locked herself in your bathroom. She won't come out."

I needed a second to calm myself down before I went in there and I also needed as much information as my mom could give me because I didn't want Isabelle to have to repeat it.

"Where were you, Caleb?" my mom was saying now and I didn't appreciate the accusation in her tone. "Why didn't you pick up the damned phone?"

I'd been at the gas station picking up that goddamn Nicotine gum and those patches, but that wasn't important now, and I just waved a hand dismissively. "It was Padilla?"

My mom nodded tightly. "She said she recognized him from the patch-over party."

"He didn't touch her?"

"If he did, she isn't saying. Maybe she'll tell you more, but she said she got him good with pepper spray, so it sounds like he didn't chase after her."

"Good," I huffed darkly. "I hope she sprayed the whole damn can in his face. Anyone been to the house yet?"

"They're waiting for you."

With a quick nod in her direction, I knocked on the door.

"Iz," I called gently. "It's me. Open the—"

The door flew open, cutting me off mid-sentence, and my arms were around her before either of us could say anything else. Jesus, she was shaking like a leaf and when I lifted up her chin to get a better look at her, I wanted to punch right through the mirror above the sink. Isabelle bit down on her bottom lip to keep herself from crying and her lip quivered. Her eyes were wide and haunted; her face was pale and blotchy at the same time, like the adrenaline coursing through her wasn't quite sure how to manifest itself.

"Iz," I whispered hoarsely as both hands closed around her face and I backed her into the bathroom to lift her up onto the sink. "I got you, okay?"

Isabelle nodded tightly into my hands and bit her lip again as her eyes welled up. "I had a panic attack. I couldn't breathe and my chest still feels really tight. I still feel like I can't breathe."

Her breath was coming in stunted and staggered, like her lungs were working overtime to take in air, but her body just wasn't having it right now and my arms tightened around her.

"Just breathe slow," I told her. "In and out. Focus on that."

She nodded tightly and leaned into my chest. After a few silent moments, all the tension in her body seemed to gradually slip away and her chest was rising and falling a little more normally now.

"I was so scared," she whispered into my chest. "I thought he was gonna kill me."

It was just one thing after another. It was just like Dom had said the night before: everything was snowballing. Left, right, and around every goddamn corner. I was done letting my life shit all over her, stress her out, and scare the living hell out of her.

"Hey," I murmured to her, running my thumb over her cheek to reassure her. "You're tough as shit, Iz. You got away. You kept yourself and our kid safe. That's all that matters. I'll take care of everything else."

She nodded into my hands and I wiped away a stray tear with my thumb.

"Did he do anything, Iz? Did he grab you? Say anything to you?"

Isabelle swallowed tightly with an almost imperceptible nod and laughed a little. "He called me a fucking bitch. That was about as far as he got."

My jaw clenched and I had to bite back the rage threatening to boil over. It all played out in my mind and that alone was enough to seal that asshole's fate. It didn't even matter that Padilla hadn't touched her. He'd violated our home. He'd forced Isabelle to have to protect herself. He'd scared her so badly she'd had a panic attack in the bathroom of my dorm. He'd sworn at her. As far as I was concerned, he'd better hope I never found him.

"Did he have a gun, Iz? A knife? Anything?"

She just shook her head and I leaned forward to kiss her forehead. I'd heard everything I needed to know.

"Stay here with my mom," I told her quietly. "I'm gonna go take care of this."

She nodded again and smiled weakly at my mom from over my shoulder, who had dutifully maintained her post outside the bathroom. My mom looked halfway between relieved and irate, but I guess I couldn't really blame her.

"How long are you gonna be gone?" she asked and I tucked some blonde hair behind her ear.

"I don't know, babe," I murmured back. "Just stay here. Get some rest and I'll get back to you as soon as I can, okay?"

She nodded slowly. "Okay. Please be safe."

"I always am," I grinned back at her and leaned forward to press a quick on her lips. "See ya later, Iz."

As I passed through my dorm, I kissed my mom quickly on the forehead to both thank her and reassure her before motioning with my head to Dom and Casey, who were already waiting for me outside the door.

"Heading to your house?" Dom asked, clearly ready to follow into step behind me.

Somehow in the midst of this white-hot rage, I managed to shake my head. "I'll worry about the house later. I need to have a word with Padilla first."

Dom's eyes went wide with alarm and he immediately held up his hands. "Caleb, you gotta bring this to the table. You can't go flyin' off the handle here—you're just gonna make this shit worse."

"This isn't club business," I spat. "I don't have to bring *shit* to the table because this is about me and him."

I moved to start down the hallway, but Dom stepped directly in my path and held up his hands to stop me.

"Slow down, Caleb. Think this through. You go on a manhunt for Padilla by yourself with a vendetta and that could go south real fast," Dom told me in a calm and even voice I couldn't have faked if I tried.

"Yeah, well, I'm not going by myself," I cocked an eyebrow at him. "'Cuz you two are comin' with me."

Dom exhaled roughly and scrubbed a hand over his face. "I think you might end up regretting this, you know."

I just shrugged and pushed past them both to hike through the debris. While reason ebbed at my conscience, the only thing I could focus on for longer than a second was putting my fist right through that asshole's jaw and shattering it all over the floor. Never in my entire life had I felt this bloodthirsty, this violent, this driven by blind rage. I didn't care. I didn't care if the club came down on me for going after Padilla without permission. As far as I was concerned, permission was the last thing I needed right now.

"Dom," I called over my shoulder as I stalked down the hallway. "If it was *your* house and *your* old lady, you'd feel a little differently, don't you think?"

I nodded to myself when I heard Dom's sigh of surrender and then there was some shuffling behind me as Dom and Casey followed me out of the clubhouse without so much as a protest from anyone else watching this scene play out. I didn't stop until I was standing in front of my bike again to turn to Dom and Casey to bark out some orders. This was my business and if either of them didn't like it, they could get on their bikes and head back inside.

Hell if I cared right now. That wasn't going to change shit because I was going with or without them.

"Get Ortega on the phone," I instructed pointedly and clenched my fists in anticipation. "Let's see if he knows where his old lap dog has been lately."

. . .

My eyes just about glazed over as I rose my fist to knock on the door. Once Ortega was brought up to speed about what his former associate was up to, he rattled off all the places Padilla was known to frequent without hesitation. As luck would have it, we'd found him at the first place we tried—his house. Padilla was either incredibly stupid or incredibly confident I wouldn't retaliate. Either way, he was going to be feeling every single inch of what he'd destroyed in my house and every second of fear he'd inflicted on Isabelle.

Padilla probably thought all our shit was settled and over now.

Asshole had another thing coming.

I pounded fiercely on the front door, shrugging off the way Dom and Casey shifted anxiously behind me. They didn't want to be here right now and I didn't really give a shit. The club didn't have anything to do with this—this had everything to do with all the times me and Padilla had stared each other down, each time I had worked overtime to report back to Ortega all the ways Padilla was screwing up, each time Padilla came up empty and each time I reveled in every wrong move he made...it had all come down to this.

A few moments later, the door swung open to reveal Padilla, dressed in a dirty wife-beater and a half-empty beer in one hand. The smug expression drained from his face and then he scrambled to shut the door in my face. I slammed my foot right into the middle of it, knocking Padilla back into his living room, and charged straight ahead.

"Hey, man, listen," Padilla held up his hands in clear desperation. "Nobody got hurt. No big deal, man. We're square now."

I stepped inside the living room, with Dom and Casey hot on my heels, and cocked an eyebrow at him. "You think we're square? Man, you're even stupider than I thought."

I moved forward until I was toe to toe with the man I was going to take great pleasure in beating to a bloody pulp and my lips curled back into a snarl. "Your first mistake, asshole, was fucking with my old lady and my house. And the second, dumbshit, was sticking around long enough so I would know it was you. You think I'm just gonna stand here and let you shit all over what's mine?"

"You cost me a shit-ton of money," Padilla interjected hastily. "I was gonna make over 100 Gs from that deal and you blew it."

"100 Gs, huh?" I nodded to him and my shoulders shook with laughter. "Bullshit. Everyone knows you're not smart enough to pull somethin' like that off."

Rage flared up in Padilla's eyes and just as he was gearing up to swing, Casey appeared at his side and twisted his arm back before he could move an inch.

"Watch yourself, asshole," Casey leaned into Padilla menacingly. "You should know better than to go after a woman. You deserve everything you're about to get handed."

"I didn't hurt her!" Padilla hollered back in his face. "I didn't even touch her!"

As if on cue, a short, scantily-clad Mexican woman, the same one I recognized from the patch-over party, appeared in the hallway. "Diego, what's goin'—"

She stopped short as soon as she took in the three Horsemen cuts standing in her living room.

"Get back in the bedroom, Luz!" Padilla yelled at her. "Turn around and walk away!"

Luz's face contorted, but she stood her ground, refusing to leave her man behind. I supposed I could understand that kind of loyalty and chose to ignore her instead.

"So," I started again, leaning down to get in his face. "Let's try this again. What were you gonna do if my pregnant old lady hadn't nailed you with pepper spray, huh? You know, the one you called a fucking bitch?"

Padilla's eyes flooded with sheer panic and he didn't need to tell me what we both already knew: if just a few seconds had happened differently, Padilla wouldn't have hesitated to tear her to pieces too. My lips curled into a menacing snarl and right about now, I was surprised I was even seeing clear objects in the room I was so blinded by this overwhelming rage.

"I didn't know she was pregnant! I swear I didn't!" Padilla pleaded hoarsely, but it fell on deaf ears.

"You know," I started darkly and ignored his cries. "You were right before. About us gettin' square. We should be square. Then this shit between us can be finished once and for all."

I pulled my own Glock out of the holster underneath my cut and aimed it directly at Luz's head. I wasn't normally prone to such spiteful violence, but now that the wrath-fueled floodgates were open, there was no stopping the rush that followed.

"How do you like it, huh?" I snarled back at Padilla, still holding my Glock trained on his woman. "How do you like someone comin' up into your space and scarin' the shit out of your woman? Doesn't feel so good, does it?"

"Caleb..." Dom's voice called out to me to bring me back from the brink. I didn't miss the warning in his tone, but right about now, that was the least of my concerns.

"I got it, Dom. Just keeping this shithead in his place," I shot back tightly, keeping my focus trained on the man shaking with anger in front of me.

"Now," I turned back to Padilla. "We're almost there. Just about square."

I tucked my Glock back in its holster and then swung my fist until it connected right in Padilla's jaw. With my fury now completely unleashed, I kept swinging and kicking, oblivious to the shouting around me, until my knuckles were torn and bruised and covered in Padilla's blood and until Casey finally dragged me away.

My chest heaved violently as I watched Padilla crawl around the bloodied floor and spit a tooth out two feet away from my shoes.

I crouched down and grinned at the mangled mess I'd made.

"Now we're square."

CHAPTER NINE
Worth The Wait

Isabelle

I ran a hand over my tired eyes and gratefully took the bottle of water the prospect slid over to me. Lexie was bouncing Chloe anxiously on her hip next to me as Skyler eyed us both warily. Becca was still nowhere to be found, but that was honestly the least of my worries right now. I'd tried calling her a little after Caleb left the clubhouse and once I'd finally started to feel normal again, but had only gotten her voicemail.

Just the fact that I'd left my best friend a message to say my house had been broken into and now, it'd been almost two hours and still, nothing...there was something seriously wrong with that. I just didn't have the energy or the presence of mind at the moment to dwell on it for too long.

My number one priority right now was Caleb. Or rather, where he was, what he was doing, and what kind of state he going to come back in. I knew him well enough to know that Diego Padilla was going to be looking a hell of a lot worse than him, but still, the barely-bridled violence and rage burning in his eyes before he'd left with Dom and Casey was scary as shit. And for a moment, I'd panicked that I was going to lose him, that he wouldn't come back to me in one piece, and sitting here waiting was just cruel and unusual punishment.

Thankfully, it wasn't much longer until the tell-tale roar of motorcycles echoed through the quiet clubhouse. I jumped at the sound and Lexie cast a sympathetic glance my way.

I didn't have to wait long because Caleb strode into the clubhouse with Dom and Casey right on his heels. The triumphant smirk on Caleb's face wasn't hard to miss and just as I'd started to relax, my eyes settled on his bloodied and torn knuckles. While I'd known exactly what he'd done and why, I still hadn't been prepared to see the physical evidence.

I didn't want to think about what he'd done with those fists. What he'd done with the Glock I knew he had in that holster underneath his cut.

Caleb's dark eyes roamed the clubhouse hungrily and when his eyes found me, his lips twisted into a smile, silently telling me that everything had been taken care of, that nothing was going to happen to me again. Just as he stalked toward me, Marcus stepped in his path.

"Everything handled, Caleb?" Marcus asked gruffly, clamping his teeth around his cigarette as he spoke.

Caleb nodded quickly, his eyes darting between his club president and me. "No problems."

Dom huffed roughly next to him and Caleb rose his eyebrows at his best friend. I watched them carefully, trying to decipher the meaning behind their silent communication, even if part of me wasn't so sure I really wanted to know.

Marcus cocked an eyebrow at Caleb, his black eyes shifted quickly between them. "I respect your decision to handle this outside the club, Caleb. This was personal between you and Padilla and I get that. You brought back-up with you and you handled your shit, so you got no problems on my end as long as there's no blowback."

"There won't be any blowback," Caleb pushed out through tightly clenched teeth. "He got the message."

"Alright," Marcus dipped his head down in approval.

Caleb didn't waste any time and I bit down on my bottom lip to keep my emotions in check as he closed the short distance between us. My arms were around his neck before I could even fully register that he was standing right in front of me and then his lips pressed into mine hungrily. For a moment, I forgot we were standing out in the open, right at the bar where everyone could see us, and I quickly broke away so I could inspect the damage to his hands.

"Caleb..." I whispered softly as I brushed my fingertip on a piece of torn skin.

"You wanna go clean me up?" he asked in that husky voice he knew drove me up the wall.

I laughed and playfully smacked him in the chest. "Any excuse to get me alone, right?"

"You know it, babe."

"Okay, but after that," I told him pointedly. "I want you to take me back to the house."

His face twisted with anguish and immediately shook his head. "Iz—"

"It's our house, our things. I just want to see it."

Caleb ran a hand over his face, despite the pain he had to be feeling in his hands, and grimaced harshly. "I don't know, Iz. Maybe we should wait. We have to stay at the clubhouse until everything's cleaned up anyway, you know. I haven't even seen it yet and I don't want you to—"

"Caleb," I cut in. "I just want to grab some clothes."

He frowned down at me and I could see the wheels in his head turning, weighing the pros and cons of what I wanted to. It was interesting...all the things I'd learned about being in a relationship with the hard-edged, tough-as-nails biker that he was. He might like to show that tough exterior when other people were around, but when it was just him and me, the tenderness softened out those rough edges. Sometimes, it was like he was two different people—the outlaw biker and the sweet, attentive guy I'd fallen head over heels for all wrapped up in one pretty package.

"Well," he started slowly like he was mentally chewing on the words to see how they tasted. "I suppose we could swing by the house *if* you promise me you'll see our doc as soon as she can fit us in."

Of course he'd give me an ultimatum. Damn him and his super-intuitive, alpha-male tendencies.

I was *fine.*

"Iz," Caleb started again, this time his voice was cautious. He was well aware treating me like some kind of invalid who couldn't take of herself was not the way to get me to agree to just about anything. "You can't deny you had a pretty good scare today. Add the panic attack into the mix and I think it's better to be safe than sorry."

I guessed he had a point.

"Fine," I grumbled and jabbed a finger at him. "But only because I love our child. This has nothing to do with you being right."

His shoulders shook with laughter as he swung an arm around me to tuck me into his side. That guy was lucky he was so cute when he laughed.

. . .

"You sure you wanna do this, Iz?" Caleb murmured in my ear as he led me up the walkway to the front door, the same walkway I'd sprinted down just two hours before as my life flashed before my eyes. "I can just go in and throw some shit in a bag for you. You don't have to go inside."

I knew what he was doing and understood why he was doing it. He was protecting me. Just like he always did and even though that just made my heart swell at the thought, he couldn't protect me from everything. This was our house. These were our belongings. And thank God for homeowner's insurance.

"No," I shook my head, resolved to see this through to the end. "I need to go in. It'll just drive me crazy if I don't see it."

Caleb swallowed hard and then I felt his hand rest on the small of my back to lead me inside the house. Once we approached the door, he promptly pushed it open to reveal the disaster inside. For a few moments, I just stood there, frozen in place with my trembling hand covering my mouth. This couldn't be real. This couldn't be our house. This was someone else's life.

With a gulp, I stepped around Caleb, who'd skidded to a stop at the sight, and surveyed the damage. Our TV and my computer were demolished. All the shelves of books and movies had been upended. The curtains were ripped to shreds. Our couch and chair were slashed up like Freddy Krueger had been there. The kitchen table was overturned and crushed, like someone had stomped on it. Every drawer, every cabinet...everything was destroyed.

This was what I signed up for when I'd agreed to be Caleb's old lady and somehow figure out how to fit in this life. In *his* life. This was the consequence. Or at the very least, one of them. With a deep exhale, I squeezed my eyes shut and told myself that what had happened to our house wasn't actually about me, but that didn't make it hurt any less.

Against my better judgment, I started heading for my studio.

"Iz," Caleb called out desperately and I could feel him right behind me. "Let me go in first. Just—"

I just pressed forward and flung open the door anyway. At first, relief flooded through me and almost knocked me sideways. Everything was fine. Padilla hadn't gotten far enough to destroy all my hard work...and then I smelled that pungent, sour odor that could only be one thing. In complete disbelief, I turned back to Caleb only to find him pale with grief.

Every painting I'd ever done, save for the ones still hanging around the house and the three still at school, were in this room.

And now, they were all destroyed because Diego Padilla had pissed on every single one of them.

Unable to control myself any longer, I lurched forward until my hands came in contact with some canvas and I kicked right through it before heaving it into the wall. I'd gotten my hands on another one when a pair of strong arms closed around me and gently tugged the ruined painting from my grasp. I collapsed into his chest, allowing him to bear the brunt of my weight, and finally released all the anger, frustration, devastation, and terror I'd felt since the moment I stepped up to my front door earlier today.

I had nothing left to do but weep in his arms. I just felt so violated. And, really, these were just possessions and materials. Everything could be replaced, with the exception of my paintings, and I knew I needed to just be grateful I'd managed to get away when I did, but the impact of this, the hatred and animosity it must have taken for anyone to do something like this, it just wouldn't compute.

He let me cry it all out before tenderly taking my chin in his hand. "You're okay, babe. This is all gonna be okay."

"What happened, Caleb?" I whispered hoarsely. "Why would he do this?"

He blew out a deep breath before cradling me against him and tangling his hands in my hair. "This is my fault. This had nothing to do with you, Iz. Long story short, I got Padilla kicked out of the Lobos because he sucked dick at his job. He blamed me for it and even though it was his fault, he came back at me personally, through you, through our house."

"So what did you do to him?"

In light of everything already knocking at our door, we both understood how important it was that he tell me exactly what was going on and why.

He exhaled deeply and ran a hand over his face before finally speaking. "I tracked him down through his old prez, kicked down the door, and taught him never to mess with a Horsemen's old lady, especially mine."

There was a part of me that was more than a little thrilled he'd clearly beaten Diego Padilla to a bloody pulp for me. That he'd went into a rage and tracked down the man responsible and brought him to outlaw justice. The alpha male act was one Caleb knew well and the more I was exposed to it, the more I wanted it. And there was another part of me that didn't know how to feel about that. Didn't know how to feel about the fact that he was capable of that kind of violence.

"Is that all, Caleb? You beat him up. That I can see," I gestured to his bandaged knuckles as I spoke. "But is that it?"

I watched his Adam's apple bob up and down, instinctively knowing I wasn't going to like whatever was coming next. At this point, I was ready for it.

Just keep it coming. How could things get any worse?

"I held his girlfriend at gunpoint in front him," Caleb murmured hoarsely next to me, unable to meet my eyes. "He needed to know what it felt like."

That wasn't exactly what I'd been expecting to hear, but it was more or less on par with my understanding of the way the club operated and the way Caleb operated within the club. There was most definitely a catch-22 when it came to the club—being around them was both the safest and the riskiest thing a person could do in this town, but it was better than the alternative. It was better than living without him.

"Thank you for telling me," I pressed my face into his neck and all the tension in his body seemed to slip right through my fingertips as I wrapped them around his waist.

He kissed my hair and I could feel the relief radiating off him. "Let me get you outta here, Iz."

. . .

Caleb snapped his phone shut and tossed it a few inches away from where I sat on the bed. I gestured with my head toward the spot next to me and he flopped down on the mattress. He leaned into my shoulder, wrapping an arm around me, and I scooped up my bare legs underneath me so I could rest my head on his shoulder.

"Pizza'll be here in about 45 minutes," he told me. "I'm gonna have to make a mad dash for it though so Tiny doesn't get to it first."

I smiled into his shoulders, but that was the most I could muster. My body was too tired and my mind was too spent.

Tomorrow, we'd have to begin the process of going through the house to see what could be saved and what needed to be replaced, but I guess that was the least of my worries right now.

"I'm going to make that doctor appointment tomorrow," I murmured into his shoulder. "I promise."

He nodded and kissed my hair. "Good."

"Hopefully they'll be able to get me in right away. I'm sure everything's fine though. When you think about it, given everything that's happened the last couple days, I think I'm doing pretty good."

At least he was still in good enough humor to huff out a laugh before blowing out a deep breath. He had to be as tense and as worn out as I felt, so I reached out to gently knead the tight muscles in his neck.

"Hmm," he murmured. "That's nice, babe. I should really be doing this for you though. Or, you know, rubbin' your feet or some shit like that."

"Not tonight," I smiled. "You're always taking care of me. Why don't you just let me take care of you for once?"

"You know, I think there might be a double meaning in that, Iz."

I cocked an eyebrow at him. "Do you want the neck massage or not?"

"Do I get another kind of massage after?"

"Shut it."

He just shrugged. "Okay."

After a good 10 minutes, his calloused fingertips grazed my hands to tell me it was okay to stop and then he shifted on the bed, sliding his hands down my bare thighs, until he faced me on the bed. A slow grin tugged up his lips and he leaned forward to kiss me, gently pushing me back onto the bed.

Caleb hovered over me as he situated himself between my legs and skimmed his hands up the Horsemen T-shirt I wore.

"I like seeing you in my clothes," he murmured, leaning down to press his lips against my stomach. "But I think my shirt'll look better on the floor right now."

"Oh wow," I laughed. "What a line."

"Hey, that's not even my best stuff," he rested his chin on my stomach as he spoke.

It was his eyes that got me every time, those deep sapphires that shimmered with love, devotion, and a healthy dose of mischief. I wished I could swim in those eyes, drench myself in their warmth, and sink into that liquid silk.

As if he could read my thoughts, Caleb shot me a wolfish grin before shifting his attention back to my stomach.

"Hey there, little buddy," he told my stomach. "Mommy did a pretty good job protecting you today, didn't she?"

I just laughed. "I see you haven't accepted that it's gonna be a girl."

"Okay, fine," he relented and gestured back down to where our baby was resting. "Hey there, little princess. If you turn out to be anything like your mom, and I suspect you will, I am shit up a creek. Seriously. You and your mother will be the death of all my hair.".

"Oh God," I shook my head. "You're crazy."

His lips found my stomach again before he rested his chin against my skin. "Yep."

The smile that slipped across his face now was softer than before and had me reaching down to touch his cheek.

"Caleb?"

"Yeah, Iz?"

"Make it go away," I whispered.

He nodded. He knew exactly what I was asking and I knew that anything I asked for, anything I wanted, he was going to give me. And even if his mind had been on a rougher, faster track tonight, even if he'd needed to work out a little more aggression from the day's events, I needed him to go slow, to be tender with me, and to just love me.

"Okay, Iz," Caleb murmured.

He leaned forward and gently brushed his lips against mine, his fingers skimming all the way underneath the shirt to slide it over my head. My legs wrapped around his waist and a moment later, my fingers were pulling his own shirt over his head. He bent down to place feather-light kisses on the insides of my thighs, my stomach, my chest, my neck, before finally settling over my lips.

I loved this about him—matter what was going on with us, whether it was the club, school, or just plain old life, sex was always something that just worked between us. It was where we met up at night. Where we found each other again in spite of whatever happened that day. Tonight, even in his worked-up state, was no exception.

He swirled his tongue in long, leisurely circles inside my mouth, taking his time in getting me to relax. I needed him to take his time, but I also needed him to get somewhere else first and slipped both his shorts and his boxers down to his ankles so he could kick them off. I hoisted myself up on my elbows and watched him with hooded eyes as he lazily freed himself from the layers keeping us apart. Two seconds later, he thrust his hands underneath me and playfully yanked me closer to him.

He gripped my hips, digging his fingers into my skin and he easily slipped inside me. My hands tangled in his hair and he rocked against me, finding that easy rhythm and hitting exactly where he knew he needed to go. It was slow, lazy lovemaking and it was exactly what both of us needed tonight. His lips never seemed to stray far from an inch of my skin, trailing up my neck, pressing into my mouth, lingering around my jaw.

We'd done this leisurely, easy pace before and we had all night to enjoy it, but this was different.

Every movement, every kiss, every touch seemed to heighten the emotions we were feeling—the love, the need, the desire. It felt like a piece of my soul had splintered and his had meshed in with mine to fill in the empty spaces. We were forged as one, melded together in the heat surrounding us.

And when my release shattered through my body and Caleb trembled above me, I knew that, in spite of the day's drama, we were going to have the best night of sleep we'd had in months. All the weight had been lifted and now, we could finally breathe.

"I'm gonna marry you," Caleb hummed against my ear.

"Uh huh," I sighed lazily. "You are."

"When?"

"Soon."

"Tomorrow?" he asked hopefully and his tone suggested he wasn't being entirely facetious.

Somehow, I still had the energy to laugh. "Not tomorrow. Soon though."

"Fine," he huffed and tugged me against his chest as we settled back into the pillows. "I guess I can wait."

"You're going to have to."

"Well, it's a good thing you're worth the wait, Iz."

This time, I totally had enough energy to smack him right in the chest.

CHAPTER TEN
Sit Down, Part Three

Caleb

There were a lot of things I'd rather be doing right now. Tuning up my bike, for instance. That seemed like time well-spent. Or maybe working out. Again, time well-spent. Painting my house. Mowing my lawn. Patching up that crack in our driveway. Eating Isabelle's cooking. Yeah, I'd rather be doing that too. Watching *Project Runway*. Yep, I said it. Pulling out my own teeth with a rusty pair of pliers. Oh yeah. Letting Chloe give me a hair-cut. That'd be okay too. Or, even better yet, I could finally join the 21st century and sign-up for Facebook. And Twitter while I'm at it because, why not?

All of that was better than how I found myself spending this particular Saturday afternoon: sitting at my table with its mismatched chairs, directly across from Isabelle's dad. The business I had with him was something I could've easily done over the phone or hell, I could've just sent it to him in the mail. But that wasn't what Isabelle wanted and, to be fair, she had no idea that I planned on asserting my role in her life today. She probably wasn't going to be very happy with me—okay, she was going to be *pissed* as *shit,* but if I told her ahead of time, she'd argue and fight with me beforehand.

Seeing as how she was just going to argue and fight afterward, I figured this way she only got upset once instead of twice.

It wasn't until we went to the doctor earlier this week after the break-in that I realized just how much this new responsibility was going to cost me. Not gonna lie, I felt pretty goddamn stupid when I figured it out and I felt even stupider when I had to go to my mom for help with a solution. Needless to say, her solution probably wasn't going to make Isabelle very happy either, but until we finally got married, my hands were tied.

Isabelle was just going to have to deal with it.

So here I was, sitting across from Samuel Martin. Isabelle, in a futile attempt at keeping the peace, smiled nervously and her eyes kept darting from me to across the table almost as if she was readying herself for some sort of epic battle royale. I didn't necessarily want to get into a fist-fight with him. I just wanted him the hell out of my house.

"Dad, um," Isabelle gestured to the glass in front of him. "Do you need some more water? We have soda, too, if—"

Samuel just shook his head. "I'm fine."

A long, awkward moment settled heavily in the air and I shifted uncomfortably in my chair. This whole thing was just getting worse with every second we sat here, all three of us staring at each other expectantly, but unable to get any words out.

I heard Isabelle suck in a deep breath and let her take charge.

"Thanks for coming, Dad," she started a little shakily. "I know we've been in the house for a couple weeks now, but I wanted to wait until everything got settled a little more before we invited you over."

He just lifted a shoulder and even now, less than 10 minutes into this disaster in the making, I did not appreciate the calculating glint in his eyes, not to mention the way he stared at me like *I* was the one who'd done something wrong, like *I* was the one who had something to apologize for.

"No, I understand," he told her and shifted his eyes back to me a second later. "I heard you had a break-in."

My fists were already clenched into tight, white-knuckled balls underneath the table when Isabelle's hand rested on my thigh. She shot me a warning glance to tell me to back the hell off and I clamped down on my bottom lip to hide my reaction as much as possible.

"Yes, we had a break-in," Isabelle tried again, her voice calm and level in a way I had to give her credit for. "That's been handled and," she waved a hand in the air for emphasis, "I guess you can see everything's back to normal now."

It took the prospects almost a full week of work to get the house back in living order again, but it was done. We still didn't have any furniture in the living room you could really sit in anymore, but Isabelle, like everything else, had taken care of that and ordered new furniture the day after the break-in. In hindsight, I think she'd just needed something productive to do to keep her mind off everything the prospects had had to throw away—namely, all her paintings. Everything else, though, was pretty much as good as new or as good as it could be after a son of a bitch with a bullshit vendetta trashes your home.

"Right," Samuel replied slowly. "Back to normal. Good to hear," then he leveled his gaze right on me. "What are your safety precautions now?"

I cleared my throat of as much animosity as I could muster for Isabelle's sake. "I've got a prospect at the house whenever I'm not here, which isn't often. I've been taking her to and from campus and when I can't, someone else, whether it's a prospect or another club member, will do it for me."

Isabelle absolutely despised not being able to drive herself, but it was a necessary evil. I wasn't taking any chances with Padilla. Even though he'd gone MIA since our little chat and even if I was about 99.9 percent certain he wouldn't be stupid enough to try anything again, that didn't mean I was willing to put Isabelle any more at risk than she already was.

"I see," Samuel nodded carefully. "Is that it?"

My eyes narrowed dangerously and just as I was about to pounce, Isabelle interceded.

"Dad, there's not much else we can do. Caleb's doing everything he can to keep me safe and you know that. And look, Dad, the real reason I—*we*—wanted you to come by the house was because we have something we need to tell you."

I swallowed tightly and shifted a hard glare at him, meeting his challenge head on. The sooner we got this shit over with, the better.

Isabelle turned to me expectantly and I twisted my fingers around hers for moral support. With another quick inhale, she turned back to her dad and just let it fly.

"Dad, I'm pregnant and we're getting married."

Jesus, she probably didn't have to let it fly all at once like that, but now that it was out there, Samuel didn't really look all that surprised. In fact, he looked more pissed at me than anything with the way his eyes darkened into tiny slits, but I guess that made sense considering he just found out I'd knocked up his daughter.

"Yes, I saw something about a prenatal screening and ultrasound on our insurance statement last month," he said evenly.

I bristled at the mention of insurance, but it wasn't the right time to throw that into the mix yet.

"You did?" Isabelle asked weakly and her shoulders drooped a little at the admission.

Samuel pushed out a rough exhale. "I figured you would tell me when you were ready."

Again, a long silence followed. I don't know what I was waiting for, but it wasn't this. His cheeks were turning red, most likely from anger directed toward me and frustration directed toward his daughter, but this quiet acceptance wasn't something I'd prepared myself for.

Finally, Isabelle broke through the emptiness. "Is that all you have to say,

Dad?"

He just shrugged. "What else do you want me to say? That I'm happy for you? That I'm proud of you?"

That got the fire started and I was leaning forward in my chair, despite Isabelle's hand shooting right to my shoulder to stop me. "I don't appreciate you coming into my house and speaking to her like that."

"I can leave."

"Maybe you should," I nodded tightly.

"No, no, no," Isabelle shook her head and shot me another warning look. "Dad. Don't leave, okay? I didn't ask you to come over so we could fight. I thought you deserved to know you're going to have a son-in-law soon and that you're going to be a grandpa and I thought you deserved to hear it from us. I'm sorry you had to figure it out the way you did."

"Don't apologize to him, Iz," I told her through clenched teeth.

"Stop it," she whispered loudly. "You're not helping."

This time, it was my turn to shrug.

Isabelle sighed and ran a hand through her hair, the agitation pouring off her in waves. The break-in and the panic attack hadn't caused any damage to the baby that we knew of, but our doctor told us stress needed to be avoided as much as possible, which really had me wondering why I'd agreed to meet with her dad in the first place.

But because I loved her, because I wanted to see her happy and stress-free, I was going to have to play nice with her dad. I needed to get along with him like I needed a hole in the head, but there was just no way around it now.

"Look," I couldn't believe I was about to say this. "I'm sorry I didn't sit down with you first and, you know, ask your permission, but I hope you can see why I didn't."

The words stung a little more than they probably should have. Samuel Martin's permission was the last thing I needed to marry his daughter. If he was smart, he probably knew well enough that the only reason I'd said it was for Isabelle's sake.

"Yes, I suppose I can understand why you wouldn't see the value in discussing this with me beforehand," he allowed and that was probably all I would get from him on that front.

Which was fine.

We didn't need to hash that out here and in front of Isabelle.

"So," he held his hands out in front of him to gesture toward us. "When's the wedding then?"

"We haven't set a date yet," Isabelle told him carefully, like she was gearing up for yet another battle. "I'll let you know when we do though."

"And the baby? How far along are you if you don't mind me asking?"

"About 10 weeks."

He sighed and ran a hand over his face. "Well, I suppose there's nothing that can be done about it now."

Playing nice be damned. He'd overstepped his boundaries in a big way.

"What's that supposed to mean?" I bit out.

Samuel shot me a wary glance and then turned his attention back to his daughter. "You remember what I told you?"

I balked at those words and my eyes flew to Isabelle, who had gone still as a statue next to me.

"What the hell, Iz?"

She swallowed hard, her eyes flicking to me for just a second and then snapped back across from us. "Dad, that's a little uncalled for, don't you think?"

"What are you talkin' about, Iz?"

Isabelle just shook her head, her attention still fixed on her dad. "It doesn't matter, Caleb. Just forget it."

I opened my mouth to tell her there was no way in hell I was going to just forget it when this was obviously something I needed to be brought up to speed on, but one glare from her was enough to shut me up.

"Dad," she started again. This time, though, her voice shook with emotion. "I know you're disappointed and I understand, but you also need to understand that I'm happy. I have a good life with Caleb, whether you accept that or not, and it isn't going to change. We're getting married. We're having a baby. I'd like for you to be a part of that, but if you can't be civil and if you can't respect the father of my baby, then I don't know what else there is to say."

Finally, something broke through that hard exterior, that cold, detached demeanor melted down a little to reveal something that actually looked human. Maybe Samuel Martin wasn't a robot after all. Go figure.

His face drained of any color and it was clear he'd taken Isabelle's threat to essentially cut him out of her and his grandchild's life seriously. He sighed again and any resolve he might have had to object must have died in his throat. After all, he wasn't exactly the poster-boy for positive life choices.

"I'm sorry," Samuel murmured and leaned an elbow against the table to support his head. "I really am. It shouldn't have come down to something like this...you feeling this way. Feeling like I can't be a part of your life. That's my fault, not yours."

She nodded tightly. "Okay."

"And while I can't lie to you and say I'm happy with what you've chosen, it's not my place to tell you any different. You're an adult. If this is what you choose, if this is what you want, I can't tell you I support it, but I want to be part of your life. I'd like to be part of my grandchild's life..."

He trailed off and I just about fell out of my chair when I saw a little smile tugging across his normally hard face. This was weird. Really fucking weird. Should I feel grateful Isabelle's relationship with her dad was finally turning a corner or pissed as shit that I'd actually have to put up with being around him now?

I didn't trust him with my kid anymore than I trusted him with my old lady, but judging by the smile already spreading across Isabelle's face, the answer was kinda in the question and the answer was that I was screwed.

Now, my future father-in-law looked to me.

"I know I probably don't need to say this anymore than I have much of a right to, but you'll keep them as safe as you can? I know it's not exactly a secret that I wish the Horsemen weren't in this town and let's face it, this break-in is just another example of what happens to people connected to your club. Whenever there's any trouble, it always seems like the women and children are the first and most vulnerable targets, aren't they?"

I knew he was trying to make peace. I knew he was trying to find some sort of common ground, but the reality, the truth saturated in those words didn't sit well with me. In a roundabout, not-so-subtle way, he was basically telling me, to my face, that he didn't think I'd ever be able to completely protect Isabelle and our kid.

"The only way anything would ever happen to them is if someone got through me first," I told him, forcing each syllable to drip with all the seriousness this conversation needed.

He smiled sadly and nodded. "I figured you'd say something like that. At the end of the day, I just want to see Isabelle happy and safe. I think we can agree on at least that, can't we?"

"Yeah, we can," and on that note, I dug into my pocket for the envelope I needed to give him and slid it across the table. "While we're on that topic, I need to give this to you."

We both ignored Isabelle's confused expression and when Samuel got a good look at what was inside the envelope, his head shot back up to me.

"I can't accept this."

"Yes, you can," I told him tersely. "You shouldn't have to pay for Isabelle's doctor appointments. I think that should be more than enough to cover what your insurance has already paid for this last month or so."

Samuel swallowed hard, both of us still ignoring the way Isabelle's jaw dropped to the kitchen floor, and slid the envelope back to me. "I don't need you to pay me back. I have no problem with Isabelle staying on my insurance as long as you need her to."

At that, Isabelle sprung to life. "Wait a minute. Caleb, I don't understand what's happening here."

"We'll talk about it later," I told her. "But I don't want you on your dad's insurance anymore. I can pay for it. I *should* be paying for it."

Her eyes widened and then they flashed with that fire I knew a little too well. "Excuse me, but I don't think this is the kind of decision you should be making without talking to me first."

"Like I said, Iz, we'll talk about this later. Right now, Mr. Martin," I gestured towards the envelope still on the table. "I would really appreciate it if you took the money. Isabelle and the baby are my responsibility and any doctor bills she has should be paid by me, not you."

Samuel eyed me warily and squinted at me a little like he was trying to figure me out. His gaze shifted to the envelope again and then he tapped it with his fingers.

"So how will you be paying her doctor bills then?"

I cleared my throat, having mentally prepared myself for this question already. "Isabelle can get insurance through the shop. It's not great 'cuz she's just part-time, but it's something until we get married and until she can get on my insurance after we get married."

"Your insurance through the club, you mean?" he cocked an eyebrow at me.

"The shop," I clarified tightly.

I was technically full-time at the shop and so, just by default, my insurance was better than Isabelle's would be anyway. At least that was the way my mom explained it. As shameful as it was, I hadn't really paid much attention to things like health insurance and Medicaid and monthly payments before. My mom just always handled everything for me. The bills were always paid and that was pretty much because she'd set it up so it came out of my bank account without me having to do anything.

Now it was time for me to start footing the work and the accountability and all that shit. Be a family man and everything that went along with it. I was burning through my money too fast, but what else was I supposed to do? Let someone else take care of my family?

"And you'll be paying her monthly payments and everything?" Samuel asked and the question seemed like it was more of a formality now than anything.

"Yeah," I nodded. "And anything else she needs. Anything she wants. Like I said, she's my responsibility."

I could feel the steam practically pouring out of Isabelle's ears, but whatever. I'd expected that and then some.

"And you can afford to do that?"

I huffed out a laugh. I hoped he didn't know how right his assumptions about my bank account probably were at this point. "Well, I could afford this house, couldn't I? I'll worry about that. So, will you just take the money and we can call it even?"

Now, Samuel was looking to Isabelle, whose jaw was clenched so tightly I was a little worried it might break right off.

"And given the way he makes his money," he told her. "You're okay with him paying for your insurance, your house, your tuition, anything else with that money?"

Even though she was red all the way to the top of her ears, to her credit, Isabelle nodded as calmly as she could probably manage. That seemed to be all her dad needed to see and then with one last heavy sigh, he tugged the envelope toward him again so he could slip it into his pocket.

"I should probably get going," he was saying now as he stood up from the table. "I think we've all probably said everything we needed to say today anyway. Thank you for inviting me over. I can't tell you how much I appreciate that."

Isabelle stood to walk him out the door and I scrambled out of my chair to trail after them. We followed him out the door, walking with him down our little walkway towards where his car was parked in our driveway. Isabelle waved a little to her dad and he shot her a quick, grateful smile and even though it had stung, even though the whole thing had been pretty painful for me, if it made her happy, if it helped her stay relaxed and calm, I couldn't really complain.

Just as long as her dad didn't make a habit of stopping by our house whenever he felt like it.

As we turned back to head inside the house, I wrapped my arms around her, despite the fact that she was probably madder than all hell at me right now and let my hands drift from her stomach to her back and all the way up to her hair once I knew her dad was out of sight and down the street.

"We need to talk," she muttered harshly into my ear.

"I know."

"You should've told me about all that insurance stuff *before* my dad came over."

"I know."

"You can't keep making decisions like this without talking to me first. That's a really shitty habit."

"I know."

"Will you stop saying I know? It's really pissing me off."

Just as I was about to say *I know*, I caught myself and changed tactics. "I'm sorry, Iz."

"Yeah, well, sorry isn't really good enough right now. Look, I get what you're saying about the insurance. I understand why you don't want my dad paying for anything for the baby. I really do. But I just...I just can't believe you just..."

I sighed and tugged a hand through my hair as I pulled her against my chest with the other. "You weren't gonna talk me out of it. And, honestly, I just didn't want to upset you. I knew you'd be mad at me about this before and after we talked to your dad and I just wanted to try to minimize that as much as I could. You're havin' my kid, Iz. The only person who should be footin' that bill is me."

She shot me a wary look, but still leaned against my shoulder. "I guess I see your point. But babies are expensive, Caleb. I don't think either one of us really gets that right now. And we have the house. I'm trying to plan the wedding. Maybe we should—"

"Iz, I'm gonna stop you right there. You're not staying on your dad's insurance until we get married. I don't need any charity."

My wife. My kid. My family. My responsibility.

She gripped the front of my T-shirt and pulled me down to her level a little more. "The next time something like this comes up you need to talk to me about it first. I understand why you did what you did, but we need to make these kind of decisions together."

Fair enough.

She had a point, but I knew mine was pretty damn valid too.

"I will. This was the last time, okay? I promise. You know I just wanna take care of you, right? I just wanna make sure both of you have everything you need."

Her resolve to be pissed at me crumbled a little and her entire body seemed to soften under my hands. "I know. You're lucky you're so cute, you know? Man, if you were ugly..."

"You wouldn't be living in my house, having my kid, and wearing my ring and my ink."

She smacked me on the shoulder and I knew we were back on track now. She was on board with this, even if she wouldn't admit it just yet.

"I love you," I whispered into her hair. "All this is for you. You know that, right?"

"I know," she relented and buried her face in my chest. "I love you too."

"That's all I needed to hear, Iz."

CHAPTER ELEVEN
Recon

Isabelle

I clicked to the next page on the website and ran a hand over my face. The lace, the beading, the silk, the organza—I wanted them all. It really wasn't fair. Staring at something I couldn't have was a waste of time.

But they were just so *pretty*.

So, because I was a glutton for punishment, I let my eyes roam all the way down to the bottom of the page and then everything blurred around me. That was it. That was the one...if I would ever be able to have it.

The airy skirt had just a touch of fullness, a beautiful, intricate sheer lace overlay from the shoulders down to the wrists, some crystals around the silk belt around the waist. Classy. Different. Unexpected. It was definitely not something I would've thought I wanted, but the second I saw it, I knew it was the one.

A pair of hands ghosted over my shoulders and I shivered a little under his touch.

"That's pretty," Caleb murmured in my ear, resting his chin on my shoulder as we stared back at the picture of the wedding dress together.

"Yeah, it is."

"Is that the one you're gonna get?"

"Probably not," I sighed.

"Why? I can totally see you in that dress. You should at least go try it on or something."

I glanced up at him warily. He had good intentions. He really did. But he could be such a guy sometimes. With a little wave of my hand, I gestured down towards my stomach.

"Well, let's just say that by the time we get married, that dress won't exactly come in my size, you know?"

His hand drifted down to rest over my stomach, which was just looking a little swollen now. All my jeans were getting too tight, so I'd resorted to wearing yoga pants until it was time to break down and start buying some maternity clothes. Right now, stretchy was good.

He leaned in more to press a gentle kiss into my neck. "Well, maybe they have something like that in, uh, your size. Did you check yet?"

Just to humor him, I clicked over to the maternity tab and scrolled down so he could see all the options.

"Jesus, that chick kinda looks like a whale in that dress," his eyes widened when he realized he'd said that out loud and shot me a quick look. "Uh, I mean, you wouldn't look like that, Iz. You'd rock that dress."

I cocked an eyebrow at him. "Nice try."

"Sorry."

I just shook my head and clicked on another tab I had open in my browser. While I had him here, I figured I might as well show him everything I'd found. "So, in between feeling all depressed about wedding dresses, I was looking through some sites for reception halls and I found this one on a farm outside of town. Lots of gardens and wooded areas. It kinda has a rustic feel to it, you know?"

He lifted his chin off my shoulder so he could lean in to get a better look at my screen. "That looks nice, babe. It's all outside?"

"Yeah, we could have the ceremony outside if the weather's okay. They have big tents and everything for the reception."

"Okay," he nodded. "Let's go take a look at it."

Another sigh pushed from my lungs and I just couldn't help it. "We could look at it, but they're booked solid pretty much through the end of the year."

He frowned down at me. "So...?"

"That means if we waited until November or early December, I'll be..." I gestured out about a foot in from of my stomach to illustrate just how pregnant I would be by then. "I just don't know if I want to be *that* pregnant at our wedding."

"Why did you show this to me then?"

That was a good question. I was wallowing a little in this pity party. That's what it was. Hormones. I was just going to blame it all on hormones right now.

"I don't know," I sighed and leaned forward to rest my chin into my hand. "This is just a headache, you know? Everything...the catering, the flowers, the dress, the reception, getting everything booked in enough time before the baby comes. Can't we just go get married at City Hall or something? I'm sick of this already and I just started."

Caleb brushed his lips against my cheek and reached forward to shut the laptop we'd borrowed from Eli. "Let's do it."

My mouth dropped open a little in surprise. "What?"

"Yeah," he shrugged and rested his hands over my shoulders again so he could knead the tight muscles there. "We go to City Hall, get married, have a little party at the clubhouse and then, maybe a couple months or so after our kid gets here, we do it the way you wanted to."

It was such an easy solution I almost couldn't believe he was the one who thought of it. But then again, I'd been learning a lot about him ever since the impending parenthood bomb dropped. He was pragmatic and logical about these kinds of things in a way I never would've expected from him...buying our house, all that business about the insurance, and now this. As much as his tendency to make these decisions without talking to me first drove me up the wall, he'd been right about pretty much everything. To be fair, it was almost a little *too* easy. There had to be some sort of catch.

"Everybody wins," Caleb went on, a broad smile spreading across his face. "I get to make you my wife like tomorrow. You get to have the wedding you always wanted. Compromise, Iz. That's what this is."

I shifted in my chair and arched an eyebrow at him. "If you're really promising to give me everything I want for our wedding, that's going to cost you a lot of money."

He just shot that crooked grin at me and shrugged. "I got it. Don't worry about the money."

I narrowed my eyes. "Tomorrow?"

"Okay," he laughed. "Maybe not tomorrow. Next weekend?"

"Hmm," I needed to chew on this for a little while.

It was pretty damned impulsive, but then again, two ceremonies and two celebrations, albeit on different scales, actually seemed like a pretty good idea the more I thought about it. And, most importantly, we'd be able to get married without all the stress and all the drama as soon as possible.

After that, I'd have as much time as I wanted to plan our all-out celebration, let alone lose the baby weight, without nearly as much pressure...which was probably all part of Caleb's master plan. Was he always this smart and I just never knew it?

It was strange to feel nervous about something like this, when I had no doubts about whether or not I wanted to spend the rest of my life with him, but a major life event deserved at least a little thought and a little planning.

"Well," I bit down on my bottom lip. "My semester showcase is in three weeks. I think I should focus on that first, get it out of the way and then yeah, after that, let's get married."

He stalked around my chair and practically tugged me off it so he could wrap his arms around me.

"One month, babe," Caleb murmured against my neck. "The weekend after your kick-ass showcase, you're gonna be my wife."

"Yeah," I laughed. "I can't believe we set a date. I kinda thought we'd disagree a little more about it, but this is good. This is really good."

"You bet your sweet ass it is," he grinned down at me and then lowered his head to kiss me. "I feel like we're married already. We should make it official, you know?"

I nodded. "I know how you feel."

Caleb smiled that crooked, sexy grin that always landed right on its target and I slipped a hand underneath his T-shirt so my fingers could skim across the hard planes of his abdomen.

His muscles rippled a little under my feather-light touch and then he was reaching around to tug my tank top up over my head. By the time I sent his T-shirt floating to the floor, his hands closed around the backs of my thighs to set me down on top of our table. And just as my hands started working his belt buckle, the door bell tore us out of this heat-fueled haze.

"Shit," Caleb muttered against my neck. "That's probably the prospect. I gotta get to church soon."

"It's okay. We'll just finish this when you get back."

"Hell no," his eyes glinted at me hungrily with that devilish glimmer I knew well and I didn't even bother protesting as he dug his phone out of his pocket. After he flipped it open, he pounded out a quick text, snapped the phone shut, and tossed it onto the table behind me.

"Ten minutes, Iz," he whispered as his mouth descended on mine.

I just laughed and then my yoga pants slid down my legs right along with my panties. He sure didn't waste any time. And after that, I let him carry me away. The heat of his body against me, his skin melting into mine, his lips sealing over as many inches of me as he could get...there was nothing better than this.

Every touch set my body on fire until I was practically whimpering for that sweet release, that desperate free-fall with his name on my lips.

His hips were torture. They knew just what to do, how to tilt, how long to linger, how quickly to pull back. Every rock of skin against skin carried me further and further away until stars were all I could see, his breath was all I could hear, and his strong arms wrapped around me was all I could feel.

. . .

My paintbrush twirled around the canvas, hugging the sides and sweeping back towards the middle. I blew out a breath and leaned back, my head tilted to the side as I surveyed my work. Well, it definitely wasn't my best work, but that was probably because I was trying to recreate something long gone. Dr. Jacobs, although sympathetic to the situation, still expected the ten pieces I was required to submit for the showcase and had explicitly instructed me not to attempt recreation of any kind. So, basically what I was doing right now.

"*Art is meant to be felt in the moment, Isabelle,*" she'd told me in that pleasant French accent. "*You cannot recreate a moment. You cannot recreate a feeling. You must create new moments, new feelings.*"

Luckily, I'd had three finished paintings for the showcase already in storage at school when the break-in happened and the one I'd since finished that I'd dropped when I found Diego Padilla in my house, but that still meant I owed Dr. Jacobs six more paintings in three weeks.

My heart ached at the thought of everything we'd had to throw away.

Hours of work. Hours of *meticulous* work. Hours of *thoughtful* work. I'd only cried after I knew they were all tossed out with the trash. At least I'd been smart enough not to watch the prospects carry them all out of my house and right to the side of the road. There was no way I would've survived seeing them all lined up like that, one after the other, just waiting for incineration.

You never plan on disaster. You focus on how things are *supposed* to unfold, what you *assume* will happen and you don't even think about the alternative because no one wants to walk around with a cloud of doom hanging over their head.

I was going to drive myself insane trying to recreate those paintings I'd lost. Whatever I'd felt in those moments, whatever force had pushed my paintbrush around the canvas, it was gone now.

Damn, they were good though. Probably some of the best work I've ever done, too.

Maybe I just needed to take a break. With that thought, I pushed off my stool and headed for the hallway. Seth, the prospect Caleb had left behind in his absence, dutifully sat on the floor in the living room watching the Braves get their asses handed to them by the Cardinals. He shifted on the floor and waved to me when he saw me.

Just as I'd gotten out the paint and laid down some plastic tarp on the carpet so I could get to work on the baby's mural, the doorbell rang. The TV in the living room went on mute almost instantly and I heard some shuffling towards the door as Seth moved to answer it. When I stuck my head out of the nursery to see what was up, I found Becca standing in my doorway with her hands stuffed into her pockets and apology written in her dark eyes.

What she was sorry for still remained to be seen.

"It's okay," I told Seth and waved Becca inside the house. "This is my friend, Becca. It's fine."

Becca stepped inside tentatively, looking around like this was the first time she'd ever been here. I wanted to believe it was more about her uneasiness over the break-in and about the oddity of seeing my living room all but empty, save for a coffee table resting awkwardly in the middle of the carpet.

Now Becca was watching Seth anxiously in a way that had me fighting the urge to narrow my eyes at her.

"Do you think we could...?" she gestured with her head towards the kitchen and then glanced back at Seth again.

"Yeah, sure," I shrugged and headed towards the kitchen, calling over my shoulder, "We're fine, Seth. You can go back to the game."

I half-expected Becca to plop herself down at the table, but instead, she propped a hip against the counter and folded her arms around herself. I hadn't seen or heard from her since the last time we'd stood right here, when she'd put me in the middle of something I still didn't understand. Now her sudden appearance at my house unannounced less than an hour after Caleb left was suspicious, to say the least.

I hated that I was looking at her like this now, watching every nervous tick, the way she kept her eyes trained on the floor, the way one hand wrapped around her body like she was shielding herself and the other hand clenched the strap of her purse in a white-knuckled grip. She was supposed to be my best friend. We were supposed to be able to tell each other anything.

There were only five feet between us right now, but it felt cavernous. Wide and reaching into a darkness I knew I wouldn't be able to save her from. If she leapt into that darkness, I wouldn't be able to jump in after her. I just couldn't.

"I tried calling you," I started quietly, taking my place on the other side of the kitchen. It was fitting that we were here, each on our own separate sides, each having made a decision the other didn't agree with. "You never called me back."

Becca sawed on her bottom lip for a few moments before finally lifting her eyes from the floor. "I'm sorry. I got your message. I wanted to call. I guess I..."

She trailed off, fiddling with her earring as her eyes fell back down to the floor. We stood there for at least a good 30 seconds, with her boring holes into my kitchen floor and me nervously twirling my engagement ring around my finger.

"You know, it's crazy," Becca laughed a little and for the first time since she showed up, a faint smile touched her lips. "The last time I saw you, you didn't look pregnant at all. Now, a frickin' week later and you've got this little curve in your stomach. It's super tiny, but it's totally there."

"So, basically you're telling me I just look like I need to workout a little more?" I threw out lightly and hoped this would be enough to shift the mood.

"Total food baby," she laughed. "But seriously, Belle, you look great. You have this *glow*. I know all pregnant women are supposed to get that, but it looks good on you. You look happy."

"I am."

Please don't do anything that could mess it up. Please don't be stupid, Becca.

"That's good," she smiled back, but the smile didn't quite reach her eyes. "So, um, what else is new?"

Was she fishing for something? Or was she just trying to make small talk to cut this awkwardness? I couldn't make heads or tails of it and all I could really do at this point was play along.

"Well, we set a date."

Becca's eyes lit up. "You did?"

She nodded quietly like she was mulling through all the details as I shared them with her and I had a bad feeling that the details she'd wanted me to share weren't ones about my upcoming wedding.

"That sounds like a good idea," Becca told me in that quiet, ghost-like whisper I was starting to loathe.

Then her hands shot up to cover her face and her shoulders shook. Her entire body seemed to convulse, completely overpowered by this guttural sobbing and before I could let myself consider the repercussions, I stepped forward until I could wrap my arms around her. She crumbled against me and just my touch alone had her body trembling with a fresh wave sobs.

"It's okay," I whispered to her. "Everything's gonna be okay, Becs. Just tell me what's going on. Please. I won't be mad."

"I'm just so sorry," she sobbed. "When I came over here last week, I was such a bitch. I didn't mean to be. I swear I didn't. I was just so scared. I'm *still* scared and I took it out on you."

I wanted to believe that was all this was about. I really did. But I also knew she'd gone to The Sundown Saloon right after she left my house to buy cocaine. Trusting anything she said right now would be a mistake. As much as it hurt, as much as I ached to help her, I couldn't believe a word she said. Our lines were drawn in the sand now and I couldn't step over that line.

"I know," I told her instead. "That was a really shitty day and neither of us were thinking clearly, you know? We were both scared. We were both emotional. It's okay, Becs. I get it."

She didn't respond and abruptly pulled herself out of my arms so she could brush away her tears with the heel of her hand. A long, harsh exhale blew out from her mouth and then she was staring up at me, trying her best to mold her lips into something that resembled a smile.

"I wish I could just hit rewind or something and do it differently," Becca murmured. "I shouldn't have said all that shit to you and I shouldn't have put you on the spot like that. It wasn't fair."

"Water under the bridge, okay?"

"Right," she laughed and wiped one last tear away from her face. "Can we just forget that ever happened?"

It would be nice if I could actually do that.

"Hey," I shifted gears and gestured with my head to where Eli's laptop still sat at the table. "You want to see this dress I like?"

And for the next half hour, it was like I'd gotten my best friend back. She ooo'd and ahhh'd over the dress and a few others we found on a different website, genuinely excited for my wedding, genuinely happy for the changes happening in my life. We didn't talk about the fact that I hadn't asked her to be my maid of honor because I wasn't sure I wanted her to have the title. We didn't talk about her drug use. We didn't talk about Caleb. We didn't talk about Eli. We didn't talk about the club.

My friendship with Becca had eventually led me to my future husband and the father of my baby. For that, I would always be grateful to her, but I just didn't trust her anymore.

So, when I left the table to take a bathroom break, I should've known better. But I wanted to believe she was still the girl I'd known since we were five-year-olds in matching backpacks and pigtails. I wanted to believe she would do the right thing because by betraying Eli, Caleb, and the rest of the club, she was betraying me too.

As it turned out, I was wrong. And stupid. And gullible.

Both of us closed doors at the exact same moment. Her eyes flew up to me, frozen like a burglar caught under a spotlight, her hand still on the doorknob to the garage. My body stilled, already on high alert, and I couldn't put one foot in front of the other because my feet were just rooted to the carpet.

"What are you doing, Becca?" I whispered.

I didn't even recognize the sound of my own voice. It was foreign even to my own ears. I think my ears might have been buzzing too much to even realize it. The TV suddenly went dead and Seth scrambled into the hallway, positioning himself directly in between me and this potential new threat.

"I'm so sorry," Becca pushed out roughly, tears already welling up in her eyes. "I didn't know what else to do."

"What were you doing in my garage?"

That must've been all Seth needed to hear to dig manically for his phone, but I rested my hand on his arm to stop him.

"Miss, I gotta call—"

"This is still my house, Seth," I instructed quietly. "I can handle this."

He looked terrified, but he backed down nonetheless, unearthing his hand from his pocket without his phone. I didn't even bother telling him to go back into the living room because for the first time in my life, I wanted this buffer between me and my former best friend.

"Becca," I turned my eyes back to her and everything just went cold. The hollowness and dark circles around Becca's eyes, her pale cheeks, the way she was nervously chewing on her bottom lip...guilt was written all over her face.

"You told them something, didn't you?"

Becca's eyes widened and another tear slipped down her cheeks as she shook her head furiously. "I didn't tell them anything, I swear. I have nothing to tell. Eli never talks to me about the club, never tells me anything. I just...I needed to give them *something*."

My body wrestled free of this shock-induced coma and I was shaking with anger now. "What the hell were you doing in my garage then?"

Becca's eyes darted down to the table as she whispered: "I'm not supposed to tell you anything."

My eyes narrowed dangerously.

"Let me guess," I spat furiously. "They offered you immunity and the drug charges are off the table now, right? All you had to do was what? Snoop through my house?"

Becca's eyes widened in alarm. "How did you know—"

"The ATF aren't the only ones who've been tailing you, Becca."

That did nothing but send her even further down the rabbit hole.

"It's...you...you don't understand, Belle," she stammered. "They said I was gonna go to prison. I can't go to prison! They said I could go away for the maximum sentence. That's 15 years! I can't..."

I felt my lips curl up into a snarl and fought back the urge to slap my former best friend right across her double-crossing, deceitful face.

"Oh, okay," I shot back icily. "Sure, because you're the only one with something to lose? Who cares about anyone else?"

"I'm so sorry," Becca whispered. "I didn't know what else to do. They knew everything, they followed me, they had pictures of me buying...you know. There was no other way out of it. I'm so sorry."

Becca's jaw trembled and as she sucked in a shaky, stunted breath, and I could barely even breathe, let alone understand what I was hearing.

"Why didn't you tell me? I would've tried to help you. God, if you would've just *told* somebody what the ATF wanted from you, if you'd been honest about it, Becca, I think they would've—"

"They would've killed me!" Becca cried. "I didn't think I had a choice."

"You had a choice," I shot back darkly. "And you chose wrong."

Becca nodded sadly and just squeezed her eyes shut as another tear fell down her cheek. I was suddenly aware there could be more happening here than I'd initially assumed. Becca could be wearing a wire and she was holding her cell phone in a death-grip, so who knew if she was taking pictures or recording, who knew what the terms of her deal were.

"Get out of my house," I whispered.

I hoped I never saw her again. I *knew* I'd never see her again. Even if she got away, even if they whisked her away to witness protection, if she'd even still get it, Becca was already gone.

Now I had to watch my former best friend pass right by me down the hallway and walk out my front door for good.

I shuffled down the hallway toward the garage and stared numbly ahead of me, vaguely aware that Seth was on the phone in the living room. My hand crept down to protectively cover my stomach as I pushed open the door to step inside the garage. Somewhere, deep in the recesses of my mind, I was very aware I probably shouldn't have let Becca leave like that.

A split-decision ruled by my conscience and one I'd probably have to answer for later, but right now I didn't care. Becca would never get very far anyway. Maybe, whether it was subconscious or otherwise, all I'd done was give her a head-start.

Now, my hands were in everything, skimming across every surface, dipping into every box, every drawer, searching for whatever Becca had been looking for. On my hands and knees looking underneath Caleb's workbench. Digging into the consoles of my mom's Trans Am and Caleb's truck, sifting through the glove boxes, ducking to look underneath the seats...nothing. At least nothing that could even be a little incriminating. Nothing out of the ordinary. Nothing but old motorcycle manuals, tools, boxes of junk we didn't really need, a few rakes, two sprinklers, and a lawn mower.

What did she think she was going to find in here?

I popped up from underneath the driver's seat in Caleb's truck just as the garage door flung open to reveal Caleb, Dom, Eli, and pretty much every other member of the club crowding into my kitchen and gaping back at me. After a beat, Caleb bounded down the short steps from the kitchen into the garage to stalk over to his truck and pull open the door. I braced myself for malice, anger, *something* for what had happened in our house tonight, but instead, his forehead creased with worry and his hand reached for my shoulder.

"You okay, Iz?"

I shook my head, choosing to wave a hand around the truck instead. "I'm trying to figure out what the hell she was doing, what she was looking for."

My head snapped to the side at some shuffling to my right and I was met with a somber-faced Dom, an irate Marcus, and a pale, grief-stricken Eli. Caleb just nodded, ignoring the presence of the three Horsemen cuts behind him. He hitched both hands on his hips as he surveyed the space around him and all its contents.

"There's nothing," I told him. "I've looked everywhere. I just can't figure it out. Why would she come in here? She had her cell phone with her, so maybe she was taking some pictures or video? I just can't figure out why."

Caleb shot Dom a quick glance, his eyes squinting in thought and then he crouched down, dropping to the ground so he could slide his entire torso underneath the truck to sweep both hands along the inside of the frame. In reality it only took him a few minutes, but it felt like hours as the rest of us waited in various degrees of impatience, fury, and disbelief.

It wasn't until his long arm reached up inside the tire well directly above the passenger seat that I heard it.

"Shit," Caleb muttered under his breath. Then he slid back out from underneath the truck and held up a tiny rectangle-shaped black box.

A low string of curses erupted from the cuts around me and everything went a little hazy. It was like that scene in a movie where the main character has that *moment,* that moment of realization, that moment of absolute and complete terror when the frame around them zooms out in a flash—I was living that moment. That realization. That terror.

I went completely numb as Caleb strode around to the Trans Am, repeating the exact inspection he'd done to his truck, and reappeared minutes later with a second identical black box in his hand.

Even I knew what those black boxes were used for. GPS trackers. Put under both vehicles in my garage by my former best friend.

Somehow, I managed to slip out of the truck, shut the door, and find my way to Caleb, my eyes fixed on the two black boxes in his hands the entire time.

"I can't believe it," I whispered.

Now a pointed finger jabbed in my face.

"You wanna explain to me why you let that fucking rat just stroll out of your house?" Marcus spat in my face.

He was red in the face, practically foaming at the mouth with fury, and all that venom leveled right in my direction knocked the wind out of me, but Caleb was in between us in a flash, holding up both hands to force Marcus to step back.

"She didn't know what was going on," Caleb told him in a calm, even tone with just a hint of warning.

Marcus narrowed his eyes into tight slits. "I don't give a shit. There's a right way to do things and tonight, your woman did shit the wrong way."

"She didn't know," Caleb told him again, this time his voice cracked with more than just a warning. He took a small step forward, but it was enough to reinforce he wasn't backing down.

"I just wanted her out of my house," I interjected quietly, even though I felt Dom's mammoth-sized hands on my shoulders to hold me in place. "The only thing I could think of to stop her was to get her out of my house."

And because I couldn't stomach the sight of her.

And because I couldn't stomach watching them descend on her like the pack of wolves I knew they were.

Marcus leaned to the side to get a better look at me from over Caleb's shoulder, his eyes darkening with calculating appraisal. I knew what I'd done wrong, but I couldn't apologize for the knee-jerk reaction and for ultimately following my instincts.

I especially wouldn't apologize for something that had happened in my own house, but I also wasn't stupid enough to say that to his face.

The only reaction I got from Marcus was a grunt in my general direction and then that was it. Caleb's hand had replaced Dom's and then he was leading me up the steps to the kitchen. All the rest of the club members had packed into the space, filling the area from wall to wall as Marcus dropped down into a chair at the table.

"Hey, Blondie," Marcus called out to me, lifting a hand to wave me into the hallway. "Why don't you go to your room and find somethin' to watch on TV? We got some club business to take care of here in your kitchen."

His words might've been directed at me, but his eyes were squarely on Caleb the entire time as if he was challenging him, goading him to see how he would react. Caleb stood still next to me, a tight line ticking down his jaw and the hand on my shoulder clenched ever-so-slightly. It was right on the tip of my tongue to defend myself, to tell him he couldn't kick me out of my own kitchen, but then I remembered who I was dealing with. What I knew he wanted to do to Becca.

Lipping off to the club president seemed like a pretty poor choice right about now.

Everyone was just standing here, waiting for the next move, and since this whole pissing contest in the middle of my kitchen had gotten old after about a second, I was done with all this for the night. I'd already shut the door to my home studio before I heard any murmurs from the kitchen.

So, those moments I was looking for, those feelings I'd needed to create art?

It looked like I'd just stumbled on those in abundance tonight.

CHAPTER TWELVE
Clean-Up

Caleb

Everyone knew what needed to be done. Now, it was just a matter of making quick work of the details. But when Marcus slipped his cigarette pack out of his cut, I took that opportunity to remind him whose table he was currently at.

"You're not smokin' that in here," I told him as I dropped down into a chair across from him. "You need to smoke, you step outside."

He arched an eyebrow at me in challenge, but I shrugged it off.

"My house, my rules."

He shot me an exasperated glare, but I wasn't backing down on this one. Not after the way he'd spoken to Isabelle, the accusation in his voice, the harsh, aggressive tone, and the way he'd disrespected her.

Her instincts were different than anyone else's in this kitchen and she was a little more emotionally invested in keeping Becca in one piece than any of us combined, including Eli. I never wanted her to lose the part of herself that was good, decent, and honest, especially not because of the club. All she'd done tonight was be the person I'd fallen head over ass for. All she'd done tonight was be a decent human being.

That was more than I could say for the rest of us.

"Now," Marcus pressed on. "Who's going with Eli on garbage duty? The longer we sit here, the longer it'll take us to send that trash where it belongs."

From the corner of my eye, I could see Eli grimace and run a hand over his face. Life as he knew it was over.

"I'll go," I volunteered quietly.

Becca had come into my house and planted two GPS trackers in my garage to set me up. Putting the tracker on Isabelle's car might as well have been the nail in her coffin for me. I didn't care who she was. As much as her connection to Isabelle would make putting this matter to bed uncomfortable and that much more difficult, she couldn't be allowed to just walk away. Clean-up duty wasn't something I relished, but we had no other choice.

Eli nodded to me, his face stony and expressionless and I had to give him credit for that. Maybe he wanted to make her look him in the eye, to force her to explain herself. If I were him, I think that's what I would need too.

Dom leaned down to me, "I can hang here with Isabelle until you get back."

I nodded to him and scrubbed a hand over my face as my gaze shifted to Eli. "They've obviously got nothin' 'cuz they wouldn't have had her doing this shit if they did. I doubt they'd give her any real protection now, so she's gonna be runnin' on her own. Any ideas where she would go?"

Eli blew out a deep breath. "I have no idea."

Marcus gestured with his head toward the hallway and catching his drift, I begrudgingly rose from my chair to go get the one person in this house that could actually help us, the same person Marcus had just dismissed from the kitchen like a house servant. After a pause, I pushed open the door to find her sitting on her stool with her back to me, earbuds lodged in her ears with her paintbrush sweeping furiously around the canvas.

Shit. Whenever she was in a mood like this, it was usually in my best interest to keep my distance and not interrupt her. It was sort of like poking a sleeping bear, if the bear was a 5'6, blonde, hormonal pregnant lady wielding a paintbrush.

"Hey, Iz?"

Either she was ignoring me or just couldn't hear me because her shoulders were still square with the canvas and her paintbrush still swung around from side to side like there was no tomorrow. Preparing myself for the tongue-lashing I was about to receive, I closed the space between us until I could rest my hand on her shoulder and crouch down to her level.

She started a little at the touch of my hand and then she stared up at me expectantly, tugging her earbuds out of her ears and dropping her paintbrush into the mason jar at her side.

"Iz," I began carefully. "Marcus wants to talk to you."

Isabelle rolled her eyes. "Oh, now little ol' me is important enough to keep around? I'm not going back out there."

I tossed a glance over my shoulder, grateful to see the rest of the club had respected our privacy.

"Where would Becca go, Iz?"

She lifted an eyebrow and now the light blue of her eyes twisted into a cloudy, black storm. "So now I'm supposed to help you catch her too?"

I knew exactly what she was thinking, why she would object. This was her best friend—well, *former* best friend, someone she'd known for years and if our roles were reversed and Dom was in Becca's shoes, I didn't know if I'd be able to bring myself to lead the club to him either.

"Iz," I sighed. "You know her better than anyone. You know we can't let the ATF get to her. Where's she runnin' to?"

Isabelle squeezed her eyes shut. "I used to think I knew her better than anyone. Now I have no idea."

"I know," I nodded and shot her a weak smile, my hand squeezing her shoulder just enough to prompt her.

She blew out a deep breath and then glanced at her phone, which was resting right next to her easel. "It's only been what? Twenty minutes since she left? Do you think the ATF would help her if she called them?"

"Depends on what their deal with her was. If all she was supposed to do was plant those trackers, who knows. They might not care about her anymore since she technically didn't deliver. Either way, Iz, we gotta get to her first."

She chewed on her bottom lip in thought and the pain in her eyes twisted my heart. This wasn't going to be easy for her, but after this, no one could ever call her loyalty into question again, especially not Marcus.

"Her family has a house in Wilmington right on the beach," she told me softly and she squeezed her eyes shut the moment she realized what she'd just done. "We used to go there sometimes during the summer. I don't think she ever told Eli about that because she never mentioned them going there before. If he doesn't know anything about it, that's probably where she's heading."

"You know the address, Iz?"

"I don't remember it," she shook her head. "But I could give you directions."

"Does anyone live there year-round?"

Her eyes widened a little as the true reasoning behind my question sank in and she swallowed tightly. "No. It's her parents' place, but they live here in town. They only go there in the summer on the weekends."

"Okay. Thanks, babe," I leaned forward to kiss the side of her head. "Dom's gonna stay here with you until I get back. It'll be late, so don't wait up."

"How could I possibly get any sleep tonight?" she muttered and reached for my hand. "Please be safe."

"I always am."

Once all the details were settled and we figured out that Eli did not, as Isabelle predicted, know about this summer house, I slid into my truck, threw the duffel bag we needed in the passenger seat, tucked Isabelle's written directions into the console next to me, and pulled out of the driveway with Eli right behind me.

. . .

Two and a half hours later, I pulled my truck into the driveway of a modest-size, single-story house right on the beach, just like Isabelle had described, and pulled my hood up over my head. It was already pitch-black and late enough at night that any neighbors wouldn't be up to see us coming and going. We didn't plan on being in this house for long, but the less people around, the less trouble that could end up blowing back on the club.

Eli leapt up the stairs, taking the lead and I was happy to hand over the reins on this one. This was his problem just as much as it was the club's, if not more so, and it was his right to confront her, to demand the answers he deserved before we cleaned this mess up. He tried the doorknob and got nothing. Becca was smart enough to lock the door behind her, but stupid enough to choose the Feds over her local MC.

He reached behind him and I handed him the leathermen he needed to jimmy the lock. Having done this very thing many times for the club already, Eli was a pro, despite the way his gloved hands shook as he jerked the tool into the lock and the way his chest heaved up and down. After about 15 seconds of work, the lock gave way and Eli pushed through the door. He flipped the light off in the kitchen as we moved through the darkness, both of us just needing to get this over with as soon as possible.

Just as we rounded the corner of the kitchen, Becca materialized in the hallway, stopping dead in her tracks at the sight of the two hooded men in the house.

Her eyes widened with terror. Even in the darkness, she knew who we were. She knew what we'd come here to do. Instinct kicked in and she turned on her heel to sprint back in the direction she'd came, but Eli's cold voice called out to her.

"Don't run, Becca. It's not gonna help you."

She froze mid-step, her entire body trembling as she hyperventilated right where she stood. That was all the time Eli needed to advance on her, clamping both hands on her shoulders and shoving her into the wall. Becca cried out, tears already streaming down her lying face and she tore and clawed at Eli's iron-grip.

Fighting wasn't going to help her any more than running would.

"Why did you do it?" he asked, his voice cracking with desperation and grief. "Tell me why, goddammit!"

She choked out a sob, shaking and convulsing underneath his hands, but Eli, to his credit, never flinched. Never moved a muscle except to keep her right where she was, right where she belonged. Now she was shaking her head like *we* were the bad guys. Like *we* were the ones who'd done something wrong.

"I didn't know what else to do," Becca pushed out in between sobbing gasps. "I'm so—"

Eli slammed her into the wall to cut her off. "Don't fucking say it. You don't mean it."

As much as my sympathies were with him, we needed to get this moving. So I shifted until I was shoulder to shoulder with Eli and close enough to look Becca right in the eye.

"Your deal with the ATF," I started evenly, my eyes locked on Becca with every word. "What were the terms? What did you give them besides agreeing to put those trackers in my garage?"

She squeezed her eyes shut. Eli snarled at her and slammed his hand right next to her head to force her to answer us.

"I didn't...I didn't give them anything," she stammered and swallowed hard. "I didn't know anything. Nothing they cared about, at least."

"What were the terms of your deal?" I tried again, this time letting some menace slip through.

Becca's eyes widened and they darted anxiously from me to Eli and back to me again as if struggling and crying for mercy would somehow convince us to back down.

"If I put the trackers on," Becca pushed out in between heaves. "They wouldn't charge me with anything."

Yeah, that's what I figured.

"And you thought you'd get away with it?" my eyebrows rose at the stupidity of the whole thing. "No harm, no foul?"

Becca shook her head furiously.

"Is that it?" I growled.

She swallowed hard. "I was supposed to see if Isabelle knew anything, if she'd tell me something that would help. They knew you might've told her something, that maybe you talked to her about the club. I was supposed to go over there and try to get her to talk."

Yeah, that's what I figured too. The second she'd agreed to that, she might as well have just signed her own death warrant.

"I didn't wanna do it," she whispered. "I knew she'd never say anything that could get you in trouble. I didn't even try that hard."

Like that was supposed to make what she'd done less deceitful. Less disgusting.

"Let me guess, you recorded the conversation too," I didn't even wait for her to nod. "Where's your phone?"

She gestured to the bag sitting underneath the kitchen counter that both Eli and I had missed in the darkness.

"Recording your best friend's conversation and trying to get her to talk," I shook my head at Becca. "That's some nasty, evil shit."

"I thought—"

"You could've told me!" Eli charged in, twisting his fingers into her shoulders and practically lifting her feet off the ground. "You could've told me what they wanted. What they were threatening you with."

"You wouldn't have trusted me anyway," Becca whispered, her voice trembling in fear and something that sounded a little like resignation. "I did the only thing I could."

He shoved her backward in the wall one more time, knocking her head violently into the drywall behind her. "I loved you, Becca. I would've tried to help you. We could've figured something out. It didn't have to be this way. You didn't have to do this."

"You never loved me. You never trusted me," she murmured hoarsely. "If you did, we wouldn't be here."

Eli dropped her, and she slid to the floor in front of us, covering her head with her arms and crumbling with heavy sobs. There was nothing else to say. Nothing else that could be done. We got the information we came here for. Just one last order of business left to do.

My eyes lifted up from the pathetic excuse for a human being below me and found Eli, whose eyes had glazed over in a flurry of violent, grief-fueled rage. I nodded to him, signaling that it was time, and gestured with my head to the duffel bag at my side. There was a little bit of quick prep work to do, so I headed for the nearest bathroom down the hall to get my part ready. All I had to do was lay out the five-foot square of heavy plastic, grab the first pillow I could find from a bedroom down the hall, attach the silencer to the Glock, and set it down on the counter for Eli.

Right now, I was just back-up. Not even 10 seconds after the Glock rested on the bathroom counter, Eli shoved through the door with Becca in tow. She kicked and bucked and struggled against him with every ounce of strength left in her, but that was just adrenaline. There was no use fighting or struggling.

Eli hauled her up and slammed her down onto the plastic to hold her against the floor with a pointed elbow. Becca's pleas and cries for mercy would fall on deaf ears.

I handed him the pillow and the Glock and stepped back to watch the sentence get carried out. Eli pressed the pillow against Becca's head, muffling her terrified screams for help. She kicked, bucking into the floor, and nearly knocking the Glock out of Eli's trembling hand, so I leaned forward to hold her legs down—anything to make this easier, anything to get this behind us.

He pushed the Glock's short barrel into the pillow and I could see his bottom lip quivering, both hands shaking, his entire body trembling and struggling to follow through. His lips pulled apart in agony and he squeezed his eyes shut before finally letting out an anguished, tortured wail.

With an abrupt sob, Eli shoved her even deeper into the floor and sprung up to his feet to push his way through the bathroom.

"I can't," he muttered helplessly as he passed me. "I just can't do it."

I nodded, more to myself than anything, when he shut the door behind him and focused on the buzzing in my ears instead of the crying girl just a few feet away from me. I couldn't think about how she was my future wife's best friend. Or about the fact that the only reason Isabelle had ever come back into my life in the first place was because of Becca's indirect involvement. Or about how Isabelle had always talked about the way Becca was there for her after her mom's death in a way her dad hadn't been able to. And I couldn't think about the fact that Isabelle might look at me differently after this. That she might, once the shock and the betrayal wore off, only see me as her best friend's executioner.

I just couldn't let myself go there.

Because a traitor was lying at my feet. One who, if Eli *had* been upfront with her the way I was with Isabelle, wouldn't have hesitated to sell out the club and her best friend. I couldn't let myself forget that.

I reached into the duffel for the second pair of leather gloves and leaned against the wall across from her as I readied myself.

"I guess I shouldn't have been surprised she told you about this place,"

Becca's hoarse voice called out to me from the floor.

"No," I told her as I slipped the first glove over my left hand. "You shouldn't have been. I'm pretty sure any loyalty she had to you died the night you showed up at my house last week and forced her hand."

Her eyes followed my movements, watching me wearily as I slid on the right glove and then untucked my own Glock from underneath the back of my jeans. If I was really going to have to do this, I would use my own piece. That's just the way it had to be. Her eyes clouded over as she silently observed me dip into the duffel bag one last time for that second silencer I'd packed away in there just in case this very thing happened.

"Just make it quick," she whispered.

My eyes lifted to her for just a second as I screwed the silencer on over my barrel.

"You know, I have a lot of regrets, Caleb," Becca called out to me again and I stilled where I stood, letting the hand gripping my Glock fall down to my side for the time being. I knew this part well too. This was the part where they made their peace with their life, where they confessed to whatever sin they'd been holding on to, where they made their last mark on this life for whatever it was worth.

"Yeah?"

I'd play along, let her say whatever she needed to say.

"I wish I'd never met Eli."

I lifted a shoulder. "Yeah, I guess I can see that."

"I wish I'd never brought Isabelle to the clubhouse."

My eyes shot up from my gloved hands to find her staring me down defiantly, challenging me to say otherwise.

"I'd wish I'd never brought her around you people," Becca pressed on from her spot on the floor. "I wish *I'd* never been around you people. All you care about is yourselves, keeping yourselves safe, yourselves out of prison. You don't care about anyone else. And then I do the exact same thing and I get tossed out with the trash."

I shot a hard glare her way. "Maybe. I'll give ya that. But you had every opportunity to go to someone for help and you didn't. You chose to sell your best friend out hoping you'd get something good enough to save yourself. Think about that for one of the three minutes you have left and tell me you aren't just as selfish as the rest of us."

Becca just shook her head, sniffling a little as a lone tear trailed down her face. "You know, one of these days, Isabelle's gonna realize what you really are. She's got you up on this pedestal like you're some kind of Superman," she laughed mirthlessly. "Being with her doesn't make you a better person—it's just makes her a worse one. And sooner or later, she's gonna realize you're not the good guy she thinks you are and she's gonna hate you and she's gonna leave your ass in her dust. The only thing she'll ever want from you then is child support and if she's smart, she'll never let you anywhere near that baby."

She must've known she hit a nerve because her eyes, still streaked with tears, went wide with awareness. Her words had sliced right through the most tender spot in my conscience. That gaping black hole that just kept pulling me in, carrying me away, and eating its way through all my guilt, all my doubts, and all my fears. I tried to tell myself I had to be all about business. That this was protocol. That this was just how we handled situations like this.

But before, I hadn't had Isabelle in my life. I hadn't had any other priorities than the club. Things were different for me and they were changing in a way I didn't quite understand. Marcus had said to me once, a long time ago at Dom and Lex's wedding, that problems at home would mess with my priorities in the club. Assuming the club always had to come first. Assuming I always had to follow orders without questioning anyone's motives or calling anyone onto the carpet.

The longer I stared at Becca with my gun in the my hand, the more I just didn't recognize myself. I was about to kill my future wife's best friend. Somewhere along the way, I'd deluded myself into thinking this was the right choice. That putting the club first above everything else was *always* the right choice—it was what I'd been programmed to believe.

Tonight, though, I didn't really want to put the club first.

I looked down at the gun in my hand again and I wanted to vomit. Why was no one thinking about the fact that the ATF could be waiting outside this house right now, just waiting for us to carry out a dead body? It was so easy and even if setting this kind of trap hadn't been their plan all along, we'd handed them the opportunity right on a platter without even thinking twice.

If I pulled the trigger tonight, what were the odds that I'd find myself handcuffed minutes later and shoved into the back of a squad car with murder charges wrapped around my neck?

Why did no one else in the club seem to care about that?

The right thing to do tonight was to renege on protocol and follow my own instincts.

I didn't hesitate now. I tossed my gun back into the duffel bag and hauled Becca up to her feet.

"Wha—" she stammered.

"Shut up."

With a tight grip on her elbow, I pulled open the bathroom door to find Eli leaning against the wall with his head in his hands. When his face unearthed from his fingertips, he blinked back at me in shock.

"What are you doing?" he choked out hoarsely. "We have to—"

"We don't have to do shit," I growled. "You and I both know you don't really wanna see her in a hole somewhere. So this is what we're gonna do..."

. . .

I pulled my truck into the precinct, jerked into a space, and shifted into park. Sure enough, just like I'd predicted, we had a sedan tailing us all the way back from Wilmington right up to the precinct's parking lot. If I'd gone through with this the way I was supposed to, I'd probably be sitting in holding right now, getting fingerprinted, and forced into a nine by nine cell until I could get sentenced for murder.

Come hell or high water, I'd made the right fucking decision.

With my eyes locked onto the double-doors in front of us, I shifted just enough to make sure she wouldn't bolt on me.

"You clear on what you have to do?" I asked her in a calm, even voice.

Becca swallowed tightly and wiped a stray tear from her cheek. "It's either this or you guys kill me right?"

I shot her a wary glance.

"I think I can live with this," she whispered.

"Me too," I exhaled.

"You're sure they won't—"

"They were blackmailing you, Becca," I cut in abruptly. "There's no way any judge would give you a maximum sentence after the way they played you. They made you feel like your back was against the wall, like you had no choice. So now, they've got nothing and you've gotta face the fallout."

She drew in a deep breath, her eyes still focused on the precinct's double doors when they darted back to me. "Thank you."

"I didn't do this for you."

She nodded sadly, her eyes still shining with unshed tears. "I know."

I tipped my chin to her and held out my hand. Becca quickly slid her phone into my palm and that was all I needed from her. The last order of business where she was concerned was walking her into the precinct and sitting with her until a deputy escorted her into a holding room.

Prison was the right place for her now. A place she'd earned. But she didn't deserve to be in a hole in the ground, especially since she'd been right about us. We'd turned on her the second we found out about her drug habit. Instead of containing the issue, getting her ass out of town or at least offering some damn support and trust, we'd been immediately suspicious, immediately willing to throw her to the wolves to save ourselves, just like she'd said.

I was no better than the rest of them, but at least now, I'd saved someone's life instead of taking it.

This was the first time in my life I've ever blatantly disregarded orders or even blatantly *questioned* those orders and in going against the grain, I'd followed my gut and kept myself out of prison.

This was the first time in my life where I'd put myself before the club. Where I'd put my *own* family before the club. Right about now, I wasn't sure if any of them, save for Dom, even really understand what having a real family meant.

. . .

When I finally pulled back into my driveway, I turned the ignition off as my eyes drifted to my duffel bag, the same one that contained the gloves, cleaning supplies, and silencers we would've used to get rid of Becca.

I scrubbed both hands over my face and pulled the driver's side door open to head inside the house. It was done. It was over. And I'd come out of it the other side with life as I knew it still intact.

Not that I'd expected anything less, but Marcus wasn't happy. We'd had orders and we'd disobeyed. *I* had disobeyed. I'd do it again if I had to and he knew it. For all the swearing and stomping in rage I heard from his end of the phone, the second the word *tail* had left my mouth we both knew he didn't have a leg to stand on. I'd made the right call, whether he liked it or not.

I shuffled through the kitchen and into the living room to find Dom and Isabelle sitting shoulder to shoulder against the wall across from me. The second Isabelle's eyes locked with mine, her entire face crumbled. She covered her face with one hand, her shoulders trembling with silent sobs, and Dom reached out to put his hand on her shoulder to give her what little comfort he could.

"Iz," I called out softly, but her shoulders just kept shaking. "Iz, look at me."

I waited just long enough for her eyes to fly back up to me before delivering the news, "She's fine."

Her eyes widened and Dom's mouth lobbed open a little in stunned silence.

"What?" Isabelle whispered, staring back at me like the words just didn't compute.

"Becca's okay," I told her as I headed for her.

Dom waited long enough until I slid down next to her before rising to his feet to give us some space. His job was done here anyway; it was on me to pick up the pieces now.

I pulled Isabelle's shaking body to my chest, holding her to me as tightly as I could, to give her as much as I could. "Long story short, babe, they tailed us all the way to Wilmington and were waiting for us to bring out a body. I figured it out before it was too late. It's over now, Iz."

Dom's eyes were still on me, digesting my words and then his eyes narrowed. "So what did you do?"

"I made her turn herself in at the precinct," I shrugged and tugged Isabelle a little closer to me. That seemed to be enough to appease him and he nodded before walking out the front door.

I leaned down to brush my lips against her forehead. "I couldn't exactly let her just walk away after what she did, but she didn't deserve what the club wanted to do to her either."

Her eyes glimmered with tears and she leaned into me, as if holding on for dear life. "You did the right thing. I'm so glad you did the right thing."

"Me too," I murmured.

"So Becca's gone?"

"I don't know exactly what they'll charge her with, but it's not gonna be the maximum sentence. Not after the stunt they pulled and gambling with her life like that. She'll do some time, get what she earned, and then if she's smart, she'll never step foot in this town again."

It wasn't until Isabelle had cried herself into exhaustion, whether it was from relief, grief, or both I still wasn't sure, and until I'd carried her to bed that I found myself back out in the garage and slid into my truck. I reached for Becca's phone before I could stop myself and carried it over to my tool bench, where the two black GPS tracking boxes sat waiting for me.

Now that it was in my hands, I wasn't sure what I wanted. Right up until this moment, I thought I'd known exactly how I would handle this, how I would feel. But now that I had it, now that the temptation was there, it would be easy to just press the home button to at least see if she had a passcode. If she did, all I'd have to do was ask Eli to jailbreak it and I could access anything she'd recorded without a problem.

There was a part of me, a shameful, deep-seated part, that needed to be 100 percent positive Isabelle hadn't fallen into the same trap that Becca had, that she'd remained loyal until the bitter end of this whole mess. The undertow of this temptation was just too strong and I knew I'd get carried away and drown if I fed into it.

My hands gripped a hammer a second later and then I gave it hell, pounding the shit out of Becca's phone until all that was left of it were tiny scraps of metal and dust. I needed to demolish it until all the temptation was gone.

Listening to that recording would be a violation of everything we were building together.

I chose to trust and to protect her instead.

And so, I carried the ashes of Becca's pulverized phone and Isabelle's handwritten directions to that beach house out to the makeshift fire pit in my backyard and burned every last scrap.

CHAPTER THIRTEEN
On Call

Isabelle

Becca's happy face smiled up at me and my heart knotted violently. I hit delete. Then I swiped my thumb to the next picture in my camera roll: one with Becca and me cheek to cheek and smiling brightly into the camera. I hit delete. I didn't know how many times I repeated that motion, but each time I did it, it was just as cathartic as it was agonizing. Each time I hit the delete button, the knife in my heart twisted a little more, but deep down, watching the pictures disappear was a relief.

I had to forget her. I had to erase her memory as much as I could. Holding onto it wouldn't help me move forward.

My eyes fell to the clock on my phone and then I tossed it down onto our bed. Caleb should be home from the shop anytime now. We had a big night ahead of us and here I was, clouding the mood and wallowing in a pit of despair and depression that still wouldn't change the outcome.

Becca was gone. It was over.

I needed to find a way to move on.

I needed to find a way to forget that I'd been just as willing to write Becca off as the rest of them, that I'd basically handed her over to them, written directions and all, with barely any hesitation. The second she'd asked me to choose between her and Caleb, I was done with her. Now, I was just as callous, as ruthless, and as selfish as the rest of them. I could've tried to help her, but I'd turned my back on my best friend instead and I still couldn't reconcile the repercussions of what I'd done.

I just didn't recognize the person staring back at me in the mirror sometimes.

Life, for the most part, was moving on, so it was for the best I move with it. Caleb and I went about our normal routines, juggling work, school, and the club. We didn't talk about the fact that Dom had barely spoken to him these last three weeks. We didn't talk about the fact that Eli had blasted out of the clubhouse on his bike two days after that night and hadn't been back since.

I didn't really want to talk about anything involving the club anymore. Sometimes, I wished I could forget it even existed.

As I slipped my dress for tonight off the hanger, my eyes fell to the other one covered up by a garment bag and a light smile touched my lips.

One more weekend and I'd be wearing that dress at City Hall.

Maybe that's all I needed to do now: just focus on the positive, the things I should be looking forward to anyway.

Those two dresses were the first maternity clothes I'd purchased, which I figured was a celebration in itself. I set the black dress on the bed and then let myself unzip the garment bag for a quick look at my dress for my first wedding to Caleb. It was simple, but beautiful. The beaded, strapless bodice dipped into an empire waist with flowing layers of organza skimming my knees. The layers would lay right over my little baby bump, not necessarily to hide it, but to accentuate these new curves.

My hand drifted down to my stomach, covering the gentle curve and I smiled. A light fluttering right in the center of my stomach had me chuckling; she was definitely making her presence known, as if I could ever forget about her.

With that thought, I zipped the garment bag back up and tucked it into the back of my closet again. The black dress for tonight slid on pretty easily, given that my stomach was a little more rounded since the last time I tried it on. It was just a simple black dress with a high-cut tank-top style neckline with racer-back scoops cut out in the back. I liked it because it was form-fitting and I found myself chomping at the bit to wear it around for everyone to see.

Just as I finished touching up a few long curls with my curling wand, that tell-tale roar of a motorcycle ripped down the street and right into the driveway. Butterflies flurried in my stomach and I gave my hair one last spritz with some spray before changing course to the hallway to find Caleb tossing his cut over the side of the couch with a shopping bag in his hand.

His eyes flicked to me for a just second and then slammed back to me, a slow, sexy grin spreading across his lips as I met him in the living room. He gave a low whistle and shook his head, promptly tossed the shopping bag on the couch, and reached for me to pull me into his arms.

"Iz," he murmured and pressed his lips into my neck. "You look..." he trailed off and tilted his head just enough to address Seth, who was perched dutifully on our couch, "Prospect. Get outta my house."

Seth scrambled off the couch and hightailed out the front door, but neither one of us was really paying all that much attention to him. My lips curled up as Caleb's hands slipped around my waist to pull me against his chest. His mouth was on my neck again, leaving little trails of hot fire in his lips' wake and I shivered in his arms as his hands skated down my hips to skim the edge of my knee-length dress up my thighs.

I laughed, pushing him back with both hands before we got too carried away. "As much as I would love to take this further, you need to change and we have to get going otherwise I'm gonna be late."

Caleb groaned and knocked his forehead into my shoulder. "Ten minutes?"

"No," I shook my head, still laughing, and shoved him backwards so I could grab the shopping bag and sneak away. "We needed to leave 10 minutes ago. What is it with you and 10 minutes anyway? Whatever happened to 15? Or 20? Or some foreplay, maybe?"

His lips twitched with amusement. "You can have all the foreplay you want. Just as long as you keep that dress on."

I was already backpedalling into the kitchen to put some space between us and called over my shoulder, "Isn't the whole point to get my dress *off*?"

"Oh, don't worry, Iz," Caleb called back to me from the hallway, where he was, thankfully, heading towards our bedroom. "It'll come off. Doesn't mean I don't wanna enjoy that dress though."

"Wow," I muttered, shaking my head as I hopped up on the counter and rifled through the shopping bag, my eyes lighting up at what was inside. By the time Caleb re-appeared in the kitchen, still buttoning up his white collared shirt, I'd already dug away at a good chunk of the mint chocolate chip ice cream he'd brought home for me.

When I hopped off the counter to put the container in the freezer, he was hot on my heels with his lips on my shoulder. His hands slid around my stomach, easily finding the swollen roundness there.

"I felt that little fluttering again today before you got home," I told him. "She's just getting comfortable. You know, stretching out, making a little more room."

Caleb laughed, gently turning me around in his arms until I faced him. "It's a good thing we'll get all that resolved once and for all soon enough. Then you'll eat your words, Iz."

"Shut it. I'm right. You're wrong."

"Okay. Whatever you say."

I leaned back a little to take him in and ran my hands over the hard planes of muscle underneath his shirt. "You look nice."

He took a step back and spread his arms out wide to give me a better view. "So I pass?"

"Oh yeah," I nodded. "You'll do."

Caleb leaned forward to kiss me, thought better of it, and opted to plant a quick kiss on my forehead. But when his phone buzzed in his back pocket, my heart skidded and plummeted right into my stomach. I knew what that meant and I blew out a shaky breath as he shot me a worried glance before digging for his phone. I didn't even need him to tell me what the text said—the way his face fell and the way he squeezed his eyes shut pretty much said it all.

"You have to go, don't you?" I whispered.

"Church in 10," he nodded soberly. "I'll get there in time, Iz. As soon as I can, I'll get my ass to the gallery. I promise."

All I could do was mask my disappointment as best I could and watch him head back into the living room for his cut, his phone to his ear while he made some last-minute arrangements. My frustration wouldn't do anything but make Caleb feel even more guilty than he already did and make me feel even more stressed out than I already was.

With his keys in one hand, he swung his cut on over his shoulders as he strode back into the kitchen. It was a jarring image: that clean-cut white button-down tucked into black dress pants with his leather Horsemen cut thrown over the top. It didn't quite mesh, but it didn't quite look out of place on him either. The two sides to him were more apparent now than ever, the outlaw and the sweet, sensitive father of my baby.

Two sides of the same coin.

Two completely different lives.

"I don't have time to change," Caleb told me quietly and then bent down to press a quick kiss onto my stomach. "Gotta get you to the clubhouse so you can hitch a ride with the prospect."

At the very least, I was grateful he hadn't called Skyler or Lexie to take his place until he could get there. I just didn't want to turn my first showcase into a bigger deal than it needed to be because I kind of just wanted to get it over with more than anything. Besides, I'd just wanted to be alone since Becca's exit from my life and Skyler and Lexie had been just as distant as Dom since everything had went down.

"I'm not gonna miss any of it," he promised me again. "Even if church runs a little long, I'll get there as soon as I can. I'll do 150 on the highway if I have to."

"Can your truck really go that fast?"

"She will if I tell her to."

We'd meant to cut the tension, to lighten up this dismal reality, but it didn't work. Even as he ushered me into his truck, I just couldn't shake this sick feeling in my stomach.

The club was his full-time job and he was on call 24/7. If he got the call, he had to go. No matter what was happening, no matter what responsibilities he had at home with me, one phone call and he'd have to be on his bike en route to the clubhouse. The club didn't give a shit that we had somewhere important to be tonight because it wasn't important to them.

I had a sinking feeling that I could be in labor, ready to deliver, and Marcus would still feel like he could call him away and Caleb would still feel like he had to go.

That was just something I'd never get used to.

. . .

Caleb

I pulled out my chair at the table, ignoring Casey's eyebrows wiggling idiotically at my shirt and pants, and I chose to pop a piece of nicotine gum into my mouth instead of giving him any sort of reaction.

Damn, this gum tasted like shit. Like mint and piss. Moldy piss. Well, it looked like I'd found something that tasted worse than Isabelle's cooking. At best, this was just a distraction until church started and until I could get my ass back on the road. I had a 45-minute drive ahead of me and I needed to get this over with *now*.

I already felt like a big enough asshole the way it was. The longer I sat here, the worse I felt for basically throwing Isabelle to the prospect and ditching her for the clubhouse. Now I couldn't stop thinking about what I had to miss because I was sitting here instead. About where I'd rather be than here at this table.

My eyes fell to the empty chair just a few paces down the table from me and I pushed out a heavy sigh. Eli was still MIA, still out on the road, on his own, trying to sort out his demons. I didn't envy him for a second, but after a three-week absence with virtually zero contact with anyone, the mere mention of his name was becoming almost as taboo as the would-be-rat I'd dropped off at the precinct.

Finally, Marcus dropped down into his seat at the head of the table and pounded the gavel, eyeing my attire with one skeptical, cocked eyebrow. Whatever. They could rag on me however they wanted as long as we moved this along.

"This'll be a quick one, boys," Marcus huffed out gruffly with one last glance my way. "There's just one order of business to handle tonight, but it's a big one. Got a call from Wallace, says the Warlords are lookin' for a delivery ASAP for a buyer and are willing to pay for our speedy service."

I straightened up my chair and asked the question on everyone's mind: "How much are we talkin' about here?"

"$30K bonus for the delivery. Whoever goes splits it," Marcus related.

Shit.

I didn't even need to look at Dom to know he was on the same page as me. Everything I'd had to pay for in the past few months and all the bills that would rack up on me in the next few years too, flashed through my mind all at once. The house payments. Isabelle's engagement ring. The $5K I'd handed to her dad in that envelope. Jesus, the last health insurance bill I'd paid had been nearly $700 thanks to Isabelle's shit insurance through the shop. Apparently, a pregnancy was a 'pre-existing condition' in their minds and so I'd footed almost 75 percent of that recent bill.

I'd feel a helluva lot better going into our wedding next weekend with that extra cash in the bank. All the things I'd promised her and all the things I wanted to give her...I could start reaching for it with this money.

"What about the ATF?" Heath asked quietly from his end of the table.

"Nobody's seen or heard from them since I left Becca at the precinct," I offered. Right about now, I was willing to do and say just about anything to get my ass added to this run. "Kelly told us himself they packed up their shit and lit outta here, what, not even three days after? They threw all their chips down on a dark horse that never had a shot at winning and they lost. We were careful, we covered our asses, and it paid off. They're long gone."

My gut was telling me I was right and the last time my gut told me to do something, I was the one who'd been careful when everyone else sitting at this table did nothing but blindly follow orders.

Heath took a long pull from his cigarette in thought. "Yeah. But we don't know they're gone for sure. How do we know they're not just hidin' out somewhere and waitin' for us to make our next move?"

"They didn't get what they wanted from us," Dom tossed out, casting me a careful glance as he spoke. "They moved on. Pulled out and cut their losses. There's no sense in us bleedin' cash any longer than we have to."

I nodded to him. It was reassuring to hear, out loud for the rest of the club to hear, that I wasn't crazy. This was the type of deal that set my family on the path to an easy, comfortable life where they would want for nothing.

"Do the Warlords know we've had the ATF sniffin' around?" Casey wondered out loud.

Marcus shook his head. "Not as far as I know."

"Doesn't matter anyway," I told the table. "They won't be a problem."

"From what I'm hearin', it sounds like Caleb and Dom are volunteering," Marcus surmised ruefully with a weariness that told me he wasn't exactly keen on the idea.

"The Warlords aren't exactly a club we want to piss off," I shrugged. "As far as I'm concerned, *not* takin' this deal puts us worse off than if we don't. We can't afford to get on the Warlords' bad side. We say no now and how do we know they won't pull back on more offers and give them to a competitor until we got nothing up north?"

The Warlords were one of the most in-demand and powerful distributors with wide-reaching connections north of Tennessee. They had as many connections there as we did and for that reason alone, both of us needed to stay in each other's good graces.

Marcus' eyes fell to Dom, who nodded tightly in the affirmative.

"Alright," he shrugged. "Looks like Dom and Caleb are taking the cargo up to Pittsburgh tomorrow."

As far as I was concerned, the ATF was all but a distant memory. Besides, even if they weren't, we'd lost them easily before. We'd take a different route to Pittsburgh, crash in Cincinnati again if we had to just to be on the safe side, just like we'd done last time. This was nothing but business now. They'd either been reassigned or quit while they were ahead.

Finally, Marcus swung the gavel down to end church and I practically leapt out of my chair to head right for the exit. Church had, as I'd predicted, gone for longer than I'd anticipated and now, I was right on track to show up at least 20 minutes into the showcase. The gallery was open for two hours, but I didn't want to miss even a minute more than I had to.

My hand was already on the doorknob when Marcus' voice called me back, "Caleb. Got a minute?"

"Shit," I muttered under my breath. No, I didn't really have a minute, but

I couldn't exactly blow him off either.

Still, I reared back to face him while the rest of the club cleared out of the chapel. "Alright. What's up?"

Marcus gestured for me to have a seat at the table, right in the chair Heath had just left vacant and the implication wasn't lost on me. Someday soon, this would be my chair. My responsibility. My time away from my wife and my kids. My eyes flicked to the chair, just waiting for me to occupy it, and I hesitated. My fingers tingled a little—this wasn't a big deal. It was just a chair. That's all it was. A chair rooted in the legacy hovering over my shoulders now like an anchor, weighing me down, keeping me in place and in line.

His dark eyes locked on me as I dropped into the chair and he smoothed a hand over his salt-and-pepper ponytail before reaching into his cut for his cigarette pack. After tapping one out of the pack, he offered it to me.

"Nah," I shook my head and dug into my pocket for my nicotine gum instead. "I'm tryin' to quit. You know, 'cuz of the kid."

"Right," he nodded to me, gesturing towards my chest. "You got somewhere to be tonight?"

"Iz has a showcase at her school. We were on our way out the door when I got the text for church."

"Fair enough," Marcus shrugged. "I'll make this quick then. You havin' money problems, son?"

I balked at the question, rearing my head back and huffed out a laugh. "Where's this comin' from?"

He just lifted an eyebrow. "When I brought this deal with the Warlords to the table, I honestly didn't think anyone would jump on it. I figured it'd just be a formality and then I'd make the call to Wallace to turn him down. I never thought anyone, *you* especially, would take the risk."

"What's that supposed to mean?"

"It means I think you're takin' a stupid risk by takin' this job."

I swallowed hard. "We won't have any problems. We'll deliver the cargo, get paid, and keep the Warlords happy. Everybody wins. And besides, I didn't see you sittin' me down like this before all that shit went down a few weeks ago. That was a pretty goddamn big risk, too, wasn't it? Look how that turned out. Maybe I actually know what I'm talkin' about here."

And maybe that's what was really bothering him—the fact that *I* might be right and *he* could be wrong.

Marcus observed me carefully for a long moment and then leaned forward in his chair. "I know we haven't exactly seen eye to eye on shit lately. I also know you've got a lot of new responsibilities right now and I know all that shit got sprung on you pretty much all at once. You wanna take care of what's yours and provide for them and I'm sure all you're seeing is dollar signs right now. The last thing I wanna see is you doin' something stupid just to make a quick buck."

I laughed bitterly. "Okay. If that's really the way you feel, why the hell didn't you bring this up at the table?"

"I figured you wouldn't want me asking you these kinda questions in front of the club. All I gotta do is call Wallace and tell him we're sittin' this one out. As soon as I tell him about our reservations, he'll probably be grateful we turned him down."

Right, because then I'd look like a complete pussy for backing out now.

"I think you're making a bigger deal out of this than it needs to be," I told him, choosing my words carefully.

There was a long pause before Marcus spoke again. "You need money, all you gotta do is ask. You can pay me back when things get going again and I won't say a word to anyone."

The last thing I needed or wanted right now was a handout. Marcus would call it a loan, but I knew better.

"I appreciate the offer," I told him tightly. "I really do, but I can take care of my family on my own."

"C'mon," he shot back. "You're my family, too."

Am I really?

It was right on the tip of my tongue, but the words never gained any ground. Between all the added tension surrounding this table, the term 'family' didn't really sit well with me here.

When I didn't respond, Marcus held up both hands in surrender. "Alright. If this is the call you wanna make, I'm not gonna stand in your way."

"Good. Are we done here? I gotta get my ass on the road."

Marcus dipped his down, signaling I was free to go, and I shot off the chair, heading right for the exit. I practically sprinted through the clubhouse and the parking lot until I was slipping back into the driver's seat of the truck. As I sped out of the lot toward the highway, I pushed Marcus's offer out of my head.

I didn't need his help.

I didn't need anyone's help.

CHAPTER FOURTEEN
Commitment

Isabelle

I glanced over at the gallery's main entrance one more time before turning my attention back to my exhibit. There were plenty of people coming and going through the doors, but I'd yet to see the person I was looking for. There was still a half hour left of the showcase, but that also meant he'd missed an hour and a half of the whole thing too.

The butterflies bouncing around in my stomach weren't helping. I'd always thought finally getting to display my work in a real gallery for a real audience would be one of the biggest highs of my life and now that it was here, I thought I might throw up all over my stilettos, and not because of morning sickness. That tightening in my throat, the clammed up, sweaty feeling in my palms...it was too similar to what I'd felt right after the break-in and I did everything I could to swallow it down, to get it under control.

Somewhere in the back of my mind, I knew my work wouldn't be in the semester showcase tonight if it sucked. I knew I was talented and my work was worthy of showing; my professors all semester had told me as much and then some.

But now that an actual audience had become a very real reality, I wanted to bolt. I wanted to throw up. I wanted to lock myself in a bathroom until the showcase was over. So much for getting myself under control.

Not having Caleb here to anchor me just multiplied that feeling exponentially.

I blew out a deep breath and my eyes immediately flew back to the main entrance. Still nothing. More people were starting to filter out of the gallery as things started to move toward a downswing and I felt my heart sink a little.

Our life together would never be normal. I was still sorting out how I felt about that just when I thought I'd started to come to terms with it. In light of everything the last few weeks had thrown at us, I just felt so *tired*. I just wanted to crawl into bed with Caleb and let him hold me until everything calmed down, until everything just became a little bit easier.

Luckily, Dr. Jacobs, of all people, yanked me out the black hole I was teetering over.

"Isabelle," she smiled broadly, spreading her arms out into the space around her. "What a wonderful turn out, no?"

"Yeah," I grinned back. At this point, I'd take any distraction I could get and if it had to be Dr. Jacobs, then so be it. "It's pretty great."

"I noticed there was quite the crowd around your pieces tonight," Dr. Jacobs nodded. "And rightly so. Where is your young man? I was under the impression he'd be here tonight."

"He will be," I pushed out a little too quickly. "He's just running late."

"Of course," Dr. Jacobs nodded, but this time, her eyes narrowed ever so slightly. "Now, Isabelle, since we have a moment, I wanted to speak to you about setting up an appointment next week. We should discuss your options for the rest of your coursework as soon as possible now that this semester is behind you."

I frowned back at her. "What do you mean?"

Dr. Jacobs' eyes dropped to my stomach. "You're due in December, correct?"

"Yeah," I nodded weakly.

"Your due date takes you right to the end of next semester. I'm sure we'll be able to get your studio hours and everything else completed before then, but there's still the issue of what you'll do the following semesters. We really should discuss how much time you'll want off, how you'd like to schedule your studio hours and I'm not sure if you were aware of this or not, but we also have a daycare here on campus that you may want to utilize. There's always the option of adding in courses and studio hours this summer to move you along before your due date."

I hadn't thought of any of that. I'd been so focused on the present, so focused on getting through these last few weeks that I hadn't really thought about what my life would look like once the baby was here.

The reality was overwhelming.

"Um," that was the best I could come up with on the spot. "I'll have to talk to my fiancé about all of that."

"Of course. Speak with him first and then email me when you'd like to set-up the appointment," Dr. Jacobs pressed a tight smile on her face, her eyes serious and concerned in a way I'd never seen them before. "You are one of the most talented students I've ever had the pleasure of working with, Isabelle. Your work comes from a different place than most students. Most focus on technique and form, but there's an emotional connection you have to it that's real and raw and beautiful. That's what people respond to. I would hate to see you throw away any opportunities because of..."

I was expecting her to say because of family responsibilities. Because I'd put my family before myself. Because I'd sacrificed my career for my family...but then I turned my head and found the person I'd been waiting for striding right up to me.

Still dressed in that crisp white button-down tucked into well-fit black pants, he'd appropriately left his cut in the truck, but my heart still stuttered and skipped at the welcome sight of him. Caleb anxiously tucked some stray hair behind his ear as he approached us, already reaching out to wrap an arm around my waist.

He kissed the side of my head, oblivious to anyone around us, and murmured in my ear, "I'm sorry I'm late. I got here as soon as I could."

"It's okay," I told him with a quick smile.

Dr. Jacobs cleared her throat, and just like all the other women in the gallery and some of the men too, she regarded Caleb appreciatively.

"Well," she stated simply. "This must be the young man I've heard so much about."

I nodded quickly, feeling a blush creep across my cheeks, and gestured to Caleb, who cast me a wolfish grin before extending his hand in greeting.

"Dr. Jacobs, this is Caleb Sawyer," I introduced them quickly. "Caleb, Dr. Jacobs."

"Isabelle's told me nothin' but good things about you," Caleb started, winking at me as he spoke. "Nice to finally meet you."

Dr. Jacobs, clearly charmed by his effort, placed a hand gingerly over her heart. "Well, I'd hope so."

With a sincere smile, Dr. Jacobs' hand found my arm and I jumped a little at the contact. "I'll leave you to enjoy the rest of your evening. Don't forget to email me."

"She didn't seem so scary," Caleb whispered in my ear as Dr. Jacobs moved away from my exhibit. "Guess that must mean you're doing something right, Iz."

I just blew out a deep breath in reply and squeezed his hand as Caleb gestured with his head toward my display. All ten paintings had been set up with the proper lighting and organization I'd asked for. I'd been obsessing about the arrangement for the two last months when I first found out my work had been chosen for the semester showcase. The light really did highlight all the textures, colors, and you could even see the angle I'd used with my paintbrush.

Caleb stepped even closer until he was close enough to touch them. His Adam's apple bobbed in his throat a few times and his hands sunk deep into his pockets as he took in each stroke and each dash of color. It was fitting that the first one he stood in front of was the one inspired by the new life we were building together.

"What do you think?" I murmured to him, taking my place beside him.

His eyebrows rose and his gaze flicked back to me for a second before returning back to the painting in front of him. "What do I think, Iz? I think it's absolutely beautiful. I mean, I still don't really understand what I'm looking at here, but I know I love it. I know it's special."

"Well," I laughed and leaned into his shoulder. "It's abstract. It's supposed to be all about the feelings, the emotions."

He grinned down at me proudly and then his eyes fell back on the canvas filled with bright, happy twirls in splashes of yellows, blues, and greens. "So what were you feeling when you painted this one?"

My eyes flew back to the display and my hand reflexively landed right on top of my little baby bump. "I was thinking about the baby."

Caleb turned his head to face me again with a tender smile spread across his face and he draped an arm around my shoulder to tuck me in close. We stood there for a little while, staring dreamily up at my painting, and finally, I felt myself relax.

"You're gonna put that in the nursery, right?"

"Oh yeah. Definitely."

"Good," he grinned and then we moved on to the next piece, my earliest attempt at a nature scene depicting a lone figure walking through a maze of autumn leaves and earthy tones. "What about this one?"

"My mom," I exhaled and quickly jumped to explain when his face fell a little. "When we got home from the doctor's office right after she found out she had cancer, she didn't say much. She just announced she wanted to go for a walk and left."

His eyebrows rose at that and I smiled back absentmindedly as the memory washed over me again.

"I kinda freaked out," I went on, my lips quirking up when he grinned knowingly. "I guess I just didn't want to be anywhere she wasn't. I also didn't see the benefit of someone with stage four lung cancer going for a walk anywhere by herself. But when she came back, she just seemed so peaceful. So accepting. Almost happy, too, if that makes any sense. I couldn't understand it. I *still* don't really understand it. I guess I just wanted to see if I could figure out what she was feeling when she went on that walk, how she could set aside all the bad and choose to just focus on the good and be happy. I don't know if I'll ever understand that."

Caleb tilted his head to the side a little, his eyes trained on my painting as he spoke. "I don't know what your mom was thinking that day, but if it's anything like that," he gestured with his head to the canvas, "I think I can see where she was coming from."

I smiled softly. "Thanks."

His eyes gave me the strength I needed to continue on and I walked him through the rest of my exhibit, the one inspired by my conflicted emotions surrounding my dad, one inspired by Chloe that I planned on gifting to her as soon as the showcase was over, a few pieces detailing both my anxiety and my passion for this new career path I was heading down, the ones inspired by him, and finally, the one about Becca with its slashes of crimson.

He wrapped both arms around me, enveloping me in warmth and safety.

"I'm so fuckin' proud of you I can barely see straight," he whispered into my hair. "Every single one, Iz...they're all you. You blew all these other sorry assholes here tonight right outta the water."

"You didn't even see the other exhibits."

He shrugged with his arms still around me and bent down to press his lips against mine. "Didn't have to."

"I love you."

Caleb smiled against my lips. "I love you, too."

. . .

Caleb

I wasn't exactly looking forward to having this conversation with Isabelle, but I didn't really have a choice either. We were leaving for the run tomorrow and the details were already set in stone. The drop-off location and time were ready to go. Marcus had pretty much immediately decided that our 'usual' meeting location was a no-go this time around and I could see his point. Better to be safe than sorry.

We'd be making the exchange with the Warlord's VP, Theo Wallace, as well as two other club members. This was just typical shit, nothing new, nothing to be worried about and come Tuesday, I'd have an extra $15K sitting in my hands.

The problem now would be Isabelle.

I watched her take her high heels off and toss her purse down on the kitchen table; it was that moment that I made the immediate decision to butter her up as much as I could. When I handed her the ice cream she'd all but annihilated before we left the house earlier, she cocked a suspicious eyebrow at me.

"What?" I shrugged innocently. "I thought maybe you wanted a snack or something before we went to bed."

"Sure," she drawled and hesitantly took the ice cream from me. "This is weird."

All I could do was watch her hop up on the counter and brace myself for the inevitable fall-out while she dug in. I let her get a few healthy bites in before I took a deep breath and came out with it.

"Iz, I need to talk to you about something."

The ice cream carton immediately dropped down to the counter.

"Okay."

I took a deep breath. "Dom and I are goin' on a run tomorrow."

Her mouth dropped open a little and jumped on the opportunity to explain before she could beat me to the punch.

"I know what you're thinkin', Iz," I held my hands up in defense. "I'll be back in plenty of time before Saturday. It'll just be a few days and I should be home by Tuesday—Wednesday at the absolute latest, okay?"

Isabelle stared back me, her mouth still lodged open in surprise and then she started shaking her head in disbelief.

"Wha...wait. I don't understand. Why are you doing this?"

"Marcus brought it to the table tonight. That's what church was about. We'll get to Pittsburgh and back in plenty of time before the wedding and Dom and I are gonna get $15,000 out of the deal, Iz. That's kinda insane, right?"

"Yeah," she replied in a tight, flippant voice that already had me wincing. "It is insane. Very insane. And what happened to us talking everything through before making a decision that affects both of us?"

I frowned back at her. "We are talking, Iz."

Her face turned stony as she hopped off the counter. "No, we're not. This isn't us having a productive discussion. This is you making up your mind *again* before talking to me about it *again* and now you're just telling me after the fact...*again*."

"This is club business. It's not the same."

"So you're saying you leaving for this run tomorrow doesn't affect me at all?"

I blew out a hard breath and tugged a hand through my hair. "No, that's not what I'm saying. I knew you weren't gonna be happy, but, Iz, this is for the club. This is to help keep the peace between us and one of our business contacts. I hate to break it you, but those kind of decisions don't really concern you."

Her eyes flashed and now she was leaning against the counter with her arms folded across her chest defiantly. "The fact that this is stupid and risky and just dumb when the club has been having all these problems lately—that you could get *caught*—that doesn't concern me at all?"

"I never said that."

"Yes, you did. And that's really not fair, you know."

"We already made the arrangements, Iz," I lifted a shoulder. "And we'll be back before you know it. Would you just calm down?"

Oh shit. I'd just made a huge mistake.

Her arms fell from her sides and she was advancing on me now, fire raging in those blue eyes, until we were toe-to-toe.

"No, I will not calm down. I just don't get it, Caleb. Why does it have to be *you* taking this kind of risk?"

I sighed again and tugged another hand through my hair, reaching for her with my free hand, but she batted it down. "We could really use that money right now, Iz."

Her eyes widened. "That's what this is about? Money? Are we...wait a minute. Is there something else you haven't told me?"

"We're not exactly in the red or anything, but think about all the money I've had to spend recently. The house. Everything in our house. Everything we need for the baby."

"We can figure something else out," she whispered, her eyes still wide with awareness. "We can cut back. I can work more hours at the shop. I can—"

"You're not working more hours at the shop," I cut in and rested both hands on her waist before she could stop me. "I'm not gonna let you."

"Oh?" she shot back and pushed both hands into my chest until her hips slipped out of my grasp. "You're not gonna let me? That's such bullshit, Caleb.

You have to let me contribute a little bit. It shouldn't have to come down to doing something dangerous like this just so we can make ends meet."

"Look, Iz, you said so yourself that babies are expensive. Now that all those doctor bills are coming in, I'm seeing how right you were. We need the money and this is how I make my money. This is how I pay for the house you're living in, the food you eat, the bed you sleep in, the couch, the TV, everything in this goddamn house, your doctor bills, everything you want for the baby, that wedding you wanna have."

I hadn't meant for my anger to bleed through this way, but I just needed her to understand. I needed her to understand this wasn't really about her. It was about me taking care of her the only way I knew how. And even though I hadn't meant to hurt her with those words, the pain and animosity in her eyes still blazed an angry blue.

"Okay," she whispered furiously. "I see how it is. If you want me to pay you rent or something, I can do that. I have my own money, too, you know. Not a lot of it, but I can help. I don't see why you feel like it has to be you that pays for everything. Like I'm never going to make my own money, right? Like I'll never be able to help provide for my family too?"

"No, Iz, that's not what I meant—"

"I understood you perfectly, Caleb," she cut in. "The last thing I want is to be a freeloader. We should've talked about this when we first moved into the house, but there are other ways we can make ends meet, okay?"

"That money could get us more things we need," I told her, desperate now for her to just get it. "Furniture for the nursery. That dress you want for the wedding after the baby gets here. That place you found online for the reception. The mortgage on our house. Your tuition—"

"You're *not* paying my tuition, Caleb. You shouldn't have to do that. I have student loans and—"

"And," I told her pointedly. "When we get married, your debt will become my debt too, won't it?"

She sucked in a shaky breath. "That's not fair."

"That's the way it is," I shrugged. "And don't get me wrong, I don't have a problem covering any of it. I want to. That's the point, Iz. I want to provide for you and our family and get you anything you want. But to do that, I have to take these jobs. I have to go where the money is."

Isabelle blew out a breath and shook her head. "I can take a semester or two off after the baby comes. Dr. Jacobs was talking to me at the showcase about getting my studio hours done before the baby's born, taking time off, and daycare options. I don't know. Maybe it'll just be easier if I take some time off. Then I'd be able to work more hours at the shop and—"

"You're not taking any time off from school, Iz. At least not a full semester. You can't."

Now, her eyes were blazing again. "Don't tell me what to do, Caleb. You're perfectly willing to walk around and do whatever the hell you want without consulting me first, so why can't I do the same?"

"After the baby gets here, you'll just have, what? Three semesters left? You can't take a break, Iz. You need to finish. If you take a break, who knows when you'll be able to go back?"

She had to know I was right about at least that. The last thing I wanted was to see her give up her passion because I couldn't be the man I needed to be and put food on the table. Instead, she just backpedalled until her hips hit the counter.

"That's not your decision to make," she told me icily. "You don't get a say in *my* career."

"I just want the best for you, Iz," I held my hands out in the air and lifted a shoulder. "That's all this is about. I don't wanna fight with you, but I need you to understand this is just something I have to do."

Her chest was heaving now as she glared back at me, hot, angry tears welling up in her eyes. "I get where you're coming from with the money and the bills and the house and everything else that goes with it. I can't understand *this*. I can't understand something that would put you in danger—something that would put you at risk."

"I'll be fine. There's no risk. No danger."

"I don't believe that," she shook her head. "And you're an idiot if you do."

"Iz," I sighed, my hands on my hips and at the end of my rope. "I need you to get behind me on this."

She swallowed hard and wiped a tear from her cheek. "So that's how it's going be? If I got on my hands and knees and begged you not to do it, you still would, wouldn't you? It doesn't matter what I think. You're still gonna do it."

"I have to."

Her teary eyes rolled up to the ceiling as she shook her head. Now she pushed past me and headed right for the hallway, calling angrily over her shoulder: "You don't *have* to do anything, Caleb."

I squeezed my eyes shut and scrubbed both hands over my face. Then I took off after her, hot on her heels to follow her to our bedroom only to have the door slammed right in my face. My hands immediately shook the knob and I pounded on the door.

"Iz, come on. Don't do this. Just let me in, okay?"

The cold, muffled voice through the door pretty much solidified how I'd spend the rest of my night: "You can spend the night at the fucking clubhouse for all I care."

I sighed and leaned my forehead against the door. I'd expected her to be upset. I'd expected a little bit of an argument, a little bit of fighting, but I definitely hadn't expected this. As I ran a hand over my face, I shuffled down the hallway, grabbed a spare pillow and blanket from the closet, and tossed them onto the couch.

Maybe in the morning, maybe when I got back from the run, she'd see how she'd completely blown this out of proportion. When I came home and when I handed her that envelope, she'd be grateful and happy to have the extra security just a few days before our wedding.

Tonight, unfortunately, I was sleeping on the couch.

CHAPTER FIFTEEN
Coup de Grâce

Caleb

I leaned back against the driver's seat and squeezed my eyes shut. The last 24 hours had been filled with restless tossing and turning and hours on the road. Dom and I buckled down in Cincinnati the night before and then hit the road early this morning to meet up with Theo Wallace and finally get this shit over with. Like I'd predicted, we had no issues. No signs of any problems.

Once Wallace showed up and the exchange was made, we'd be free and clear.

But now that we were just sitting here waiting, that sick feeling I'd spent most of these last 24 hours trying to bat down reared its ugly head again. It didn't help matters that Isabelle had all but shut me out since slamming our bedroom door in my face. Right before I left the next morning, she finally opened the door, let me kiss her goodbye, and whispered to me to be safe. That was pretty much all I'd gotten from her since, too.

Part of me knew how right Isabelle was, and how right Marcus was too, but I'd put my foot down. I'd made a decision and now I had to see it through. How would it look to the rest of the club if I swore up and down that there was no risk, that I would have their backs and protect our deals with the Warlords only to just back out at the last second?

I couldn't back out now for that very reason even if I wanted to.

"Jesus, this is takin' forever," Dom muttered next to me. "I just wanna get this over with."

I nodded tightly. "Yeah. You and me both."

We'd really only been sitting here not even a full five minutes, but each second that ticked by just upped my panic, my dread. I just wanted to be home right now. Even if it meant admitting I was wrong. Even if it meant getting on my hands and knees and kissing Isabelle's feet until she forgave me.

Just following through with this job, just sitting here in the van waiting for the Warlords to get here—it just all felt wrong.

"Honestly," Dom told me quietly, as if he'd heard my thoughts and decided we both needed a distraction. "If things weren't so tight money-wise, I never would've agreed to this. Lex is already talkin' about another kid. Can you believe that shit? Our first one isn't even close to a year old yet and you'd think she'd want to wait a little while since it wasn't exactly like we planned the first one, you know?"

"Yeah, that's something I'll never understand," I huffed out a laugh and shook my head. "It's like a switch just turns on. When Iz first found out she was pregnant, she was the one who completely freaked out, not me. All this stuff about how we weren't ready, we were too young, it was too soon and then...bam! She's sketching a mural in the nursery and getting on my ass about smoking."

"That sounds familiar," Dom nodded ruefully.

"Now she's talking about taking some time off from school after the kid gets here."

Dom cocked an eyebrow. "That sounds like something she'd say, but I take it you don't agree."

"Nah. I don't. She worked too hard to get where she is. Besides, what will she do if she doesn't end up going back?"

"I don't know," he just shrugged. "What will she do even if she finishes?"

"What do you mean?"

Dom scratched his beard in thought. "What does someone with a degree in painting do in a town like Claremont anyway?"

I frowned, my eyes flying back to the gravel road in front of the van. What *would* she do after she graduated? I didn't know much about the art scene or how an artist even attempted to get a career going, but I knew enough to know you couldn't do it in Small Town, USA. That was why I'd wanted her to end up at that school in Richmond anyway.

All my good intentions, all my selfish happiness at her decision to stay in town back in January, all my concerns that she was giving up something she shouldn't just to be with me...I was starting to think that maybe she'd inadvertently sacrificed it anyway without either of us even realizing it.

The reality was difficult to reconcile. I didn't want her to have to give anything up, but if we were living here, raising our family, what options did she really have? Working in the office at the shop? Opening her own gallery in town where hardly anyone here was equipped to really understand her talent, where she'd barely get any recognition or any money for her hard work?

I swallowed back more panic, fighting the urge to stick my head out the window and puke.

Luckily, my stomach was saved when another black van rolled down the gravel road and parked right next to us.

Everything sprung to life just a few moments later as the three Warlords we were meeting jumped out of their van. Following their lead, Dom and I opened our doors and stepped onto the gravel to meet Theo Wallace.

I stepped forward, my hand outstretched to him and Wallace promptly shook it, regarding me with a tight nod.

"Nice to see you again, Sawyer," Wallace greeted me, gripping my hand a little tighter as he spoke.

"You, too," I retorted and quickly gestured to the back of the van. As far as I was concerned, there was no time for small talk.

Wallace seemed to agree and skirted around to the back of the van, where Dom was already waiting with the back door open so Wallace could inspect the product before he took it off our hands.

Wallace ran a hand over his shiny bald head and then stroked the dark scruff on his face as he perused the contents of each barrel, double-checking to make sure we'd held up our end of the deal, just as he should.

"Looks like everything's there."

I squinted at him, a little surprised that he would even imply it wouldn't be. "Of course it is. So we ready to do this?"

Wallace tipped his chin down in a nod, never one to mince words, and then gestured to the other two guys with him towards the van, stepping back so they could jump inside and start moving the product into their transport.

Once the barrels were safely inside the Warlords' van, Wallace reached inside his cut and held an envelope out to me. I'd barely gotten the envelope inside my own cut when five sedans tore out onto the gravel road from around the corner and skidded to a stop just a mere 10 feet away from where we stood.

There was no time to react. No time to even think about reaching for the Glock tucked behind my jeans. No time to even think about hopping into our van to make a run for it.

Because the doors to each sedan flew out and 10 agents aimed cocked guns at us, screaming to get our hands up and on our stomachs.

We were surrounded.

We were caught.

I was numb. Paralyzed by shock. Stunned into immobility. But when Agent Jordan's smug, triumphant face came into clearer view, that was when everything snapped back to life. That was when my blood boiled over, when loathing took the reins and spilled over, drenching the smirking bastard stalking toward me and most of all, on myself.

I should've known better. I should've listened. I should've backed out when I had the chance.

Now I was completely screwed and I'd taken Dom down with me.

Even as Jordan hovered over me with handcuffs in his hand, even as he slapped those same handcuffs over my wrists and knelt down, I didn't care.

"I bet you thought you'd never see me again, huh?" he chuckled in my ear. "Good thing you ended up being exactly what I thought were: stupid and predictable."

All he was doing was rubbing salt in an open wound. Kicking me while I was already down. Throwing sand in my face.

All I could see now was Isabelle. All I could think about now was our baby.

The timing was just a sick joke. Part of me wanted to raise a fist to the air and scream: *Congratulations, universe. You win. Thanks for giving me everything I've ever wanted and then ripping it away.* The other part of me wanted to curl up into ball and wail like a baby. This was my fault. I was the one in control of this situation. I was the one who'd made this decision and followed through with it.

And for that, I was going to miss everything. Every kick, every doctor's appointment, every time she needed me to do something for her, I wouldn't be there. Someone else was going to have to do it. I would miss the birth of my own kid just because of greed. Because of my ego. Because of my pride.

My stomach swirled and nearly emptied itself right here on this gravel road, right over Jordan's scuff-free leather shoes and I let him haul me off the gravel, yank me to the nearest sedan, and throw my ass in the backseat.

. . .

Isabelle

My paintbrush moved in broad strokes, up and down in the wall, covering my pencil markings effortlessly and a little too absentmindedly. I wasn't in the right frame of mind to do this right now. I really *shouldn't* be doing this right now, but I needed something to take my mind off all this ugly, to focus on something positive, something that was still good in my life.

Painting the baby's mural today of all days was a terrible idea.

Now, every time I looked at it, I'd forever be reminded of this day. The fear. The pain. The heartache. The loss. How much I wanted to murder my baby's father right now.

I just shook my head at that thought. I wanted to hit him, not murder him. Scream at him. Kick him. Throw something at him.

He was probably on his way back from the clubhouse right now after being released from holding in Pittsburgh. More than likely, he'd taken one look around the parking lot, saw that I wasn't there and jumped back on his bike to head right to our house.

I didn't want to see him, mainly because I was terrified of what I would say to him, terrified of what I *wanted* to say to him and right now, I just wasn't sure if I could even stomach looking at him.

Over the last two days since he'd called me from holding in Pittsburgh, I'd gotten a crash course in navigating the dark waters of legal representation. My whole life I'd only seen it from from my dad's point of view as a lawyer himself: his view of the cases, the defendants, and the rulings. Now, here I was on the complete opposite side of it and barely able to keep my head above water.

I now knew way more than I'd ever thought I'd have to know about gun trafficking laws, too. Apparently, there was no federal statute in writing which was a good thing, the lawyer, Ross Hinkley, had said. Thinking about how it was a *good* thing not to have a federal statute standing against you, that we should be grateful Congress couldn't agree on a law...it was mind-boggling. I couldn't wrap my head around something like that. To make my head swim even more, there was the whole issue of the fact that Caleb and Dom had crossed state lines.

If they'd gotten caught in North Carolina, they would've been looking at a much shorter sentence. Since they'd gone all the way up to Pittsburgh, not that the distance mattered, they were looking at a maximum sentence of five years. The three Warlord members who'd been arrested with them would get less time just on that technicality alone, and in spite of my fury, even I had to admit that didn't really seem fair when all five of them had basically committed the same crime.

The second Hinkley had said the words *maximum five years*, I'd felt my eyes practically roll back in my head and I'd almost passed out right on the clubhouse floor.

Of course, he'd been quick to add that the best course of action was to plead guilty, which would automatically lower their prison sentence, even if it raised the length of their probation, and since this was their first charge 'of this nature', as Hinkley had so eloquently stated, and since they hadn't been transferring any assault weapons, it was likely a judge might be lenient. Hinkley was going to ask for a reduced sentence of 12-18 months with parole at Caleb and Dom's sentence hearing in two weeks.

But still.

Prison.

Caleb was going to prison.

There was no way around it. No magic *deux ex machina* that could sweep in at the last minute and prevent it from happening.

It was most definitely happening.

The irony, of course, was that Skyler and I had had to scrape together every last penny and all but emptied Caleb's bank account just to bail him out of prison. Karma, in all her infinite, bitchy wisdom, really knew how to kick you right where it hurt.

We were supposed to go to City Hall in two days to get married and now, I just didn't know how I felt about taking that step with him.

And more than anything, I needed to just stop working on the baby's mural. Creating it under all this negative energy wasn't good for anyone. A spike of pain flashed across the length of my stomach and I winced, rubbing the spot on my baby bump a little.

That tell-tale motorcycle roar came screaming down the street and I closed my eyes to brace myself. I didn't want to see him. I did, but I didn't. About a minute later, the front door opened and closed and I knew I just had seconds to calm down long enough to tell him to get the hell out before I did or said something I'd regret later.

As it turned out, I had only about half a second before a gentle knock rapped at the door.

"Iz?"

I squeezed my eyes shut, blew out a deep breath, tossed my paintbrush into the mason jar at my feet, stood up my stool on shaky legs, and flung open the nursery's door with one swift motion. Caleb was standing in front of me, both arms splayed over the doorway as he leaned into the open space.

It was his eyes that knocked me sideways. I didn't know what I'd been prepared to see, but this softness, this apology, this genuineness, this *anguish* had me momentarily forgetting why I was so furious with him in the first place.

"Iz," he started softly before darting his eyes over his shoulder to the prospect behind him and nodding to him, signaling it was time for him to leave. "Can we talk?"

My chest was heaving wildly now and I couldn't make it go away. So, without as much as a word, I gripped hold of the door and started to slam it right in his face. When his hand shot out to stop me, putting just enough force to gently nudge me backwards, the soft, concerned eyes reflecting back at me still didn't change.

"Iz, please," he tried again, this time more urgently. "Just let me in. Don't do this."

My nostrils flared at his choice of words and his eyes widened when he realized his error.

"No," I bit back. "I can't even look at you right now, let alone even think about talking to you."

Pain flashed across his face, but he didn't take another step. He knew what he'd done, he knew he'd completely destroyed everything we'd been working toward, and he knew there was nothing he could say that would make this better.

His head tilted to the side in agony and he reached for me, but I just batted down his hand. If he touched me, I'd let him in. I'd talk to him. I'd forgive him. He didn't deserve any of those things right now.

"I'll call you when I'm ready to talk to you," I told him icily. "Until then, I think you should leave."

Steely resolve clouded his eyes and for a moment, I thought he would protest. I thought he would fight a little harder. Instead, he nodded sadly and stepped out into the hallway. I watched him walk out the door and locked it behind him just for good measure. Sure, he had a key, but I wanted him to hear the lock click. I wanted him to hurt just as much as I was hurting right now.

I stumbled back until my calves hit the back of our couch and tried desperately to control the thundering inside my chest. About two seconds later, my phone chimed from the nursery and I headed back down the hallway with a sigh.

As I swept my phone off the carpet, ignoring the little pricks of pain in my stomach, and frowned down at the screen.

Not leavin you, Iz. I'll just wait til you wanna talk.

Swallowing tightly, I leaned across the window and pulled the blinds down. Caleb sat on the edge of our porch, hands clasped in front of him as a cloud of smoke puffed out into in our yard.

My phone buzzed again.

Sorry about the smoking. It's just been a shitty day. This is my last one today. Promise.

I pushed out a heavy sigh and let the blinds fall back in place. He knew me too well. And he knew exactly what to do to crumble my resolve. Still, if he wanted to wait, then I'd let him wait. I just didn't know if I could have a rational conversation with him without throwing something at his head or screaming obscenities at him until I was blue in the face.

With new resolve, I headed straight for my home studio, plopped down on my stool, and shoved my earbuds in, and cranked up the volume as loud as my eardrums could tolerate. Twenty minutes later, I roughly pushed off the stool and stalked back to the window. White shoes were still directly in my line of vision, but now, both of his hands were clasped over his knees, and he was leaning forward enough off the porch that I could clearly see his stricken, tightly drawn features. He really was going to sit out there and wait until I decided to let him back in the house.

I squeezed my eyes shut and rubbed a hand across my belly to try to lull the sharp pain there. In two weeks, Caleb would be checking into prison and I'd be lucky if I saw him once a week. Shouldn't we be making the most with the time we had left together?

That dull ache in my stomach had spread all the way around to my back and I sucked in a breath when that dull ache sharpened into a shard of pain. It almost reminded me of some of the worst period cramps I'd ever had, but that couldn't be what this was. I inhaled again, a little more slowly this time to try to soothe whatever was going on inside my stomach, but it didn't work.

At first, I thought I had to be dreaming, but then little pricks and tremors erupted and pulled at the inside of my stomach.

My eyes flew open as the pain subsided for just a moment and my hands subconsciously flew protectively over my tiny baby bump. What had started as a slight tugging sensation had quickly escalated to a sharp, stabbing pain and now there was no denying it.

Just as I leapt to my feet to head for the front door, another wave of pain nearly knocked me to my knees. Somehow, I managed to scramble to the door, wincing and gritting my teeth through the sharp edges of pain spreading across every inch of my stomach, and threw open the door. Caleb had his back to me and whirled around from his perch with a relieved smile on his face.

But just as quickly, that gorgeous smile faded into deep lines of worry and disbelief. He shot up to his feet, practically tripped up the stairs, and his eyes widened when I winced yet again and hunched over from the pain.

I squeezed my eyes shut and tried in vain to breathe through the pain, but it felt like my stomach was spasming and closing in on itself and I finally cried out through clenched teeth as Caleb's hands closed around my shoulders to steady me.

"Iz, what's happening?"

"I don't— " my voice died out on me when a rush of warm wetness soaked between my legs. I looked down in disbelief, unable to let myself even consider what was really happening here, but I knew.

Somewhere, deep down, I knew.

"I think..." I struggled for the words.

If I said it then it would be real. I guessed I just needed to live in a fantasy world for as long as I could, but when another wave of needles swept through my stomach, I couldn't deny it any longer.

"I think my water just broke."

CHAPTER SIXTEEN
Blowback

Isabelle

When we finally got to the hospital, Caleb sped through the entrance, ignoring every stop sign and speed limit warning in our path, until he skidded the truck to a stop directly in front of the emergency room's main entrance. In a flash, he shot out of the truck and sprinted around the side as an attendant met him at the passenger side door with a wheelchair.

Caleb carefully lifted me out of the truck and set me gingerly down in the wheelchair. When the attendant moved to take hold of the steering, Caleb roughly shoved him aside and wheeled me inside the emergency room, where a nurse was already waiting for us.

All I had to do was sit there numbly, twisting my engagement ring around my finger while Caleb, following the nurse's lead, wheeled me right through the hallway and into an elevator that would take us to the maternity ward.

After Caleb helped me out of my clothes and into the hospital gown, he carefully lifted me onto the rickety bed as a doctor and nurse pulled the curtain back to enter.

"Alright," the doctor began easily, despite the tension in the cramped space. "My name is Dr. Reynolds and I'll be your attending physician tonight. So," he gestured for me to put my feet into the stirrups as he spoke. "You're 15 weeks along, correct?"

"Yes," I nodded anxiously. "We just had an appointment a few weeks ago. Everything was fine then."

Caleb squeezed my hand supportively while Dr. Reynolds positioned himself and the fetal monitor next to us.

"When did the cramps start?"

"Maybe an hour ago. I didn't really think much of it at first, but the pain just kept getting worse and..." I trailed off, unable to force myself to say any more.

"You did the right thing in coming in," Dr. Reynolds nodded tightly, his lips set in a grim line. "With your water broken, I need to listen to the baby's heartbeat first and then we can decide what steps to take from there."

There was a part of me, even as Caleb squeezed my hand and kissed my forehead, that knew no amount of denial or distraction would make this go away. Even I knew, as the doctor dutifully got to the task of trying to hear the baby's heartbeat, that the odds of the baby even surviving a delivery, if there had to be one, would be slim to none.

I winced and shifted uncomfortably on the squeaky bed, but my eyes never left the fetal monitor screen, waiting desperately to hear something similar to what we'd heard at my gynecologist's office. Everything just seemed to stop as Dr. Reynolds waited and waited for the screen to focus on something other than waves and emptiness.

As Dr. Reynolds gently moved the fetal monitor away from my body, all the blood drained out of my face. I knew what was coming now. It was only a matter of time before the doctor told us what I already knew and had known from the moment I'd first felt those little pinpricks of pain before Caleb came home.

"I'm so sorry," Dr. Reynolds looked at us somberly. "There's no heartbeat."

Hearing the words, the confirmation, was more devastating than I'd expected. It felt like I was submerged underwater and everything felt hazy, like I'd just been shot with a tranquilizer. I felt heavy, despite the way my heart thundered violently in my chest and I was vaguely aware of Caleb's tortured, hoarse voice above me.

"What do you mean?" Caleb asked desperately, disbelief flooding into his voice. "How can it just be gone? I don't understand."

"Well," Dr. Reynolds cleared his throat painfully. "Unfortunately, premature labor like this isn't uncommon and when that happens at this early stage, there's very little we can do to stop it once the water breaks. I wish I could tell you the exact reason..."

At this point, I knew I was better off just tuning out the rest of this terrible conversation. I didn't want to hear any more. I *couldn't* hear any more. Now, there was just this heaviness weighing down inside me and I didn't know how much more of this shit I could take. There was just nothing now. Nothing but emptiness.

After the nurse pumped me with some pain medication, my body finally caught up to my mind.

I finally allowed myself to take a deep breath for strength that never came. A beat later, as Dr. Reynolds once again expressed his sympathies, he launched into our 'options' and my heart sunk lower and lower with every second.

"In circumstances like these, the baby is just too big for us to allow him or her to naturally pass," he started and whatever life that was left in me withered away. "We have several options: the first is to allow labor to continue. You're already dilated several centimeters, so the delivery would be fairly quick. After an epidural, you wouldn't feel any pain and in most cases, it's one push and it's over."

On some level, I appreciated the doctor's no-nonsense, yet sympathetic approach and the way he referred to the baby as a him or her, but that didn't make the reality burn any less. Just as I was finally beginning to wrap my head around what I might actually have to do, I dared a glance at Caleb.

He'd gone white as a sheet next to me and he rubbed his mouth with the hand that wasn't locked around mine. But it was his eyes that nearly me brought me back over the edge—mostly because the anguish and the devastation and the disbelief and the guilt mirrored everything I wouldn't let myself feel.

"What's the other option?" Caleb murmured hoarsely.

Dr. Reynolds pressed a quick, albeit grim, pained smile on his face. "We can do a procedure to remove all the remaining tissue."

I winced at the word, *tissue,* and glanced at Caleb again, who still clung to my left hand like his life depended on it. His watery eyes softened and he pressed a kiss into my fingertips.

"It's an invasive procedure, that's for sure," Dr. Reynolds went on. "But it would allow you to bypass having to go through a delivery. I know this is extremely difficult, but the best advice I can give you is to do what you feel you're most physically and emotionally able to handle. Every couple chooses a different course for their own reasons. Some people want to be able to hold their baby and others prefer to move through this stage as quickly as possible."

My head shot up at the mention of being able to hold the baby and I sucked in a sharp breath as everything finally began to sink in. The doctor seemed to pick up on this almost instantaneously and he flashed me a quick, supportive smile.

"If you choose to deliver, you'll have some time with your baby."

Even as the doctor excused himself to give us a few moments to talk it over, I couldn't let myself think about everything a delivery would really entail. I just wanted to hold her and I wanted Caleb to hold her too—it was all we'd ever get with her.

"Iz," Caleb called out hoarsely to me.

I shifted my gaze away from my feet and slowly toward Caleb's pale, grief-stricken face. His face twisted in anguish when our eyes met and his cobalt eyes shone with unshed tears. With a free hand buried in my hair now, he drew me to his chest, squeezing his arm around my shoulders, and leaving me no other choice but to be comforted. Breathing him in helped a little. The familiar scent of musk and gasoline flooded my senses just enough to make me forget for a moment and that was almost enough.

"Iz," he murmured in my hair. "Whatever you want, that's what we'll do, okay?"

He wiped the few stray tears that slipped down my face as he lifted my chin up and pressed both hands against my cheeks. Watery, devastated blue eyes found me and I had to squeeze my own eyes shut to keep from weeping openly. There wasn't even a question of what I wanted to do. Even if I wasn't in the right mental state to be making these kind of decisions, my heart still knew what to do.

Somehow, I managed to find my voice long enough to say the words I knew I'd never regret as long as I lived. "I want to hold her, Caleb. I want to see her."

"Iz," he swallowed hard, his hands trembling around my face. "You don't have to—"

"Don't you want to see her too?"

Tears welled up in his eyes and his face twisted in pain. "Of course I do. I want to see her and hold her more than anything, but I don't want you to have to go through this either. I can't...I can't even wrap my head around it."

I wasn't about to let him talk me out of what I knew, beneath all the numbness, all the heartache, and all the pain, was the right decision for both of us.

"We have to see her, Caleb. We have to hold her."

He nodded into my hair and kissed my forehead. "Okay."

I didn't know how long he held me, but I was barely even able to register that human contact. Before long, a nurse pulled the curtain aside so the doctor could once again step through. He winced a little at the sight in front of him: a grieving couple clinging to each other for dear life. Probably just another day in the maternity ward for him, but for us? It felt like the floor opened up underneath us, threatening to swallow us whole and send us tumbling down into the throes of black despair.

Dr. Reynolds waited patiently for our decision and when I couldn't find the words, Caleb squeezed my hand and nodded to me with tears in his eyes.

"She's gonna do the delivery, doc."

"Okay," he affirmed with a tight nod. "Is there anyone you'd like to call before labor progresses any further?"

Caleb shifted his gaze back to me. "Iz, do you want me to call my—"

"No," I whispered, looking to the doctor now. "I just want to get this over with. It'll be quick, right? I won't feel anything?"

Dr. Reynolds shot me another sympathetic smile. "You should be able to push soon."

He went on to explain how the delivery would go, but I'd tuned him out at that point. There was no stopping it anyway, so what was the point in delving into the gory details of how my baby would enter this world five months too soon?

True to his word, the doctor worked fast and since my body was already too shocked to feel just about anything, the epidural came and went without much of a whimper. After that, I didn't feel anything from the waist down, not like I was really capable of feeling much anyway. Everything just sort of tingled like the feelings were there underneath the surface, but a solid wall kept them from bubbling over the top, where I'd have to finally face them.

With Caleb clutching my left hand and a nurse attached to my right, Dr. Reynolds positioned himself at the end of the bed and once again lifted my legs into the stirrups. It all seemed to be happening in equal strokes of speed and slow motion and there just wasn't enough time for my emotions to play catch-up.

"You can do this, Iz," Caleb whispered in my hair and kissed my forehead as the nurse leaned me forward just enough to get into pushing position.

"Okay, Isabelle," Dr. Reynolds instructed gently. "You're ready. Just one push. That's all we need."

I dipped my chin down in a nod, barely aware that Caleb had wrapped his free arm around my waist to help prop me up as much as possible, and I swallowed hard, readying myself for the dark abyss I was about to dive into headfirst. So I closed my eyes, squeezed Caleb's hand, and pushed.

The doctor was right. One push and it was over. Well, the delivery was over. All the rest of it...

I didn't know what I was waiting for. I didn't know what I was even listening for. There would be no baby crying, no nurse cooing over my beautiful newborn, no doctor checking any vitals, and no Caleb cutting the umbilical cord.

There was just the quiet, persistent ticking of the machine next to me and Caleb's ragged breath in my ear as he held me close.

But when the doctor held a towel out toward us, the wall keeping me upright crumbled onto the hospital floor.

There she was.

Beautiful and macabre all at the same time.

Somewhere above me, I heard a strangled sob and turned away from my baby long enough to see Caleb, his eyes fixated on her with one hand covering his mouth as tears flowed freely down his cheeks. Then, my attention moved back to Dr. Reynolds, who leaned forward to gently slide her into my waiting palm.

Her skin was glossy and tinged purple. She was curled into herself with one tiny hand and it almost looked like she was sucking on her thumb. Every part of her was misshapen and malformed somehow, but I didn't care. All I could see were fingers, toes, sweetly-closed eyes, a curved mouth, and a dainty little nose.

She was beautiful. She was perfect. She was gone.

She'd never take a breath. Never open her eyes. We'd never see her smile or hear her laugh. I'd never hear her call me Mommy. Never see her in Caleb's arms.

This moment was all the three of us would ever have together.

I reached out to run my index finger down her cheek and closed my eyes at the feel of her rubbery skin underneath my fingertips. Somewhere along the way, my shoulders began to shake and tears streamed down my cheeks.

"Iz," Caleb whispered next to me as he held out his hand. "Can I...?"

I obliged him silently and slid her tiny, curled body into Caleb's waiting palm, where she looked even smaller than she had in mine. Another hoarse cry tangled in Caleb's throat as he curved his fingers around her tiny frame and touched his fingertip to her mouth. Tears flowed freely now as we took turns alternating between getting to know her and saying goodbye to her.

It wasn't enough time, but the universe was a fickle bitch. Always giving and taking on a whim. Sooner or later, Dr. Reynolds returned with a nurse to take her away.

"No..." I murmured and shook my head, fresh tears slipping down my cheeks. Caleb shifted next to me with our baby still in his palm, his gaze flicking up to me and back down to her again in anguish.

The nurse looked to Dr. Reynolds nervously, who flashed me that ever-present sympathetic smile.

"If you need more time," he told me gently. "We can come back—"

"No," I whispered again just as suddenly.

Even I knew prolonging this would only make it harder in the end. I couldn't keep her. I couldn't bring her home. They'd already respectfully given us ample time with her and now I gave myself one last moment that would just have to last me a lifetime.

I leaned down and kissed my baby, who was so small she barely covered the length of Caleb's palm. Then I leaned into Caleb's arm for strength as he pressed his lips right where mine had been and carefully handed her back to the nurse.

Someone said something about a sleeping sedative, I wasn't sure if it was one of the nurses or Dr. Reynolds, and Caleb murmured a quiet response. It didn't matter. I was in a dark tunnel now, digging deeper and staring numbly at my feet.

There was no end in sight.

There was just nothing now.

. . .

Caleb

The entire hallway felt like it was spinning and for a moment, I wasn't really sure where I was as I stepped up to the nurses' desk. I felt like I was pushing through a clammy, dense fog with no hope of ever seeing daylight again. The moment that doctor shut off the monitor and stared back at us with that tired and sad expression, I'd fleetingly wondered if this was just all some horrifying nightmare, one Isabelle would shake me awake from and then everything would just go back to normal.

After what I'd just witnessed, after what I'd just seen Isabelle do, after what I'd just held in my hand...there would be no waking up from this ever.

The fog momentarily lifted as I rested my hands on the desk. Shortly after Isabelle fell asleep, I'd managed to have enough sense to call my mom before a nurse came in to tell me all the paperwork was ready. Whatever this paperwork was, it didn't really matter. I just needed something to do—to be of use somehow, instead of just helplessly, powerlessly clinging to Isabelle's hand.

The nurse passed me a few forms with a sad smile on her face and I buried myself in the paperwork. It was all pretty no-nonsense, just some insurance forms, a medical release, and then I flipped to the last page.

Certificate of life.

Whatever was left of my heart splintered across the floor.

My hands shook and I had to set the pen down. I squeezed my eyes shut and scrubbed both hands over my face. I didn't know if I could do it, but then I thought of Isabelle sitting in that hospital room, going through labor, getting stuck with that monstrous needle, and delivering our baby and I was pathetic.

Pathetically paralyzed.

That shit needed to stop now.

And then I really looked at what was written on that page and shattered all over again.

"Excuse me, nurse?" I asked and she was already walking around the side of the desk before I finished. "It says here that the baby was female," my voice cracked on the word *was,* "and I know Isabelle—"

"Dr. Reynolds said the sex organs were visible," the nurse told me gently and placed a hand on my shoulder as she spoke. "The form is correct."

Tears pricked my eyes yet again as I whispered, "She was right. She's always right."

"Sir," the nurse started again. "If you need more time, the form can wait right now. Your wife will be asleep for awhile and you should rest too. Can I get you anything? We can get you some coffee or—"

"No," I shook my head and swallowed hard. I wouldn't correct her because deep down, I knew this might be the only time I'd ever get to hear Isabelle referred to as my wife. "Thanks though."

She nodded sadly, squeezed my shoulder, and then returned to her post behind the desk. It was just as well that when I finally picked the pen up again, I heard those tell-tale sounds of heels clicking against the floor. My mom was on her way.

Just as I turned around to face her, my mom's warm, comforting arms enveloped me and pulled me close. I needed this and I didn't. Tears pricked my eyes yet again and I quickly shook free of her arms to compose myself. The last thing I needed to do was start crying again.

"Caleb," my mom whispered in my ear, her voice fracturing with grief. "I'm so sorry. I just can't...I'm just so, so sorry."

"I know," I tried to smile, to show I really was grateful she was here, but I couldn't summon any other emotion but raw misery. "Thanks for being here, Mom."

"Where else would I be?" she told me through her tears. "Is she...?"

"She's sleeping," I gestured with my head toward Isabelle's hospital room. "They gave her something to knock her out for awhile."

"Good," my mom nodded tightly, her eyes flitting to Isabelle's door and back to me again. "She should rest. I just can't..." she shook her head again as more tears streamed down her face.

Because I just couldn't handle any more outpouring of emotion right now, I turned back to the form sitting on the desk and picked up the pen again. My hands trembled as I brought the pen down to the page and began filling in the blanks the hospital needed. I could feel my mom's hand on my shoulder, silently supporting me so I could get through this, and that was exactly what I needed.

I wrote the name *Ava* in the first name space and after a moment's hesitation, wrote the name *Katherine* in the middle name space.

"That's a beautiful name," my mom murmured to me as she leaned into my shoulder.

"Iz picked it out," I sucked in a deep breath and scrubbed my free hand across my eyes. "We never talked about middle names, but I think she'd be okay with Ava taking her mom's name too, right?"

My mom's face twisted and she bit down on her bottom lip to keep from crying again. "I think it's perfect."

"Right," I murmured, but I didn't really know who I was talking to right now. I was nodding, but I didn't know why. Nothing was right. I didn't know if it would ever be again.

After I wrote our names in the mother and father lines, that was it. I was done. Emotionally and physically spent.

"We got to hold her, Mom," I murmured hoarsely and I barely recognized the sound of my own voice as I gestured to my right hand, which had held the contents of all my hopes and dreams just less than a half hour ago. "She was so small, Mom. Her little head barely even came up to the end of my thumb and I..."

I trailed off, unable to force myself to say anymore. There was no point in relaying the gory details. It was already devastating enough on its own and my mom's arms enveloped me tight like I was 5-years-old again.

"I'm so, so sorry," she whispered in my ear. "What can I do? What do you need?"

I just shook my head and pulled away, running both hands through my tangled hair for lack of anything better to do. "There's nothing you can do. I just need some air."

"Okay," she nodded, eager to help, eager to come along, but that was the opposite of what I needed right now. "Let's go—"

"Mom, I just need to be alone for a second, okay?"

Her face fell and I scrambled to give her something to do.

"Why don't you go sit with her? She's gonna be sleeping for a while, but I don't want her to be alone any longer than she has to be."

That lifted some of the fog as my mom scurried off to let herself into Isabelle's room and I sighed heavily, scrubbing my face with my hands one more time before turning on my heel to head down the hallway.

I made it all the way to the nearest men's room. That was it.

Pushing through the door, I stalked around a moment, pacing the tiled floor and tearing my hands through my hair and I had a feeling the urge to hit something was just going to multiply as soon as the initial shock wore off. Because that's what I was really feeling right now: shock and complete disbelief. Fucking horror.

All I could think about was how she was in some box in some room of this hospital now. I'd never see her again. Never hold her again. Never watch her grow. Never see her laugh or smile. There was nothing I'd wanted more than to be that tiny baby's dad.

I pulled my hands through my hair and squeezed my eyes shut as the little control I had left faltered and tears tumbled down my cheeks.

Then my mind sifted through everything that had rained down on Isabelle at breakneck speed: the ATF, the club's suspicions, the break-in, Becca, school, our fight. Just one blow right after the other, with each one lined up to take its turn with me delivering the final death blow in getting my stupid, arrogant ass arrested.

All that stress...God, no wonder the baby didn't make it. The odds had been stacked against us before we'd really had a chance to get started.

And at the end of the day, the common denominator was me.

Every single thing that happened had my fingerprints all over it. If I'd never goaded Padilla, if I'd been smarter, if I'd listened, if I wasn't part of the club, maybe...

And here I thought there'd be no blowback.

This was the consequence. *This* was the price I'd had to pay for my short-sighted, devil-may-care, shoot-first-ask-questions-later attitude toward just about everything in my life.

I could play the 'what if' game until I was blue in the face, but it still wouldn't change the fact that the only real reason Isabelle was lying in a hospital bed and our baby was lying dead in a box was because of me.

At some point, my shoulders shook with sobs and my hands gripped the edge of the sink until my knuckles turned white as I finally gave in. I couldn't handle this shit. I didn't know *how* to handle this shit. What was we supposed to do now? How did we even begin to move on?

I was no better than her piece of shit father. Always wreaking havoc, always leaving chaos in my wake. Unreliable and disappointing.

Maybe that ATF agent was right all along: maybe this life was just a bitter, fucking cycle. I might be going in for a couple years this time, but it could be longer next time and there *would* be a next time.

Isabelle would be a normal art student in Richmond if it wasn't for me and none of this would've ever happened to her. Her life would be so much better if I just wasn't in it and she deserved so much more than the lifetime of shit I had to offer. And then I heard Becca's bitter, spot-on voice in my ears and I shook my head. *Being with her doesn't make you a better person—it's just makes her a worse one.*

As my legs gave out on me, I stumbled backward until my back hit the wall behind me and I sank down to the tiled floor, one arm folded across my knees while the other flew up to cover my face. The tears wouldn't stop and I didn't really care. It was all I could do just to keep myself sitting upright against the wall.

I was so lost in the grief, so carried away by the torrential waves crashing through me, that it took me a few moments to realize my mom had discreetly texted me to let me know the doctor needed to talk to me.

After shoving myself up to my feet and wiping my eyes one last time, I pushed through the bathroom door and headed back down the way I'd come before. Dr. Reynolds was already waiting for me right outside of Isabelle's room with his hand supportively on my mom's shoulder, but the better part of my attention fixed right on the door. It didn't matter if she slept through the next week, she needed to know I was right here in this with her.

Dr. Reynolds nodded to me politely and then over to my mom, who reached out to slip her fingers around my hand.

"I know how difficult tonight has been for you," Dr. Reynolds started slowly, genuine regret filling his quiet voice. "So I'll make this as brief as possible and then you can get some rest. I'd like to keep Isabelle overnight for observation. There's some bleeding that needs to be monitored and if it should get worse, it's better if she's already here so we can act quickly if needed."

All the blood drained from my face in alarm and the doctor jumped to explain.

"There's no need for immediate concern," he told me gently. "Given everything her body's been through, not to mention the emotional toll, I'd rather play it safe."

Dr. Reynolds paused for a brief moment to consult something on his chart and as I cast a sideways glance at my mom, I could see the visible relief cross her face. I didn't really understand everything the doctor had just said, and while bleeding seemed like something I *should* be worried about, if my mom's reaction was any indication, I would just have to take the doctor at his word.

"Lots of women go through this," Dr. Reynolds continued. "It's not uncommon, unfortunately, and those same women go on to have successful pregnancies afterward when they're ready. You're both young and healthy and you've got time on your side for that."

My heart plummeted at the doctor's words. There was no way he could possibly know that time, in fact, wasn't on our side. In two weeks, I'd have to go in front of a judge, plead guilty, and pray to all things holy the judge would throw a little mercy my way and accept my 12-18 months plea.

It wasn't likely.

If Isabelle and I were a normal couple in normal circumstances, we'd be able to start trying again when Isabelle was ready. Now, whenever that happened, I probably wouldn't be around anyway.

"Thank you for everything you've done tonight," my mom called out to the doctor in a quiet, somber voice.

I immediately extended my hand. "Yeah, thanks, doc."

Dr. Reynolds smiled weakly as he shook my hand. "You're welcome. I just wish I could've done more. One of the nurses can bring you the memory box whenever you want."

"I can stay the night with her, right?"

The thought of leaving Isabelle here alone tonight sent terror rippling down my spine and I squeezed my mom's hand searching for anything to make this easier. I never found it.

"Of course you can," Dr. Reynolds nodded.

When the doctor left and my mom left with plans to come back with a change of clothes for us and some food, all I wanted to do was just get her home. Right up until they pumped her with sleeping meds, she'd been trying so hard to to be strong.

And then I realized I'd been standing here like a zombie and that Isabelle had been alone for too long already. I needed to get to her; I needed to hold her; I needed to let her know she could cry and scream and throw things and do whatever else she needed to do.

I needed to hang onto her for as long as I possibly could.

So I creaked open the door, tip-toed to the bed as quietly as humanly possible, and crawled into the hospital bed with her.

. . .

Isabelle

I shifted uneasily in the hospital bed, wincing at the stiff soreness in my abdomen. Everything still felt foggy as my body slowly began to wake up again, but that glaring absence in my stomach wouldn't go unnoticed. Was it always going to hurt this much? Was I always going to feel so *empty* now?

Rough fingers moved gently through my hair and then I couldn't stop myself from shifting on the bed so I could really see him.

"Easy, Iz," Caleb murmured against my cheek. "You probably don't need to be moving around so much."

"It's okay," I winced a little and finally relented, letting him turn me until we were lying face to face on the bed.

"Hey," he smiled softly and moved forward just enough to kiss my forehead.

"Hi," I tried a smile, but it didn't feel right. "How long have I been out?"

"A couple hours. My mom was here before with some food and some clothes. She wanted to let us rest for a little while, but she'll be back."

Smiling was a wasted effort, so I opted to lean into him instead. The second my cheek made contact with his chest, my entire body convulsed with sobs. I just couldn't hold it in any longer. There was nothing that could stop it. Nothing that could make this go away, not even Caleb's tender touch or his gentle kisses in my hair.

The feel of his hands on me, in my hair, pulling me against him made me forget for just a moment. For that moment, it was just the two of us here, holding each other, and without the emotional baggage of this night. And then everything came rushing around me. The searing emptiness in my stomach, the agonizing pain, the anguish of what we'd lost tonight and another wave of sobs racked my body.

"I got you, Iz," Caleb whispered in my hair. "I got you."

My body just completely gave out on me now as tears pooled into Caleb's T-shirt and I was vaguely aware he seemed to have drawn me in deeper and somehow closer against him. All I could do was bury what was left of myself against him and allow him to catch me.

I didn't know how long we laid here wrapped around each other. The only things my mind allowed me to focus on were his gentle massaging into my hair, his lips pressed against my forehead, and the wetness on my cheeks. Slight tremors shook Caleb's body and it was then that I realized the moisture on my face and in my hair wasn't just from my grief. We were both suffering and in two weeks, we'd would both have to suffer alone.

Now I snapped out of it a little and reached up to gently wipe his cheek clean of his fresh tears. I pulled away from him just enough to really get a good look at him and what I found sent me plummeting back to the depths of despair. His normally bright and vibrant cobalt eyes were now an ashen black, tortured and anguished, and lined with tight, red creases.

My fingers lightly traced the skin where the compass I'd drawn for him was inked on his forearm and his hand quickly closed around my own.

He opened his mouth to speak, but his face fell. I wasn't even sure if my voice would actually work, but I had to try. He deserved this, especially after the way he'd swooped in, just like he always did, and put my needs and my well-being before anything else. He'd never hesitated to reach for me and I knew I needed to give some of that back.

"I love you," I whispered, my voice cracking from the sheer weight of it all.

His face twisted in anguish and then his lips pressed gently against mine.

"I love you too," he murmured against my lips. "So much."

I sucked in a sharp breath and allowed my fingers to continue their ministrations across his tattoo. "And here I was starting to feel like we could do this, that we could be parents and maybe not completely screw it up."

He smiled sadly and his Adam's apple bobbed violently as tears welled up again in his devastated eyes.

"Do you think it'd be alright if I waited a little while to finish the mural?"

Caleb nodded immediately through his tears. "Absolutely, Iz. Whatever you want."

I knew how stupid it was that, out of everything, the mural was the thing that had bubbled to the surface, but maybe that was just the safest thing to fixate on right now.

He grasped my fingers again in between his hands and pressed a long, meaningful kiss into my fingertips. "Just tell me what you need and I'll do it. If I can't do it, I'll get it for you."

I laughed in spite of myself, relieved I really was able to feel something other than pain and numbness.

"I need you to keep holding me and kissing me like this."

He nodded, immediately kissing me again. "I can do that."

We stayed like that for a few moments longer until his voice cracked against my hair.

"I named her, Iz."

My head jerked away from his chest. "What?"

Caleb swallowed tightly. "The doctor said you were right. She really was a girl and I—I named her Ava like you wanted."

There was just no way to ever prepare yourself for something like this. I'd always known I was right, even when it was too early to truly know, but hearing the confirmation...the sledgehammer that had flattened my heart got back to work again.

"I put Katherine for her middle name," Caleb went on quietly. "You were sleeping and I didn't want to wake you and I figured that was what you would want—"

I cut him off with my lips, my heart swelling at yet another reminder why he was absolutely everything I needed. He was and always had been everything to me. With him, all the pieces of my shattered existence could be pieced back together again. It would take time, but I knew that at the end of the day, as long as I could lean on this man, who was the glue that held everything together, there would be light at the end of the tunnel.

There would be life after this night.

CHAPTER SEVENTEEN
Cancelled

Isabelle

The music thumped in my ears, effectively drowning out everything else, but the beat, the paint, and the canvas. My brush swirled and swayed to the rhythm, but what I was doing right now could hardly be categorized as art. Leaning back to study the muddied shapes on the canvas, I cringed at the sight.

It had been over a week and I'd spent most of that time right here, perched on my tiny stool as I attempted to exorcise the demons threatening to consume me. Which also meant my interactions with Caleb had really been few and far between. He was giving me the space I craved right now and I knew it, but the timing couldn't possibly have been worse. Caleb was due in court in three days and here we were, as far apart as ever.

When the day we were supposed to go to City Hall came and went, neither of us even acknowledged it. And now that we were staring down a separation, the length of which still had to be determined, this distance was only going to make things worse.

With a sigh, I gingerly set the paintbrush down and rubbed my hands anxiously against my thighs. Shutting him out wasn't going to help anything. What I really needed right now was for everything just to go back to normal. But, the problem was, with all these impending changes in my life, I had no idea how to define normal anymore.

The idea of having to confront these changes and work through this emptiness without Caleb there beside me was excruciating. How could I possibly expect to heal without being able to lean on the other half of my soul? How could I possibly expect to move on without Caleb moving in step beside me?

That last thought was all the motivation I needed to propel me out of this room and out into the rest of the house. I hadn't seen Caleb since earlier this morning, when we'd had a quiet, almost awkward breakfast. Our interactions had been tentative at best with Caleb mostly treating me like glass and with me mostly keeping my distance.

The time for separation was over.

Figuring he was most likely working on his bike or something along those lines, I rounded the corner to head towards the garage only to find Caleb already stepping into the kitchen. It was hard not to see him like this, in just a pair of red Nike shorts with sweat and grease streaked across his bare chest, and not drop everything to wrap my legs around his waist. I hadn't realized how much I'd missed him until just now.

That familiar stirring pulled at my stomach and I had to swallow down the urge to sprint toward him. While my doctor had cleared me for things like exercising and general day-to-day activities, sex was not on that list yet and it wouldn't be for another week or so, which was really a week too late. Still, I found myself chewing absentmindedly on my bottom lip with my eyes focused on those taut muscles.

"Hey, Iz," he called out to me as I slowly closed the distance between us. "I thought you'd be working a little longer."

"I did too," I shrugged. "But it was starting to look like a huge blob of nothing, so I thought I'd see what you were up to."

"Okay," Caleb nodded softly and ran a hand over his scruff.

We stood there awkwardly for a few long moments and I chewed on my bottom lip as he nervously tugged a hand through his hair. He was just standing there looking so hesitant, not wanting to make the first move and wanting to give me whatever I needed, but not completely sure what that exactly was. I couldn't wait any longer. All I needed right now was just to be close to him.

But when I got close enough to wrap my arms around him, the typical warmth I was used to seeing in his eyes wasn't there. He was smiling, but it didn't quite reach his eyes. For a moment, he even seemed frozen by my touch. Then a beat later, his calloused hands grazed my waist before pulling me flush against him as he buried his face in my neck. With a deep exhale, I leaned into him, reveling in the feel of his bare skin against my cheek.

One of his hands was gently massaging my head now as he drew me in closer and I squeezed my eyes shut. Our foreheads found their way to each other and I lifted my head just enough to search for his lips and carefully pressed my lips into his. Caleb jumped a little at the sudden contact, but it only took him a moment to recover from his surprise.

Instead of pulling me in, like he always did, his fingers tenderly grazed my cheek and I wanted to cling to him for as long as I could. He released me almost immediately, rubbed his hands anxiously on his thighs, and gestured to our kitchen table.

"Iz," he started unsteadily as he pulled out a chair for me. "I think we should talk about what's gonna happen when I'm inside."

I swallowed hard and nodded despite the fact that all I wanted to do right now was forget about everything and just be with him.

But when I sank down into the chair across from him, something shifted between us. I stared back at him in a daze, searching his face for the cause. This was more than just the weight of the last few weeks. I knew his expressions like the back of my hand and right about now, the steeled, blank resolve in his eyes sent my heart plunging down into my stomach.

We sat there like that for a few long, silent moments as Caleb quickly averted his eyes away from me and the longer I sat across from him, the more I felt like everything was about to come crashing down around us again.

He squeezed his eyes shut and rubbed a hand roughly over his face. "I don't think it's a good idea for you to visit."

Those words had me frozen to the chair and I couldn't move even if I wanted to. Suddenly, my eyes darted around the kitchen, searching for the easiest way to cut and run. Maybe if I could get out of here and bail before he had the chance, maybe I could stop this.

Caleb swallowed tightly and when he forced his gaze back on me, his eyes had glazed over. I furiously shook my head at him and just as I started pushing back from the chair to run, his cold voice stopped me.

"I don't want you to wait for me, Iz."

My mouth dropped open in protest, but my throat was hoarse and dry, unable to form the words I needed. I stared back at him in shock, my heart thundering wildly in my chest.

"I don't understand."

I understood full well what he wanted, but I needed to hear the words. I needed to make him say it.

He glanced up at me for just a moment and then tore his eyes away. It felt so foreign to see him this way, so spineless, so cowardly, and I couldn't reconcile *this* man with the man I fell in love with a year ago.

"Iz," he started again shakily, still unable to meet my eyes. "I—"

"Why are you doing this *now*?" I sputtered furiously. "And you know what? If you're gonna lay this on me now, at least fucking look at me!"

His cloudy blue eyes shot up at my outburst and the blank expression there quickly eroded into clear pain. At this point, I couldn't have cared less.

"Iz—"

"Don't call me that," I snapped.

He shifted nervously in his seat and chewed on his bottom lip with a brief nod. "Alright. I know the timing doesn't make sense to you, but I wanted us to have a couple of days to sort everything out before I leave. Like I said, I don't want you to visit me. I'm not gonna," he swallowed hard as his voice caught on the words, "I'm not gonna put you on my visitors list."

I leaned away from the table, feeling like the walls were starting to close in on me and now, I just wanted to scream.

"What about us getting married? The baby? All that just never happened?"

He couldn't hide the pain that flashed across his face, but he recovered quickly. "It's just better this way. You can stay at the house for as long as you need to, but—"

"So that's it, Caleb? Just like that?"

He shook his head and leaned forward. This time, the steel had slipped back into his eyes.

"I know this isn't what you wanna hear right now," he charged on. "But I'm not gonna let you put your life on hold. I'm not gonna let you waste years sitting around waiting for me."

Now I had half a mind to wind up and punch him right in the face. Now I just wanted him to put on a stupid T-shirt already so I didn't have to look at my name written across his chest. I just couldn't reconcile that tattoo with everything he was telling me.

"That's bullshit," I pushed out through clenched teeth. "And I missed the part where you had any say over how I spend my time while you're in *prison.*"

Resolve clouded his eyes and he sat up a little straighter. "I know you don't see it now, but this is for the best. If you're not tied to me, you're not missing out on anything. You won't be—"

"What happens when you get out?"

He swallowed tightly and folded his hands in front of him at the table. "I don't know."

"So you're telling me," I narrowed my eyes at him as I spoke, determined to make him squirm as much as possible. "That when you get out and I'm with some other guy halfway across the country and a kid on the way, you'll be completely fine with that?"

Pain flashed across his handsome face and disappeared just as quickly as his jaw clenched. "It's just like you said. I don't have any say in how you spend your time while I'm gone. If I get out and you've moved on just like I'm telling you to and you're happy...yeah, I'm good with that."

"Really."

He squeezed his eyes shut and ran a hand over his face. "Iz—"

"You don't get to sit here and tear everything apart and still call me that," I spat.

Because he didn't have a leg to stand on, he just shook his head and rubbed his eyes again. "Okay. Okay. I get it. We don't have to make it harder than it has to be."

I huffed out a bitter laugh and leveled a hard glare his way. "Let's do it the hard way, huh?"

A ghost of a smile flashed across his face, like this was exactly what he'd expected me to say. There was a hint of pride there, too, but it vanished a moment later.

"You always do this—you always do whatever you think is best without ever bothering to actually talk to me about it first," I raged on. "All that insurance crap, buying our house, going on that stupid run, not talking to me about money *and* conveniently forgetting to mention all the other times you've been arrested, hell—I would still be at school in Richmond if you had your way."

"I wish you *had* stayed in Richmond," he nodded firmly. There was no apology. No acknowledgment that I was right. He just kept his hands on the wheel, steering this train right off the track. "I wish you'd never started working at the shop. I wish you'd never started coming to the clubhouse last year. And I wish we'd never gotten together in the first place."

I knew what he was doing. He was breaking us apart, shattering whatever was left of us, rubbing salt in the open wound all so I would hate him. All so I would stay far away.

"You don't really mean that, Caleb," my voice was trembling now, but I couldn't fight it anymore.

"Yeah, I do," he murmured and scrubbed his face with his hands again. "Being with me, Iz—Isabelle, I feel like I ruined you. I'm the worst thing that's ever happened to you."

Tears pricked my eyes and no amount of willpower could keep them at bay. They flowed down my cheeks like a river, pouring out all the things I couldn't bring myself to face.

"That's not the way I see it," I whispered through my tears. "You're the *best* thing that's ever happened to me. I don't understand why you can't see that. You've given me—"

"What, Isabelle?" Caleb cut in abruptly, his voice steeled with resolve. "What exactly have I given you?"

He didn't give me a chance to respond.

"Look at everything that's already happened in the last year alone," he sucked in a ragged breath and swallowed hard.

I leaned forward, ready to reach out to him, to do something to keep this from happening. "It's not your—"

"Yes, it is," he cut me off yet again. "It is my fault. I know I couldn't control Padilla or the ATF or Becca or even the club, but at the end of the day, none of that would've ever been within miles of you if it weren't for me. And honestly? You never belonged around any of it in the first place. It's just not who you are. And you need to get out while you still can and before it gets worse."

"And what about you? Being around the club and everything that goes with it is too dangerous for me, but it's totally fine for you?"

A sad smile flashed across his face and his knuckles turned white. "This isn't about me. And you and I both know I'm never leaving the club. What else would I do? I don't know how to do anything else."

"That sounds like bullshit to me. You're smart. You're resourceful. You could figure it out and I'd support you every step of the way."

He lifted a shoulder and blew out a deep breath. "Look, none of that matters right now. The point is I'm going to prison in three days and I deserve to be there. I can do my time because I earned my punishment, but what I can't do—what I *won't* do—is force you into prison too. You don't deserve to be punished with me."

Caleb swallowed hard, as if he was summoning the strength he needed to carry on. "I know this isn't what you wanna hear, but when I'm gone and after some time has passed, you'll see I'm right. You'll move on and you'll forget about me, and it'll be like all this never happened. You'll meet some good guy—trust me, they'll be lining up at the door to have a chance with you—and he'll treat you right, keep you safe, give you a family and a life and all the things I just can't."

I was practically shaking with fury by the time he was done with his little speech and didn't even know if I wanted to find the strength to put him in his place. I wasn't sure I would even know where to start.

"You don't know what the hell you're talking about, Caleb," I pushed through gritted teeth. "I know what you're trying to do. You think you're protecting me, but this isn't your decision to make."

I'd been prepared to put everything on hold, to wait *years* if I had to because I loved him and because I wanted to spend the rest of my life with him. He wasn't as convincing as he thought he was, but I couldn't deny that the angle he'd played hadn't hurt like a bitch. And somewhere, deep down, his argument really did carry some weight. I just wasn't interested in hearing it.

Caleb's jaw clenched tightly and he leaned forward a little. "I don't know what else you want me to say here."

"You're an asshole," I hissed hoarsely as another fresh round of tears slipped down my cheeks.

He just shrugged, his eyes betraying zero emotion. "Just go live your life, Isabelle. Move on, okay?"

Suddenly, I wanted to reach across the table and punch the son of a bitch. How dare he make assumptions about what I wanted and what was best for me? He wanted me to live my life? To just move on? Fine, asshole. That was just fine. The rage coursing through me made me tremble with an unadulterated need to slap the shit out of him. To shake him. To make him snap the hell out of it.

"Fuck you," I spat venomously as another traitorous tear fell down her cheek. "I love you and you're throwing it all away for nothing. My dad was right about you. I never wanted to believe it because the Caleb I know would never pull this kind of bullshit, but he was right. Because you know what he told me? He told me all you were going to do was get me pregnant and leave me. And you know what? He was right."

He remained silent across from me with his hands folded tightly in front of him, but for a split second, pain flashed through his eyes and his jaw clenched. It didn't matter. Nothing mattered anymore. He'd taken the future I'd imagined for us, the life I'd wanted with him, and he'd burned it to a crisp for misguided, selfish reasons. And now, after everything that was said, after seeing the cold, detached expression in his dead eyes, I just wanted to leave.

With an abrupt, anguished breath, I pushed out of my chair and stumbled backward, shifting on my heel just as quickly to get the hell out of there.

"Isabelle," Caleb called after me. "Wait—you don't have to leave right away."

I whirled around. He might as well have just slapped me in the face. "Are you kidding me? You really think I'm going to stay here with you?"

He was up on his feet in a flash, reaching out, and heading straight toward me. "Don't leave like this. Please, just— "

"Just what, Caleb?"

When his rough fingertips gripped my forearms to pull me closer, that was it. I'd officially reached my breaking point, not like I hadn't already been there for the last two weeks. I shoved him in the chest with all the strength I had left, letting adrenaline take the reins, and then when he *still* reached for me, my hand flew out to crack him right across the face.

I watched him rear back with a hand covering the red mark on his face. His chest was heaving and he squeezed his eyes shut, but didn't make the same mistake for a third time. He kept his damn hands to himself.

"You got what you wanted," I whispered as I backpedalled toward the front door. "Now you'll get to go to prison with a clear conscience, right? Congratulations."

I didn't turn back as I pushed through the front door, practically hitting him in the face with the screen door as he trailed behind me.

It wasn't until I backed my mom's Trans Am out of our driveway that I saw him. This was the last time I'd see him for years, probably, and this moment would forever be burned in my memory. His fists balled up at his sides, the way he slumped down on the patio steps to watch me leave, the torment striking across his face, the defeat in his eyes, and finally, his head falling into his hands and his shoulders heaving.

He wouldn't chase after me. I didn't want him to anyway. Instead, I forced myself to drive, furiously wiping away tears so I didn't die in a fiery car wreck on my way to God knows where. Every place I could think of to go was connected to Caleb and the life I'd had with him and I couldn't go to Lexie or Skyler. I didn't need their sympathy and as terrible as it was, I just didn't really want to see them either. Becca was gone. There was no one else, wasn't there? How pathetic was that?

And here I thought I'd never be the girl who got so wrapped up in a guy she had no friends or real family outside of him. I guessed the joke was on me.

So I pulled into the one driveway that didn't hold as many memories attached to Caleb and the life he'd just torn to pieces. I knocked on the door with tears still streaming down my face and winced at the shock on my dad's face. I could only imagine the mess he'd found on his doorstep.

This was the last place I ever expected to go, but I also never thought it was possible for the person I loved more than anything to hurt me this way.

"I'm sorry for just showing up like this without calling first," I murmured through my tears. "I don't have anywhere else to go."

My dad hesitated for just a moment and then whatever held him back disappeared just as quickly. He gathered me in his arms, ushered me inside, and quietly closed the door behind us.

CHAPTER EIGHTEEN
Interstice

Caleb

Three Months Later

Time inside moved fast and just as slow. There were days where I felt the excruciating passing of each second until my mind went numb. And then there were days where my mind was moving so quickly I barely noticed any time had passed at all. As much as I hated to admit it, having Dom with me helped. Having someone to watch my back did wonders for my peace of mind, but of course, didn't really do much for my conscience, considering that Dom had had a hell of a lot to leave behind.

The first week was the hardest. All the goodbyes, the adjustment to life inside, figuring out which guard was on our side and which fellow inmates could be trusted, and hell, even the routine had been an adjustment. I was used to keeping my own schedule and doing shit on my own time, so my body had had a difficult time adjusting to 'inmate schedule'.

But none of that was the most difficult adjustment I'd had to endure. In the three months since I'd become a long-term ward of the North Carolina Department of Corrections, Isabelle had never strayed far from my thoughts. At first, I'd spent the better part of my time alternating between restraining myself from punching anything I could get my hands on and from sobbing like a baby.

Every time I closed my eyes, her face flashed across my mind. Her beautiful smile, so full of life, her vibrant blue eyes, the deepest blue I'd ever seen, the feel of her soft skin against mine, her warm, lean body curled up next to me, flowers and vanilla—all of it crashed over me in waves and I couldn't stop it even if I wanted to.

The problem was simple: I was a criminal who deserved to be exactly where I was and that would never be good enough for her.

My hands were tied—the club was all I knew and all I would ever know. Isabelle, on the other hand, had the potential for a wonderful future and staying with me would only turn it into an ugly nightmare.

So even though I didn't know how to get myself out, I had to see her safely into a lifeboat, away from this sinking ship, away from this chaos. With the club, there would always be *something* going on beneath the surface and behind closed doors, always some new threat, always some new business deal that could just as easily go awry, and always the potential that I might not come home that night in one piece. That was something I couldn't change.

But Isabelle's association with it? *That* was the only hand I'd had to play.

"Yo, Caleb!"

I turned my head at the voice and found Dom staring back at me expectantly.

"Is today the day?"

I blew out a deep breath and threw him a glance over my shoulder as we walked up to check in for visiting hours. "Does it really matter, Dom?"

"Sure it does," he shrugged nonchalantly. "'Cuz if it is, I'd like to make sure Lex and me are sitting as far away from you two as possible today."

"Well, maybe you'd better rethink your reserved table," I muttered over my shoulder. "Because this is gonna be ugly."

I shifted anxiously from side to side as we waited our turn to pass through and glanced at the clock directly above the visitors' entrance. Any moment now, I'd be face to face with her and I honestly didn't know how I felt about it. It didn't exactly help that she'd flatly refused to see me for the last three months and had only recently agreed to take my phone calls.

She was punishing me. And she was essentially telling me that it didn't matter if I still had 21 months left of my sentence or if I was suffering because she thought I was the dumbest, most insane, asshole bastard she'd ever met. And of course, she was right. I deserved to suffer. I deserved to spend every second in agony.

I barely slept, barely ate, and the only real reason I was surviving at all was because Dom had my back. If not for his intervention, my ass would've been shanked by now. I honestly just didn't really give a shit anymore. At this point, I couldn't care less if I ever got of prison.

So when my mom's icy, black-rimmed eyes focused sharply on me as she perched on the bench across from me, I was having a hard time feeling anything less than apathetic to her stare-down. She made no moves to hug or even touch me, but my mother's touch wasn't what I needed right now.

"Hi, Caleb," she bit out finally through clenched teeth.

"Hey, Mom," I sighed and stared down at the table in front of me.

The next few moments passed by with slow, steady beats and I wasn't looking forward to hearing the inevitable emotional beat-down she was about to lay on me. It wasn't that I didn't deserve it. I just didn't want to hear it.

"You look like shit," she stated quietly, her hawk-like eyes scanning over me.

"Yeah, well, I feel like shit, so I guess that sounds about right," I mumbled back and slid down a little lower on the table.

My mom nodded tightly. "Good."

My eyes lifted to the ceiling at that last comment. It wasn't like I expected her to be sympathetic.

Still, I had to ask. I had to know.

"How is she?"

The words hung in the air like a plague, sinking deep inside my soul and poisoning me. But I had to know that she was surviving, that she was moving on, that she wasn't as broken by this as I was.

My mom's eyes narrowed dangerously and she leaned forward like a cat about to pounce on her prey. "You cut ties with her, Caleb. And now you wanna know how she's doing? You can't have it both ways."

"Mom," I pleaded, surprising both of us with my desperate tone. "Can you just give me something? Anything?"

She regarded me silently for a few moments, weighing whether or not this was a good idea and then she exhaled exasperatedly.

"Well," she pushed out slowly. "You shattered her heart into a million pieces and then stomped all over it. How do you think she's doing?"

I flinched and swallowed hard.

"Is she..." I murmured hoarsely. "Is she still at the house?"

"No, she's not," my mom answered simply and showed zero signs of offering any other information.

My mind immediately leapt to all the alternatives, of where she could be living or what she was doing. Part of me wouldn't be surprised if she'd just picked up and moved closer to campus. The truth was I'd been going a little crazy wondering if she was okay, if I'd been too cruel and impassive, if I'd done more damage than I'd intended and I just had to know. And although I'd pushed her away, I couldn't push away what I felt for her. That would always be there, trailing after me like a ghost until the day I died.

"Is she still in town?"

My mom eyed me carefully and leaned forward. "I'm not gonna tell you shit. I know what you want and right about now I'm not so sure you deserve it."

"Wow," I exhaled with a huff. "Thanks, Ma. Love you too."

"I never said I didn't love you," she shook her head ruefully. "You wanna know what I think?"

All I could do was stare. She was just going to tell me anyway.

"I get you didn't want to see her waiting for you, but I think you let your grief do your talking for you. It'd only been two weeks since you lost the baby," her voice caught on that last word and I pushed out a heavy sigh. "And neither of you had enough time to really process that, Caleb, to really deal with it together. That girl has done nothing but love you unconditionally and you bailed on her when she needed you the most. You walked away and left her to clean up your mess."

My head dropped forward, barely hanging on its hinges as her words washed over me. I knew all this already. But hearing it out loud—she might as well have just thrown a bucket of ice water over me.

When she finally had enough, murmured a quick goodbye, and left the table, I sat there alone, feeling like someone had just walked up behind me and shanked me right in the back. Even as a guard motioned for me to get moving, I still sat there stiffly, frozen to the metal bench underneath me.

It wasn't until I was back in my cell and sitting on my bed just as powerlessly and helplessly as before, that I finally did something about it. I didn't even know where to start. Didn't know how to even begin to tell her I'd made the biggest mistake of my life. All I knew was that I'd pushed away the best thing that ever happened to me and I'd get on my hands and knees every day of my life to beg if there was even a chance she could forgive me.

So because I had no other way to reach out, I grabbed some stray paper and a pencil and started to write:

Hey Iz...

. . .

Isabelle

One Month Later

"Well," my dad put his hands on his hips and surveyed the small space. "I think that's everything."

My tiny one-bedroom apartment seemed even smaller filled with all these boxes, but I couldn't put a price on its biggest and most important highlights: it was only a half mile away from campus and it got me out of Claremont. I was sold before I even saw the place.

I'd spent the first week basically a walking zombie, barely sleeping, hardly eating, and not even really human. Getting off the couch long enough to go to the bathroom was difficult enough and my dad had to practically lock me in the bathroom just to get me to take a shower.

Somewhere between crying myself to sleep, waking up in the morning in tears, and wallowing in self-pity, I'd gotten angry. Pissed as hell was more like it. And then, after speeding over to the house and tearing apart our bedroom in a fit of blind, red-hot rage, I'd had the worst panic attack of my life with numb hands, shaking limbs, dry throat, feeling like the walls were rushing in on me—a million times worse than the one I'd had after the break-in.

Somewhere along the way, I'd settled on an epiphany: it was time for a fresh start.

I wouldn't give Caleb the satisfaction of acknowledging I was doing it because he'd told me to. There was nothing I could do about it anyway, considering that I'd been barred from visiting him in prison. Now I could see it for what it was: the final nail in the coffin of our relationship.

Still, I knew, the same way I knew I couldn't go a day without holding a paintbrush in my hand, that I would never be able to shake my feelings for him.

I could have kids with another man and wish Caleb was their father instead. I'd always wonder what my life would look like if I hadn't lost our baby, if he hadn't gone to prison, and I would be 90-years-old with an entire lifetime behind me and still know that the short year we'd spent together had been, regardless of what happened, the only time I'd truly been happy.

With a long exhale, I ran my left hand through my auburn locks and took in the small space that would be my home from now on. The hair color change had been the first of many changes I knew I needed to make to find some semblance of a life after Caleb. Right after my breakdown in our bedroom, I carefully set my engagement ring on the kitchen counter and hadn't stepped foot in the house since.

Ten minutes later, I'd hopped into a salon chair and made the most drastic change to my hair since, well, ever. I'd just needed to do *something*. Anything to have some control again. Anything to take a step towards normalcy and recovery.

That's all I really wanted at this point. Just to feel normal again. Just to feel human again.

"It's not as small as you said it was," my dad told me and, thankfully, interrupting my grim thoughts.

"It's not exactly all that great either," I cocked an eyebrow at him even as he leaned forward to look out the nearest window.

My dad glanced at me over his shoulder. "Nice view."

"Sure," I shrugged.

"You know," he turned around to face me again. "I'm going to miss having you at the house, but you're making the right choice here, Isabelle. You really are. I think this'll be exactly what you need. A change of scenery...a fresh start...I know it's not ideal, but you have to start somewhere."

I smiled sadly and sucked in a deep breath. "Thanks, Dad."

He reached out to squeeze my shoulder and then released it just as quickly.

In the four months since I'd shown up at his doorstep, he'd weathered the storm with me exactly the way I needed him to. Even though he'd already known about the baby, he hadn't pushed for the rest of the details and I'd told him enough to fill in the blanks.

And the most surprising part of all?

There were no "I told you so's" and no bad-mouthing of Caleb at all. Instead, he almost seemed impressed that Caleb made the decision he did and had been nothing but respectful of him the few times we talked about Caleb, even if all that did was piss me off even more. But he'd been a rock, a place I could hide from the tornado that had ripped through my life, and for the first time since my mom's death almost two years ago, I finally felt like I had my dad back again.

He shuffled over to my makeshift kitchen table—I'd left every single piece of furniture inside the house because I didn't even want to touch it—and swept a large manila envelope off the table.

"You left these at the house," he told me as he held the envelope out to me. "I'm sure you left them on purpose, but they've just been piling up on the kitchen counter and besides, some new ones came in the mail this week and I don't know. If you decide to read them, I think you should have them all. And this came in the mail yesterday. I wasn't sure if you'd want it or not—"

My eyes widened at the North Carolina Department of Corrections insignia on the envelope and snatched it out of his hands. This particular one was different than all the others I'd gotten from this address—*this* one was from the DOC directly. I tore it open and skimmed it as fast as my eyes would allow.

"Inmate no. 32689, Caleb Sawyer, has requested your name to be added to his approved visitors list. Should you choose to visit, the correctional facility's visiting hours are Saturday and Sunday..."

A million thoughts ran through my mind at once: he was okay, he wasn't hurt or sick, but what the hell? Why now? After all his grandstanding about me needing to move on with my life and how he wasn't going to put me on the list, what the hell was his problem? Part of me wanted to crush the letter in my hand or at the very least, tear the thing to pieces so I didn't have to look at it anymore.

"What a dick," I muttered under my breath.

"Everything alright?" my dad asked me from over my shoulder.

"Yeah," I sighed. "He's fine. I guess."

Silence fell between us as my dad cocked an eyebrow at me and gestured to the letter in my hand with his head. "You sure?"

"He wants me to visit now. Can you believe that?"

My dad rubbed his mouth and winced a little. "Yeah, actually I can."

With another sigh, I crumpled the letter and tossed it into the closest garbage bag I could find.

"So I take it you're not planning on seeing him anytime soon?" his soft voice called out to me.

"No," I told him curtly. "I'm not. He can't keep jerking me around like this. It's so unfair it's not even funny."

He lifted a shoulder with a deep sigh and set the large manila envelope back on the table. "Well, I think you're well within your rights to feel that way. But someday, you might at least decide you're ready to read them, don't you think?"

I couldn't do or say anything except allow my eyes to rest dangerously on the large manila envelope on the table.

"You changed your address at the post office, didn't you?"

I nodded numbly.

"So," he shrugged. "They'll get forwarded here now. You can do what you want with them, Isabelle, but I think you'll regret it if you throw them out."

Maybe, but I couldn't let myself see him anymore than I could let myself read his letters.

. . .

Four Months Later

Hey Iz,

Have you been getting my letters? I guess I just wish there was some way I could know for sure if they're even getting to the right place. I know you haven't been living at the house for a while and that's why I started sending them to your dad's. I just don't want them to get lost in case you really are reading them.

You're never going to believe this, but I've been doing a little reading. I know, I know. You probably thought I was illiterate or something (hey, I know big words too), but I can sort of read. My counselor told me I needed to occupy my time here in a 'positive way'. Whatever that means. Anyway, I figured, I got nothing but time, so why not give this reading thing a shot? So I went to the library, checked out some old-ass books, and started reading. I really don't have anything better to do when I'm not in the yard.

I started with Huck Finn. That was actually pretty good. Then I read Fear and Loathing in Las Vegas and the guy in the cell next to me started pounding on the wall because I was laughing so loud. Then I started reading The Autobiography of Malcolm X. I had no idea that guy was ever in prison and then I felt kind of stupid for not knowing that. Did you know he read tons of books and worked on his vocabulary when he was in prison? I didn't know that. Then I didn't feel like such an idiot about all this reading. I read a few books by Stephen King too. I really liked those, especially the one about those kids who follow the train tracks to find a dead body. I don't know why, but it kind of reminded me of when me and Dom were kids, getting dirty and getting in trouble, but not the kind of trouble that lands you in a place like this.

I don't know. I guess I picked things I thought you'd like to read too.

You want to know something else? I read some Shakespeare. Yeah. You can get off the floor now, Iz. One of the guys in the library told me to read Romeo and Juliet because it's one of the most famous stories ever or something like that. I didn't make it past Act 3. God, that was the most frustrating thing I've ever tried to read. I mean, why can't they all just speak English?

I got to the part where Romeo kills Juliet's brother (or was it her cousin? I can't remember) and then he gets banished and he's in the Friar's room crying like a little baby and that's when I threw it across my cell. It just felt too familiar, you know? The guy getting everything he wants and screwing it all up because he's a hot-headed asshole. There's this line, I think it went something like, 'what says my lady to our cancelled love?' and my hands started shaking when I read it. That's exactly how I feel, Iz.

I feel like everything we had just got cancelled, like it all just got ripped away from us. It was like Shakespeare wrote that picturing all the bullheaded, reckless, and completely stupid things I did as much as I don't like comparing myself to some sappy teenage tool.

Not to mention the fact that those losers kill themselves in the end. Who wants to read a love story that doesn't have a happy ending?

I guess my problem isn't really with Shakespeare, but you knew that already. I didn't realize reading can have this kind of impact, that I'd actually feel something, you know? It's weird. I'm going to keep reading though. I think I'll just stay away from Shakespeare for awhile.

It'll just make me miss you more.

Love you always,

Caleb

. . .

Isabelle

Six months later

This was a terrible idea. Necessary, sure. But headed straight for disaster.

I'd been fine with it right up until I was sitting at the bar, waiting for my date to show up. I'd been calm and collected as I drove here, making sure to text my dad to let him know I was really going through with it. He didn't believe me and given the circumstances, I couldn't exactly blame him.

But the second I sat down on the stool and ordered a drink, my chest tightened like a vice, sucking what little air was left right out of my lungs. It was like all the agitation, unrest, and torrential heartbreak seeping through every crack in my heart threatened to implode. The weight of that implosion would break me completely and my eyes darted around anxiously for a route to the fastest exit.

Before I had a chance to make a clean getaway, a guy dressed in jeans and a polo shirt approached me.

"Hey, Isabelle!" he called out to me, his green eyes filling with genuine hope and anticipation.

"Hi," I pressed a tight smile across my lips when his face lit up.

"I'm so glad we finally decided to do this," he told me as he closed in on me.

My eyes narrowed a little. *Finally*? And I didn't like the way the word, *we,* rolled off his tongue so comfortably. I'd known Alex in passing for a few months mainly through the coffee shop where both of us got our daily dose of caffeine in the morning. Through some small talk, a few too many run-ins, and more than a little persistence on his part, I'd agreed to meet him out for a drink. I hadn't wanted to say yes, but I also felt like I couldn't say no either. This was an opportunity to try again, to really start over, and like my dad always said, I had to start somewhere.

Alex was, for all intents and purposes, the exact opposite of Caleb. Clean-cut, preppy, no leather in sight..the only reason I'd agreed to this in the first place was because Alex was exactly the type of guy Caleb wanted me to end up with. That thought alone sent a rush of nausea right through my stomach.

Our conversation started off awkwardly after he ordered himself a beer and hopped up on the stool next to me at the bar. He prompted me with a few generic questions about school and all I could think was: *you're not Caleb.*

When he asked me if I wanted another drink, I almost said, "You're not Caleb."

As he asked earnestly about my upcoming gallery showing—something I now seriously regretted telling him during one of our random 'run-ins', which I suspected weren't really that random—all I could think about was how Caleb wasn't going to be there...and Alex just wasn't Caleb.

Well-intentioned and well-meaning, but not the person I really wanted to be sitting next to.

It was around that time the nausea and utter horror of my situation sent me high-tailing it to the ladies' room and I threw my head in the toilet where I dry-heaved for a good five minutes. When my stomach finally stopped rolling long enough to let me to slide down to the ground, I leaned heavily against the divider, trying not to think about the stickiness underneath me. This was never going to end. Why the hell did I ever think it could?

Life after Caleb didn't even seem like a possibility anymore. This wasn't actual living. This was just existing.

My fingers brushed my stomach and tears stung my eyes.

I was completely pathetic. Pining away for a guy who didn't want me. Still loving him and still hurting because of him. Still wishing everything could've been different for us. And it didn't matter that he'd already been gone for 10 months and that he kept writing and started calling, too, because it was over.

The only thing I could do now was just keep moving forward, at least as much as possible. So this date hadn't exactly panned out. I'd dry-heaved in the toilet at barely 20 minutes of small talk with a guy who wasn't Caleb and at some point, I was going to have to figure out how to do this. I was going to have to figure out how to date other guys, be with other guys, and eventually, love another guy.

With a sigh, I squeezed my eyes shut and pressed my head against the metal divider. Who was I kidding? There would never be anyone else.

I would always love him.

It was just that simple and that devastating.

. . .

Six Months Later

Hey Iz,

How's your summer break going? I know you were in the semester showcase again. Why would they choose anyone else? People were probably crowding around all your pieces just to get a closer look. I tried looking it up online to see if I could find any pictures, but they don't let guys in prison use the internet. I can pretty much only use the computer to type and I'd rather just write you these letters. It just feels more like I'm actually talking to you this way.

Getting past the halfway point feels weird. These last 14 months have felt so long and so short, if that makes any sense. I've got 10 months left in here and I feel like I haven't really slept, I mean <u>really</u> slept this whole time. It's hard and it's not just about being trapped in a cell. It's about everything I know I'm missing. Your birthday. All of your shows. Christmas. Waking up with you in the morning. Touching you. Just getting to see you and hear how your day was.

I need to move on to a different topic, don't you think?

I have something to tell you actually. I waited a little while because I wasn't sure I would actually keep up with it and I didn't want you to get all excited and proud only for me to tell you in a couple months that I quit. But here it goes. I started working on a degree. I guess the reading thing was working out so well that my counselor got me started on an accelerated program. I might have a few credits left to finish when I get out, but that's not a big deal.

Business sounded pretty boring at first, but I figured that's the one thing I might actually be able to use when I bust out of this place. The classes are okay. Lots of economics, accounting, and marketing. Some psychology too. I actually don't mind it. I'm not as bad at math as I thought I was, so that means there's still some hope for me left, right?

I guess I just wanted to see if I was smart enough to do it and this is a different kind of school than I'm used to. I can do it all at my own pace and there's still a teacher there to help me if I have questions. I like this a lot better than high school, that's for sure. Knowing this will help me, that I'm doing something I can put to use, it makes me actually try and concentrate. It's better just keep to myself as much as possible anyway and there are plenty of quiet places to sit and study in peace.

Dom said I'm the only person he knows who'd go to prison just to end up in college, but I don't really see it that way. I think the problem is that guys like me and Dom, who don't know anything different than life in the club, we think that's all there is. We don't think we have any other options when we do. We just don't know how to figure out what those options are. It's not like anyone in the club is going to help us.

Sometimes I wonder what my life would be like if I was someone else, someone who wasn't raised in this. I don't think I would've chosen it if I hadn't grown up around it all my life. I don't know how I feel about that and I don't really know what I'm supposed to do about it either.

I started talking to this guy I met in the library (he's the one who told me to read Romeo and Juliet) and he told me he wakes up everyday and wishes he was dead. He's finishing up 10 years in here for vehicular manslaughter and you know, I get where he's coming from.

He said he feels like his whole life was leading up to the moment he got in the car and if he'd made one different decision somewhere, somehow, maybe he wouldn't have gotten in that car.

It's crazy because that's exactly how I feel. I feel like my whole life was leading up to the moment I decided to go on that run. If I was a different person, if I lived a different life, I never would've even been at the table having that conversation with Marcus. I think I'm starting to figure out that I can sit here with my head in my hands and wish away all my mistakes or I can do something about it. At least that's what I told him when we got to talking. I'm still working out how to do that.

I told him about you. I hope that's okay. It was just nice to talk to someone who understood how I'm feeling.

Anyway, I have to get going so I can study a little bit. I have a test later today in my business marketing class and my buddy from the library is going to quiz me. I bet you never thought I'd ever say something like that, huh? It's weird, I know.

I hope you're okay. I hope you're happy. I hope...I don't know. I just hope.

Love you always,
Caleb

. . .

Isabelle
Eight Months Later

"This is the one, Isabelle," Dr. Jacobs pointed abruptly to the painting to my left, her flowery French accent making her sound a little more nonchalant than she really was.

I flinched at her choice. Why, oh why, did I bring it in? All I'd wanted was some feedback. That was it. A few critiques here and there about my technique and I would've been perfectly happy with that. But no. She had to push and push until she got her way. That way, it seemed, involved putting my most personal painting to date on display for everyone to see.

With only two months until Caleb was released, my emotions had been getting the better of me. And, true to form, I'd let those emotions manifest themselves across the canvas in splatters and swirls of blue.

To me, it was grotesque and seeping with self-loathing. To Dr. Jacobs, the painting was raw and 'crackling with pain'. Those were her exact words. I'd wanted to throw my paintbrush at her. Maybe I should've.

"I don't know," I sighed. This was a wasted effort. She would not be reasoned with. "It's just too personal. I don't feel comfortable opening myself up this way for everyone else to see."

She just lifted a shoulder, her eyes never leaving my painting. "Your first showcase, if I remember correctly, was stuffed full of personal pieces."

My first showcase, and I *did* remember correctly, was also during a time in my life when I'd had a solid foundation to stand on. I'd been able to let go more easily because, other than the pieces inspired by my mom and Becca, everything else was positive. Happy. Contented, if not a little anxiety-ridden. But it was okay then. *I* was okay then. Now, I felt like I was just stumbling around the wreckage, slipping and sliding on the rubble with little hope for rebuilding.

"Isabelle," Dr. Jacobs rested a hand on my shoulder and gave it a quick squeeze. "Raw emotion, whether it's good or bad or happy or devastating—that's what life is all about. You must have the courage to reach out and grab it while you have the chance. And you can't worry about what other people will think. True artists channel their pain because pain is something we all feel every single day."

I didn't like the sound of that. And I really didn't like the idea of my personal devastation being printed in the university magazine. The exposure was insane, but any other painting and I'd be all over it. But this one? The one I'd painted after a particular sleepless night where I'd missed Caleb so badly, where I'd let pain and depression swallow me whole, and I'd sobbed for hours, hugging my pillow and imagining it was him...this one wasn't really intended for anyone else to see.

The worst part was that I'd painted this just a month ago, so that pretty much spoke volumes for how much I'd figured my shit out. Basically, not at all. I was existing, sure. Going back and forth between classes and work. Getting coffee on the other side of campus so I didn't run into Alex. Meeting my dad once a week for dinner halfway between campus and Claremont. It wasn't much of a life, but it was mine.

"Think about it, Isabelle," Dr. Jacobs stressed and gestured toward my painting again. "Pieces like this? They're not meant to stay locked inside you. They must be shared. They must be seen."

My eyes fell to the painting and I pushed out a deep breath. This was probably a losing battle.

"And," she went on as she pushed a file folder into my chest. "I printed a few things for you to take a look at. I think there might be some options you'd be interested in."

I numbly slid the folder away from my chest and flipped it open. It took me a moment to realize what she'd given me, but my eyes darted back up to her just as quickly.

"Internships? Really?"

She just shrugged. "Yes. You need to start building relationships with galleries that can continue to give you the exposure you need to have a successful career. Many galleries, particularly the ones there in that folder, choose to work exclusively with artists they have a history with. Internships with most galleries are thankless work, but if you intern at any of these places, you'll automatically have a foot in the door for gallery space."

We'd spoken about this before, but at that point, graduation hadn't seemed so imminent. She was right. I needed options and I needed to find them before I graduated and before Caleb got out of prison. If I didn't have some sort of plan, even if it was vague and poorly-drawn, I just didn't know how I'd ever really be able to gain any traction on my own.

It wasn't until I was back in my apartment and sitting at my kitchen table that it really sunk in.

To my left sat a shoebox full of unopened letters. To my right, the file folder stuffed with opportunities. My past and my future lined up right next to each other.

I blew out a deep breath and flipped open the folder. Dr. Jacobs had been thorough. Raleigh. Chicago. Los Angeles. New York. Washington, D.C. Boston.

New York called to me in all its art-scene glory. I could already imagine myself walking through Central Park with my sketchbook and trekking through fresh snow to get to a gallery. New York was a place where this thing inside me, this passion, this creativity, could thrive and grow and maybe even make me some money if I was lucky.

Then, as if my fingers had a mind of their own, they trailed over the top of the shoebox and pushed it off. They dipped inside the box and lifted one off the pile. It was like clockwork—a new letter came every Monday and Thursday and he called every Friday at 3:00 on the dot. I always let it go right through the automated message asking me if I wanted to accept a call from an inmate at the North Carolina Department of Corrections and that was always when I hung up.

I just couldn't let myself go there. I couldn't give in. If I read one letter or took one phone call, that would be it. I'd forgive him. I wasn't sure if I could ever do that even if I wanted to.

So, with a heavy sigh, I opened up my laptop instead and Googled the first gallery in the folder.

. . .

Six Weeks Later

Hey Iz,

Two weeks. That's all I have to survive now. Just two weeks. I made it this far, so this should be a walk in the park, right?

I just have one more test to take and I'll officially have an associate's degree in business. I still can't believe I actually did it. I guess I still don't really know what I'm going to do with that when I get out, but I'll figure it out. If anything, I'll probably be able to earn my keep a little more at the shop. It's crazy to think that I started out working on this degree just because I needed more things to do to pass the time, not thinking any of it would ever matter, and now I feel like I really did something worthwhile with my time here.

Maybe Dom was right. Maybe the only way I was ever getting to college was by going to prison. But I didn't waste these two years. I read a lot. I learned a lot. I definitely never thought I'd ever actually like school. So it wasn't all bad, not like it was really all that good either.

I have a plan, Iz. When I get out, the first thing I'm going to do is corner Lex and I'm not moving until she tells me where you're living now. I'm sure you live on campus, but I still need the address so I can get to you. I know my mom won't tell me, but I'm hoping Lex will tell me just to get me off her back. Then I'm getting on my bike and I'm coming to you.

I don't care where you are or how far I have to go, I'll get there. I don't care if all I get to do is walk you to class. I'll take it if it means I get to see you. I'll walk you to class every day if it means I still get to be part of your life. I know I don't have any right to do that, but I just need to see you, Iz. I can't wait any longer.

I really hope you're reading this.

Love you always,

Caleb

CHAPTER NINETEEN
Fickle Fortune

Isabelle

I blew out a deep breath and glanced at the digital clock above my stove. Another half hour and I'd have to leave for work. On any normal day, I wouldn't be just sitting here, staring at the clock and swallowing back butterflies in my stomach, but this wasn't just an average day. Today was the day Caleb got out of prison.

Today was also the day I knew I'd have to see him.

I didn't know how and I didn't know when, but I knew he'd find me.

Even I knew those thoughts were along the lines of *Sleeping With The Enemy* meets *Fear,* but this was Caleb. Finding me today wasn't about anything other than groveling. I knew this because even during this last week, his letters and his calls still came like clockwork.

All I had to do was make myself scarce today. Go to my studio space on campus or even just get in my mom's car and drive. If I wasn't here, I wouldn't have to see him. Even if he somehow figured out where I worked, I doubted he'd show up there unannounced and uninvited. But instead of doing any of those things, here I was, fidgeting at my kitchen table and waiting.

The whole thing was just so pathetic. I just spent the last two years trying to find a way to move forward, but on the day I really needed to be strong and show some backbone, I couldn't move. Sure, if we missed each other somehow today there'd always be tomorrow and the day after that and the day after that until we finally reconnected, but that was exactly what I was afraid of.

Reconnecting. Seeing if we could reclaim a little bit of what we lost. Picking up where we left off.

That just couldn't happen. Life just didn't work that way. My eyes fell to the small stack of envelopes sitting on the table in front of me and I sucked in a harsh breath. A few of them I'd opened. The rest were the last ones I'd gotten from Caleb. My fingers itched to rip them open, but I'd held out this long. I couldn't break now when it mattered the most.

But when that telltale engine roared down my street, all the hairs on my arm stood on end. Reason told me it could be anyone because plenty of motorcycles had driven down this street before. Instinct told me something else. My body, my senses, my heart...they all knew.

Everything was on high alert and working overdrive as I raced headfirst toward the inevitable, listening for the buzzer, and skating dangerously between feeling like puking and darting around the room like the crazy person I'd become.

Two seconds later, the buzzer rang out through my apartment.

My chest heaved and tightened, but I froze. I could still ignore him, couldn't I? It would be so easy to just pretend I wasn't here. He'd never know. But then he'd just keep coming back and keep calling.

So against my better judgment, I hit the talk button on the intercom.

"Hello?"

Not even a beat later and I heard the voice I'd only heard in my dreams, the same voice that could elicit emotions in me I'd rather keep buried.

"Hey, Iz. It's me," he paused for a moment, his voice a little breathless and a little deeper than I remembered. "Can I come in?"

My hands twisted into knots at my waist, hesitation weighing me down. I took a breath and hit the button to unlock the main door in my shared entryway. No going back now.

He sure as shit didn't waste any time and I could hear him bounding up the steps right before the hard knock at my door. If that wasn't a harsh dose of reality then I didn't know what was. I stared at my door, swallowing tightly and finally, I had to squeeze my eyes shut just to keep the room from spinning as I reached for the door handle.

The door opened and there he was, crowding my doorway with his presence, which right about now, felt bigger than my whole apartment complex and the neighborhood combined. He seemed taller somehow, leaner yet brawnier at the same time and his hair was tied back behind his head. All his tattoos, including the upside down compass I'd designed for him, were on display over the sinewy lines of his forearms. But once I recovered from the initial shock of being so close to him after all this time, my attention never waned from his face and the way his lips curved up into a hopeful grin.

I sucked in a tight breath and it was all I could do to keep my feet planted a safe distance away.

It was his eyes that nearly did me in. Relief. Happiness. Exhaustion. Anticipation. Worry. Apology. Love. It was all there in those gorgeous blue eyes I saw every time I closed my eyes.

"Hey, Iz," he smiled softly and leaned forward a little, wanting to be asked inside, but trying not to overstep.

It was right on the tip of my tongue to ask him not to call me that, but I couldn't deny the way my heart leapt into my throat at that name on his lips. I hated and loved that name all at the same time.

"Hi, Caleb," I whispered.

Pure elation spread across his face the moment I spoke like it was the sweetest sound he'd ever heard and in that moment, I imagined it was.

He gestured with his head towards my apartment. "Is it alright if I come in? We can talk out in the hallway if you—"

"No, it's okay," I cut in before I could stop myself and opened the door a little wider so he could step inside. "You can come in."

After he took a few hesitant steps inside, an awkward silence permeated the air between us. Neither of us really knew what to do, what to say, or where to even begin.

"So, um," I tried to smile, but I couldn't decide whether smiling at him was good or bad for me. "When did you get out today?"

His eyes trailed over me, drinking me in, and I felt it almost as if he'd actually reached out to physically touch me. It singed my skin and left me gasping for air, desperate to touch him back.

Then his lips curved up in a knowing smile. "A little over an hour ago."

There was a part of me, the same part that refused to go ignored, that was thrilled beyond belief that the first thing he did when he got out was come see me. That he'd literally gotten to the clubhouse, interrogated someone for my new address—I felt really bad for Lexie right about now—and raced through the 45 minutes it took to get here from Claremont. Then the other part of me remembered him telling me to move on, to go out and live my life without him, to find some guy who could give me all the things he couldn't all because he'd gotten himself sent to prison.

"Okay."

I didn't know what else to say.

He shoved his hands deep inside his front pockets and chewed nervously on his bottom lip. "So, um—"

"I have to go to work," I butted in. "I just wanted to let you know I have to leave soon."

He nodded immediately, undeterred. "No problem, Iz. I just wanted to see you."

Another awkward moment passed and he ran a hand over his head, a gesture I was well-acquainted with.

"Where do you work?"

I glanced down at my usual work uniform, just a black pencil skirt and matching peplum tank top, and bit my lip. "I don't know if I want to tell you."

Alarm flashed across his face and I jumped to clarify.

"I just mean," I pushed out a rough breath and laughed unsteadily. "You're gonna make fun of me if I tell you."

That initial alarm vanished and relief flooded his face as his lips curled up into that crooked smirk that always had the power to make me weak in the knees.

"Come on, Iz," he tilted his head to the side a little as he grinned. "You can tell me."

I knew I could tell him anything and that was what scared me. Pushing that aside, I laughed again and lifted my eyes to the ceiling.

"I work at one of the makeup counters in Macy's."

His lips twitched in amusement and he had to bite down on his bottom lip just to keep from laughing right in my face. "Of course you do."

I shook my head and smiled right back at him. "Shut up."

Even as his smile seemed to grow even wider, Caleb took a tiny step closer to me. "I'm sorry. I won't say another word about it. Promise."

I wanted to reach for him and I didn't. Instead, I found myself gravitating toward him, letting myself get drawn back in like a stupid, masochistic moth to a flame.

"Did you get my letters?" his soft voice called out to me as he took another step closer.

"Yeah," I nodded.

"Did you read them?"

In spite of everything, I didn't have it in me to lie to him, especially not to his face. So, I shook my head, unable to bring myself to say the words.

He nodded slowly, rubbing his mouth with one hand and stared at the floor for a few moments. Then his eyes snapped back up to mine with new determination. "That's okay. I'm glad you got them at least. That's all that really matters."

His fingertips grazed my arm and my eyes flitted shut at the contact. I inhaled suddenly and the words sputtered out in a desperate attempt to give myself a little more time.

"I got some internship offers."

His fingertips just kept their exploration of my forearm as he closed the distance between us and he beamed a proud smile my way. "That's great, Iz. I bet they were all just biding their time until you finally graduated, huh?"

"I guess," I laughed, breathing in that familiar scent of musk and gasoline and feeling a little light-headed. "So, um, I got offers from galleries in Raleigh, Boston, New York, and Washington, D.C."

His face was an open book of raw emotions and with each turning of the page, a new emotion—pride and happiness for my success, dejection and grief, and finally, acceptance.

I didn't tell him that I hadn't even bothered to apply to the galleries Dr. Jacobs had suggested in Chicago and Los Angeles simply because L.A. was too far away from my dad—and Caleb if I was being completely honest—and the lure of New York's art scene was just too great. My heart wanted to choose Raleigh just as much as it wanted to choose New York. I just wasn't ready to talk about that yet.

Still, despite the news I'd just dropped on him, his thumbs brushed my cheek. I leaned into him, inhaling one more time, and feeling my heart finally tear through the wall I'd carefully constructed around it. I couldn't hold out anymore. I'd missed him too much. I loved him too much.

My arms wrapped around his neck as tears pricked my eyes. This was what I needed—feeling his strong arms holding me tight, protecting me, loving me. I couldn't stop now even if I tried. Our foreheads found their way to each other and his fingers ran along the edges of my hair like he was reminding himself what it felt like. Both rough hands closed around my face as he pressed his lips into mine, moving his mouth slowly to savor this moment. My hands skimmed around his shoulders and grasped the labels of his leather cut to pull him in even closer, drunk on the taste of his lips and the feel of him underneath my fingertips.

He hummed against my lips and pressed himself even closer until I was flush against his chest. I wanted to be closer. I wanted to just wrap myself around him and forget the last two years ever happened. It just felt so good...it felt like home. Like everything might be okay again. Like I might actually be whole again.

And then the fog lifted as my thoughts caught up to me. I gently pulled away, but not before kissing him one more time.

"I have to leave for work," I murmured against his lips.

He nodded, his hands still cupping my cheeks and his forehead still connected to mine. "Can I see you tomorrow?"

I closed my eyes and nodded before I could stop myself, my emotions once again getting the better of me. "I have class at eleven and then I have to work at one."

"Okay," he told me with a firm nod. "Maybe I could walk you to class?"

My heart flip-flopped. He was willing to turn around and drive back here tomorrow just to walk me to class? Now I just wanted to kiss him again. So, it was really for the best that his calloused fingertips slipped away from my face and he took a small step back as his hands found their way to his front pockets again.

"So I'll see you tomorrow?"

"Right," I smiled through my hesitation. "Tomorrow."

Hope and happiness flared in his eyes and he leaned in to kiss me one more time before stepping back out into the hallway. I watched him leave, shutting the door behind him when he descended down the stairs with a wave, and I leaned heavily against my door, my hands wringing in front of me.

I didn't know how I'd ever recover from that.

As I shuffled back to my kitchen table to grab my purse, my eyes fell on the stack of letters again. My past and present, still rearing their ugly heads, and I scrubbed my hands over my face. New York and Boston needed an answer soon and I couldn't put off the inevitable forever.

The problem was that up until 10 minutes ago, I'd been absolutely firm in what I wanted *and* needed to do. And then Caleb showed up and everything flew off-kilter again. Just when I was finally ready to take the necessary steps in order to actually move on—the timing couldn't have been worse.

I never thought I'd ever be the girl who made all her decisions because of a guy. Even when I'd chosen Winston-Salem over Richmond, I'd talked myself into believing it really was the best thing for me. Maybe that had been the right choice at the time, but now I was in a different place. Now I needed to move in a different direction.

If I stayed in North Carolina, I'd be holding myself back for the sake of working on a relationship I wasn't sure could be saved. I'd be sacrificing yet again. Putting someone else above myself. Making decisions with a *we* mentality.

At some point, I needed to figure out what was really best for me and the course of my life. I wasn't so sure I could afford to make the same mistake twice.

. . .

I sat in my mom's Trans Am in the driveway with my hands clenched tightly around the steering wheel. What the hell was I doing here? This was just a bad, bad idea. Nothing good was going to come of this, and yet, here I was, parked in the driveway of the house I'd only lived in for a few months. It seemed like so long ago since I'd lived here I was beginning to wonder if I'd only dreamt it.

Calling would've been so much easier and way less painful, but instead, I was parked in the driveway, unable to stay, but unable to leave just yet.

I just needed to see him. That's what this was really about.

I didn't know how my brain was still somehow able to command my finger to press the doorbell when I finally got the nerve to get out of the car. Now all I could do was wait.

Nothing.

I waited a few moments longer, shifting anxiously from side to side and still, nothing. Maybe he wasn't even home in the first place. It was early and maybe—God, what was I doing? I was hovering out of my body, watching helplessly as I rang the doorbell again.

Before I even had a chance to back away in a panic, I heard Caleb's gruff, muffled voice from behind the door and I froze to the ground again. And then the door opened.

"Alright, alright, what the hell do you..." Caleb trailed off, his arm stretched out to hold the door open and his eyes wide with surprise. "Iz? Wha—is everything okay?"

"Everything's fine," I jumped in to appease his obvious worry. "Can I come in?"

Oh shit. Why did I say that? Why couldn't I have just said what I needed to say out here on the safety of the porch?

His eyes softened right before they landed on the box under my arm and he swallowed tightly before nodding, stepping to the side just enough to give me room to pass by him. My eyes roamed the house hungrily as my heart twisted with regret. Everything looked pretty much the same way I'd left it, minus the stale pizza box and empty beer cans that littered the coffee table in front of the couch. Other than that, everything was still eerily the same, which given the fact that my relationship with Caleb was anything but the same, just made this all the more painful.

"I'm sorry to bother you," I told him now in a voice I barely recognized. "I know you planned on coming to campus later today."

Caleb's eyes bore into me with the same kind of intensity he'd brought with him to my apartment yesterday, the kind that sent a flutter deep into my stomach. "You're not bothering me, Iz."

"I'm taking the internship in New York," I blurted out suddenly, surprising us both. That was what I'd come here to say and now that it was out there, I wished I could snatch it back and pretend it wasn't happening.

His face twisted in agony and all that hope that had radiated in his eyes from the moment he'd opened the door withered and died. He nodded simply, like he'd already expected it, but that didn't make it hurt any less.

My arms somehow managed to hold the box out to him.

"I kept every letter you sent me," I told him shakily. "I couldn't throw them away, but I can't read them either. You should have them back. They're not really mine anyway."

It was too dangerous for those letters to end up in New York with me. Sooner or later, my willpower would give out and some random, drunken night in the not-so-distant future, I'd tear through them one by one until I found myself at his doorstep again so I could jump right back into his arms. From where I was standing, my world was a whole lot safer if those letters were in their rightful owner's possession.

Without a word, he gently slipped the box from my hands and promptly set it on the back of the couch.

I didn't owe him anything. I knew that. But despite all the shared history between us, despite the pain and the heartache and the devastation we'd left in our wake, I still needed to explain.

"I can't stay," I whispered hoarsely as one traitorous tear slipped down my cheek. "It just hurts too much. And I need to do what's right for *me*, not anyone else."

His eyes watered with unshed tears and he nodded dejectedly.

"I'm so sorry, Iz," he murmured. "I know there's nothing I'll ever be able to do or say that can make this right, but I understand. I really do."

"I wish I could stay. It's just that..." I willed myself to press forward and push through the speech I'd practiced in my head during the drive here. "I know that if I do, we'll fall back into something and it'll never be the way it used to be. I can't just forget everything that happened to us. It doesn't work that way."

I paused and found him focused on me intently, hanging on every word to brace himself for the inevitable blow he was about to receive.

"Caleb," my voice shook as I went on. "I understand why you didn't want me to wait for you. It took me awhile to really see it, but you were right about everything. It's not fair for you to just show up at my apartment after you told me not to wait for you. I'm just doing exactly what you told me to do and it took me awhile to get there, but I'm moving on."

Clear resignation reflected in Caleb's eyes now and I could almost feel the defeat just radiating off him. His shoulders slumped and his face crumpled in obvious anguish.

I blew out a deep breath, overcome with the weight of what I was about to say. I never thought we'd ever be standing here having this conversation, but there was no point in ruminating on the how and why. Our dreams had been crushed right before our eyes.

"I know you blame yourself, but I need you to know that *I* don't blame you. Well, I guess it was your fault for ending up in prison, but everything else...it wasn't your fault. You were the best thing that's ever happened to me and I know you don't see it that way, but I don't regret any of it. Not even for a second. It's just over now."

This internship in New York would open up a world of opportunities I might never get again. If I wanted to be a serious artist with a real career, I needed to reach for that future with open arms and nothing holding me back. I didn't know what my future had in store me, but I was finally beginning to accept that maybe Caleb just wasn't in it. That thought was devastating and freeing all at the same time.

Caleb shuffled backward, wiping his eyes with the back of his hand, and once his face was scrubbed free of his tears, he inhaled sharply. His eyes snapped up to me, but there was no bitterness. No disappointment. Just acceptance and grief.

"I need to leave, but, um, I was wondering if I could take a few of the baby's things," I called out to him, shifting anxiously from side to side as I watched his eyes widen and soften at the same time. "I didn't take anything with me when I moved out because I think I just wasn't ready to even touch it, but I can't go to New York without it. I just can't."

His Adam's apple bobbed up and down and then his head dipped into a tight nod.

"Of course, Iz," he murmured and motioned with his head toward the hallway.

I trailed after him, not wanting to get too close, but still craving that heady intoxication all the way into that third bedroom. This was the last thing I had to do here before I could finally leave and really start a new life, but it was just so much harder than I'd expected. I'd known stepping back into the nursery would throw me back into the dark abyss I'd somehow climbed out of, but the second my eyes fell on that half-finished mural, tears flowed freely down my cheeks.

Caleb reached up to get the memory box he'd pushed into the furthest depths of the closet the morning I came home from the hospital. I'd only opened the box one time and had barely survived it. The only way I'd survive it a second time was because Caleb was standing next to me.

He opened the box with a shaking hand as I leaned around his shoulder to see inside, shuffling through a few items so he could pass me the certificate of life.

"Take it, Iz," his voice was rough, but firm. "Please. You should have it."

As if they had a will of their own, my fingers reached out to slip it from his hand. From there, the rest happened naturally as we split the remainder of the box: a tiny pink blanket, a few pictures of her, the sympathy card signed by our doctor and nurses, a card with her footprints on it, a little pink onesie, and our hospital bracelets.

Caleb wiped his eyes and put the box with its cute pink bunny on it back deep into the closet. When he turned to face me, before I could even catch my breath, he was heading right for me. I closed my eyes as his lips brushed against my forehead and his fingertips gingerly trailed across my face. Every moment, every touch was equal parts pain and comfort and I hated every second of it. When I forced my eyes back open, tears spilt down my cheeks in waves and Caleb caught them with his thumbs.

My body was working against my mind now, but none of that mattered until I felt his strong arms wrap around my waist. Nothing else in the world would ever make me feel this safe, this protected, this loved.

Lifting my face out of his shoulder just enough to brush our cheeks together, I shivered when Caleb's lips caressed mine, gently moving and coaxing all the emotions out of me I'd fought to keep at bay.

"I love you," Caleb murmured hoarsely against my lips and it was only now that I was able to see the wetness shining in his own eyes. "I'll never stop."

These overwhelming sensations had just brought up everything I knew, deep down, was true: I didn't really want to leave because I loved him.

Please ask me to stay, I thought as tears streamed down my face. *Ask me to stay and I'll do it. Fight for me. Please.*

"I love you too," I whispered in between kisses, just letting him hold me tighter as my tears mingled with his.

He never asked.

And it was for the best. Love was never our problem and now, in spite of my moment of weakness, love just wasn't enough anymore.

So I let myself revel in his touch and his kiss one last time because now, this was goodbye.

. . .

Caleb

I turned my face into her hair and breathed in deeply, taking in everything about her while I still had the chance and burned this moment in my memory. Every soft rise and fall of her chest. How soft her skin was. Her warmth. Her beauty. Her everything.

I hadn't earned the right to keep her. I had to let her go instead.

Asking her to stay would be just like slapping shackles around her ankles.

But when she stepped into the hallway, panic leapt up into my throat.

"Iz! Wait!" I called out and desperately reached for her before she could make it to the door.

My hand closed around her elbow and gently turned her around, only to find her cheeks stained with freshly-shed tears and her shoulders trembling. Her head was buried in my shoulder before I had a chance to say anything else and I wrapped my arms around her, drawing her in closer, deeper while I still had the chance.

I took her face in my hands, brushing away her tears with my thumbs and gently pulled her chin up to look at me.

"I'll never love anyone else," I told her through my tears. "It'll *always* be you."

Her beautiful face crumbled as a new wave of tears tumbled down her cheeks and she covered her face with her hands. After I gently pried her fingers away from her face, I brushed these new tears away too.

"Please don't cry, Iz," I tried to smile through the wetness on my own cheeks but couldn't muster the strength. "You're gonna go to New York and you're gonna be famous. People are gonna be lining up just to get a glimpse of your work. I know it. They'll probably pay millions of dollars, too, just to be able to have a piece of it."

She laughed in spite of her tears and I swept my thumb across her cheek just so I could keep touching her for a little bit longer. She swallowed hard and with a tight nod, gingerly stepped backward, out of my grasp, and toward the door.

"I need to leave, Caleb."

"I know."

She backpedalled until our hands slipped away from each other and she was right at the front door. This was it and my heart thudded desperately in my chest just to prove it. She was really leaving now. And I had no one to blame for this but myself.

By the time the door opened, she turned back one last time with a devastated smile just barely touching her lips.

And as she sent me one last, soft smile, she stepped through the doorway and then she was gone.

I shuffled to the kitchen window to watch her rush to her car and tear out of the driveway. The blinds in the window slapped back down in place and I stumbled backward. My heart stuttered and then plummeted right into my stomach.

She was really gone. Just like that. Something that was never meant to last, but had irrevocably left its mark on me. I was forever altered. Forever scarred.

Things might've been different for us if I hadn't failed her so miserably. Because of my actions and my stupidity, the only woman I'd ever truly loved and would ever love, had just pulled out of my driveway for good.

I earned that.

It was that last dark thought that sent me digging in the pantry for the bottle of Jack I'd bought on impulse just a day before. I may have learned the hard way that booze and women didn't solve shit and didn't make that shit go away any faster, but because the blame rested solely on my shoulders here, I figured there was nothing wrong with torturing myself just a little more.

Before I could stop myself, my feet carried me back to the nursery and as I pushed open the door, I took another swig from the bottle for added liquid courage. I sunk down right across from the mural, half-finished and abandoned just like all my hopes and dreams. I shook my head at the irony and leaned my head back against the wall. This room was once filled with so much hope for our future, for our family...both of which, now, would never be.

She would've been such a good mom. *She was still going to be a good mom,* I thought bitterly. I'd just never get to see it. I'd never get to see any of it. Instead, I'd sentenced myself to a lifetime of unhappiness and emptiness.

My phone buzzed in my pocket and I scrambled to flip it open, irrational hope flooding me that maybe it was...nope. Just the club.

Church in 10.

I snapped my phone shut and slammed it down into the carpet. The clubhouse was the last place I wanted to be right now.

Church would go down just like every other time and the end result would always be the same. My life, my safety, and my freedom all at risk once again. Everything I'd ever done for the sake of the club ran through my mind—every bullet, every run, every crime, every day in prison. Always taking. Always wanting me to give more.

At this point, I didn't know what else there was to take.

Except the rest of my miserable life.

Hadn't I already given them enough? Every time they called, I was there. Anything they needed, I did it. And for what? So I could sit my sorry ass in prison for two years, so I could put my life on the line every single day, so I could lose the only real family I'd ever had all in the name of brotherhood.

Sure, they'd all paid their condolences when we lost the baby and promised to help us anyway they could, but the only time Marcus, Tiny, Casey, or anyone else had ever paid me a visit when I was inside was when they needed something. Whether it was inside information about a fellow inmate or to consult about new club business, they never showed up for visitation hours unless I could be of use somehow.

That's all I was. An instrument for their purposes and their plans. I had no real identity outside of the club. No other way to make money to support myself and my would-be family. And that was exactly the way they liked it. They needed me to be dependent on the club and all the while, they just poisoned my life with false promises of wealth, partying, and freedom.

I didn't care about any of that anymore. At the end of the day, the common denominator in all my problems was still me, but I'd shoved aside the other factor in the equation—the club. If the club had had their way, I'd still be in prison, but not just for something small-time like running guns. Nope. I would've wasted away sitting in a cell for murdering Becca and they all would've been completely fine with that if it meant their asses were safe.

I'd followed the club's orders blindly all my life up until that moment and in *this* moment, the fracture splintered deeper.

Somewhere along with the way, my priorities had shifted. Isabelle had always been an asset, but the club had become my weakness.

They didn't *really* care that I'd lost not just two years of my life, but the love of my life too. In fact, if circumstances had been different and Isabelle had made a deal with the ATF, they would've been chomping at the bit to get rid of her, just like Becca. And they would've expected me to pull the trigger, just like Eli, as part of my duty to protecting the club. They would've happily handed me the gun and helped me bury the body, too, if it meant they all stayed out of prison a little longer.

At the rate I was going, I'd be lucky if I made it to 30 before I ended up with a bullet in the head or another prison sentence.

Things would never change. I'd always be expected to stay on my leash, even if I ever did get that president patch. I didn't have it in me to want that anymore. The things I did want now? Those things were long gone and they were gone because of me and my involvement with the club. I'd lost myself in the club long ago and I didn't recognize this empty, broken person I'd become.

Then I heard Isabelle's voice:

"You're smart. You're resourceful. You could figure it out and I'd support you every step of the way."

I didn't know what other options I had two years ago because then, I was just another convicted criminal with a prison sentence hanging over my head. I was still just another ex-con trying to piece his life back together, but I had options now.

I might not have Isabelle or the family I thought we'd have together, but I didn't *have* to end up in prison again either. I didn't have to feed that endless cycle and fill my role as just another cog in the wheel. I didn't have to blindly follow orders. I didn't have to constantly put myself at risk, not if I'd get nothing but loss in return.

There had to be another currency besides bullets, guns, and violence.

My phone continued buzzing on the carpet next to me, but I ignored it.

And as my eyes memorized that half-finished mural, some hope finally began to take root. All my life I'd thought I was living on my own terms, but that couldn't have been further from the truth. Maybe there was still time to turn things around, maybe I could somehow earn back all the pieces of myself I'd lost, and maybe someday, Isabelle would come home to see it.

Part Two

Six Years Later

"Where thou art—that—is Home."
—Emily Dickinson

CHAPTER TWENTY
No Direction Home

Isabelle

"Oh, come on," I muttered and rubbed my temples as I flipped through the next page.

Seriously.

How was someone this smart *this* freaking unorganized? My dad had years, and I mean *years,* worth of documents, all of it really important right about now, just crammed in file folders. Some of the folders were labeled, some just randomly shoved in equally random folders in no particular order. He couldn't have at least put them in chronological order? Even a little bit?

I needed a bottle of Tylenol to go along with this monstrosity.

Cooper lifted his giant head off my foot and glanced at me side-eyed, as if to remind me I only had about another hour or so to chip away at the mess in my dad's office until he woke up.

"I know, Coop," I sighed and reached down to scratch between his ears. "Just bear with me, alright?"

The only real man in my life, aside from my dad, swept his tongue over my open palm and resumed his quasi-protective position at my feet.

With another sigh, I glanced at the clock and squeezed my eyes shut. We'd fallen into this daily routine too quickly: meds, nap, some TV, maybe a walk if he was up to it, more meds, another nap, some more TV, a little bit of eating here and there, and finally, lights out for the night. And in between the many naps he took throughout the day, I sat here in his office, mostly to get all our ducks in a row before the inevitable, but also just to keep myself busy.

I couldn't exactly let him watch me prepare for his death when he was awake, so I opted to get my work done while he was sleeping.

After a long road of rehabs and relapses, my dad's body finally gave out on him. While he'd fought it with everything he had left, the damage was already done. When you have stage four liver cancer with an undetermined expiration date, you're not exactly an ideal candidate for a transplant. And now, as his illness advanced every day, his doctor was just trying to keep him comfortable via a hospice nurse who visited us once a day.

In a way, waiting for this parent to succumb to illness was a little bit easier than the first. With my mom, I'd always held onto the hope that something would sweep in and save the day, like some experimental, miracle treatment that would kick the cancer right in the ass. Even at the end, I'd had to believe there was a chance, especially when my mom outlived her initial expiration date.

My dad was a different story. There was no hope now. There would be no miracle treatment or eleventh-hour liver transplant. It was almost easier to accept that it was going to happen no matter what.

Maybe, when I was younger, optimism wasn't just wishful thinking. When I was 20, when my mom first got sick, I hadn't yet suffered any major tragedies in my life. The idea that anything bad or even potentially fatal could happen to one of my parents, or to me for that matter, was completely out of the realm of possibility. Tragedies only happened to other people in my 20-year-old mind. Not to my family. Not to me.

Now my 30-year-old self knew better.

So, after getting the phone call that his illness had moved to the end stages, I dropped everything and practically sprinted from my brownstone in Chelsea to the airport. My dad, of course, fought me every step of the way, insisting I stay in New York where my work and my life was. Since he had no interest in even meeting with any doctors in New York and because he wanted to, and I quote, "die in my own home", my hands were tied. There was no way I wasn't coming back to North Carolina.

Then there was just that little issue of the ghosts, one in particular, still lingering here in town. And now that I actually was here in Claremont, there were only so many places I could hide in a town this small. Eventually, we would cross paths. All I could really do was avoid it for as long as humanly possible and hope that ghost just kept his distance.

I'd spent the last six years trying to convince myself that the life I'd had here was nothing but a distant memory. Now the memories, the pain, and the bitterness I'd fought so persistently to erase nagged at me like a scab that just wouldn't heal. Of course, it didn't exactly help matters that the one day a year I dreaded more than anything was just two weeks away.

So when the doorbell rang, I jumped in my seat. Cooper leapt up at the same moment, but wisely obeyed my loud *shush*. My heart was racing at the possibility that my thoughts had somehow made the inevitable materialize at my dad's doorstep. No, he wouldn't be that stupid. I'd already been in town for a week and there'd been nothing but silence between us, just like the entire six years before. Why would he bother now?

Despite my better judgment, I trudged over to the front door and opened it only to find Skyler Sawyer on the stoop with a covered casserole dish in her hands.

Even though I hadn't really seen the woman the entire time I'd lived in New York, she still looked like she hadn't aged a day. Whatever her secret to eternal youth was—a cream, a serum, a certain kind of lease on life—it just didn't make sense given the environment she surrounded herself in. How could all the worry, the stress, and the danger *not* age you?

Now, Skyler stood in my dad's doorway with those same black-lined eyes I'd used to know so well fixed on me. Her dark eyes softened the moment I opened the door and...I didn't know what I'd been expecting. Just a little hint of bitterness maybe? Some standoffishness? False concern? After all, I never called. I never saw her on the rare occasions I actually visited Claremont. She had every right to feel slighted, but if she did, she didn't show it.

"Hey honey," she called out to me softly with a sad smile on her face. "It's good to see you."

"Hi," I murmured, suddenly overcome with the reality that I hadn't really seen this woman in six years.

Skyler's eyes fell to my black lab, who sat at my feet. Cooper stared right back at her, watching her every move, but perceptive enough to know she wasn't anything he needed to be worried about. As far as I was concerned, she wasn't wearing enough leather to be considered a potential threat.

"That's some guard dog you got there," Skyler laughed uneasily. "Wow. He's huge."

I swallowed back the lump in my throat, gestured for Cooper to go upstairs, and nodded to the dish in her hand.

She just shrugged. "I wanted to come over sooner, but I didn't want to impose. I figured you'd need some time to settle in and didn't need me rushing over here like a bat outta hell."

Since my voice still wasn't working properly, I just nodded and made way for her in the doorway, gesturing for her to come inside.

"Well," Skyler soldiered on as we walked through the hallway and headed for the kitchen. "I'd ask how you're doing, but I think I already know the answer to that question."

I wished that wasn't so true and I still couldn't, for the life of me, figure out the right thing to say to her after all this time.

"I was hoping you'd call," Skyler sent me a kind smile as she set the casserole dish on the counter. "But I get why you didn't. Lexie's hoping to hear from you, too."

Just hearing her name had me wincing from the impact. Lexie's friendship was just another casualty of my past and just another thing I hadn't been able to hang on to in all my vain efforts to really move on with my life. I'd needed to cut myself loose completely when I left for New York and that, as much as it stung, also meant breaking ties with the people I'd really come to love like family.

Finally, I found my voice. "I figured that and I'm sorry I didn't. I guess I've just had a lot going on since I've been back, you know?"

Skyler nodded sadly and turned just for a second to put the dish in the refrigerator for me. When she turned to face me again, that somber, regretful expression still hadn't dimmed on her face. I guess I hadn't realized just how much I'd missed her until she was finally standing right in front of me again.

"How's he doing?"

I just shrugged. "He's dying, so there's that. But for the most part, he's still pretty alert. Everything just moves a little slower now."

Skyler blew out a deep breath and pressed another pained smile on her face. "I'm so sorry, Isabelle. I know you're probably sick of hearing that, but I really do mean it. If there's anything you need, anything I can do or the club can do, you know you can ask, right? That's all you have to do and we'll be there for you."

I bristled at the mention of the club and she picked up on that immediately, her eyes clouding ever so slightly as a frown creased her forehead. The club was the last thing I wanted to talk about. They weren't my family and they weren't my friends. Other than Skyler, Lexie, and Dom, they never really had been in the first place. And judging by the sad awareness in Skyler's dark eyes, she knew it too.

"I know it's not my place to ask," she paused for a moment and I didn't know why she even bothered because I knew what question was coming next. "Have you seen him since you've been back?"

It wasn't lost on me that even just the mere mention of him, let alone the fact she couldn't even bring herself to say his *name*, shifted a wave of darkness and tension in the air. From the little I'd let my dad tell me, Skyler, understandably and predictably, hadn't handled her son's decision with any decorum or grace. Instead, she'd chosen to fight him tooth and nail until it was really final, until it was actually done, and I guess the final blowout hadn't been pretty. All the rest of the club had seemed to handle it with various stages of disgust, disappointment, and acceptance. Skyler, on the other hand, raged a war and then wrote off her only living family member for what, in her mind, was the ultimate betrayal.

On some level, and given everything I knew about the woman, I couldn't really blame her for feeling that way.

Finally, I managed to shake my head. I couldn't say his name either.

"No," I told her quietly. "I haven't."

"It's probably for the best you two just keep your distance," she nodded tightly. "Trust me, it's easier that way."

I inhaled sharply and started chewing on my bottom lip because I just didn't know what else to do.

Skyler blew out another deep sigh and leaned back against the counter. "Sorry. I shouldn't even be...it just never really gets any easier. No matter how hard I try to really wrap my head around his reasons, I just can't. I mean, if he'd followed you to New York to try to work things out, I might've been able to understand. But he didn't. I just can't understand why he didn't."

There was a part of me, a deep, ugly, and bitter part, that thought the exact same thing more times than I was willing to admit. But I wasn't going to go there now, especially not in front of Skyler.

"Sorry," she told me again and winced, like just the *thought* of him hurt. I knew the feeling. "I'll stop talking about him. It's stupid. Once I start, I can't stop, you know?"

I didn't know because I never talked about him, but I gave Skyler what she wanted and nodded.

She shot me a kind, reassuring smile and then squeezed my shoulder. "You know, honey, I know you and I both wish the circumstances were different, but I'm glad you're finally home."

I flinched at that particular word. Home wasn't something I had associated with Claremont in a long time. My studio at the gallery was home. My brownstone in New York was home. My dad was home. Cooper was home. I'd be hard-pressed to find much in town here that I could truly affiliate with that particular noun.

"Well," Skyler clapped her hands together as she pushed off the counter. "I should get going. I didn't come over here to commiserate or make all this harder on you. I just wanted to—"

"I know, Sky," I reassured her and surprised us both by stepping closer until my arms closed around her shoulders just long enough to appease her. "Thank you for stopping by. I really appreciate it."

I let myself have this one moment as the woman I'd once loved like a mother held me tight. The feel of her arms, comforting me, embracing me, loving me, it all felt so familiar, but the problem was that it took me back to a place I couldn't go and even if I could, I didn't want to. It wasn't Skyler's fault, at least not directly, but letting her back in my life would be letting myself fall back into old habits.

It was just as well that she left quietly and with only a promise to bring back more casseroles if I wanted them. We didn't need to pretend we were something to each other that we just weren't anymore.

After checking on my dad and leaving Cooper to dutifully keep watch over him, I padded back down to the office with an odd sense of foreboding snaking down my spine. My body was on high alert, fully aware that while I'd been able to run, I still had never really been able to hide.

So, when I started flipping through yet another unlabeled folder only to come across a piece of paper that made my blood run cold, I probably should've seen it coming.

"You've got to be freaking kidding me," I muttered through gritted teeth.

At first, it took me a moment to realize just what this paper really meant. But after the fog lifted, there was little I could do to convince myself otherwise. The evidence was right here in my hand.

The contract was simple, straight-forward, and easy to follow. Just an average payment schedule with standard dates and figures laid out on the chart. And right at the bottom were two signatures: Samuel Martin and Caleb Sawyer.

From the looks of it, Caleb had been helping my dad make payments on the house for nearly two years.

Right after I'd learned his diagnosis, I'd asked him point-blank about the house—specifically, what he wanted to do with it. He'd told me to sell the house and keep the money. Not one word about money problems. Nothing about having trouble making mortgage payments. And certainly not a single thing about having any kind of contact with the one person he knew I never wanted to see again.

Just when I thought I had everything worked out, just when I thought my dad and I had really set our past behind us, this bullshit happens. Did he not trust me enough? Or did he just think I couldn't handle his illness and the house all at once? And then another terrifying thought gripped me. It was very possible my dad had known about his illness much longer than he was letting on and it was even more likely Caleb had known about it while I sat obliviously in the dark.

I just...I just so *pissed*. I couldn't even see straight. My hands were shaking as everything went a little hazy around me. Alarm bells sounded off in my head, but I went on auto-pilot, taking off down the hallway and skidding to the garage with my dad's keys in hand before I could really take a moment to catch my breath.

This might be one of the worst ideas I'd had in a long time, but I was on the warpath now. God help the man who got in my way.

. . .

The parking lot of Sawyer Custom Builds, lined with rows of motorcycles, trucks, and pristine, fresh pavement, wasn't even half-full yet.

This wasn't the plan.

This was the exact *opposite* of the plan.

And something about this felt awfully familiar.

In another life, I'd sat in a parking lot not so different from this one clenching my hands around the steering wheel until they turned white just like I was doing right now. Even then, I'd known I was on the precipice of something. I couldn't have known what would follow the moment I stepped foot on that parking lot all those years ago, but I knew better now.

Being older should've made me wiser. If anything, I'd just become more reckless because I had no business being here right now.

I'd told myself that I would never, under any circumstances, find my way to this parking lot during the entire time I was in Claremont, however long that was. I'd only held out for a week. No good could possibly come of this and yet here I was, the careless moth floating helplessly towards its irresistible, seductive flame.

At least I had the foresight to pull down the visor to look in the mirror before I started my inevitable descent into self-destruction. Since I took off from my dad's like a bat out of hell, I hadn't really stopped to consider the fact that I was showing up here after six years in an old pair of yoga leggings, an oversized tank top, and a rat's nest head of hair without a stitch of makeup on. Why it mattered that I slightly resembled a walker from *The Walking Dead*...I shook my head at myself in the mirror.

Nope. Not going there. And I definitely wasn't going to ruminate on how I knew *exactly* where the shop was without needing to cue up maps on my phone, not to mention just how many times I'd pored over the website or the fact that I'd chosen to drop everything and drive over here first instead of waiting to talk to my dad like a rational person. Instead, I raked my hands through my short, messy hair and called it good. This was about getting answers, finding a quick and painless solution to the problem, and nothing more.

With a deep breath, I pushed all the warning bells going off in my head aside and stepped out of my dad's aging BMW. My eyes drank in the building's clean, red brick lines, the bright blue curls around the 'S' on the sign directly above the shop, and as I got closer, dared to let my eyes wander deeper inside the open garage, where business certainly looked to be booming.

There had to be at least 15 separate projects going on inside the garage at once and even above the cacophony of machinery and music, I could still hear the muffled voices from inside—laughing, discussing, observing, and clearly enjoying their time spent here. Judging by first impressions alone, Caleb had built himself a thriving, professional business.

As I passed the garage's entrance, everyone else was so engrossed in their work they didn't so much as glance my way. But when the time came to actually pull open the office door, knowing full well who I was bound to find inside, I almost bailed and high-tailed it back to the car. Then I remembered why I was here, and surged ahead, swinging the office door open before I could stop myself and swallowed back another nasty taste of deja vu.

Two things assaulted my attention at once: neither of the two men inside were Caleb and, more disturbingly, the sketch I'd given Caleb years ago of his bike sat framed on the desk for anyone to see.

I froze right in my tracks, my eyes locked on the careful strokes of the stretch and I could practically see myself hunched over my old bed in my dad's house, working tirelessly through the night to get the lines perfect. I blew out a harsh breath and blinked a few times just to make sure my mind wasn't playing tricks on me.

Nope. It was still there. I wasn't going crazy, but right about now, I sort of wished I was. Then all this would make a little more sense.

A deep voice called out to me through the fog and my head jerked up at the sound. "Can I help you, miss?"

The owner of the voice, the taller, older of the two men—and who reminded me a little of an aging Denzel Washington with his salt and pepper beard and weathered good looks—smiled back at me politely. The younger one gaped at me for a long moment and then his dark eyes flashed as a slow smile crept across his face.

"Yeah," he grinned at me. "Please. Let us help you. Anywhere you want it. Seriously."

The older guy smacked him in the back of the head and shook his head at me. "I'm really sorry about that, miss. This one here," he jerked his thumb at the other guy, "hasn't really been housebroken yet. He doesn't play so well with others."

"That's okay," I shrugged, shifting from side to side on the checkered tile, uncomfortable with all this attention.

"Let's start over, okay?" he didn't wait for my response and gestured to himself. "I'm Saul. That idiot right there is Lucas. We would both be happy to help you however we can in a completely professional, non-threatening way. Right, Lucas?"

The younger guy ran a hand through his dark hair and grinned back at me sheepishly. "Right."

I gulped and winced. "Thanks. I'm, um, I'm looking for Caleb Sawyer. Is he here today?

Saul laughed a little before that smile dipped into a frown as he lifted a shoulder. "Of course he is. Where else would he be?"

Oh right. That made sense, considering the fact that Caleb, according to my dad, lived in a little apartment he'd built for himself right above the garage. Where else *would* he be?

"Right," I laughed and even though I did my best to mask the awkwardness and the nervousness, I wasn't fooling anybody, especially not myself. "I just really need to talk to him."

Saul eyed me carefully, like he was taking stock of everything, my demeanor, my intentions, all in under a second flat.

"Sure," he drawled with an easy nod. "I'll get him for you. Who should I say is looking for him?"

My fingers twisted into a tight knot. "You can just tell him it's Isabelle. He knows me—"

I didn't get a chance to finish because both men stilled in front of me, their eyes bugging out of their heads, and the pen Lucas was holding dropped to the ground with a loud clink.

"Holy shit," Lucas muttered under his breath and then he shot Saul a panicked glance. "I'm so dead."

Saul's expression, on the other hand, turned up until a slow, knowing grin spread across his handsome face. Instead of acknowledging Lucas directly, Saul just clapped a hand on his shoulder and beamed back at me.

"Well, Isabelle, it's great to meet you," he told me and that smile just seemed to get even bigger the longer we stood here. "I'm gonna go get the boss now. You just sit tight here."

With that, he winked at me and proceeded to push Lucas towards the door leading inside the garage.

"I can stay—" Lucas protested.

"Like hell you are," Saul murmured to him and just tightened his grip on Lucas's shoulder to shove him forward.

"Please don't tell him I—"

"Oh, you know I will."

Lucas paled, panic flooding his eyes, and he tried to turn around again, but Saul kept right on pushing. "Oh God. I'm dead. Make sure my mom and dad get what's left of my body, okay? I'd like to sort of be buried in one piece."

I didn't know if I was supposed to laugh at this pseudo-slapstick act they had going here or if I was better off just observing in stunned silence. Saul flashed me yet another grin over his shoulder as he finally shoved Lucas out.

"Don't mind us," he called over his shoulder. "Just hang on, okay?"

I smiled tightly and my chest started heaving right around the time the door closed behind them. This was it. Even if I bailed now, he'd still find out I was here. Mind as well suck it up and get this over with.

But the longer I stood here in the office—which, to be fair, probably wasn't *really* that long—the more that telltale tightening in my chest sent pricks of anxiety skating over me. Through some work, and admittedly, some medication, I'd somewhat conquered those good old panic attacks that seemed to sneak up on me at the most inopportune moments. Until now. Of course. It was just my luck. I'd barely gotten a handle on my shit when the doorknob turned.

I wasn't ready for this.

I didn't think I'd ever be ready.

All the time, distance, loss, tragedy, and heartache separating us faded for just one blinding moment. For that one moment, my heart stomped through the walls I'd built to keep it safe. For that one moment, my heart sang and leapt for joy.

And a moment later, Caleb walked through the office door.

Six years later and just one glimpse of him could still send every single one of my senses into overdrive. Focusing on the physical changes was all I was really equipped to handle: his hair was significantly darker and shorn close to his head. The scruff was still there, but had grown-out into a lazy goatee.

The leather cut he'd worn like a second skin was long gone. Instead, he wore a simple, if not slightly rumpled, white button-down with the sleeves rolled up at his elbows, exposing those familiar tattoos on his forearms, especially the upside-down compass I'd designed for him. There was a new one, too, right below the compass on his wrist, but I wasn't close enough to make it out, which was a good thing. And was he walking with a little bit of a limp, too?

Everything about him seemed more world-weary and more mature now. He was still just as handsome since the last time I saw him, but then that boyish, youthful charm had been right at the forefront. Now all of that had been replaced with the lethal and magnetic lure of a man.

And his eyes...they were exactly the same as I remembered. Deep oceans glittering with pain, a little bit of concern, some happiness, and most of all, that boundless, unconditional love I used to know. I could've swam around in those eyes all day, wading in their warmth and basking in their love. But that wasn't what I was here for.

His lips curled into that crooked grin that once had the power to make all feeling in my legs just disappear.

"Hey, Iz," Caleb murmured as his hand reached up to skim his buzzed head and it was then that the three letters tattooed right above his wrist finally became clearer.

Ava.

And just like that, I was right back where I started.

CHAPTER TWENTY-ONE
Ghosts

Caleb

At first, I wasn't sure she'd actually heard me. All she seemed to be able to focus on was my left wrist and as my eyes followed hers before finally resting on those three letters, my jaw clenched. Now, the dazed, bewildered expression in her deep blue eyes had me worried she might just up and bolt on me before I even had a chance to really talk to her.

Her beautiful mouth dropped open and then abruptly closed shut. She bit down nervously on her bottom lip and I would've given anything to reach out to her, even if it was only to just graze her arm.

She swallowed tightly and then finally, I heard the voice that only found me in my dreams, and sometimes, in my nightmares.

"Hi, Caleb."

I fought the urge to close my eyes at the sound of her voice and instead, stared back at her intently, willing her to keep talking. Anything just to keep her here a little bit longer. Anything just to be able to see her a little bit longer.

"Can I talk to you?" she asked me now and I didn't hesitate to nod immediately.

I only had a moment to really take her in, but if this was all I was going to get, I had to take it. At first glance, I almost didn't recognize her and it wasn't just her appearance. Her cropped blonde hair, with the front a little longer than the back, made me just want to run my fingers through it to see if it was still as soft as I remembered. The black yoga leggings and loose tank top showed off the body I'd missed, but there was something else that I couldn't put my finger on. Something harder about her that hadn't been there before.

The years we'd spent apart had only made her more painfully gorgeous and even though every second I spent watching her stung, I still couldn't pull my eyes away from her. I just couldn't help myself. She was like a balm to an open wound and suddenly, all my anxiety and all my underlying fear of what would happen when we actually came face to face just vanished.

She was here. She wanted to talk to me. And right now, that was all that mattered.

Suddenly, her hand abruptly dove inside her purse, pulled out a piece of paper, and then thrust it out to me. My fingers closed around it blindly and it wasn't until I glanced down that I realized she'd just handed me the contract I'd signed with her dad nearly two years ago.

"So I was going through my dad's office," she started a little unsteadily and raked a hand through her hair to shove it out of her face. "I'm sure you can imagine my surprise when I found that."

I just lifted a shoulder. I knew exactly where this was headed, but this was one argument she wouldn't win.

"Look, Caleb," she pressed on and my heart seized at the sound of my name on her lips. "I don't even know where to start with all this. I had no idea he...I mean, what happened?"

As much as I wanted to keep her here for as long as possible, the answer to that and all the other questions that would follow wasn't something I could give her. It just wasn't my place.

"Don't you think you should be having this conversation with your dad?"

She blew out an exasperated breath, perched her hands on her hips, and stared me down. This sure looked familiar. Still just as beautifully stubborn as ever.

"I'd like to talk to *you* about it right now if that's okay," she shot back.

I held my hands up in defense and cocked an eyebrow at her. "Alright. Fine. You wanna talk, let's talk."

"Good," she nodded tightly and gestured to the contract still in my hand. "Let's start at the beginning then. Why did my dad come to you for money?"

Again, that just wasn't a question I was in a position to answer for her.

"Honestly, Iz, I don't know."

Her eyebrows lifted in annoyance and I just shook my head at her.

"I mean, come on," I tossed the contract down on the desk, shoved my hands in my front pockets and rocked back on my heels. "It's not like your dad and me exactly have the best track record. I was just as surprised as you were. Okay, probably not as much, but you know what I mean."

She eyed me carefully and let her gaze drift down to tattoo on my wrist one more time. "Fair enough. But why did you even agree to it in the first place? I figured my dad would be the last person you'd ever want to help."

"He was worried about losing the house, Iz. What was I supposed to do? Tell him no?"

"You could've minded your own business, for starters," she replied coolly.

"Yeah, well," I shrugged. "He kinda made it my business when he came to me for help."

"You didn't have to say yes," her lips set in a firm line and then she squeezed her eyes shut with a shake of her head. "I'm sorry. I didn't come over here to fight or to be a bitch, even though I'm sure it doesn't seem like that to you. I just don't see what you could possibly have to gain by helping my dad make payments on the house."

"You're right. I don't have anything to gain," I allowed easily. "But that's not really why I did it either."

The truth didn't seem to sit well with her because she flinched at those words.

"*Well,*" Sam had told me when he'd shown up at my shop out of the blue two years ago. "*I know you won't tell me no.*"

I'd cocked an eyebrow at him, more than a little ticked he'd just walk in here and assume I'd even consider doing anything for him just because he asked.

"*Oh yeah? And why's that?*"

He'd just smiled at me. "*Because you love her. That's why. And because I think it's about time both of us finally figured out how to do right by her.*"

Coupled with the sucker-punch of his declining health, I would've moved heaven and earth, downsized the shop, sold off whatever I had to, and anything else I could possibly do to keep that house afloat. After that, my uneasy, but necessary alliance with Samuel Martin began. It wasn't about the money. It wasn't even really about the house. It was just about her. It was always about her.

"So what were the terms? You just make the payments until he dies? What happens then, huh?"

My eyes narrowed at her tone. "That contract was between me and your dad, but since I have a feeling you're not gonna drop this until you get what you want, the agreement is that after he passes, I'll sign my part of the house over to you and then you can do what you want with it."

Isabelle gaped at me like I'd just sprouted a second head. "You're just going to...*give* it to me? You're not going to let me pay you back?"

"No," I shook my head. "I'm not. Did you really think I would?"

She paled and sank down on the leather couch just a few feet away from her, putting some more distance between us, which only made me instinctively move closer. Her head fell into her hands and then she started murmuring so softly, I had to take a few more steps closer to the couch just to make it out.

"I had no idea he was having any money problems," she whispered. "Why wouldn't he talk to me about it? Why couldn't he have just gone to a bank? I don't understand any of this..." then her head shot up to meet me right in the eye. "He already knew he was sick then, didn't he? That's why he came to you for help."

That last part caught me off-guard. I didn't know exactly how long he'd been struggling financially, but I did know that within days of his diagnosis, he showed up at my shop looking to right some wrongs—almost a full year before telling his daughter he had cancer. Isabelle probably didn't need to know that and even if she did, I wouldn't be the one to tell her.

She also probably didn't really need to know that ever since we'd struck that deal, her dad made a point to stop by my shop a few times a month to 'catch up', as he called it, and sometimes, we even had dinner together, too. I had a feeling telling her all that would make her head explode.

"Iz," I started shakily, but she beat me to the punch.

"Don't even bother," she sighed and pushed herself off the couch. "I'm sorry for barging in here and demanding answers for something that didn't really have anything to do with you. And I appreciate what you did for him. I really do. I just wish you hadn't. I can't exactly write out one big check to you for what you've already paid, but I'll figure something out, okay?"

I appeased her for now and just nodded. I'd never take a cent from her and instead of telling her that, I dared another step closer to her just because I had no idea when I'd get the chance again.

She frowned at my movements and tilted her head a little to the side. "Are you limping?"

I glanced down at my legs and laughed a little. Sometimes, I didn't even notice the stiffness in my knee—it was just so familiar to me now I pretty much forgot it was there.

"Yeah," I grinned at her and scrubbed a hand over my head. "I, uh, got into an accident on my bike a couple years ago and pretty much landed right on my knee."

Her blue eyes widened and immediately fell to my legs again. "Were you —"

"I'm fine, Iz," I just batted a hand at her. "It could've been worse, you know? I wasn't paying attention, took a turn too fast, and skidded into the shoulder. My knee took most of the impact and I had to have surgery on it, but it's just pretty stiff now most of the time."

She nodded carefully, like she was still trying to digest all this new information.

"And, you know," I laughed again. This time it felt a little too forced even to my own ears. "I guess I'm lucky I knew a pretty decent bike shop in town that could handle all the repairs for me."

A slow smile spread across her beautiful face and my fingers itched to touch her. "Yeah, I guess that would come in handy."

I grinned right back at her, silently memorizing the way her lips curled up and the little wisps of blonde hair that kissed her shoulders.

Because I needed to stop openly staring, I gestured toward the door leading to the garage. "Do you want a tour? I've got plenty of time—"

"I should probably get going," she smiled somberly. "The hospice nurse is stopping over soon, so I should really get back before she gets there."

"Right," I nodded and shoved my hands back into my pockets to force them to behave. "Maybe some other time."

"Yeah. Maybe."

There wasn't much of a promise there, but I'd take it. Hell, I'd take anything she was willing to throw my way.

"I should let you get back to work," Isabelle whispered and when she started moving to the front door, I couldn't stop myself from reaching out to her.

The moment our hands touched, Isabelle jumped as if I'd burned her and tore her hand away. My hand dropped back down to my side, but I wasn't sorry I did it. I was just sorry my touch affected her this way.

"Iz," I exhaled and my heart twisted when her eyes finally met mine. "If you need anything, all you gotta do is ask."

She winced and just shook her head. "I don't know if that's such a good idea."

"Yeah, maybe not," I shrugged as I hustled over to the table and grabbed one of the shop's business cards so I could scribble on the back. When I handed it to her, she stared at the card for a little too long. Finally, she slipped it from my fingers and flipped it over to see what I'd written.

When her eyes snapped up to mine, I just lifted a shoulder. "That's my cell. And all the shop's numbers are on the front."

Since she'd without a doubt deleted my number a long time ago, I didn't feel the need to tell her I'd gotten a new number and a new phone after trashing my club-issued phone years ago. I also didn't really believe she'd actually use any of the numbers I'd given her, but that was beside the point. I just needed her to know I was still here.

She just smiled sadly. "I should go."

Swallowing back my defeat, all I could do was nod and watch her walk out the door one more time. I lifted a hand in an awkward wave and she shot me a pained smile before disappearing out the door. While I'd been holding out unfounded hope that we would cross paths while she was back in town, I had no idea it would be this soon or this excruciatingly difficult.

I wasn't sitting here waxing poetic about second chances at love, how my world revolved around her, or any of that sappy shit, but I also wasn't going to pretend that less than 10 minutes in her presence was only a painful reminder of how much I still loved her. Of how much I would always love her.

That last thought trailed after me as I walked into the shop to retreat into my back office where I could shut everything out, including the prying, curious eyes watching my every move like a hawk.

. . .

My chair creaked and groaned underneath me as I rocked back into the carpet, trying and failing to focus on the spreadsheets on my computer screen. Isabelle had been gone for at least 10 minutes now and I still hadn't recovered from the shock of seeing her. It was like a ghost had suddenly materialized right before my eyes, one who'd only haunted my dreams and my nightmares before today.

My eyes squeezed shut as the memory of my last dream about her washed over me. Just the night before, I'd tossed and turned in my apartment right above the shop before finally falling into a restless sleep. Surrounded by nothing but penetrating darkness, Isabelle's tear-stained face called out to me, reaching for me while some unseen force pulled her just out of my reach. No matter what I did, how fast I ran, or how loud I screamed for her, I just couldn't get to her before the darkness tore her away.

And just like every morning after I dreamt of her, I woke up with a panicked start, frantically searching the room for her. Nothing had been able to shake that feeling of desperate helplessness and I'd carried it with me for the rest of the day, feeling off-balance and nearly out of my mind. But the second Isabelle appeared in the office, it was like everything else just fell away. Just being within reaching distance of her again snapped a few of the missing pieces right back into place.

Part of me wished it hadn't been so instantaneous because what the hell was I supposed to do when she just left town again?

It was just easier to go about my day knowing she was in New York, living the life I'd always wanted her to have, and completely out of reach. Close proximity was a real bitch.

My fingers twitched on the armrests, itching for a cigarette, but I needed to do something productive. So I cued up a Google search on my computer, bypassing the real work I should've been doing instead, and like the stupid masochist I was, pulled up the website for the gallery that showcased Isabelle's work.

The Warehouse was the same gallery she'd interned at and like the smart, business-minded people they were, the powers-that-be there had wisely decided to forge a long-term professional relationship with her. I scanned on older blog post from a few weeks ago, one I'd already read more than once, that detailed the cancellation of an upcoming show due to 'family issues' and that Isabelle was taking a leave of absence indefinitely.

Her dad definitely hadn't been happy about that development, but like I'd told him, there was no point in reasoning with her. Isabelle was coming back to Claremont come hell or high water.

My eyes fell on the picture accompanying the post that highlighted Isabelle at her most recent gallery showing. Dressed in a black knee-length dress that hugged her lean curves, she laughed at something an admiring guest had just told her and the happiness and triumph in her glittering blue eyes was unmistakable, even in a picture.

I'd never get to bask in my happiness at her success or stand proudly next to her while guest after guest complimented her work. Instead, I was stuck creeping on her from behind my computer. And as I rubbed my eyes in disgust, it was just as well that a knock on the door interrupted this little pity party.

Before I had a chance to do or say anything, Saul poked his head in with a big smile on his face.

"So."

That was all I got as he stepped inside my office and leaned back against the wall with his arms crossed over his chest. The shit-eating grin on his face didn't budge and that pissed me off.

"So what?" I shot back testily.

His eyebrows waggled a little from side to side. "Interesting day, huh?"

I shot him a mirthless glance. "Sure. Whatever you say."

"Well," he shrugged. "It's not everyday a girl like that shows up around here. Especially, you know, considering she's the one who got away."

My jaw clenched and I promptly swiveled around in my chair so I didn't have to look at him anymore. There was no one I trusted or respected more than the man standing in this room, but right now, I kinda hated him too because I knew he was about to hand me a truth I wasn't quite ready to hear.

"I take it she found out about that little arrangement you made with her dad?"

"Yep."

"And she was pissed as shit just like you thought she'd be."

"Yep."

"So what happens now?"

I scrubbed a hand over my eyes and sighed exasperatedly. "I don't know, Saul."

"Well, instead of sitting here with your dick in your hand, you should probably figure it out, don't you think?"

The no-nonsense attitude was something he'd brought with him all the way out of prison and the only time I wished he wasn't so spot-on was whenever we talked about Isabelle, which wasn't often.

"She's not gonna be in town forever."

"I know that, Saul," I bit out through clenched teeth.

"Alright," he just shrugged again and pushed off the wall as he waved a hand in the air. "I'll leave you alone in here to sulk if that's what you really want, but I gotta tell you, she's exactly the way you described her. I can see why you—"

"You talked to her for what? Two minutes?" I cut in and cocked an eyebrow at him.

"I don't know. I like to think I'm a pretty good judge of character. Ah, but you already knew that."

Yeah. I did know that, which was part of why I'd trust him with my life if push ever came to shove. That intuition had a lot to do with why he'd recognized a kindred spirit in me and taken me under his wing in the library. The least I'd been able to do to repay his friendship and his guidance was offer the man a job when he'd gotten out of prison six months after me.

"And your girl's just as hung up on you as you are on her," he went on matter-of-factly. "Just figured I'd point that out and earn my paycheck around here."

I shook my head at him. "She's not my girl, Saul."

Not anymore at least.

"Sure, boss," he called over his shoulder. "Whatever helps you sleep at night."

Just as he got to the door, he abruptly spun around to face me again. "Hey, you know what Shakespeare said about fate? He said it's not in the stars to hold our destiny, but in *ourselves*. You remember that shit. It's good advice."

I narrowed my eyes at him right before chucking the closest thing I could find at him, which just happened to be a pen. Fucking Shakespeare.

Saul easily ducked out of the way with a laugh and smirked at me. "Ah. I hit a nerve. Figures. Oh, and before I forget to tell you, Lucas made a fool out of himself hitting on your girl before. Just figured you'd wanna know."

Something ugly and dark clouded my judgment and I shot up from my chair, stalked to the door and threw it open. It just took a quick scan of the garage to find my target and when I did, all the blood drained from his face and he started shaking his head furiously as Saul chuckled behind me.

"Hey, Lucas!" I barked across the garage.

He gulped and winced. "Yeah, boss?"

I grinned back at him maliciously. "Bitch duty for a month."

Lucas's eyes popped out of his head as a round of snickers echoed around the garage. "Wha—"

"Don't even start," I cut in sharply and jabbed a finger at him. "If that's the way you talk to all the female customers who come in here, you and I need to have a serious conversation."

Lucas shook his head furiously, but it was too late.

Another round of cheers and jeers passed around the garage as Lucas ran a hand over his face and swore under his breath while Jared, one of my mechanics, gleefully tossed him a broom.

With that business taken care of, I shut the door behind me again and sank down heavily back into my chair. I didn't even bother messing around on my computer anymore—I wasn't getting any work done for awhile.

Now, as I sat here in silence, I still had to shake my head in disbelief that I was even sitting here like this in the first place. It was sort of a miracle. No. It really *was* a miracle. And while everything professionally was going my way, personally, I was still in pieces. I'd accomplished almost everything I'd set out to do, but it wasn't enough.

Because the truth was, nothing felt right without Isabelle here next to me. Nothing felt complete. Nothing felt like it even really mattered. Even the triumphs and successes I'd achieved along the way felt deflated without being able to share it with her.

I knew, with clear certainty, that what I needed in my life was her. Seeing her again today just reinforced what I'd always known. I needed her support. I needed her guidance. I needed her love. I needed her to be my wife.

None of that was going to happen and no amount of wishful thinking would ever change it. I'd seized my own destiny long ago, shedding the chains that held me back and building something real for myself with my own two hands, but maybe it was for the best if I just accept that fate would never really be on my side. The stars, it seemed, still held a little of that control when it came to Isabelle.

Since nothing else was getting done, I unlocked the bottom drawer on my desk, pulled out my notebook, and flipped it open. I skimmed through the last entry I'd made the night before where I'd related the details of the new addition I was planning for the shop. I'd long switched to just keeping everything in a notebook since I never actually sent them, but it was a habit I'd never been able to shake. And I was okay with that.

So I put my pen to the paper and scribbled out the way I started all my entries:

Hey, Iz...

CHAPTER TWENTY-TWO
Familiar Territory

Isabelle

I gave my dad a full hour after the nurse left before I descended, which given the circumstances, was pretty damn patient. The nurse did her thing, checking all his vitals, and reminding me to pick up his prescriptions today and then she left.

Just another day in the Martin household.

When he finally settled down on the couch and flipped on the History channel, I knew it was time to strike. I swooped down, grabbed the remote out of his hand, and turned the TV off before he had a chance to even get a word out.

"Dad, we need to talk."

He shot me an exasperated, tired glance like he already knew how this was going to go down and sighed. "Alright, Isabelle."

"I found that contract you signed with Caleb."

He didn't even have the decency to look surprised. "Okay."

I blew out a deep breath, gritting my teeth in frustration. "You need to tell me what's going on and you need to tell me now."

My dad just lifted a shoulder. "Where would you like me to start?"

"How about at the beginning? You know when you got your diagnosis almost a whole year before you even bothered to tell me?"

"Well," he exhaled loudly. "I know you're upset and I understand that. I just didn't want to burden you with any more of my problems."

My heart twisted violently in my chest. "Dad, I—"

"No," he shook his head. "Just listen, okay? I waited to tell you because my doctor still wasn't sure if I could get on the transplant list. I didn't want you to get your hopes up and I didn't want you to be more upset than you had to be. I was just trying to spare you more pain, Isabelle, that was all."

I couldn't necessarily argue that if he'd told me earlier, we could've found out if I was a donor match sooner. It hadn't mattered because I wasn't a match. That alone was a shock—I'd completely expected to give my dad part of my liver because I just couldn't fathom any other alternative.

"*It doesn't matter anyway,*" my dad had told me when he'd finally been honest about his failing health. "*I did this to myself. I'd never risk your health to pay for my mistakes.*"

And as his doctor had explained with careful sensitivity, it wasn't uncommon for parents and children *not* to be matches for each other, which sent me spiraling down into a tornado of rage and grief.

Story of my life.

An endless black march of tragedy after tragedy and disappointment after disappointment.

"Look, Isabelle," my dad sighed as if he could read my thoughts and he covered my hand with his. "I've been a terrible father— "

"Dad," I cut in, ready to protest, ready to tell him it wasn't quite as awful as he remembered, even if it really was, but he just shook his head with a grim smile.

"I've neglected you. I've disappointed you. I've hurt you in more ways than I can stomach, let alone even think about. I didn't even really support your art and your talent until you were almost done at UNC. I think I was just too wrapped up in my own demons to really see what I was doing to my only family."

"Can we please focus on something else?" I squeezed my eyes shut. Hearing him list it all out like that brought back too many painful memories. He was right about everything, but what was the point in rehashing all these things that couldn't be changed?

"You're right," he nodded tightly. "We should focus on the time we have left and we will. But before we do that, I need to say this to you: it's taken me too long to figure out how to be a real father to you, the kind that loves and supports and protects you no matter what. And I wish the reasons for it were better than they were, but I thank God everyday we finally figured it out. I have so many regrets, Isabelle, and I don't want to die with them. I want to let them go, but I can't do that without your help."

I sucked in a harsh breath as tears pricked my eyes. This was just one more thing I wasn't ready for.

"Okay," I croaked through my tears.

"And I promise that me going to Caleb for money wasn't about manipulating either of you. After a while, my insurance wouldn't pay for any more rehab or counseling and I guess, when you consider how much I needed through the years, I can't really blame them. It all ate up my savings and I legitimately couldn't make the payments on my own. If I hadn't done something, we would've lost the house and after everything I've put you through, I didn't want to burden you with my debt. This house is all I have to give you after I'm gone and I want to make sure you get it."

For the life of me, I couldn't come up with a counter-argument, save for one little detail.

"I guess I can understand all that," I allowed carefully. "But I still can't understand why you went to Caleb. I mean, you've *never* liked him. The two of you could barely stand to be in the same room together. It just doesn't make sense."

"Well," my dad lifted a shoulder a little too nonchalantly for my liking given the topic of conversation. "I'll be the first one to admit I never thought he was good enough for you and I still think that's true when you first got together. Between his reputation and the club, I didn't want you anywhere near him. And I can still remember him threatening to throw me in an unmarked grave very, very clearly, even though he wasn't exactly wrong to feel to feel that way."

"So what?"

He just smiled at me. "I know you don't want to hear this, but I knew I was wrong about him right around the time he went to prison. And ever since then, he's done nothing but continue to prove me wrong because the cocky, womanizing kid with danger and guns trailing after him just doesn't exist anymore. Everything that scared me about him, how he might use you, how he might hurt you, how he might put you in danger, it's just not an issue anymore. He's a man now and a hell of a good one, too. I know you don't want to see it, but you also haven't been around to watch the changes in him like I have."

I didn't want to think about Caleb any longer than I had to, so I moved to wrap this up already. "Alright. Maybe he has changed. I don't really care about that. What I want to know is why you went to him and not me or a bank or any other option out there besides him."

Maybe I already knew the answer, but I was too far gone to back down now.

"I knew he wouldn't say no," he just shrugged.

Right. Even though he'd claimed he wasn't trying to manipulate me, I'd be an idiot not to think he was completely full of shit. He'd had plenty of other options, but he'd chosen the bank of Caleb Sawyer instead for one very specific reason that I couldn't say out loud. It would just hurt too much.

Not to mention the fact that he put that contract right where he knew I'd find it.

"Besides," my dad laughed heartily, showing a little bit of rare energy I hadn't seen in him for awhile. "He can definitely afford it."

I laughed in spite of myself and shook my head. "Yeah. Right."

"It's pretty amazing, isn't it? For him to do what he did, leave everything behind, and build that business from the ground up, not to mention make it actually successful. Talk about beating the odds."

My eyes narrowed. "Right."

I didn't need a history lesson. He'd already related the details as they went down and I didn't see the point in hearing them again. When I'd first heard he left the club, I just couldn't believe it. In fact, I'd thought my dad was flat-out lying to me. But after a little time passed, the evidence was too real to ignore. I never thought he'd actually do it, but somehow, he'd shaken the life that could've easily destroyed him, the same life that had destroyed us.

At the end of the day, I just couldn't understand why he'd go through the painful, and potentially fatal, process of breaking ties with the club just to set up shop here in Claremont. He could've gone anywhere and probably should have, but why the hell did he choose to stay *here*?

I'd be lying if I said him leaving the club hadn't sparked a glimmer of hope, as selfish as it was, that I hadn't thought about what would happen if he actually showed up in New York, free of the chains keeping him in a life neither of us deserved and ready for a second chance.

He never called. Never wrote me another letter. Never texted. Never reached out. And I was irrationally and foolishly bitter about that. It wasn't fair—after all, I left and I never called, wrote, or texted either and it was just as selfish as it was immature to assume his decision to leave the club had anything to do with me or why our relationship had crashed and burned the way it did.

All he'd done was given me the space I'd needed, but there was still something comforting about getting those letters in the mail. It meant he was thinking about me. It meant he cared about me enough to take the time to put his thoughts on paper for me, even if I never read them. It meant we were still connected somehow.

Yeah. I knew how insane that sounded. But when those letters stopped coming in the mail, it was really over. It all just felt so *final*. As if it wasn't over already. And I'd cried myself to sleep for a whole week after I realized I'd never see one of those letters in the mail again.

I guessed I just thought I meant more to him than that. I guessed I just thought he would fight a little harder for me.

Story of my life.

"Isabelle," my dad's soft voice ripped me out of those dark thoughts. "What I'm trying to say is that all I want is to see you happy and at peace. Let's face it, you haven't been either of those things in a very long time."

My eyes narrowed into dangerous dark slits. "And you think pushing Caleb on me is the solution?"

"That's not what I'm doing," he shook his head carefully. "I know that's exactly what it looks like, but you're 30-years-old. I can't fight your battles for you and I'm not sure I ever really did. I just think you and him have unfinished business and you'll never really move on until the two of you sort it out."

I gritted my teeth and huffed out an exasperated breath. Unfinished business my ass. As far as I was concerned, the only unfinished business between Caleb and me was the house.

"You know what, Dad?" I exhaled as I pushed myself heavily off the couch. "I think I need to go for a drive and clear my head. I need to pick up your prescriptions anyway. I'll be back in a little bit, okay?"

He nodded sadly. "Alright. I'll just...you know, be here."

I smiled in spite of our sad existence and headed back to the driveway where I'd parked the BMW.

. . .

Once I was rolling down the street, I cranked up the radio and just drove, which didn't exactly work out so well for me because each mile brought with it a new flash of an old memory—ones I'd previously cemented way up high in that compartment of my mind housing all my pain.

So going for a drive back-fired on me. Go figure.

Once my dad's many prescriptions were tucked safely in my purse on the passenger seat, I still needed to kill some time and found myself at a gas station right on the edge of town.

Driving around aimlessly and just as purposelessly had landed me right where I was and no closer to resolving this lingering frustration, confusion, and plain, raw heartache. What I needed was a distraction and as I pushed through the door and the cashier, the same one who'd worked here for years, smiled at me with happy surprise.

"Hey, Isabelle Martin! I heard you were back in town. It's great to see you!" he waved to me.

"Hi, Denny," I smiled back weakly. "It's good to see you too."

I started my trek toward an aisle before he could jump even deeper into conversation. He was a sweet old man, but I just wasn't here to chat. All I wanted to do was walk around and for some reason, I'd picked this gas station today.

I walked laps around the gas station in a fog right up until the bell over the entrance chimed and three leather cuts walked in the door.

All the hairs on my arms stood on end and I nearly dropped the bottle of Mountain Dew I was holding. Instead, I clenched my hands around it, willing myself to stay hidden somewhere, that maybe they were like the dinosaurs in *Jurassic World*—maybe if I didn't move, those predators wouldn't be able to see me.

When I finally turned my head to get a better look at them, my eyes widened. Those were no Horsemen cuts. Instead of a fiery, devil-eyed black horse stitched onto the back, a skull wielding a machete laughed in my face.

Warlords.

They were a long way from Pittsburgh...what the hell were they doing here?

It'd been a long time since I'd been anywhere near a leather cut and I'd forgotten just how powerful one could be. Everything stopped in that gas station the second they walked inside. Denny stood at attention, watching their every move with fear in his eyes and the two other patrons inside were doing exactly what I was: trying to stay hidden and out of view. My fingers dipped inside my purse to brush my knife just to remind myself it was there.

Living in New York had taught me to take precautions because you just never knew what might happen to a single girl living in a big city. Keeping a knife and my mammoth black lab on me at all times, not to mention taking self-defense classes with my PR girl from the gallery, gave me the little bit of security I needed to feel safe living on my own. I'd just forgotten I wasn't necessarily safe in a small town like Claremont either.

Suddenly, one of the Warlords rounded the corner, heading right for me. I sucked in a breath and pretended to read the label on the back of my Mountain Dew and this man, with his shiny bald head, stocky build, and roguish smirk, wasn't convinced.

"Excuse me, miss," he told me with a wink as he side-stepped around me to get to the beer section.

My heart pounded furiously in my chest as I watched him reach up with a tattooed forearm to grab a six-pack from the highest shelf. I got an eyeful of his president's patch and quickly turned my head before he could catch me staring. Without another glance around the store, I walked to the front as calmly as I could. The last thing I needed was to draw unnecessary attention to myself and putting my soda back and hightailing it out of the store would do just that.

I set my soda on the counter smiled tightly at Denny, whose eyes met mine for just a moment before flicking back to the three leather cuts behind me.

"You okay, Isabelle?" he asked me quietly.

I nodded right away and when I turned my head ever-so-slightly to my left, the Warlords' bald president was staring right back at me with narrowed eyes.

Denny's gaze flew to where mine had been only to find the Warlords' president murmuring lowly to his two minions.

"Maybe you should wait until they leave," Denny whispered to me.

"It's fine," I laughed a little, trying and failing desperately at any ounce of normalcy.

This was just paranoia. That's all it was. They couldn't possibly know anything about me, especially since I'd never seen any of those men before in my life. I just knew enough Horsemen history to know I didn't want to be anywhere near them, let alone any other club affiliated with them. But the longer I stood there, the more I felt those calculating grey eyes seize me like a shark circling its prey.

Yep. Time to get the hell out of here. I finished paying, grabbed my soda from the counter, and despite Denny's quiet protests, hightailed it back into the parking lot and didn't stop until I locked myself inside my dad's car.

But when I put the key in the ignition, a funny thing happened. The fucker wouldn't start. I just kept turning and turning, willing the stupid piece of junk to pull its shit together, and jumped with my heart in my throat when someone rapped on the driver's side window.

The Warlords' president grinned back at me through the glass and gestured with a ringed hand toward my ignition.

"Need some help?" he called out through the window.

I shook my head and plastered on a smile. Maybe if I was polite, he would just leave me alone.

"I'm alright. The engine takes awhile to turn over sometimes."

It wasn't completely a lie, but right now, I was all about getting those leather cuts back on their bikes and as far away from me as possible.

"You sure? I could, you know, give you a ride somewhere or somethin' if you need. It'd be my pleasure."

I just batted a hand with a tight smile and pushed away whether or not that offer was a thinly-veiled threat.

"Nah. I'm good. If I can't get it started, I'll just call my dad," who wouldn't be able to get me since I was currently sitting in our only mode of transportation, but the president of the Warlords MC didn't need to know that.

"Alright," he shrugged. "Suit yourself then. Just tryin' to do my good Samaritan act of the day. Good luck to ya, Isabelle."

My eyes flashed at him in surprise and he just winked before cocking two fingers at me in a mock-salute as he backpedalled toward his bike. I held my breath until all three swung their legs over their bikes, revved the engines, and left the parking lot. As soon as they were down the street and out of view, I blew out a deep breath and leaned forward until my head rested against the steering wheel.

I turned the ignition again. And again. And again. And again. And again. Finally, I had to admit defeat.

Of all the random, terrible luck...

Before I could stop myself, I dug into my purse for my wallet and pulled out the business card I'd tucked away for safekeeping. And then just as quickly, I shoved it right back into my wallet. Thinking about calling him was a disastrous idea. Actually going through with it would be an abysmal dive head-first into Crazy Town.

So I chose the lesser of the two evils instead.

I only had to wait about 10 minutes before a Sawyer Auto Repair tow truck pulled into the parking lot. And I guess, given the way my day was going, I really shouldn't have been surprised to see Dominic Fletcher climb out of the truck with his blue work shirt on.

Three blasts from the past all in the span of less than five hours? I was on a roll today.

"Hey, Isabelle," Dom waved to me with that kind, familiar smile on his scruffy face. "I heard you're having some car trouble."

"Hi Dom," I nodded to him as he closed the distance between us. "You heard right."

He shocked the hell out of me by pulling me into a tight bear hug and releasing me just as quickly. "Long time no see, right?"

"Right," I laughed. "It's good to see you, Dom."

A wide smile spread across his face. "It's good to see you too. Man, you're a sight for sore eyes. I just wish it wasn't under such shitty circumstances, you know seeing as how you're sitting here stranded in a parking lot, right?"

"Right," I nodded again.

That was the thing about Dom. He'd always been the quietest one in the room, but because of that, he was also the most observant and most perceptive one, too. He saw what everyone else didn't and him bypassing any mention of my dad was right in line with everything I knew about him.

He gestured with his head toward the car and in no time, he popped the hood and stuck his head under to inspect the damage.

"Well," he glanced at me from underneath the hood. "From the looks of it, your starter's shot."

I winced. Shit. That sounded bad. And probably really expensive.

"Don't worry," Dom laughed. "It's fixable. I just have to get it to the shop before I can do that for you."

"Okay. Thanks," I nodded and chewed on the inside of my cheek, trying to think of the best way to say what I needed to tell him. In the end, there was no sugar-coating it. "I saw some of the Warlords when I was in the gas station just now."

Dom's head shot up from underneath the hood of my dad's car, suddenly colder, tighter, and with more edge than the easy-going, kind guy I was used to seeing. "What happened?"

"Nothing really," I lifted a shoulder. It was difficult to explain just how threatened I'd felt when nobody had really done anything that could be defined as threatening. "They just made me really uncomfortable, especially since they knew me. I mean, I've never seen any of them before, especially not the president—"

"Wallace was there?" Dom cut in sharply, his hands clenching around the edge of the hood until his knuckles turned white.

I nodded.

"Did he say anything to you?"

"He just asked me if I needed help when my car wouldn't start. It wasn't really a big deal...he just scared me."

That was all Dom needed to hear. He promptly directed me to the truck's passenger seat and made quick work of loading my dad's car onto the truck, all the while scanning the roads with an eagle eye and talking to someone on his phone. It wasn't until we were finally on the road that I realized he wasn't taking me in the right direction. Or, more specifically, not in the right shop's direction.

"Dom."

He shot me a sideways glance. "Sorry, Isabelle. I don't have a whole lot of options right now. I need to get to the clubhouse now and you need your starter fixed. It's just a means to an end for both of us."

"If I remember correctly, the shop you're taking me to doesn't exactly service BMWs."

Dom grinned at me with a hearty laugh. "Yeah, well, Caleb knows how to replace a starter on a car. Trust me, helping you out won't be a problem for him."

At this point, I figured I'd do us both a favor and changed the subject to something a little more user-friendly.

"So," I started easily. "You're the big VP now, huh?"

"Oh, you heard?" Dom laughed. "That's sorta old news, isn't it?"

"I haven't seen you in awhile," I reminded him, a sad smile crossing my lips. "Is it everything you hoped it would be and more?"

I'd meant to inject some lightness into the conversation, but all that comment did was send a deep line into Dom's forehead.

"It's alright," he allowed slowly. "I can't say I mind the status. A little extra money never hurt either. It's kinda weird though, especially since I never thought I'd actually get the VP patch until Caleb was..."

He trailed off, and for a moment, the silence was deafening. None of our lives had turned out the way we thought they would, but then again, did anyone's? If someone had told me eight years ago I'd be right where I was and that Caleb would be where he was, and that we wouldn't be in those places together, I would've wanted to punch that person in the face for even *suggesting* life could go any other way than according to plan.

I couldn't take the silence anymore and seeing as how I was trapped in this truck and heading right back to where I'd been just a couple hours ago, the least Dom could do was give me some answers.

"Do I have anything to worry about?" I asked him quietly. "How would that guy even know me? Would he know Caleb and I used to..."

I trailed off, unable to finish that last sentence and, luckily, Dom jumped in to fill in the blanks for me without dwelling too much on the past.

He pushed out a rough sigh and glanced at me from the corner of his eye. "I'm gonna spare you the details, but things between us and the Warlords have been pretty tense for awhile. Pretty much since we got out of prison. Wallace was there that day we made the exchange and all of us got our stupid asses arrested and ever since then, things have been escalating. It's all been really subtle, petty kind of shit these last few years, but ever since he got the president patch six months ago, we've had some problems."

My eyes narrowed and even though I didn't really want to know the answer, I had to ask anyway. "What kind of problems?"

Dom shot me a tight smile. "Not the kind you're thinkin' of, or at least not yet. Wallace is smart. And resourceful, too, especially since he's been systematically shutting down our business contacts pretty much the day he got the gavel. We've been bleeding in the red for months. Every time we take one step forward with a new business contact, Wallace steps in and either offers them more cash or the kind of muscle we just don't have. We don't have a leg to stand on, even when we retaliate."

Thankfully, he didn't divulge those particular details.

"Why would he do that though? That just seems really extreme to have that kind of vendetta over, what? A two-year prison sentence? He probably didn't even get that much because he didn't cross state lines like you guys did."

It was strange to talk about Caleb's arrest so openly and when a thin, grim line crossed Dom's face, I knew this conversation was just going to keep heading south.

"We heard some rumors about Wallace. I don't know how true they are, but it sure as shit explains what he's doing. Apparently, Wallace had a sick kid when he went inside and another one on the way. With him gone, his wife couldn't afford all the hospital bills and she lost their house. I heard his older kid, the sick one, died before he got out, but I don't know if that's true or not. Anyway, by the time he did get out, his wife had filed for divorce and took off with his kids halfway across the country and won't let him see them."

I blew out a deep breath and shook my head. Well, if even part of that was true, it certainly explained the vendetta. Now Theo Wallace also had the power to put some real clout behind it. And then a terrifying thought gripped me.

"He blames you and Caleb for everything, doesn't he? It doesn't even have anything to do with the club."

Dom scratched his beard in thought and sighed heavily. "I suppose if I were in his shoes, I'd probably feel the same way."

The whole thing from start to finish was just so *awful.* Everyone involved in that arrest had lost something and now, everyone involved was still paying for it one way or another.

"And Caleb knows about all this, right?"

Dom nodded tightly. "We keep each other updated, yeah."

"Okay," I allowed. "But you still haven't answered my question. Should I be worried? Should I talk to my dad? I mean, if this guy—"

"Like I said, Isabelle," he cut in quietly. "Wallace is smart and he's resourceful. I'm sure he knows everything there is to know about every single current and former member of the club, including the people we love."

I bristled at that last part, but Dom charged on.

"But I also don't believe he'd go after my wife and kid or you, for that matter. He's attacking the club, not me or Caleb directly. I think if he did wanna do that, he'd be doing more than just offering to help you when you're having car troubles. He's never come within a mile of Lex or Chloe either."

That you know of, I thought darkly.

"And besides, we're on it. Wallace won't be an issue pretty soon if he keeps going after our business the way he has."

Again, Dom thankfully didn't dig any deeper. I didn't need to know and I didn't want to know either. So I changed the subject instead and immediately regretted it.

"I know you said you've been talking about all this stuff, but do you ever see him? Are you two still...."

And again, I couldn't bring myself to finish that sentence.

Pain flashed across Dom's face for just a moment and disappeared just as quickly. "Not really, no."

"I'm sorry."

He just lifted a shoulder. "It is what it is, you know? He made a decision and I have to respect it. He stays on his side of town and I stay on mine."

"That's pretty generous of you. Just from what my dad told me, it sounded like you were the only one that actually did accept it."

"Yeah, well," Dom smiled at me briefly. "If what happened to you guys had happened to me and Lex, especially the *way* it happened, I can't say I'd make the same choice, but I understand why he did what he did. I just wish it didn't have to come to that."

And on that note, it was probably for the best for both of us that he pulled up into Sawyer Custom Builds another moment later. This conversation had taken an uncomfortable, personal tone too quickly and as much as I'd always liked Dom, he was just one more piece of my past I needed to keep buried.

"Well, this is your stop," he told me lightly, but I was too busy focusing on Caleb to really hear him.

My body just didn't know what to do—did it want to run toward him or away from him? Leap into his arms or smack him? This push and pull only left more heartache and confusion in its wake and I was already sick of it.

Despite all that, I couldn't take my eyes off him even as Dom climbed out of the truck and headed to the office. Caleb was standing just outside the door with Saul, Lucas, and two other guys wearing Sawyer Custom Builds work shirts, all of them with cigarettes in their hands. It wasn't so much that he was still smoking that had me rooted to the passenger seat; it was the fact that the second he saw me sitting in the truck, the cigarette in his hand sailed through the air until the burning cherry landed on the concrete.

The gesture was so familiar it hurt.

That momentary paralysis still didn't prevent me from sliding out of the truck and making my way over to the small group assembled in front of the office. We'd clearly interrupted a smoke break, but that seemed to be the furthest thing from Caleb's mind as he concentrated on what Dom murmured in his ear. His eyes widened and then flashed with something I couldn't quite place. It wasn't worry. It wasn't quite anger either. Maybe I didn't really want to spend too much time decoding that; I had a feeling I wouldn't like what I found.

Caleb shook Dom's hand with a tight, albeit appreciative smile as I approached the office door.

"Don't say I never did anything for you," Dom told him lowly and then winked at me before clasping a hand on my shoulder.

"Give Lex a call, alright?" Dom called out to me as he backpedalled to the tow truck. He didn't wait to hear my answer, but I waved anyway. Unfortunately, we both knew I probably wouldn't be calling her.

Now that I'd joined the group, Saul took one second to grin broadly at me and then pushed Lucas and the other two guys into the garage. Caleb shoved his hands deep into his front pockets as his eyes followed them and then, when his gaze flicked back to me, that lopsided smirk that seemed burned into my memory curled his lips and something inside me curled up too.

"Hey, Iz," he murmured.

I sighed and pushed some hair out of my face in defeat. "Hi, Caleb."

"You okay?"

"Yeah," I frowned. "Why wouldn't I be?"

His eyebrows lifted in surprise and it took me a moment, but yeah, there it was. Just being within reaching distance of him again had momentarily short-circuited my brain and I'd completely forgotten the pseudo-run-in I'd had before.

"It wasn't a big deal," I recovered quickly. "Dom told me not to worry about it."

Caleb nodded slowly and his eyes shifted to the cement at his feet for just a moment. "I'm sorry that happened. That's the first time any of the Warlords have been seen in town since Wallace took the gavel."

"I guess I was just in the wrong place at the wrong time," I shrugged nonchalantly.

His frown only deepened and when his lips parted, he surprised me by changing the subject completely: "So it looks like I'll be replacing that starter for you."

"Yeah," I narrowed my eyes at him. "It looks like it."

Right away, I picked up on two things: he clearly planned on doing all the work himself and also, knowing him, he clearly planned on doing all that work for free. I didn't get a chance to call him out on that though because just as I was gearing up for another fight, he unearthed a hand from his pocket and tossed me a pair of keys.

"You better hang on to those," he told me as I caught them. "You're gonna need something to get around until I get it fixed. It might take awhile to get the parts I need, too."

I glanced down at the keys in my hand. I didn't like where this was going. "These are your keys, aren't they?"

His grin only widened. "My truck keys, yeah."

I tossed the keys right back at him. "I'm not taking your truck."

He caught them in one hand and sent them flying my way again. "Yes, you are. I've got my bike. I can get around just fine without my truck. Besides, I don't really have anywhere else to be except my shop anyway. And you're not going to rent a car or take a cab anywhere. Just take my truck."

"But—" I started, but he never let me gain any traction.

"What if I said I'd let you pay me in full?"

"For the house or the starter?" I shot back.

Caleb's lips twitched in amusement. "The starter. You take the truck and I'll charge you all the way. Labor, parts, everything."

He had me there. If I rented a car or took a cab, he wouldn't let me pay for the work. Shit. He knew me too well. God, I was really sick of men. Every single one of them. They'd been nothing but a pain in my ass today.

"I really hate this just so you know," I told him through clenched teeth.

"I know you do," he grinned.

I jabbed a finger at his chest. "And if I find out you gave me a discount or conveniently left something off my invoice, you and I are going to have some serious problems."

That smile, the same one I saw in my dreams, the same one that used to melt me down into a puddle at his feet...that smile just curved up the side of his mouth and sent me plummeting down to the concrete.

CHAPTER TWENTY-THREE
Word Vomit

Isabelle

"It's okay, Dad," I rubbed his back soothingly as he heaved into the toilet bowl. "I got you."

He squeezed his eyes shut, leaned back to ready himself, and then dove headfirst into the toilet once more. Cooper, who'd been perched just a foot away through the whole ordeal, inched forward until he could rest his head on my dad's shoulder to offer him as much comfort as he could. My dad rubbed Cooper's huge head in slow, exhausted movements before throwing his head back in the toilet one last time.

All I could do was rub his back and pretend my eyes weren't stinging. Every day it just got worse: the nausea and vomiting from the cocktail of meds he was on, the weakness and lack of energy, the appetite loss and subsequent weight loss. He was withering away right before my eyes. Deteriorating into a shell of his former self. Again. And here I was, helpless and desperate to help him any way I could. Again.

The more things changed, the more they stayed the same.

Every day he moved a little slower, ate a little less, and slept a little more. Every day brought us closer to the end. Every day tore me apart just a little bit more. Every day I just wanted to run away. Maybe then I wouldn't have to face all this bullshit and maybe, when I finally came back, everything would magically be good again. My dad wouldn't be dying. My life wouldn't be one epic, pathetic mess. Maybe I'd actually figure out how to be happy again.

But for right now, my focus was getting my dad off the bathroom floor and back into his bed where he could rest and hopefully, get a little peace for himself, too. I pulled with all my strength to get us enough momentum where he could slide to his feet, but I just wasn't strong enough.

What you need is an extra pair of hands, I thought. *Maybe a little back-up.*

I could do this—I had to. There was no else. So I gritted my teeth and lifted him up by the shoulders, but his body just slipped out of my grasp and back down to the floor with a soft thud.

"Come on, Dad," I whispered in his ear as I gripped underneath his shoulders. "Gotta get up, okay?"

He nodded weakly and squeezed his eyes shut. Then with a surge of whatever strength he had left for the day, he pulled himself off the floor with my help and together, we shuffled stiffly down the hallway until I could help him get into bed. After I tucked him in and leaned in just once to remind myself he was still breathing, I closed his bedroom door behind me with Cooper right at my side.

I leaned back against the door and my head fell into my hands. My breath came in and out in haggard, rough spurts and my shoulders heaved against the door. I didn't know how much more of this I could take. I knew this was going to be hard, but I never thought it was going to be *this* hard. This devastating. This excruciating.

It was never going to get better. He was just going to keep fading away until there was nothing left. And I would sit here until the very end, holding his hand and praying we had more time.

Then a wave of guilt washed over me.

All I wanted was more time with him while he was suffering. It was so selfish it wasn't even funny. Wanting him to finally find some relief, that it wouldn't take too long, and yet, hoping the end wasn't here just yet. I wanted to let him go, I *knew* I needed to let him go, but I just wasn't ready yet.

I covered my face with shaky hands and inhaled sharply. I couldn't do this. I couldn't sit here in this house filled with so much sickness and suffering and imminent death. And tomorrow...tomorrow was the day I dreaded more than any other day in the entire year. Tomorrow I might as well not even bother getting out of bed.

The walls seemed to be closing in on me and just as suddenly, the hallway spun, but my feet were still rooted to the carpet with my hands tingling numbly around the scruff of Cooper's neck. I couldn't move. Terror gripped me. Panic smothered me. And then my legs gave out on me as I sank weightlessly onto the floor, clinging to my dog like my life depended on it.

This feeling of debilitating powerlessness was a familiar one, but this was the first serious panic attack I'd had in a long time. The first real one I'd ever had had happened after Padilla's break-in eight years ago and they'd never really left me since then. In fact, they'd only gotten worse right around the time I moved to New York, which, in retrospect, didn't really make sense considering that entire move was centered on taking control instead of losing it. In between then and now, I thought I'd had it under control. Therapy, some counseling, Cooper, and medication had seen to that. Then I found out my dad was sick.

With slow, focused breaths, my eyes flitted shut and finally, some oxygen started flowing through my lungs. I could breathe again. They never lasted that long and after one more deep inhale, I pulled my shit together and got up on my feet. The walls didn't seem quite as suffocating as they did before and my hands weren't clammy and tingly anymore, which was all a good sign that one had passed.

But I was still terrified. Still plummeting toward something I couldn't stop and couldn't control.

"Hey, Coop?" I murmured hoarsely into his fur.

His ears perked up at the sound of my voice and his big, brown eyes watched me intently, waiting for direction.

"Wanna go for a car ride?"

. . .

"What are you *doing*?" I muttered.

I shook my head at this stupid recklessness that found me here once again. After driving around aimlessly for an hour, something snapped. Ridiculously and impossibly snapped. This was the last place I should be and the only place I really wanted to be.

Cooper glanced at me out of the corner of his eye, gave me one more chance, and then pounced, nearly knocking the drinks all over the center console of Caleb's truck. Ugh. Now I just needed to get out of this truck.

After two weeks of driving this thing around, I really should've been used to it, but every time I opened the door, the familiarity curling around it was almost too much to bear. He had a newer, fancier truck since I last saw him, but it wasn't that. It was just him. Everywhere and in everything. The presets on the radio. The pine air freshener hanging from the rear view mirror. The Harley Davidson sticker in the back window. Even the color, a deep, magnetic blue, was all him. I hated it. And yet, I was still driving the damn thing around, wasn't I?

I gave Coop what he wanted and let him out, wincing as he took off for the closest patch of grass, which just happened to be right in front of the office, and proceeded to piss all over it.

"Nice, Coop," I grumbled. "Way to make a first impression."

From the looks of it, nobody was in the office to notice Cooper's little display. Lucky me.

To be fair, Caleb had no idea I was coming. *I'd* had no idea I was coming up until about five minutes ago. Somehow, I'd just sort of found my way here, starting with my aimless drive around town and ending with me standing in Sawyer Custom Builds' parking lot with a bag of take-out in one hand and a tray of drinks in the other.

I hadn't seen him since my dad's BMW took a shit and I'd had that fun little run-in with the Horsemen's current nemesis, but he'd called my dad's cell phone three times during these last two weeks. Once to quote me a price, which I still didn't trust was completely thorough, and the other two times to give me an update on the status of the parts and progress on my dad's car.

It was just easier that way. If we kept our distance and stayed behind our carefully-drawn lines in the sand, we could each just continue on as normally and as civilly as possible. All that, of course, completely flew in the face of my current predicament. Not to mention I was still sitting here wondering just *how* he had my dad's cell number. I had a feeling the answer to that might make my head explode.

Just like the last time I'd found my way here, every single person inside was engrossed in their work. Chrome plates littered each worker's individual work space, others were welding in the corner, another pair of workers were hand-painting decals onto the length of some chrome, tires were being replaced, and in another corner, an entire engine sat on a desk as one of Caleb's employees unscrewed a piece of it. It was all so efficient and organized. Everyone in their own area and playing their part, rolling along like a well-oiled machine.

A low whistle sounded from above my head and it took me a moment to find the source. Caleb leaned over a railing with his elbows on the ledge, grinning down at me with just a hint of surprise and confusion in his eyes. Without any other hesitation, he started down the flight of stairs, which I imagined could only lead to his apartment above the shop.

"Hey, Iz," he exhaled when we were finally standing face to face. "What's up?"

I gingerly lifted the bag of food and drink tray in my hands. "I thought I'd bring you lunch. Unless you ate already...?"

His eyebrows furrowed as his eyes dropped to my hands and back up to me again. I couldn't really blame him. I didn't know what I was doing here either.

"Nah, I didn't eat yet," he rocked back on his heels and tilted his chin toward the bag of food with a smirk. "Whatcha got in there?"

"Fast food," I shrugged. "I figured if I cooked something, you'd be too afraid to eat it."

His lips twitched in amusement. "That sounds about right."

I just rolled my eyes at him and held out the drink tray, which he took wordlessly from me. That was right around the time Cooper remembered he was technically supposed to have my back as he padded over to me, sat on his haunches at my feet, and eyed Caleb up curiously.

Caleb's eyebrows lifted as he quietly observed Cooper lean into me and raise his left paw up for Caleb to shake.

"Geez," I muttered under my breath.

With his eyes glittering, Caleb crouched down to Cooper's level and shook his paw.

I rolled my eyes and gestured to my dog. "Caleb, meet Cooper. Cooper, Caleb."

When you put their names together so closely—nope, not going there. Subconsciously or not, their names had nothing to do with each other and that was what I just had to keep telling myself.

Caleb dropped Cooper's paw so he could scratch in between his ears and I thought I saw Cooper's eyes roll back into his head. Just great.

"Hey there, buddy," Caleb murmured to him. "You been taking good care of her, right?"

My eyes dropped warily to my dog, who was looking at Caleb like he hung the moon and the stars as long as he just kept scratching him like that. "It kinda defeats the purpose of having a guard dog when he just walks up to every stranger he meets like they're his best friend."

Caleb's lips twisted into a frown as he glanced back down at my dog.

"It's nice to have a little security when I'm in my apartment or just walking around the city, you know?" I shrugged.

He was silent for a moment like he was considering my words and my life in New York carefully and his eyes dimmed. "Right."

This slightly darker mood had me shifting from side to side uncomfortably and I gestured to the food in my hands so we could get moving already.

"So you wanna eat or what?"

Just like that, the cloud lifted and he flashed me a bright smile. "Yeah. Let's go. I got a picnic table behind the shop with our name on it."

. . .

Well, if this wasn't just a basketful of shitty memories. I didn't know how many times Caleb and I had sat at a picnic table eating lunch together and I'd all but forgotten how much I'd used to look forward to this whenever we shared a shift. It was weird, to say the least. And painful. And wonderful. And all the other things I just couldn't let myself feel.

If Caleb noticed my discomfort, how unsettled I felt sitting here, how desperately I wanted to just reach across the picnic table and touch him, he didn't show it. In fact, he unwrapped his cheeseburger, took a healthy bite, and watched Cooper inspect the lot without as much as a glance my way.

But any leeway and space he'd afforded me just now flew right out the window when he glanced up at me from his burger and asked, "So I'd like to believe you brought me lunch today because you wanted to see me, but I don't really think that's why, is it?"

He was closer to the truth than he knew, but admitting that out loud wouldn't help me right now. It wouldn't really help him either.

I sucked in a deep breath and smiled. It was brief and forced and it was more for his benefit than mine, but I didn't know what else to do.

I shrugged and dove into the little speech I'd practiced on my way here. "I've been a complete bitch to you since I've been back and I'm sorry."

His burger dropped onto the greasy paper in front of him and he leaned forward, opening his mouth to correct me, but I beat him to the punch.

"Come on, Caleb," I smiled softly and something shifted in his blue eyes as he leaned back. "You know it's true. I found that contract, came charging in here without even really thinking about it and blamed you for something that wasn't really your fault. I should've been thanking you, not yelling at you."

Caleb sighed heavily. "You were blind-sided by the whole thing, Iz. Your dad knew you'd feel that way and he kept it from you anyway and I played my part by agreeing to it in the first place. You had every right to be pissed at both of us."

"And what about the fit I threw about the starter, huh?"

He frowned at me. "I wouldn't exactly call it a fit."

"Fine. Whatever you wanna call it," I batted a hand at him. "But I wasn't very nice about that whole mess either. All you've been doing is trying to help me and I've just been making your life difficult every step of the way."

His lips quirked up in a smile and he lifted a shoulder as he swept his burger off the table again. "And it's been a pleasure."

In my need to change the subject, I thoughtlessly spewed out something I'd never planned on telling him.

"Honestly, I think I just needed to get out of the house for awhile," I told him quietly.

Goddammit. What the hell was my problem? Now that I'd opened it up, he was just going to ask more questions that I wouldn't want to answer. I never should've bothered coming here. What did I really think was going to happen?

"How's he doing?" Caleb called out to me from across the picnic table.

I just shrugged helplessly. "He's dying. Everyday's just a little bit worse than the last one."

He nodded and glanced down at his hands for just a moment. "If you need —"

"I got it, okay? It's not on you to take care of him."

"Right," Caleb nodded tightly.

As far as I was concerned, it wasn't really any of his business either, but we didn't need to go there. And then my mouth opened before I could stop myself.

"It was just really bad this morning," the word vomit tumbled out of me whether I liked it or not. "His medicine was making him throw up and I couldn't get him off the bathroom floor. He's just not himself anymore. It's eating away at him and I can see it. I can literally *see* it happening and there's nothing I can do to help him..."

I trailed off, sucking in mouthfuls of air but that didn't stop the tightening in my chest. Or the tingling in my fingertips. Or the dryness in my mouth. I was right back where I was this morning with trembling hands and sweaty palms only this time, I wasn't alone. This time, I had an audience.

"Iz?"

I glanced up only to find Caleb leaning into the table on his elbows, his forehead creased in a deep line, and his eyes scanning me from top to bottom.

"Iz?" he asked again when I didn't answer. "You okay?"

My throat tightened like a string and I squeezed my eyes shut, pushing off the bench so I could go...I didn't know where. Somewhere away from here. Somewhere away from him. The reality was that I'd come here today because I wanted to see him and because I knew seeing him would somehow make me feel better. And now I was running from it, scrambling away from the table and aimlessly backpedalling into the gravel at my feet.

"I just, um, I need to go to the bathroom."

Caleb, unfortunately, had already leapt up from the table and was hot on my heels. "It's the second door on your right."

I pivoted around to face the garage, telling myself he wouldn't follow me all the way inside, that he would just leave to ride out this panic attack in peace. Who was I kidding? There was no such thing as peace when Caleb Sawyer was around.

"Don't follow me," I snapped over my shoulder, but there was no point. He was right behind me, so close, in fact, that I could smell that familiar, heady scent of musk and gasoline trailing right underneath my nostrils.

It wasn't enough of a distraction though because my chest was still heaving, my throat was all dried out, and my hands had practically fallen asleep at my sides. I rushed into the bathroom and slammed the door right in Caleb's face before he had a chance to get a word out.

I leaned into the sink with both hands clasping the sides and closed my eyes.

Breathe in. Breathe out. That's all you have to do and this will just be over.

My eyes flew open when pounding thumped on the door.

"Iz," Caleb's voice, although muffled through the door, sounded almost as panicked as I felt. "I have a key, you know. I'm giving you 10 seconds and then I'm coming in."

I sucked in a haggard breath. God, why did I come here today? I should've just ridden this out in my dad's office, freaking out in silence and solitude instead of making a fool of myself here. Suddenly, the door flew open and Caleb crowded the doorway with one hand on the doorknob and the other one tearing through what little hair he had. Our eyes met and then he immediately shut the door behind him, taking a careful step closer.

I didn't know what else to do and because my legs felt weightless, just like they had this morning, I backed up against the wall closest to me and slid all the way down as my feet gave out on me.

Caleb was silent for a moment and shoved his hands deep into his front pockets, his forehead once again lined with worry. I couldn't bring myself to look at him, so I hugged my knees to my chest and rested my chin on one knee. He shuffled forward until we were toe to toe and then he gestured down to the space next to me.

"Is it alright if I sit?"

I shrugged. "It's a free country."

In spite of everything, his lips twisted up into a grin and he slid down the wall to settle in just a few inches away from me, only slowed by the stiffness in his knee. He mimicked my sitting position and leaned his head against the wall before finally turning just a hair to get a better look at me.

"I don't know what happened just now," he murmured. "But you gotta tell me what's going on."

It was only fair. I couldn't show up at his place of business, interrupt his day with a spontaneous, uninvited lunch, barely make it through the whole meal without hyperventilating, and *not* explain myself.

"I had a panic attack," I exhaled, barely recognizing the sound of my own voice. "That's what happened."

He was silent for a moment, considering my words carefully before he spoke again. "Do you get those a lot?"

"Sometimes. I had one this morning. Having two in one day hasn't happened in a while though. Apparently, they're triggered whenever I feel out of control."

I wasn't going to add that my therapist had also prescribed sleeping pills, which I rarely took even though I probably should, and anti-anxiety pills as well, which I did take as prescribed to various degrees of success. Caleb didn't need to know that.

Caleb nodded slowly as he studied the lines dividing the tiles in his shop's bathroom. "Like the one you had after the break-in?"

Of course he remembered. I hadn't really expected anything else.

"Yeah."

He nodded tightly and his Adam's apple bobbed up and down a few times before he cleared his throat harshly. "And you've had them ever since?"

"Pretty much."

He flinched and the hold he had on his hands folded at his knees tightened until his knuckles turned white. "I'm sorry, Iz."

"I don't know why you're apologizing. It's not your fault."

All I got was silence as he stared blankly into the planes of wood on the door. Now I just needed something to fill this void and as if it had a will of its own, my mouth opened and more word vomit came spilling out.

"It's just so much harder than I thought it would be," I whispered. "I mean, I knew it was going to be hard, but actually *watching* it every single day, seeing him suffer—I don't know how much longer I can do it."

He nodded again, giving me the space and the time to do or say whatever I needed to feel more normal again. And as I spoke, my body gravitated toward him like a magnet. His presence was enough because ever since he'd stepped foot inside this bathroom, my breathing slowed, my chest loosened, and my fingers didn't tingle so much anymore.

"I'm a terrible person," I murmured.

That had him shifting against the wall so he could face me and he frowned back at me. "Don't say that, Iz."

"No, it's true," I shrugged and with that, my head leaned just far enough to the right until it rested on Caleb's left shoulder. He stiffened for just a moment and just as quickly, he relaxed into me so his chin could prop up protectively on the top of my head.

"I should want it to be over," I whispered again. "It's the best thing for him to not have to suffer anymore. I don't want to have to watch it, but I don't want it to be over either. If it's over, that means he's gone. Our relationship has always been so complicated, but we finally figured it out...finally figured out how to be a family again and now, I just want more time with him. It's so horrible and selfish and cruel and—"

"Iz," his head turned just enough so his mouth could brush my forehead. "It's not horrible and it doesn't make you a terrible person. It just means you love him. That's all."

"I don't know," I sighed, leaning into him just a little bit more. He didn't move an inch. "Ever since my mom...he was just never the same. You know, I spent so much of my life trying to be him, or at least, trying to be what he wanted me to be. I don't know when he stopped being my dad and became someone so *unhappy*. You wanna know what he said the first time he ever saw my sketches?"

His lips curved up sadly and he waited for me to tell him the answer.

"He told me to stop doodling and do my homework," I laughed bitterly and shook my head. "I thought he was gonna disown me when I quit Duke. God, he was so disappointed in me, but I just wish I'd pushed harder in the beginning for rehab or more counseling or *something*. I mean, how many times did we bring him home from bars? I think I lost count after a while. I just didn't want him to lose his job and I didn't want him to lose what little dignity he had left. I was just stupid and scared and I hate that it took something so scary and so terrible for both of us to finally snap out of it."

My eyes fell to the faint scar in the middle of my left hand and squeezed shut at the memory of what had finally pushed my dad into his first rehab stint. In all the years since it happened, we'd only talked about it once in family counseling together. My dad had wept on the couch, held his head in his hands, and begged me to forgive him for both the physical and emotional attack. I'd forgiven him a long time ago, but the memory still left an ugly scar. Just like pretty much everything in my life.

"You did the best you could, Iz," Caleb told me hoarsely.

"I know it's not going to change things now," I pushed on softly. "He tried so hard. He really did. He knew things had to change, but it was just too late. I guess I should just be grateful for the time I did get with him."

I felt him nod into my hair and press his mouth into the side of my head.

"That's the way it should be, Iz."

Every time that nickname rolled off his lips, I just wanted to lean in closer. I wanted to be in deeper. There was something else, too. Something hovering beneath the surface I hadn't let myself acknowledge outright because it was always so damn painful when I did. But with him sitting here, holding me like this, comforting me like this...and then my eyes fell to those three letters inked on his wrist.

"Do you know what tomorrow is?"

He lifted his face away from my hair and leaned away as he cleared his throat. Tomorrow marked the eighth anniversary of the worst day of both our lives. There was no forgetting that kind of tragedy no matter how much alcohol, counseling, and prescription medication I consumed—not necessarily in that order.

"Yeah," he nodded numbly. "I do."

"I hate tomorrow already."

He laughed mirthlessly and then swung an arm around me to tuck my body under his shoulders. "Yeah, I know what you mean. God, I can't believe it's here again. I think I spend the whole year alternating between dreading it and trying not to think about it."

I breathed him in, filling my senses with musk and gasoline. One of his hands was in my hair now while the other clung to me for dear life and for a fleeting moment, I never wanted him to let go. It was like no time had passed, like nothing had torn us apart, and all that was left was this electrically-charged connection we both knew still existed between us.

Getting caught up in his arms like this was dangerous, but I had to take these few moments. It just felt too good.

His hands were closing around my face now so he could brush a few stray tears away with his thumbs. My eyes collided with his and his face was so dangerously close. My eyes squeezed shut again as his thumb moved across my cheek. When I pulled my gaze back up to him, my breath caught in my throat at the tender, warm expression in his eyes and everything else just stopped. He leaned forward, his calloused hands still pressed around my cheeks, and then paused, as if he was waiting for some sort of sign to go further.

My chin tilted up ever so slightly to give him better access and then my hand inched up the length of his button-down shirt. As his head dipped even lower, our noses brushed against each other. Caleb leaned back for a split second, as if to silently ask permission, and after finding whatever he was looking for, his lips grazed across my cheek. Just as his lips began a light trail to my lips, the front door burst open, startling me right out of his arms.

Saul stood before us and a brief look of apology flashed across his face when he took in our current position on the floor. He held a hand up in the air and I was faintly aware that Caleb growled in his direction.

"Sorry, boss," Saul fired off. "I didn't mean to interrupt, but Theo Wallace and two of his boys are out front. They want to talk to you."

All the air sucked right out of the room as Caleb leapt to his feet, pulling me with him, and his hand fell to the small of my back to urge me forward.

"You remember what we talked about?" Caleb asked his employee pointedly and Saul nodded without hesitation.

Everything seemed to rush in a blur around me as Caleb hurried me out into the garage, all the way looking over his shoulder and then he all but shoved me at Saul before disappearing into the room next to the bathroom. My eyes followed him and then they nearly fell out of my head when Caleb opened the bottom drawer in a desk and pulled out two handguns. I froze as he tucked one behind the waistband of his jeans and then handed the other gun to Saul, who followed suit.

"She doesn't leave your sight until you get the okay from me," Caleb instructed him in a cool, lethally calm voice.

"Got it," Saul nodded, already pushing me toward the garage's back door with a hand on my back.

I glanced frantically over my shoulder, even though I knew I had to keep walking forward, and Caleb threw me one more look before nodding and turning on his heel to stalk out of the garage.

CHAPTER TWENTY-FOUR
Lighting Fires

Caleb

Theo Wallace, with two Warlord officers, was waiting in the parking lot just like Saul said he was. I'd known this day would come, I'd just never imagined it would also be the day Isabelle randomly decided to show up at my shop with lunch and a whole shitload of issues.

When it rained, it poured. Or something like that.

But with Isabelle safe in Saul's care for the time being, I had bigger issues to worry about right now.

Wallace nodded to me as I approached and my fingers itched to touch the Glock tucked into my jeans just to remind myself it was there.

"Sawyer," he called out when we were standing just a few feet away from each other.

"Wallace," I nodded back tightly.

At this point, Saul should've gotten Isabelle off the property already, so as far as I knew, she was safe and Wallace would never know she was here. That didn't mean I wanted Theo Wallace on my property any longer than necessary.

"Long time no see," he flashed me a grin, but this was more about baring his teeth than anything. There was menace in that grin, a hardness that wasn't there the last time I saw him, and now, I knew it was all directed right at me.

"Yeah," I rocked back on my heels and shoved my hands deep inside my pockets. "How 'bout that?"

He gestured with his head to my shop and I turned just in time to see Saul's truck heading down the street in the opposite direction, away from view and getting Isabelle one step closer to safety.

"Looks like you got yourself set up here real nice," Wallace pointed right at my shop as he spoke. "I guess good things *can* happen to those who abandon their families and throw their legacy in the shitter, huh?"

My lips curled up into a defiant snarl—Theo Wallace didn't know shit about me. He thought he did, but all he knew was what he'd heard. It wasn't any different than what I knew about him, but I also wasn't sitting here, insinuating about his life either. If our roles were reversed and I was standing in his shoes, with a dead kid and an MIA old lady, I probably would be doing exactly what he was: lighting fires and burning bridges. Come to think of it, he and I were never all that different, save for a few details.

"This obviously isn't a social call," I shot back, my eyes hardened and ready for a fight if that's what he wanted. "And from the looks of it, your bike doesn't need any work done, so what can I help you with?"

That toothy, menacing grin just got wider and Wallace's eyebrows lifted into his forehead at my directness. "Alright. Fair enough. I just wanted to stop by and talk some business with you."

I cocked an eyebrow at him. "What kinda business?"

Wallace gestured with his head again toward my shop. "Your little establishment there. I want in."

A deep belly laugh erupted from my throat and I shook my head. "You're not serious, right?"

His grey eyes glinted with hostility and he took a step forward. "Like the plague, Sawyer. It's no secret you're lookin' to expand your business. You need some cash to help you back that up and I can provide it for you."

And be his bitch forever? Fuck that.

"I'm gonna have to pass," I shot back just as quickly.

"Just like that? You don't even wanna hear me out?"

"Nope," I shook my head. "I don't."

Wallace whistled lowly and glanced at his companions, who I recognized as Rubin Lloyd, his VP, and Antone Jeffreys, his Sergeant-At-Arms.

"Come on, Sawyer, everyone knows you opened up a bike shop instead of a car shop just so you wouldn't step on the Horsemen's toes. Lettin' me throw some cash your way still wouldn't matter in the grand scheme of things."

Yeah, I thought grimly, *but it would matter to me.*

I didn't want money from anyone, not the club, not Isabelle, and certainly not Theo Wallace. I'd gotten this far on my own. Armed with a helluva good business plan and good old fashioned persistence, I'd gotten all the start-up cash I needed through loans from banks and that was exactly how I planned on expanding. Besides, the last time I'd made a decision solely based on money, it hadn't ended so well for me.

Theo Wallace had no business stepping foot on my property, let alone staking any sort of claim on it. All he wanted to do was use my shop as a pawn in his game. If I let him put anything in it, he'd grind me into the ground, holding his money over my head every chance he got and in doing so, would rub salt in a festering, open wound between me and the Horsemen.

Sawyer Custom Builds was mine. I'd rather let Wallace just put a bullet in me now before I ever let him have a piece of it.

"I appreciate the offer," I drawled and dug into my back pocket for my cigarettes. I shook my head as I lit one up and took a deep pull from the burning cherry. "But I'm pretty sure I can handle it on my own."

The steel clouding Wallace's eyes told me what I already knew: this was about vendettas and past mistakes and all the things neither of us could change. He was out for payback, I was trying to move on and so, I threw my cards on the table to see where they landed.

"Let's be honest, this isn't really about you wanting to get into a legit business. This is about me, you, Dom, the club, and what happened that day in Pittsburgh."

Animosity flickered across Wallace's face for just a moment, but it was long enough to let me know I'd hit my target. He took an aggressive step right for me, but I held my ground. This was my property, my staff was watching, and I wasn't moving.

"What are you doing, man?" I tried again. "You already cut-off the club's contacts in the North and you've already derailed anything new they got going in the South. They're bleeding, just like you wanted them to. Isn't that enough?"

Someone had to be the voice of reason here. Someone had to try to talk this out because all this eye for an eye bullshit wasn't helping anyone.

"What am I doing?" Wallace sneered and strode up to me until we were practically nose to nose. "I'm getting justice. That's what I'm doing. Your fucking club is a cancer and it needs to be wiped out. Every single last one of those assholes needs a bullet in the head and you don't get a free pass just because you think you got out. They might have let you break loose, but you're an idiot if you think anyone will ever forget who you are."

All he did was voice my nightmares out loud: the things that ravaged my dreams, had me always looking over my shoulder and keeping guns in my desk.

"Why'd you even bother?" he went on with a snarl. "You stayed in this bumfuck town, right under your club's nose...for what? It wasn't to get out, that's for damn sure."

I bristled at that. As far as I was concerned, I didn't owe this asshole anything, certainly not an explanation. And the reason I'd chosen to stay here in this town had nothing to do with the club—hell, it would've been so much easier if I'd just left. But I didn't and I also didn't regret it for a second, not now anyway.

"Maybe you're right," I allowed easily. "But it's also none of your damned business."

Wallace just held up a hand and I wordlessly spiked my cigarette into the concrete at my feet.

"Alright, Sawyer. Alright. I obviously hit a nerve and that's fine. So let's just cut the bullshit. You play nice, give me what I want, and I'll call us even. If you don't, I can't make you any promises."

"Promises about what?" I lifted an eyebrow in challenge.

He just shrugged. "You know exactly what I mean."

Yeah, I did. If shit got bad with the Horsemen, I'd get lumped in with the rest of them. It didn't matter that I'd gotten myself out six years ago. It was just like Wallace said: as long as I still lived here in Claremont, I wasn't *really* out, at least not the way I wanted to be.

"Look, man, you've gotta let this go—"

I didn't get a chance to finish because Wallace lunged forward, all pretense and niceties long gone, and he shoved me in the chest.

"Let this go?" he barked back at me and shoved me one more time just for good measure. "Like hell I'm gonna just let this go. You and your club are the reason my family's gone!'

Even as I stumbled back, what I wanted to say was: *you* are the reason you lost your family. It wasn't me, it wasn't the club, and it wasn't our shared arrest that day in Pittsburgh. It was him. All his legacy, which wasn't that different from mine, and all his shitty choices, each one taking him further and further away from his family. *That* was why he'd lost his family. And I knew this because those were the exact same reasons I'd lost mine.

I didn't bother saying any of that to him. He wouldn't listen, just like Dom, Marcus, my mom, and all the rest of them.

Sooner or later, that life catches up to you and the people you love, the people who make life worth living, those are the people who get caught in the crossfire. But what did I know? To them, I was a traitor to my name, my blood, and my brothers. My sin and my betrayal was all I had—I'd gladly take that same sin again if it meant a peaceful, bullet-less life. Unfortunately, it looked like all those sacrifices meant nothing as long as I was still living here.

I spread my hands out in front of me, my expression just as sincere as my intentions. "I'm sorry. I really am. You don't know how many times I've wished I could go back to that moment and do everything differently. But I can't and neither can you."

Wallace glared at me, then he lunged forward again to jab his index finger in my chest. "Fuck you, Sawyer. That means shit to me. You knew the ATF was watching your asses and you said nothing. You had no business driving up there and putting us all at risk."

How many times would I have to pay for the same mistake?

"You're right," I lifted a shoulder. "I shouldn't have done it. And just so we're clear, you're not the only one who lost something that day."

Something that looked a lot like understanding with a little bit of regret in there, too, flashed across Wallace's face. Then it was gone just as quickly.

"You know," he rocked back on his heels and ran a hand over his face. "When I first heard what happened to you and your girl, I felt real bad for both of you. I figured, maybe I had to be in prison, but at least I still had my kids, my wife and then my kid went to the hospital and didn't come back. I didn't feel so bad for you after that."

If he was going there, then I was going there too.

"I had to watch her give birth to a baby who wasn't gonna take a breath," I growled. "Did you know that?"

His movements stilled and he shook his head almost imperceptibly.

"Don't stand there and preach your bullshit about what you lost," I pushed on, my chest heaving and my fingers twitching for that gun behind my back. "Because you don't know shit about *my* loss or *my* family."

And suddenly I was back in that hospital with my arms around Isabelle, holding her as she gave birth to our baby in one long, anguished push, and I wanted to grab my gun and pull the damn trigger. Instead of mourning the loss, taking stock of his responsibility in it, and making the changes to make sure it never happened again, Wallace was raging a war he wouldn't win, at least not without more loss and more tragedy.

"Yeah, well," Wallace bit out. "At least you got to be there. I didn't. You and your club—you stole that from me."

"This isn't gonna end well," I told him hoarsely. "You know that, right? It doesn't matter which side comes out on top because everyone'll still lose. Cut your losses, take the victories you've already gotten and just go back to Pittsburgh."

Wallace regarded me with hard, unfeeling grey eyes. I knew what he was going to say before his lips even parted.

"Wise words," he smirked at me. "You would've made a helluva president, you know."

"Doesn't matter now."

"You're right," Wallace nodded tightly. "It doesn't. So consider this your only and final chance, Sawyer. I'm not gonna show up here lookin' to play nice again."

"Heard you loud and clear," I lifted a shoulder as I lifted another cigarette to my lips. "I just can't make any deals with you."

"Figured as much."

By this point, he'd started toward his bike before rearing back with that menacing grin sliding across his face. "Hey, I think I saw your girl a couple weeks ago."

My body stilled and my cigarette dangled from my lips for a few perilous moments before my mind finally caught up to the rest of my body. The less he knew the better, especially the fact that Isabelle and I had seen each other since she'd been back.

I just shrugged and took a long pull from my cigarette. "I don't have a girl."

Wallace's eyes flashed and he rocked back on his heels with that grin still on his face. "Maybe not right now, but she was your old lady at one point, wasn't she?"

"I've had a couple of old ladies," I shot back easily and hoped my nonchalance was actually believable. "You gotta be a little more specific."

"Blonde hair, tight little body, pretty blue eyes," he tossed over his shoulder as he threw a leg over his bike. "Yeah, that was your girl alright."

"Maybe it was. I heard she was coming back to town."

"I think I might've scared her."

I gave away nothing and brought my cigarette up to my lips one more time.

Wallace just winked at me as he started up his bike and revved the engine. "Wouldn't want that to happen again, now would we?"

With that, he left me standing in the middle of my parking lot, hoping to high hell I hadn't just poked an angry bear and shoved Isabelle right in front of it.

. . .

Isabelle

I tried to focus on the road. I really did, but it was kind of hard to focus on anything but the handgun resting a little too comfortably in the center console between me and Saul. My eyes fell to the driver's seat, where Saul was whistling along to the radio and that did nothing to calm my nerves. I didn't even know where to start: the fact that club business was still a very real presence in Caleb's life or the fact that his first instinct, before anything else, was to get me somewhere safe.

"Don't worry about a thing," Saul told me, his eyes still focused steadily on the road. "This is just a precaution. Nothing's gonna happen to you, at least not on his watch."

My hands still shook in spite of his reassurance because at the end of the day, I didn't think anyone but Caleb would really be able to make me feel like I really was safe. Cooper seemed to sense my agitation and rested his head on the center console from the backseat, his big brown eyes shifting up to me and pleading for me to just touch him already.

When I gave the poor thing what he wanted, his thick tongue shot out to lick me right across the face, giving me the next best thing I needed right now.

"Thanks, buddy," I whispered and kissed the top of his massive head.

"That's a nice dog you got there," Saul smiled at me, glancing down briefly at my dog before shifting his gaze back at the road.

"Yeah, he is. Thanks," and now, seeing as how we'd been on the road for a few minutes, I figured it was as good a time as any to start getting some answers. "So you and Caleb had this planned? If anyone—"

"Like I said," Saul just shrugged. "This is a precaution. He's not taking any chances when it comes to you and I can't blame him for that."

"Huh."

Something told me that was about all I'd get from him on that subject.

"Yep," Saul replied a little too easily.

I guessed I was right.

"So, um," I tried again. At this point, small talk was the only thing keeping a panic attack at bay and if I had three in one day, I'd probably have to give my therapist a call. Not exactly on my list of things to do today. "What exactly do you do in Caleb's shop if you don't mind me asking?"

Saul shot me a knowing grin, but still answered good-naturedly, "Ah, you know, a little bit of everything, but I'm mostly his office manager and accountant. I used to do that in another life, so he pounced on that pretty quickly. I've been with him since the very beginning—the outlaw with the killer business plan, kinda hard to reconcile, right?"

"Right," I laughed. "I still don't understand how he did any of it."

"Your boy's smart, that's how," Saul told me with a firm nod. "I knew it from the very first time I met him. I said to myself, *Now there's a punk-ass kid who just needs one opportunity...think of what he could do with it.* I wasn't wrong."

I smiled softly. "No, you weren't. How did you meet him?"

Saul's eyes crinkled up at the sides, but there was a hardness in his eyes now that hadn't been there before. "Prison."

"Oh."

It was such a lame response, but I honestly couldn't think of anything else to say.

"I worked in the library," Saul clarified without offering up the answer to my silent question. "He started comin' in about six months into his sentence and I got him started on some of the classics like Twain, Malcolm X, Thoreau, Joyce...you know, that sort of thing."

"Wait a minute, wait a minute," I held up a hand just for emphasis. "Caleb was *reading*? In *prison*?"

I just couldn't wrap my head around it. Since when did he like to read anything? Let alone classic literature?

"Yeah," Saul shrugged like it was really no big deal. "Guys gotta find some way to pass the time when they're inside. For Caleb, it was going to the library and digging in a book."

"I just..." I trailed off, still feeling a little blindsided by all this. "I don't know. I have very clear memories of him cheating off me during our American Lit final."

Saul chuckled heartily and shook his head. "Yeah, that sounds like something he'd do. I bet he spent more time trying to look down your shirt than actually looking over your shoulder to see the answers, too."

Now it was my turn to laugh. "Oh, I don't know about that. He had a pretty serious girlfriend back then."

God, I felt like I'd lived this whole other life I'd completely forgotten about.

"Well," Saul went on. "I'm pretty sure that's water under the bridge for him now. You know, considering..."

He trailed off, glancing at me long enough to make me squirm in my seat. Then he threw some mercy my way and changed the subject.

"Anyway, he and I got to know each other in the library. He'd come in for another book recommendation and I'd help him study a little bit too. That's pretty much it."

"You helped him study?"

The only reason I knew Caleb had gotten his degree in prison was because my dad had mentioned it not-so-subtly in passing right after I'd found out he'd left the club and was starting his own bike shop. I'd also never really taken the time to think about what he'd done in prison or how he'd spent his time there because it was just easier not to think about him sitting there in a four-block cement cell. I would've known had I read his letters, but since that wasn't an option anymore, I'd have to settle for secondhand information.

"I did," Saul nodded.

"That was nice of you to help him."

A grim line spread across Saul's weathered face. "Gave me something to look forward to, you know?"

There were so many more questions bubbling up to the surface, but I just didn't want to make him uncomfortable by asking them, so I just chose to say nothing instead.

"Ah," Saul laughed, breaking this uneasy silence between us. "But you know, I think Caleb read just about every book in that library *except* Shakespeare. He hated Shakespeare, lemme tell ya."

I smiled as I imagined Caleb hunched over with something like *Romeo and Juliet* or *Macbeth* and huffing and puffing in frustration. Probably even tearing his hair out over it, too.

"I can already hear him complaining," I laughed and then dropped my tone to mimic Caleb's low voice. "*Why can't they just speak goddamn English?*"

A slow, sly smile spread across Saul's face and that glint in his dark eyes knocked me off-kilter for a second.

"You know, that's pretty much what he said. Word for word. You know him pretty well, don't you?"

"I used to," I smiled sadly.

He nodded as he pulled into my dad's parking lot and cut the engine on his car. "How long have you known him?"

I lifted a shoulder and sighed. "I feel like he's been in and out my life since we were kids."

It was so true it was terrifying. Caleb Sawyer had been a fixture in my life, whether I liked it or not, since we were practically in kindergarten. I didn't regret it, but it was disconcerting to think that one person held so much of my history, so much of my past, and now, here we were, right back where we started, but not necessarily better for it either.

"Well," Saul's deep, voice called out to me. "This is your stop. I hope it's okay, but I gotta stick close until I get the all clear from the boss. Well, even if it's not okay, I still gotta park it here anyway for awhile."

"It's okay," I told him as I stepped out of the car to let Cooper out. "I understand. Thank you, by the way."

"Sure," he nodded tightly. "And thank you, too."

I frowned back at him and leaned down to the window.

"For not asking me what I was in prison for," Saul clarified softly. "I know you wanted to, but didn't want to be rude. So thank you for that. That's...well, that's a story for another day. You know, I can see why he's never been able to shake you. Saw it the moment you stepped into our office a few weeks ago. You walk in a room and just light the whole place up. I think a guy would be an idiot not to reach out and try to catch some of that light."

My mouth opened to speak, but all I could come up with was: "Thanks, Saul."

"Don't mention it," he batted a hand out to me. "It's not everyday I get to chat up a famous artist from New York."

I just laughed and rolled my eyes. "Okay. Sure."

"I'm serious," he insisted and started humming something that sounded a little too much like that Frank Sinatra song about New York. "You've had how many shows now in that gallery...what's it called?"

"The Warehouse," I narrowed my eyes at him.

"Right, right. The Warehouse. Anyway—"

"Saul," I interrupted exasperatedly. "Would you like to come in? You're going to have to be here anyway. You might as well come in and watch the History channel with my dad or something."

His eyes lit up at the words *History* and *channel* and I knew it was all downhill from here.

. . .

About four hours later, I'd watched about as many episodes of *American Pickers* as I could stand. My dad and Saul, on the other hand, were relentlessly entertained. Still, it was nice to see my dad perking up a little as he discussed the pickers' latest conquest with our guest.

And I, unfortunately, was currently staring at the business card with Caleb's cell phone number written on the back. I just wanted to know if he was okay or at least, that was what I had to tell myself. He *had* to be okay—Saul was still here and nobody had tried to contact him since he'd plopped down on our living room couch. But still, my fingers twitched against the kitchen table, where I sat like a crazy person just staring at those familiar chicken scratches on the back of the card.

Being with Caleb again felt like I'd been standing in the middle of a pitch black room and the moment he stood beside me was the moment the light in my world turned back on. Being with Caleb was also like speeding towards a brick wall. The high was exhilarating, all-consuming, and filled with the kind of fiery passion people only read about in books, but all that did was distract you from the inevitable.

The only way things could end with Caleb Sawyer was crashing and burning headfirst into that brick wall. I couldn't let myself forget that.

My dad called out to me over the blare of the TV, but how could I focus when half of me sat at this kitchen table and the other half was still inside Caleb's shop?

"Isabelle?"

My head shot up at my dad's voice, this time clearer and louder, and I found my dad, Saul, and Caleb all standing in the doorway, staring at me in varied degrees of confusion. Because I'd completely tuned everything else out, I hadn't even heard the doorbell ring.

Everything around me started moving at once. Saul waved good-bye to me from around Caleb and disappeared behind the front door. My dad and Caleb shook hands like they'd been friends for years.

I'd barely gotten a chance to shove the business card in my back pocket when Caleb strode into the kitchen with my dad and Cooper right behind him. He leaned up against the island and shoved his hands deep in his pockets.

"Hey, Iz," Caleb told me with a soft smile playing at his lips.

"Hi, Caleb. What are you—"

"I just wanted to make sure you were okay after everything that happened today," he glanced at my dad for a moment before shifting his gaze back to me.

My eyebrows shot up into my forehead. "I'm fine. But are *you* okay?"

A faint smile lifted his lips. "Yeah. I'm good. Look, we need to talk about Wallace."

"What did he want?"

"That's not really important right now," he shrugged stiffly and the tension was written all over his face. He was trying to put up the front like everything was fine, but it wasn't. "What matters is that I need to keep some eyes on you right now."

I opened my mouth to protest, but he just shook his head.

"I'm sorry it has to be this way," he informed me grimly. "But I'm just not going to take any chances here."

Saul's words to me earlier echoed in my head and I squeezed my eyes shut.

"Wallace isn't going to back down, at least not until he gets what he wants," Caleb went on and glanced at my dad, who'd sunk down into the chair next to me at the table.

My dad cleared his throat next to me. "And he knows who Isabelle is to you?"

The fact that my dad spoke in present tense wasn't lost on anyone in the room, but Caleb just nodded.

"How much danger is she in?" my dad asked in a scarily calm voice. Why wasn't he more worried about this?

"I'd like to believe he wouldn't try anything with Iz or Lex and Chloe or anybody else who's connected to the club for that matter," Caleb told him. "But I'm not gonna put it past him either. He's out for blood and I'm not trying to scare you guys, but Iz can't just sit here unprotected by herself anymore. It's not worth the risk. He's less likely to do something if she's got someone with her at all times."

"I'm sitting right here, you know," I practically growled, my eyes shifting angrily from both men in the room. "You guys could at least acknowledge I'm in the room."

Caleb's eyes flicked to me and the grim seriousness I found there was something I wasn't used to seeing. "Sorry, Iz. I didn't mean it like that. I just —"

"I know," I grumbled.

His eyes softened and his head tilted to the side as he shifted against the island. "I'm not gonna let anything happen to you, okay?"

I swallowed back the lump in my throat and despite everything, I didn't doubt him for a second.

"I know," I told him softly.

His lips curved up just enough to make me want to hop off my chair and run. Whether it was as far away from him as possible or right into his arms...the jury was unfortunately still out on that one.

Then my dad called out to Caleb in a hoarse voice, effectively breaking the spell.

"So what are you going to do?"

"My guys'll take shifts keeping an eye on your house while you're here and when you need to leave, someone'll drive you."

I blew out a deep breath. I hated this. Every single part of it. I'd only been back for a few weeks and already, I was sucked right back in. The danger, the violence—it was almost like I'd never left in the first place.

"I don't want—" I started, but Caleb cut me off.

"Well, Iz, the alternatives are either you stay in my apartment for awhile or you go back to New York until all this blows over. I don't think you wanna do either of those things, so this is just what you're going to have to deal with for now. It's all taken care of. Nobody'll ever get near you, Iz. I promise you that."

There was no point in arguing. If Wallace and the Warlords were really a threat, then I didn't want to be alone either. I wasn't crazy about all this damsel-in-distress shade they were throwing my way, but that was just the world we lived in right now.

I understood now why my dad wasn't barricading the windows or driving me to the airport right now. Because Caleb was calm, my dad was calm. Because Caleb was confident in his ability to protect me, so was my dad.

I was almost too afraid to ask, but the words fell from my lips anyway. "Who's got the first shift?"

His mouth quirked up. "Me."

Of course. Why would it be anyone else? I just rolled my eyes as my dad stood up from the table on shaky legs.

"That's good enough for me. I'm going to bed. I'll let you two kids hash it out for the night."

But when he took a tiny step away from the table, his legs swayed out from under him, threatening to topple him over, and both Caleb and I shot up to catch him before he fell. Caleb swung an arm around my dad's back to hoist him up and I slipped around the other side of him to grab hold of his arm.

"Sorry," he mumbled as he tried to catch his breath. "Too much excitement today, you know? All these visitors. I just need to lie down now."

"That's alright, Sam," Caleb told him and my head snapped in his direction. "Let me help you, okay?"

Sam? Since when were Caleb and my dad on friendly, first-name terms?

"No, no," my dad just shook us off and took a few more unsteady steps closer to the staircase. "I don't need help. I'm fine. Just stood up too fast is all."

Caleb's hands fell to his side and he shoved them deep inside his pockets again. All we could do was watch my dad shuffle out of the kitchen and struggle stubbornly up the stairs at a snail's pace.

"He never lets me help him up the stairs," I whispered to Caleb. "I hate watching this, but I can't help it, you know?"

Just then, my dad stumbled a little on a step and before I could stop myself, my left hand shot out to Caleb's forearm. It wouldn't help my dad, but it made me feel a little better just knowing Caleb was there, feeling his skin underneath my fingertips. Then my fingers slipped down even further until they curled around his palm. He froze for just a second at my touch, but recovered just as quickly when his thumb rubbed the top of my hand. I leaned into his shoulder, basking in his strength and his presence and his scent and I squeezed my eyes shut just to drink it all in.

When my dad's bedroom door closed for the night, I turned just enough to wrap my free arm around his shoulders so I could press my face into his broad chest. My other hand dropped to my side as Caleb wrapped both arms around me to pull me in even tighter, to do everything he could to protect me from what was happening around us.

"I'm so sorry, Iz," he murmured in my hair. "I wish there was something I could do to make all this better for you."

Just him being here was enough, but I didn't know how to tell him that. I didn't know if I *wanted* to tell him that.

"Thank you," I whispered instead.

He leaned back and brought a hand up to my face so he could tuck some stray hair behind my ear. And then my lips parted and I let instinct take over. Something screamed at me that this would only make things worse, that I'd only get sucked in deeper, but I batted it down with a reckless hand.

"So I have this tradition."

Caleb cocked an eyebrow at me. "Okay."

"You remember what tomorrow is, right?"

He swallowed hard. "Yeah."

"Well, I always get *really* wasted the night before. I guess I just can't wait. Anyway, it's the one night out of the year I let myself get completely drunk and then I usually just sleep the whole next day away, which is kinda the point."

Given my family history with alcohol abuse and depression, I figured one night out of 365 wasn't so bad.

"Alright," his eyes narrowed a little.

"So what I'm asking is...do you wanna get wasted tonight?"

His eyebrows flew up into his forehead. "With you?"

"Yeah," I laughed. "Who else? Besides, it's no fun getting drunk by yourself. All I end up doing is crying and looking at pictures and crying some more."

He blew out a deep breath and his hands ghosted over my shoulders like he was holding me in place. "Kinda defeats the purpose of me being here to keep an eye on you, doesn't it? Besides, you, me, and alcohol probably aren't a good mix."

"Yeah," I mumbled to my feet. "I guess you're right."

He shot me that crooked grin anyway, the same one that made me weak in the knees, the same one that made me want to forget everything we'd been through, everything *he'd* put me through, and just give in already.

"But I'll tell you what. I'd hate for you to miss out on tradition just because of me. So if getting wasted tonight is really what you wanna do, then I'll happily keep you company."

A soft smile touched my lips. Yeah. I could live with that.

CHAPTER TWENTY-FIVE
The Point of No Return

Caleb

I trailed after Isabelle, taking in the way she moved with lithe steps like a dancer, and I had to swallow back the lump in my throat when she finally sank down into a swing in the backyard. Following her lead, I dropped into the swing just a few feet away from her. She was still close, just within reaching distance, but the little bit of space between us seemed to take away some of the nervousness penetrating the air around us.

Isabelle rested one hand on the metal chains, swinging her body a little, as she brought the wine bottle up to her lips.

"You sure you don't want me to get you a glass?" I smirked at her.

She just batted her free hand my way. "Nah. This is easier. And *way* classier."

"Right," I chuckled.

Now she held the bottle out to me. "Wanna give it a try?"

"Fruity girl wine?" I grimaced down at the bottle and shook my head. "No thanks, Iz."

"Fine," she shrugged. "More for me then."

She took another long swig from the bottle and I had half a mind to just take it away from her now. While she wasn't even close to being half in the bag yet, I didn't exactly want to see her drink herself into a puking stupor either. If she wanted to get drunk, that was fine, but something told me it'd be way worse if I wasn't here and the idea of Isabelle alone, drunk, and crying on this night twisted something painful inside me.

Besides, I'd take whatever she was willing to give me.

"So what did Theo Wallace want?"

I wasn't sure how much I should tell her, the details weren't really important, but judging by the expectant look in her eyes, I probably had to give her more than the nothing she'd gotten from me earlier.

"Something I couldn't give him," I sighed and ran a hand over my face. Shit, I really needed to shave.

Her eyebrows lifted into her forehead and she stared back at me for a few moments. She swiveled around in the swing to face me head-on. The one time

I got her so close I could touch her also just happened to be the one time I just didn't want to talk. But just like all the times before this one, I couldn't tell her no.

"He wanted to give me money to expand the shop," I relented.

"Wow," Isabelle exhaled and took another pull from her bottle. "I didn't know you were looking to expand."

"Yeah, well, I am. I've been shopping around some banks to see what kind of interest rate I can get on a loan."

Just when I thought her eyebrows couldn't reach any higher, they slid even further up her forehead.

"New equipment, more space, that sort of thing," I told her and batted a hand dismissively. "Anyway, I can get the money on my own just like I did the first time. I don't need anyone's help. I told myself I'd never put myself in a position again where I need to take those kind of deals to make ends meet and that's how it's gonna stay."

Her eyes flashed and I suddenly wished I hadn't opened my mouth. Given why we were sitting out here in the first place, letting all that fly was probably a bad choice.

"Why would he even offer then?" she asked softly. "There's gotta be a catch, right?"

"There's always a catch when it comes to club business," I told her darkly. "And the catch is that Wallace gets to piss off the Horsemen and he gets to shove his foot in my ass whenever he wants."

"Because of what happened, right?" she asked softly and at first, I almost didn't catch it. "With his family? He blames all of you."

"How did you know that?" I frowned.

She just lifted a shoulder. "Dom filled me in on a few things that day he picked me up from the gas station. Did he really lose one of his kids when he was in prison?"

I nodded and stared down at my feet. We were treading on some shaky ground right now and this conversation didn't need to push her even further.

"Dom said that was just a rumor he heard."

"It wasn't," I murmured.

She huffed a little angrily and shook her head. "You know, I can understand why he hates all of you, but it's not like you guys put his kid in the hospital or forced his wife to leave him. Those things might've happened even if he hadn't gone to prison."

"It's not really about that," I told her softly, my eyes still focused on the ground. "Guys like Wallace need someone else to blame for their problems. They can't accept that anything they've done is responsible. They need a scapegoat so they can sleep at night."

And *that* was exactly why I hardly ever slept at night.

"And those kind of guys," I pushed on with a heavy sigh, "are the kind of guys who can't be reasoned with."

And, I thought grimly, *those are the kind of guys who won't stop until they've gotten exactly what they wanted.*

"Did you let anyone know he was there today?"

I nodded and shot her a quick glance to reassure her that was all handled. "I called Dom after Wallace left. I'm sure the club met for church after that to talk about what to do next."

"What do you think they'll do?"

"I don't know," I shrugged a little too easily.

A few quiet, awkward moments of silence passed between us before Isabelle glanced at me out of the corner of her eye and cleared her throat.

"So, um, when do you think my dad's car is going to be done?"

I chuckled at the not-so-subtle subject change. "I think your dad's car is a non-issue since you've got your very own personal driver now."

"And here I've been so spoiled by all those *awesome* taxi drivers in New York."

"Well," I laughed. "You'll get the VIP treatment here. Trust me."

I might have been laughing, but the truth was, I trusted every single one of my guys, except for Lucas, to treat her like the precious cargo she was. They'd be polite, respectful, and most of all, they'd do whatever it took to protect her all because I asked them to.

"I figured as much," she smiled. "Saul was really nice, by the way."

"He better have been."

Isabelle laughed and in the moonlight, she looked like something out of a dream. Beautiful and just as untouchable. Just as out of reach.

"I'm serious, Caleb. He was."

"Did he happen to mention how we know each other?"

She nodded stiffly and tightened her hold on the swing's chains. "He did."

I figured he wouldn't be able to keep that to himself and it was just as well.

"Hey, um, I didn't want to ask him earlier, but...what did he do?"

I pushed out a rough sigh. That guy was my brother, my father, and my best friend all in one—if we hadn't come into each other's lives when we did, I didn't really know where either of us would have ended up. And even though it was Isabelle who was asking, I still couldn't betray his confidence.

"You know, Iz," I sighed. "That's his story to tell if he ever wants to tell it to you."

She nodded silently and I knew she wouldn't push. She was too kind-hearted and compassionate to push for more information. And now, she was quiet for a moment as she stared at the ground, letting the swing rock her from side to side a little, before she spoke again.

"I think you did the right thing."

"Even if it means giving Wallace more ammunition?"

I didn't need to add the rest because we both already knew it: *even if it means putting you in more danger?*

"You can't predict what he'll do. You also can't waste your time looking over your shoulder and letting other people dictate your life."

"Thanks," I smiled softly.

"Besides, you said yourself nothing's going to happen to me. I trust you."

She had no reason to trust me, no reason to believe in me, but she did. That was all I needed. Before I could stop myself, my arm reached out until my fingertips brushed her shoulder, sliding all the way up so I could tuck some stray blonde hair behind her ear. Then my eyes dropped to the dark lines of ink etched right below her left ear and my fingers itched to trace them. I didn't know how I'd never noticed it before, but now I couldn't stop staring at those three tiny stars.

"When'd you get that?"

She just shrugged. "A few years ago, I guess."

My eyes dropped to my left forearm, right to the upside down compass she'd sketched out for me at that patch-over party so long ago. God, that felt like another lifetime ago. Sometimes, I wondered if it even happened in the first place, if the happiness I'd felt whenever I was with her was just a figment of my imagination. My mind flew to the other place I knew she had some more ink—did she still have it? Part of me didn't want to know...I was probably better off just not knowing.

But now, with the evidence right in front of me, there had to be some sort of connection between the compass and those stars tattooed right under her ear. Even my imagination couldn't make that up on its own. After all this time, after all this distance, we'd somehow found ourselves back here again, tentatively reaching out, gravitating in each other's direction, and unable to stop it. I didn't want to stop it.

"Do you ever regret it?" her soft voice called out.

"Regret what?"

"Leaving the club?" her lips lifted in a sad smile. "Do you think things would be easier if you'd just stayed?"

I didn't even need to think about it. "No. I don't regret it. And I don't think things would be any easier for me if I'd stayed either. They'd be worse."

She frowned. "What do you mean?"

I sighed and rubbed the back of my neck in thought. "Life in the club was never really what I thought it was. I thought it was about the brotherhood and about putting that above everything else. It was something to live for, something to work for, but I just didn't know any better. Didn't know anything different. Didn't know *how* to do anything different. If I'd stayed, I'd probably be back in prison or working my way toward it at the very least."

Or six feet under in a hole somewhere, I thought grimly.

Her face tilted up to me as she listened and thankfully, she set the wine bottle down by her feet.

"At some point," I pushed on. "I guess I just realized it wasn't *really* about the brotherhood, at least not the way I thought it was. It was every man for himself, even though I'd been raised my whole life to believe we were all a family who'd do anything for each other. That wasn't true then and it's not true now."

Isabelle nodded tightly, willing me to continue and finally tell her everything I'd always wanted to say, but had only managed to get out in my notebook. There were other things I needed to tell her too, but for tonight, this would have to be enough.

"It's all about protecting themselves, and sometimes, that means people need to be sacrificed. I never realized how ridiculous that was until I was on the other side of it."

Her blue eyes shone in the moonlight and her lips parted. "You mean with Becca?"

"No," I shook my head and looked down at my feet. "I'm talking about you. All the suspicion they threw your way...it was just completely insane. None of them, save for Dom, really gave two shits about you as long as they saw you as a potential threat. It didn't matter that I was standing by you. It didn't matter that they had no reason not to trust you. And then they would've happily sacrificed both of us for the good of the order if it meant they'd all go free."

"What do you mean?"

I pushed out a rough breath and ran a hand over my short hair. "If they thought you'd done what Becca did, even if they didn't have any proof, they wouldn't have cared about anything else. They would've wanted you gone and they would've wanted me to do it."

Isabelle exhaled slowly and bit down on her bottom lip as her words washed over her. She nodded and squeezed her eyes shut.

"I didn't really let myself think about that too much when it was happening."

"That was probably for the best," I nodded. "And, not just that, but they would've let me sit in prison for the rest of my life for murder too. They wouldn't have cared because to them, it was my job to put the club above anything and everyone else."

"Who cares about your life, right?" she smiled sadly.

"Right," I nodded tightly. "I figured, if I didn't, then no one else would. After I got out of prison, I knew I couldn't spend the rest of my life doing the same shit I've always done and expecting a different outcome. My life was never gonna change unless *I* changed it."

For a brief moment, I wondered what my life would be like right now if I'd chased after her all the way to New York, if I'd told her I wanted to leave the club as soon as I made the decision, if I'd asked her to wait for me just a little bit longer, but I hadn't done any of those things because I hadn't earned it yet. I couldn't let myself forget that.

I pushed those thoughts away as she spoke again.

"And you *did* change it," Isabelle's eyes seemed to glow as she leaned her cheek against the chain. "I'm really proud of you, Caleb. You're so much smarter than you ever gave yourself credit for."

"Yeah, well," I laughed. "Considering I had to completely 'throw my legacy in the shitter', as Wallace put it, in order to get out, there had to be some sort of consolation somewhere."

"But it wasn't what you wanted anymore."

"No," I shook my head firmly. "It wasn't. It cost me everything that ever really mattered."

Her eyes flicked up to me and in that moment, I wished I could just wrap my arms around her and let everything I needed to tell her pour of me. But what was the point of drowning in regret when she was here right now, in that swing, on this night, listening to me? This kind of night and this kind of moment made every hurdle I'd climbed through worth it.

"You know," I went on. My voice cracked, but I didn't care. I needed to say this to her, even if this was as far as I got tonight. "When I was a kid, I always thought if I just had a bike to ride, a cut on my back, and a place at that table, my life would be perfect. Up until the moment you walked into the shop's office looking for a job, I was completely content to live that kind of life. Being with you made me want something else."

I squeezed my eyes shut as Marcus's cold, callous dark eyes flashed in my mind.

"*You've got a responsibility to this club,*" he'd sneered at me when I'd sat them down and threw my cut on the table. "*You're not throwin' that away over lost pussy and a dead kid, are you?*"

It had only taken a second, but that was all the time I needed to lunge forward and punch my club president right in the face. In the end, all it did was solidify what I'd already known: he didn't really give a shit about me. Not if he'd stoop that low, especially not when I'd had every intention of trying to have a civil, honest conversation about why I needed to cut myself loose. According to my mom, Dom, and pretty much everyone else, I was lucky Marcus had let me leave without any repercussions, but from where I'd been standing, and was still standing, that was nothing compared to the blows I'd already been dealt.

I walked out of the clubhouse that day without my cut and without my club and I never looked back.

"Anyway," I cleared my throat and cast her an anxious, sideways glance to find her still watching me with watery eyes. "I guess the club got me into prison, but prison got me out of the club."

"It's funny how life works like that, isn't it? Nothing ever really seems to go the way you planned..." she trailed off as the smile playing at her lips dropped.

Her eyes flew to something over my head and I turned to see some movement in one of the upstairs windows. The blinds twitched and I caught a flash of Sam's face before he realized he was caught. Those blinds slapped down just as quickly and Isabelle shook her head at the window.

"Nosy jerk," she grumbled under her breath.

I just chuckled. If I were him, I'd probably want to know what the so-called reformed outlaw was doing out here with my daughter too. My breath hitched on the last part of that and I glanced down at those three letters inked permanently on my skin. The tribute didn't do her justice, but I'd wanted it somewhere I could see it so it would be like I was carrying her with me, just like that upside down compass carried so many memories of her mother.

And now, as my eyes found her again, it was like we'd been transported back in time, before all our plans were shattered, before all our hopes and dreams evaporated into thin air.

. . .

Isabelle

"What're you thinking, Iz?" his quiet, hoarse voice called out and yanked me out of my thoughts.

I didn't even know where to start. So I decided to play it safe instead and take a page out of his book by skirting around the real issue.

"I was just thinking about how much simpler everything was when we were younger. Back when my biggest problems were pulling an all-nighter to finish a paper or getting a B on an exam and being scared to tell my dad," I laughed stiffly, acutely aware he was observing me a little too closely. "I guess I had no idea what the real world was really like when I was 20 and didn't know any better. Even after my mom died, worrying about my dad kicking me out seems easy now compared to everything else."

There was a lot left there that could be open for his interpretation, but I'd always had no problem telling him more than I'd intended to anyway. Besides, I had a feeling, with the way this night was headed, that I'd tell him just about anything he wanted to know if it meant I could spend more time with him like this.

"I think I know what you mean," he told me quietly. "If someone had told me 10 years ago that I'd be out of the club at 30 with two years of prison behind me and a new business in front of me, I think I would've laughed until I cried. But you never really think about how much those things you think you want will cost you in the end. You just think about what you want when you want it."

I nodded in silent understanding and decided to lighten things up a little more. "Just think, Caleb, 10 years ago you were wrapped around Ariel's little finger. Now look at you, all mature and grown-up with a college degree. I bet she'd barely recognize you if she saw you now."

Caleb laughed and lifted his eyes to the night sky with a shake of his head. "Wow, I haven't thought about that name in years."

"Kinda seems like forever ago, huh?"

"Shit, yeah," he chuckled.

My next words just popped out before I could even really think about what I was saying: "I saw her once in L.A. actually."

Caleb stilled on the swing and his head whipped around to face me.

"What?" he laughed, but the confusion in his voice was unmistakable.

"Yeah, a few years ago. I had a show there and she just showed up. She bought a couple pieces and we had a few drinks after the show, too."

His eyebrows shot up into his forehead and more than likely, he was wondering how in the hell the only two women he'd ever been serious about had ended up having drinks together. It was a fair question.

"Huh," was about all he seemed to be able to muster.

"It was nice," I allowed, trying to appease him. "We caught up, had a few laughs at your expense. No big deal, Caleb."

"*I just can't believe it,*" Ariel had sighed as she swirled her martini. "*I mean, if I were a betting woman, I would've put my entire life savings on you guys ending up married with lots of kids and...*"

She had trailed off, probably at the crestfallen expression on my face.

"*Well,*" Ariel had went on quietly. "*I know this is really stupid to admit now after all these years, but I was always really, I mean* really *jealous of you in high school.*"

"*What?*" I'd laughed.

"*It wasn't just the whole-everyone-loves-me-because-I'm-gorgeous-and-a-cheerleader-thing,*" Ariel had gestured toward me like that description still somehow applied. "*There were so many times when I would catch Caleb looking at you. It was like you'd come into the room or walk down the hallway and he'd be doing everything he could not to look at you and would just fail miserably. I just knew if you ever gave him the chance, he'd drop me like a bad habit.*"

"*Aw, come on. You know that's not true. He was crazy about you back then.*"

"*Yeah, well,*" Ariel's lips had twisted with a slight nod. "*I guess I knew even then I would lose him to you eventually.*"

I sucked in a deep breath to wash away that distant memory, as if that would somehow change the uncomfortable air that had settled between me and Caleb now. Suddenly, something shifted between us and Caleb was grinning down at me with that same smile that could so easily send my heart right into my stomach.

"Looks like you gave up on getting wasted, huh?" he smirked down at the near-full bottle resting by my feet.

I glanced at the bottle and shrugged. "I guess I decided I'd rather talk to you instead."

Me with a bottle was more than enough to do some damage and now that we'd gotten to talking, this was better.

"Alright," he laughed. "So talk. I feel like I've just been talking your ear off all night."

"What—"

"Tell me about New York," Caleb cut in softly. "I wanna hear everything."

His eyes were blue oceans swimming with hope, regret, anticipation, and something else I didn't want to think about. Now, with our current proximity, my hungry eyes roamed over him and what struck me the most was how he could be so different, yet still so achingly the same, so painfully familiar.

I liked this new, buzzed hairstyle—it made him look older and probably more professional too, but there were still hints of the boyish, charming 22-year-old I used to know. I'd always known he would only improve with age, but the faint lines around his eyes and forehead and the masculine goatee suited him in a way I couldn't have predicted. It was like he'd morphed into the man he was always supposed to be.

"Okay," I exhaled shakily. I took a breath and launched into the distraction we both needed. "New York is everything I thought it would be. My internship was...eh."

"What's that supposed to mean?" he laughed.

"What can I say?" I shrugged. "It was an internship. I scheduled appointments and showings for other artists, got coffee for other people, made copies, kept inventories, that sort of thing. It wasn't glamorous, that's for sure, and I knew that going into it. But The Warehouse always treated me well, I paid my dues, and when some space finally freed up, they booked my first show."

It wasn't quite as easy or as simple as I'd made it sound, but the details weren't really important. I'd done the work, put in my time, and earned my space, just like Dr. Jacobs said I would.

"And now you're raking it in, huh?" he grinned.

"Oh, I wouldn't exactly say that," I lifted my eyes up to the moonlit sky above me. "But I'm doing okay."

His lips curled up knowingly and his eyebrows lifted into his forehead.

"*Okay*? Didn't your last show sell out?"

My eyes narrowed at him playfully. Someone had clearly been keeping tabs on me long before this night. A few hours ago, I might've seen it as a slap in the face, one more reminder that he'd had every opportunity to find me in New York, but didn't. Now I just didn't want this night to end.

"It did," I confirmed warily. "My PR rep got a nice little bonus."

"Your PR rep? Hmm...that's what I thought," his eyebrows waggled victoriously.

"Hey," I pointed out. "I know how lucky I am. That whole starving artist stereotype exists for a reason, you know?"

"I always knew you'd be rich and famous," he laughed.

I cocked an eyebrow at him. "I wouldn't necessarily call myself rich or famous. Selling out my last show just means I did well for that *month*. You're on your own the other months until you do another show. You have to look elsewhere to make ends meet until that next opening happens."

"Like where?" he frowned.

"I got a part-time job at the Barney's a few blocks away from where I live and when the hours cut into my painting time a little too much, I bartended on the weekends for a few years until I could save up enough money to quit."

His eyebrows flew into his forehead and I could practically see the wheels in his head turning. The idea of me bartending in New York probably didn't sit well with him. It hadn't really sat well with my dad either, but the money I earned on those weekends was enough to float me through the time in between each of my shows and freed me up during the week to work.

Now came my lame attempt at lightening the mood.

"Hey, it was better than stripping, you know?"

All the color drained from his face at once and I had a sudden urge to lean forward and kiss him, if only it would make that stricken, forlorn expression slide off his face.

"That's not funny, Iz," he snapped back, accentuating each clipped syllable like even the possibility made him alternately want to hit something and physically ill.

"Geez, sorry," I muttered under my breath and rolled my eyes. "My dad didn't think that joke was very funny either."

Caleb shot me an exasperated glance out of the corner of his eye and leaned back a little in the swing.

"Being able to quit that job felt pretty good though," I admitted and at this point, it was more to ease his nerves about the whole thing than anything. "It felt like I was really becoming a serious artist, like all that hard work and all those dreams were finally starting to pay off. Hey and you know what? I was even able to put a little money into the gallery too. I'm the proud owner of five percent of The Warehouse. How do you like that?"

That sent a little more of the light back into his eyes and the exasperation on his face slipped into something more like pride and amusement.

"So," he grinned, bumping his shoulder into me playfully. "Rich, famous, *and* a savvy businesswoman? I'm impressed, Iz."

"Oh, shut it," I knocked him back in the shoulder. "Five percent isn't that much in the grand scheme of things."

"How does that song go? *If I can make it there, I'll make it anywhere...*"

"Oh my God. You are not singing—"

"Oh, shut it," he waved a hand at me, throwing my little dig right back at me. "Who doesn't love Frank Sinatra?"

Somehow, I think my eyebrows shifted even higher into my hairline. This was just too much.

"You know, Saul was humming that earlier today," I informed him matter-of-factly. "There's been a little too much of that going around."

"He taught me well," Caleb just shrugged. "The classics. All that shit."

"Oh boy."

His grin only widened. "So New York..."

"Right," I rolled my eyes at him. "New York."

I delved back into everything he wanted to hear—Christmas in New York, snow, my series of slightly-increasing-in-size apartments starting with a tiny studio apartment all the way to the three-bedroom brownstone I had now in Chelsea, the studio space I rented a few blocks away, the few friends I'd allowed myself to make, the coffee shop where I got my lattes every morning, the best Mexican food I'd ever had in my life, the park where Cooper and I went on walks...it was such an out of body experience to sit here like this describing the life I had to the one person I'd always wanted to share it with.

"That sounds real nice, Iz," Caleb's soft voice called out to me. "I'm glad you have a good life there."

"Yeah, I do."

It's just not the life I always thought I'd have with you.

He glanced up at the night sky and squinted in the moonlight. "It's getting kinda late, huh? You cold?"

"A little bit."

Caleb gestured with his head toward the house and stood up, wincing a little when he put some weight on his bad knee. Then he reached down to sweep up my wine bottle in one hand and held his free hand out to me to help me off the swing. I stared at his open palm for a little too long—I'd been trying so hard not to let myself touch him.

I'd slipped back in the house before when my dad went to bed and I'd slipped again in just letting him out here with me in the first place. But like my body had a will of its own, my hand slipped into his, reveling in that familiar roughness, which just sent my mind spiraling down a dark hole as I remembered all the other places those rough hands had touched before.

I dropped his hand just as quickly. Being so close to him this way was dangerous. It was twisting my mind and knotting up my emotions and that was exactly what I needed to avoid.

We walked back into the house in silence and were just met with Cooper's low *woof* as we entered the kitchen.

"So, um," Caleb ran a hand over his head and grimaced. "You know I have to crash here tonight, right? I'm not leaving."

It was so direct. *I'm not leaving.* Of course he wasn't leaving and I couldn't exactly let him sleep in his truck either. Although, on some level, that did seem a little bit safer.

"Right," I sighed. "You can sleep in the guest room if you want. It's okay."

He chewed on the inside of his cheek in thought and glanced back at me agitatedly. "I can just take the couch. It's not like I haven't done it before."

His intentions were pretty paper-thin here. If we were going to sleep under the same roof tonight, the more space between us the better. I couldn't help but wholeheartedly agree.

We stared at each other for a few awkward beats and he shoved his hands deep in his front pockets as he glanced down at his shoes.

"I'm sorry, Iz," he murmured. "I know you don't want me or any of my guys hanging around your house all the time, but this is just the way it was to be for now."

"I know," I tried to ooze as much reassurance into my voice as I could, but came up lacking in a big way. "I get it. And I appreciate it. I really do, especially given, you know, the circumstances."

His eyes steeled over. "I told you nothing's gonna happen to you and I meant it."

"I know, Caleb," I whispered and dared a step closer to the island.

My feet stilled just a few inches away from him and I reached out until my open palm connected with his chest. There was no stopping it now; my body had won over my mind for the time being.

"Are you scared of him?"

His eyebrows lifted. "Of Wallace? No. He doesn't scare me."

My fingers splayed out on his chest just as he wound an arm around my waist to tuck me in a little bit tighter against him.

"But what he could do scares you."

A grim line spread across his face and he nodded. "Yeah. That scares me."

I leaned forward until my cheek rested against his chest and squeezed my eyes shut when I felt two strong arms wrap themselves around me, cocooning me in their warmth and their safety. His lips brushed my hair and his arms squeezed even tighter around me.

"It's always gonna follow me, isn't it?" he murmured hoarsely into my hair. "I'm never really gonna be out."

I lifted my face away from my chest so I could look him in the eye. His face had gone ashen and his eyes simmered with so much regret and desperation that I couldn't help but wrap my arms around his neck just to give him something.

"All these years," he whispered. "And all it takes is one pissed-off president and I'm back knee-deep in the shit. And now I'm just sitting here, wondering who else I've pissed off and what else is gonna come back and bite me in the ass. There are so many things I've done, so many things I should still be in prison for. I mean, Iz, I've *killed* people. I shouldn't even be standing here with you right now."

"Hey," my hands flew up to his cheeks to force him to look at me. "You're here though. You gave yourself a chance to have a different kind of life and that's all you can do. You can't control anything or anybody else."

He closed his eyes and nodded. "You're right. I know that. It's just hard to look at myself in the mirror sometimes knowing some of the things I've done that I can't take back."

While he could've been talking about a number of things, I chose to just focus on his past in the club, carefully stepping around everything else.

"Can I ask you a question?"

His lips curled up. "You can ask me anything, Iz."

"Why did you stay here?" I asked, finally voicing the question I'd wanted the answer to for years. "I mean, you could've gone to freaking Australia if you wanted to, but you stayed here. I just don't get it. Wouldn't it just have been so much easier if you'd left town?"

His eyes dropped down to my face, focusing for a moment on my lips, and then he smiled sadly. "Yeah, it would've been easier, but I couldn't."

"Why?"

His thumb brushed my cheek as he spoke. "Because if I left, I knew I'd never see you again."

A million emotions whipped around me all at once—confusion, frustration, elation, anger—but it was those butterflies fluttering in my stomach that held most of my focus.

"So you didn't leave just on the off-chance that I'd come back someday and we'd...what? Run into each other?"

It was right on the tip of my tongue to ask him why he'd never come to New York or why he'd never reached out before if he'd really wanted to see me that badly, but that would be too much truth for one night. I'd already gotten more than I could handle.

"I don't know," he shrugged with a soft grin. "But I do know that if I'd left, we wouldn't be standing here like this right now and I wouldn't trade that for anything."

Both of his hands settled around my face now and overwhelmed by his closeness and drunk on the emotions he'd resurrected in me, I closed the short space between us and pressed my lips gently into his. Caleb stilled for only a moment, no doubt startled by the fact that *I* was the one initiating this, but I was way past the point of no return now, and he recovered a heartbeat later, tightening his hold on my face, somehow pulling me even closer to him.

It started slow and tender as our mouths tentatively became reacquainted with each other and I couldn't help the soft moan in the back of my throat just at tasting him again. It had been so long since I'd felt this, I'd honestly forgotten what his lips felt like...or maybe I'd just forced myself to forget. But there was no denying how good this felt, how at home I felt as his hands slid all the way around my waist.

Suddenly, I was moving in the air as he spun us around to press me back into the island. He gripped my hips to hoist me up onto the counter and my legs wrapped around his waist to help him sink in even deeper before I had a moment to recover.

His tongue pushed its way through my mouth and as his rough, familiar hands skimmed up the back of my shirt, just stopping at the edge of my bra. I shivered in his arms and wondered fleetingly if this was just all a dream. If I'd wake up any moment now, alone in my bed, and wondering what the hell just happened. But his lips were still moving over mine, tasting and taking everything I offered to him, eagerly giving it right back to me.

My hands wound their way around the back of his neck and gripped the top of his head as he ground my hips down against the hardness in his jeans. Just as I leaned my forehead against his to sigh into his lips, a loud cough jerked me out of the whirlwind I'd stumbled into it.

My hands dropped away from Caleb's face and I turned just in time to see my dad shuffling toward the refrigerator. Caleb jolted and hustled out from between my legs to put some space between us. He ran a hand over his head as if to smooth the hair he didn't really have there and my dad cast a wary glance over his shoulder at us.

"Don't mind me," he chuckled. "Just needed something to drink."

"Sorry, Dad," I murmured and bit down on my bottom lip as I slid off the counter.

My dad met my eyes briefly before turning his attention to Caleb. "Where are you planning on sleeping tonight?"

Caleb cleared his throat roughly. "The couch."

"Good," he nodded and shut the fridge door as he turned to us with a water bottle in his hand. "Probably best to take it slow, huh?"

I opened my mouth to protest, but for the life of me, I couldn't find any words to say. My dad just waved goodnight and disappeared around the stairwell. When my eyes found Caleb again, he was staring slack-jawed after my dad and he shook his head.

"Wow."

"Yeah," I laughed. "That wasn't embarrassing or anything."

Instead of responding, he tucked his hands deep in his pockets and grinned at me.

"I should, um," I swallowed hard, already backpedalling toward the same hallway my dad had just disappeared to. "I should get to bed. I'll see you in the morning?"

"I'll be here," he nodded. "Sweet dreams, Iz."

I waved awkwardly because there was no way in hell I was getting out of this gracefully and I scrambled up the stairs, practically running my dad over in the process, and didn't stop until my old bedroom door was shut safely behind me.

CHAPTER TWENTY-SIX
A Better Day

Isabelle

My eyes fluttered open and I buried my face in my pillow with a groan. God, I felt like I'd just tried to run a marathon—tried and miserably failed, that is—with heavy limbs, exhausted muscles, and a pounding headache.

The real problem was that I'd spent the night tossing and turning on my mattress, twisting the sheets around myself until my head spun, and doing everything in my power to keep my body right in this bed. All night I'd waged war with myself—stay in bed or race down to the living room to...do what, I didn't know. I just knew I wanted to find out. I just knew I wanted to be wherever Caleb was.

I glanced at the digital clock on my nightstand and blew out an exasperated sigh.

I'd already let Cooper outside a few hours ago, so I wasn't expecting to see him waiting by my door or anything, but when I made it to the bottom of the stairs, I certainly didn't expect to see my dad and Caleb sitting at the kitchen table with steaming mugs of coffee in front of them and my dog right at Caleb's side, basking in the attention as Caleb scratched behind his ears with his free hand.

"Dirty rotten traitor," I muttered under my breath and cocked an eyebrow at my dog as I headed into the kitchen.

Determined to keep my distance and stand my ground, I refused eye contact with all three men in the kitchen.

"Morning, Isabelle," my dad called out to me softly.

My heart tugged a little at his voice, so much weaker than it used to be, and I threw him a quick smile over my shoulder.

Then another equally and just as painfully familiar voice called out to me too: "Morning, Iz."

My eyes darted over to the other side of the table, where Caleb sat stoically. Was he waiting for me to climb into his lap or something? High-five him for pushing me up against the kitchen island last night and sort of having his way with me? Admit I'd spent the better part of the night wrapped up in my comforter wishing I was wrapped up in him instead?

"Hi," I replied back lamely. Even I knew that was weak, but what else was I supposed to do?

But when I dared another glance his way, my lips curved downward. The Caleb I remembered, the same one who could've easily charmed the panties off a nun if he'd wanted to, wasn't here right now.

All the swagger, the cool confidence, the cocky smirk—none of that was present at the table. Instead, his lips were pressed together in a thin line and he clutched his free hand around his coffee mug like his life depended on it as his eyes anxiously searched for something I knew I couldn't give him.

"So, uh," Caleb cleared his throat roughly and ruffled the fur on the top of Cooper's head. "I can't stick around too long this morning because I have to get back to the shop, but one of my guys should be here any minute to take his shift."

I nodded and opted to chew on the inside of my cheek instead of verbally responding. That just seemed safer.

"Jared's good just hanging out in the driveway," Caleb went on and his eyes only shifted to me once as he spoke. "You'll never even know he's there unless you need to go somewhere today."

I finally found my voice and lifted an eyebrow. "And he's gonna spend the night in the driveway too?"

Some of that anxiousness slipped away as Caleb's lips quirked up into a smile. "Nah. I'll be back when I'm done at the shop for the day."

With plans to spend the night again. Of course he wouldn't let any of 'his guys' spend the night here—he wanted that shift all to himself.

"That sounds like a good plan," my dad told him. "And feel free to take the guest room tonight. You're more than welcome to it."

The underlying sentiment, of course, being that Caleb was welcome to the *guest* room, not necessarily *my* room. Thanks, Dad.

That was about as far as this discussion got before those tell-tale sounds of an engine roaring filled the driveway and Caleb was up on his feet a half a second later, stalking toward the front door with Cooper hot on his heels.

He peered through the window right next to the door, ever on high alert, and after finding what he was looking for, his shoulders relaxed and he reached down to scratch the top of Cooper's head.

"It's just Jared," Caleb told us from over his shoulder. "I should get going."

The moment it clicked that he was leaving, and that I wouldn't see him for the rest of the day, I moved toward the front door before I could stop myself.

Caleb glanced back at me in surprise as he slipped on his shoes and reached for his keys; I couldn't really blame him. I'd been running hot and cold on him so much I had half a mind to ask him why he even bothered with me in the first place.

Today was just a day I just didn't want to think about. Any other year, I'd be so hungover, I'd sleep the whole day away until I finally got out of bed long enough to eat something and drink just enough more so I could pass out for the rest of the night. I didn't have that luxury today because I'd spent my night in quicksand instead.

As if he could read my mind, Caleb reached out until his fingertips caught my elbow and pulled me closer with gentle movements. I was falling recklessly right into that quicksand again without a net and without a care for consequence.

"Hey," I deflected, immediately darting my eyes down to our feet. It was just easier if I didn't look at him. Looking at him brought up a whole slew of shit I didn't want to touch right now. "Thank you for staying last night. I'm sure you had plenty of better things to do—people to see, that sort of thing, but I appreciate you keeping an eye on things. That means a lot, Caleb."

He eyed me carefully as if he was mentally picking apart each word and sorting through the bullshit syllable by syllable. Then he nodded, but his blue eyes still bored into me with the kind of measured intensity that had me shifting anxiously from side to side.

"You weren't keeping me from anything or anyone," Caleb murmured, but that last word was pointed and marked specifically to send a message.

There's no one else.

I swallowed hard, mentally repeating a different mantra: *he only wants you now because he can't have you.*

And when he spoke again, I just wasn't mentally prepared to handle it.

"I was thinking, Iz," he flashed me a quick, nervous smile and rubbed the back of his neck. "Maybe you'd want to come to the shop and spend the day with me? It wouldn't have to be right now. I know you just got up, but I'd really like to spend some time with you today whenever you're ready."

It was right on the tip of my tongue to ask him what spending the day with him would all entail, but I never got that far. My knee-jerk reaction was to shake my head as quickly as possible.

"Doesn't that kind of fly in the face of you not wanting Theo Wallace to see me with you? What if he comes back?"

That was the only straw I had to grasp, but I held on as tight as I could.

His lips quirked up and once again, he saw right through me. "Weren't you the one who told me last night I can't spend the rest of my life looking over my shoulder?"

There'd be a smart-ass response somewhere if I could just stop looking at his lips long enough to find it.

"I don't want to hide," Caleb went on softly. "And you'll be safe there. But you already knew that."

Yeah. I did. And that safety was almost enough to propel me right into his arms and anywhere else he wanted to take me. Almost.

I sucked in a deep breath and exhaled long enough to find my bearings. "I just don't think it's a good idea."

It was hard not to flinch when his face fell in disappointment, but what else was I supposed to do? Let myself get swept away in him again? The man standing in front of me had hurt me more than anyone had ever hurt me before in my life and handing him the opportunity to do it again on a platter was as reckless as it was asinine.

Caleb steeled an impassive expression on his handsome face and nodded tightly like he'd fully expected that response. I guessed I had to give him a little credit for trying.

"Okay," he nodded again and his thumb brushed my cheek for just a second. "If you change your mind, you know where to find me."

Then he stepped away, giving me the space I needed, waved goodbye to my dad still in the kitchen, and walked out the front door.

Several moments passed before I felt like I could finally breathe again and I stumbled backward, fumbling for some sort of reprieve I knew I'd never find. Cooper brushed up against my legs, no doubt alerted by my mood, and he swept his tongue up the outside of my hand. It wasn't enough, but I patted his head anyway. When I turned on my heel to head toward the kitchen again, I skidded in my tracks, stopped short by my dad's presence at the table.

He lifted an eyebrow as he took a sip from his coffee mug and gestured for me to sit down in the chair Caleb had vacated. I opted for the chair across from him instead.

"Let me guess," I sighed. "You heard all that, huh?"

"Every word," he smiled sadly. "You want some coffee?"

I shook my head, but he got up anyway with wooden movements and headed for the coffee pot.

"So you're not going to see him at all today?" he asked me over his shoulder as he poured me a cup.

I sighed again and rubbed my temples. "No, I'm not."

"Why?"

I shot him an exasperated glare over my shoulder. "I thought you heard everything. It's not a good idea, Dad."

"Yeah, I heard you say that, but why isn't it a good idea?"

"Because, Dad," I bit out through clenched teeth. "It's just not."

"So," he told me as he set a cup of coffee in front of me. "It's *not* a good idea to spend this day with the *one* person who understands what today means to you more than anyone else? Did I get that right?"

Ugh. Why did he always have to be right?

I snatched my coffee mug up and hightailed it out of the kitchen with Cooper dutifully behind me.

"Thanks for your help, Dad," I called over my shoulder as I took the stairs two-by-two.

When I closed my bedroom door behind me, my hands were shaking. My chest was tightening, but this wasn't the onslaught of another panic attack. No, this was something a little bit worse. This was guilt. Cold, hard, slap-you-in-the-face guilt.

My trembling fingers groped my purse for my sketchbook and I curled up on the bed with Cooper right at my feet as I let the pencil do all the thinking for me. Long strokes of lead scratched across the paper, but I had no control over it. The image took shape whether I liked it or not, whether I was exorcising demons or summoning them, and when I finally dropped the pencil and took a breath, my eyes fell to the thick, dark lines.

Eyes.

Disappointed, grieving, heartbroken eyes.

Eyes that haunted my dreams and followed me through all these years of emptiness and loneliness. Eyes that held the key to both the happiest and worst moments of my life. Eyes that had never let me go.

I'd spent so much time pushing all these feelings away since I'd come back and last night, it felt good to just *feel* without wasting so much time overthinking everything all the time.

He was my siren call, beckoning me into dark waters, tempting me to give in, promising me everything but giving me nothing.

And so I fell once again, diving in headfirst with my eyes closed and my heart wide open.

. . .

Caleb

I swung my fist into the bag, hoping this hit would finally take the edge off, but the connection wasn't enough to burn away this emptiness. The little bit of pain that cracked through my knuckles all the way up to my elbow was almost enough to break down that wall—frustration, disappointment, and pain all cemented into one.

Hitting my boxing bag usually helped me work out the aggression keeping me stagnant, but today, not so much. Landing blow after blow just made it worse. Just made me angrier. Just made me want to hurt myself a little bit more.

I landed one more furious hit into the bag and let it sway from side to side in the garage, my chest heaving, but without the release I needed.

Well, this was really fucking productive.

All I'd gotten out of it was sore knuckles and a decent workout. Still no release. No redemption. No absolution. That just left me with the sting of Isabelle's rejection. Add that to my self-loathing and I was well on my way to reaching for that bottle of Jack I kept hidden in the bottom drawer of my desk.

By the time I'd taken a shower, changed, and headed back down to the garage, I didn't feel any better. Or any cleaner for that matter. I tried to be productive and listen to Lucas report the status of specific projects, but I just ended up tuning him out instead. Aside from his shitty judgment, he was still a good kid and a good employee, one I'd incidentally just given a raise to not too long ago, and he didn't really deserve me ignoring him right now.

It was only when he trailed off that he actually had my attention and when I glanced up again, Lucas was staring off into the distance at something in the parking lot. My eyes followed his gaze and my blood simmered a little when Jared's truck pulled into a space right next to the office.

"What the hell?" I muttered. "Is someone covering his shift at the house?"

Lucas blinked back at me, probably too stunned by my hard tone than anything else.

The schedule was very clear and I'd made it just as clear that under no circumstances were they supposed to leave Isabelle's house until their replacement had arrived.

"He'd better have a good fucking reason for being here right now," I growled and set off toward the parking lot.

I only made it a few paces before I skidded to a stop with Lucas practically running right into my back. Jared had already gotten out of the truck and was grinning at me sheepishly with his hands in his pockets, but that wasn't what held my attention.

It was Isabelle.

Stepping out of Jared's truck with her arms folded protectively around herself, she glanced around the lot and I swore I felt my heart literally swell in my chest. It didn't matter that she'd had a delayed reaction. All that mattered was that she was here.

Once the initial shock wore off, my eyes drank her in. The tight black leggings coupled with her black heels and leather jacket had my mouth watering. The way her short hair curled around her neck and flipped up at the ends. The way she nervously clenched her hands around the straps of her huge purse. Every time I saw her was just another reminder of how long I'd been deprived of her. How many nights I'd spent dreaming of her. How much I'd missed her. How much I loved her.

"Hey, Isabelle," Lucas called out to her with a wave as she met us right outside the edge of the shop.

My head snapped in his direction.

"You, um," the idiot stammered on. "You look real nice today."

"Thanks, Luc—" Isabelle started, but didn't get much further when I abruptly fisted a hand into Lucas's shirt to push him backward.

"Get your ass back to work," I snarled at him, pointing into the shop.

Lucas's eyes just about bulged out of his head and he nodded anxiously, shuffling backward before turning on his heel and just about sprinting back into the shop. My eyes didn't leave him until I heard Isabelle's light laughter in front of me.

"Oh, come on, Caleb," she smiled shyly and bit down on her bottom lips as she stepped even closer. "He seems like a nice kid. A little naive maybe, but nice."

"He is," I admitted. "He just needs a few lessons in how to respect women is all."

And maybe I just don't like anyone else drooling over what's mine.

Good thing I knew better than to admit *that* particular thought out loud.

Her head tilted to the side, no doubt seeing right through my bullshit as usual, but she didn't call me on it. Instead, she chewed on the inside of her cheek, waiting for me to make the first move.

"What are you doing here, Iz?"

I already knew the answer, but I needed to hear her say it.

She swallowed tightly and pressed a smile on her face. "I changed my mind."

I wanted to grab her face and kiss her, but I had to tread lightly here.

"I can see that," I grinned.

Her eyebrows lifted at my light tone and she laughed. "Maybe we should figure out how to make this day a good one instead of a bad one. What do you think?"

I rocked back on my heels and didn't bother trying to mask the wide, happy smile that crossed my face. "I think that sounds like the best idea I've heard in awhile. Where should we start?"

The question hung in the air for a few long moments. This had to be on her terms. Every single step, every single move, and wherever this day led us, it all needed to be at her pace.

"How about a tour?"

"Well," I laughed. "What the lady wants, the lady gets, I guess."

Her eyes sparked as I gestured toward the garage and waited long enough for her to step in front of me so I could gingerly place my hand on the small of her back to guide her. She jumped a little at the contact, but relaxed just as quickly, leaning into my touch as I led her around my shop.

I needed to pinch myself. This was my reality right now. She was really here, listening with rapt attention as I explained the various ins and outs of the machinery and our routine here. And it didn't help my disbelief when she graciously shook each one of my guys' hands as I introduced them and glanced up at me with such unabashed pride.

I found myself hanging on to every word, every glance, every smile, and now that she was here, I'd forgotten why I hated this day so much in the first place. Her mere presence had eradicated all the ugliness surrounding my memories of this day and now I was just looking forward to whatever today had in store.

"So," she exhaled a little nervously when we stood right at the bottom of the stairs that led to my apartment. "You live up there, huh?"

"I do."

Isabelle kept chewing on her bottom lip as her eyes flitted up the stairs again. "Can I, um, can I see it?"

My heart stuttered in a panic because I was pretty sure my tiny apartment wasn't in any condition for her to see it. If she wanted to stay there for any length of time, I just didn't know where to go from there. But hell if I'd deny her now.

"Sure," I swallowed hard and gestured with my head toward the stairs. "Let's go."

She trailed after me, following my lead, and I sucked in a deep breath when I held open the door so she could pass through. It wasn't much, but it was all I really needed. I had a bed, a TV, a few shelves, a tiny bathroom, and an even smaller kitchen. As far as I was concerned, the downstairs of this building was the part that really mattered.

Isabelle took a few tentative steps inside, taking her time as she surveyed the small space. I shuffled in behind her and on reflex, rushed to kick a pile of dirty clothes under my bed and then made a beeline for my makeshift kitchen, which was really just a stove and a sink, and started shoving some stray dishes into the sink when Isabelle's light laughter came up right behind me.

"Caleb," she called out to me. "Don't worry about it. I remember your dorm at the clubhouse looking way worse than this. In fact, this place is pretty clean compared to that."

I huffed out a laugh and ran a hand over my head. "Yeah, well, I'm pretty sure that was when I was just a stupid kid who only cleaned his room when his mom told him to. I don't really have any excuse now."

I flinched a little at the mention of my mom. God, I hadn't seen her in months. Maybe even a full year if I was being honest. No. I shook that off. I wasn't going to let any painful memories bring us down today.

She seemed to pick up on this shift in mood and padded lightly over to my bookshelf, calling over her shoulder, "The more things change, the more they stay the same."

"Right," I chuckled and again, following her lead, moved closer until my shoulder brushed hers. "Besides, I'm totally living in the lap of luxury now. Can't you tell by all this space I've got?"

Her eyes followed my gesture out into the pretty small space, but she just shrugged. "It's not so bad. How much more do you need?"

"I guess you're right," I grinned down at her.

If I had any regrets about my shop, it was that I'd had to sell the house for some of the start-up cash I needed to get my business off the ground. It just hadn't made sense to basically pay two mortgages—one for the house and one for the building—and watching the house I'd bought for Isabelle, with all those plans we'd attached to it, slip right through my fingertips had stung more than I'd expected. But, then again, that was also part of the reason I'd been able to help her dad and I didn't regret that for a second.

When she leaned into me ever so slightly, my fingertips pressed into the small of her back. I just couldn't stop myself from touching her when she was this close and I couldn't apologize for something that came so naturally. Thankfully, she didn't shy away. If anything, she just leaned in even closer as her eyes scanned the contents of my bookshelf. She reached out to skim her fingertips along the bindings and murmured some of the titles.

"*Huck Finn, Of Mice and Men, One Flew Over The Cuckoo's Nest, The Outsiders, A Lesson Before Dying, The Shining...*" she cocked an eyebrow at me. "Classic lit and Stephen King, huh?"

"Hey," I nudged her in the side with my elbow. "Stephen King *is* classic. Don't make fun of me, Iz. I'm very sensitive."

Her lips curled up into that beautiful smile and her head dipped back a little as she laughed. "Sorry. I wouldn't dream of making fun of you for reading. This is just—I just didn't expect you to be this *different,* but in a good way. I'm so proud of you, Caleb. Everything you've done, how far you've come...I just can't believe it even though I know I should."

"I wouldn't give myself all the credit," I told her quietly. "I was just surviving. That's all."

"You did exactly what you had to do," she nodded and inhaled shakily.

"Hey, Iz?" I murmured.

"Yeah?"

"I really missed you."

She sucked in a shaky breath and I resisted the urge to run my thumb over her lips when they tilted up.

"I know," she smiled. "I missed you, too."

That was all the encouragement I needed and I closed the space between us to capture her lips, pressing into them with all the words right on the tip of my tongue I still couldn't say. Maybe she could taste them and taste what I needed to say to her, taste what I needed from her. Maybe that could be enough.

Her hands twisted around my neck, skimming up around my head, and it was all I could do to just grip her tighter, pulling her flush against my body and not pull her right onto my bed. It would be so easy to lose control right now and slide my hands down her body to take what I'd been denied for so long. But that wasn't why she was here and if I let things get too out of hand tonight, I could easily wake up in the morning to an empty bed and never see her again.

With this new conviction, I reluctantly pulled myself back and ran my thumb across her cheek.

"Can I make you dinner tonight?"

She laughed and I had to steel all my control just so I didn't ruin this moment by kissing her again. "Can I help?"

My eyes widened and my mind immediately jumped back to every single one of Isabelle's cooking disasters in the past. Chicken, spaghetti, lasagna, even homemade pizza—each one more horrific and traumatizing than the last.

"You know, Iz, I think my stomach's finally recovered from your cooking. Maybe—ow!" I ducked when she swatted at me again.

"Oh, shut up," she laughed again. "It wasn't that bad."

I just cocked an eyebrow her way. Enough said.

Her eyes lifted to the ceiling and she sighed. "Okay, fine. Maybe it was that bad, *but* I'm much better now. I can actually make an entire meal without getting anybody sick or burning down my kitchen."

"Tempting," I held my hands up. "But you're my guest. I'm gonna cook for you whether you like it or not."

"Oh boy," she muttered under her breath and whether *I* liked it or not, she sank down right onto my bed.

To be fair, there really wasn't anywhere else to sit, but I still wasn't prepared for the sight of her sitting there, waiting for...something. I took that as my cue to get my ass to work and after a quick inventory of what little food I had in my barely-existent kitchen, I got down to business. Isabelle observed me with careful curiosity as I got the sauce going and mixed up some batter before tossing the chicken in.

She leaned over my shoulder to inhale the aroma of tomatoes and Italian spices and her eyes widened. "Wow, that smells amazing. Since when do you know how to make chicken parmigiana?"

"Since always," I tossed back. "You just never got a chance to try it because you were too busy trying to kill us with salmonella."

She smacked me on the shoulder and shook her head, muttering, "Asshole."

"You know," I wagged my marinara-stained spoon at her as I spoke. "I worry about you all by yourself in New York. How have you managed to survive all these years anyway?"

"Just fine, thank you very much," she shot back. "I took some cooking classes and everything. But I guess some of us go grocery shopping a little more than others."

I laughed as I dumped the sauce and a shitload of mozzarella cheese on top of the chicken and shoved the dish in the oven. Little did she know that Saul kept all the fridges stocked—the one in our break room downstairs and the one in my apartment. Whatever he bought, I cooked.

When I turned back to her, I leaned up against the edge of the counter with my arms folded across my chest.

"So you've got cooking classes, a kick-ass art studio, the fancy apartment, and a dog," I surmised. "All the makings of a true New York woman. Now all you're missing is the accent."

"Hey, I can take care of myself. You don't even know the half of it. If anybody ever messed with me, I could totally take 'em."

"Oh really?" I cocked an eyebrow at her.

"Yep. You think Coop's all I got? I have a bat under my bed, I carry a knife in my purse, *and* I took a self-defense class with one of the assistants at the gallery a few years ago. I got a certificate from the class and everything. It's official—I'm a real badass."

"Huh."

While part of me was impressed, and a little turned on by the idea of her wielding a bat, the idea of her in an apartment all by herself didn't sit well with me. I didn't even want to think about any times when she hadn't been by herself, if she'd had anybody with her for the night...

"So, you know," she went on lightly. "If you need any protection, you know which girl to call."

That got my attention and I pushed off the counter to crowd her space a little, willingly playing along. "What makes you think I need your protection?"

"Oh, I don't know. Maybe the fact that you've got at least two guns here somewhere you're not supposed to have."

Well, she had a point. Legally, I wasn't supposed to own a gun, but since both of those guns were technically licensed to and purchased by Jared, I wasn't too worried about that. Besides, once the ATF and just about everyone else realized the club had never and would never put any money into my shop, my side of town had gotten pretty quiet.

I cocked a playful eyebrow at her, liking the turn this conversation had taken. "Oh *really*?"

"Yeah, you haven't seen my moves," she laughed, grinning up at me like we were the only two people in the world and nothing else around us existed.

"Alright, alright," I pivoted around her to put some space between us and motioned toward myself with both hands. "Bring it. Show me what you got, Martin."

Her head tipped back as she laughed and waved her hands in front of her. "Your funeral. But this only works if you come at me."

My lips twisted into a wolfish grin. Yeah, I *definitely* liked where this was headed. When I took a few confident steps into her personal space, her hands came down to rest lightly on my shoulders, putting just enough pressure on them to keep me from moving any closer.

"So if you were coming at me from the front," she breathed, her voice thick and husky. "I would probably bring my knee up like this."

When her knee lifted up to my groin, just enough to brush up against my jeans, her lips twisted into a knowing, almost powerful smirk. Her knee lingered there for a few agonizing moments, moving up and down with enough sweet pressure to elicit a low growl from me.

"What else would you do?" I murmured into her hair.

"I'd probably go for your knee next," she whispered up at me. With that, the tortured pressure left from between my legs and she playfully tapped my right knee with her left foot, twisting her hip to press into my knee from a side angle.

"That's not a bad move," I chuckled hoarsely.

"I think it's pretty effective," she retorted, even though my hand was already making a leisurely trail from her ankle right up to the inside of her thigh. When my fingers skimmed around the curve of her hip, her eyes fluttered shut at the light contact. I wouldn't let things go much further than this, but for now? I'd let us have some fun.

"Anything else you'd do?"

"Blunt objects are good too," she murmured, her eyes still squeezed shut. "I could always hit you over the head with my phone or stab you with my keys or something."

A low chuckle erupted from my throat and I placed a featherlight kiss on her neck, reveling in the taste and the feeling of her sweet skin underneath my mouth. Using my hands to guide her where to go, I turned her around so that her back rested against my chest.

"What if I came at you from behind, huh?" I hummed into her ear. "What would you do then?"

Her breath was coming in more haggard now and I suspected it had a lot to do with the fact that my hands had curved around her waist, teasing her into doing exactly what I wanted.

"I'd probably do something like this," she pushed out roughly, lifting her left leg up to lightly tap the inside of my foot with her heel. That small amount of pressure against my foot was enough momentum for her to arch her hips right into my jeans, offering up sweet payback with just a little bit of friction.

"Uh huh," I groaned into her hair, digging my fingers even deeper into her soft skin. "That's pretty good, too. Anything else?"

"Maybe this," Isabelle whispered as her right arm reached up over her head and touched her elbow to my cheek. A moment later, her arm continued its ascent and wrapped around my neck, skimming up to run along the buzzed edges of my hair.

"I like your hair like this," she murmured in my ear.

"Yeah?"

It would be so easy to take this opportunity, one she was giving me so willingly, and let my fingers do exactly what they knew how to do, but we were both too vulnerable right now, too emotional and raw, for this to go much further. But *after* tonight? That was a different story.

"Hey, Caleb?" Isabelle's voice called out to me, pulling me from the push and pull of my thoughts. "Do you smell something burning?"

I jerked out of her arms and sped right to the stove, waving away the billows of smoke wafting from it. Oh shit. Of fucking course. When I opened the stove, only to be met with more smoke and the horrible stench of salty, burnt cheese, it only confirmed it: I'd epically screwed up dinner.

My eyes narrowed on Isabelle, who'd all but collapsed on my bed in a fit of laughter. "You distracted me on purpose."

That just made her double over with more laughter. "I swear I didn't! You messed up all by yourself."

I threw a hand towel down on the floor. "Oh, that's it."

When I advanced on her, she leapt off the bed and scampered playfully into my bathroom, yelping when I wrapped my arms around her waist and hauled her back into the main room. I tossed her lightly onto the bed and even as she laughed, she'd never looked more beautiful. Her hair fanned out on my comforter, all spread out and waiting for me to run my fingers through it, and all I wanted to do was fall onto the bed with her and let it happen.

But I pulled myself back, firm in my resolve to respect the little bit of room she'd given me to move here.

So I ran a hand over my head and blew out a deep breath as she sat up on her elbows, waiting for me to make the next move.

"What should we do now?" she asked, her breath still coming in and out in short rasps.

Pretty soon she'll be back where she belongs, I promised myself. *Just not tonight.*

If she stayed on my bed like this any longer, I'd...and then my mouth quirked up.

"I got an idea, Iz."

CHAPTER TWENTY-SEVEN
Cosmic Love

Caleb

I never thought I'd feel this again. Never expected I'd be here, that she'd be here. Her arms were wrapped around my waist, the hum of my bike in my ears, and the wind whipped around us. This was the closest to flying I'd probably ever been—high on the rush, adrenaline pumping through my veins, and propelling me right up into the clouds.

Up until the moment she walked through my shop a few weeks ago, everything was running out of sync. Being with her again felt like all those missed beats and all those flubbed steps just didn't matter anymore.

Maybe the life I'd wanted, the same life that had slipped right through my fingertips, was reaching out again, just waiting for me to grab it and hold on with everything I had.

I was ready.

The only thing I was waiting on now was Isabelle.

She shifted against my back and leaned into my shoulder as we slowed to a stop light. Her warm breath surrounded my ear, and just like pretty much everything else about her, carried me away like undertow. I'd happily drown in her for—

The roar of motorcycle engines split through the night air and all the hairs on my arms stood on end. They were coming from the opposite direction, most likely from the clubhouse, but their cuts were unmistakable even from the distance. I'd grown up with that black leather, tracing the familiar lines of that devil horse on my dad's cut until I fell asleep.

Marcus was in the front, as usual, with Dom right behind him and Casey to his left. Tiny, ZZ, Heath, and Doc flanked behind them in a familiar formation I'd partaken in more times than I could count.

We sat on opposite sides of the intersection and it was almost as if time had stood still. Isabelle's arms tightened around me and Dom nodded from behind his president, but that was all the acknowledgement I got from any of them. Marcus's dark eyes flicked to me for a second, his lips curled up into a tight snarl, and then he shifted his eyes straight ahead to the road like he was trying to convince himself I wasn't really 40 feet in front of him. Like it was easier to just pretend I didn't exist in the first place.

When the light finally turned green, our engines revved and we moved forward, continuing on in opposite directions, now on separate paths.

By the time I pulled into Graffiti's, my hands were trembling around my handlebars and my nerves were fried. Somehow I still had enough sense to drop my kickstand, swing my leg around the side, and help Isabelle off my bike. I clung to her hand, squeezing my fingertips around her palm, searching for the strength I'd always managed to find when I was standing next to her, and she didn't let go.

I dug through my pocket with my free hand until I found my cigarette pack. It was clenched in my fist, but the second I glanced at Isabelle, I huffed and shoved it right back in my pocket.

"Fuck my life," I muttered under my breath.

She tugged on my hand. "Caleb."

"I'm not doing it, Iz," I sighed. "Don't even try to tell me it's okay."

She just rolled her eyes and shocked the hell out of me by pivoting around, digging her hand in my pocket to pull out my cigarettes. I didn't even have time to react before she pressed the pack into my chest.

"It's okay," Isabelle told me quietly, her eyes shining up at me with an alarming mixture of mischief and concern. "Just this once."

Seeing as how this was a battle I knew I wouldn't be winning anytime soon, I obliged her and lit up a damn cigarette. The second that first hit of nicotine shot down my body I finally felt like the weight settling over my shoulders had slipped off, like I could breathe again—ironic, of course, given the fact that I was currently smoking a cigarette. But I needed it and she knew it.

The question was there; I could see it shimmering in her eyes and honestly, I'd expected her to ask it a long time ago: *if the whole reason you left the club was to stay alive then why in the hell are you still smoking?*

I'd been over all those other vices of my past years ago: drinking, weed, and women. Smoking was just the one vice I still let myself have.

But when Isabelle's lips parted, the question that fell from them wasn't the one I expected.

"Do you miss them?"

I blew out a puff of smoke, careful to angle my lips in the opposite direction. That was a loaded question and the answer varied from day to day. So tonight, I just opted for the easiest and most honest response.

"Sometimes."

It was just too bad the only part of my life in the club that had been real was Dom.

There were plenty of times I'd reached for my phone to call him, but the only times we'd really talked recently was just to keep the other up to speed about Wallace. He was stuck in that graveyard of ghosts I dragged around with me, but I never let him get too close.

He'd told me I was making the biggest mistake of my life by leaving the club and I'd told him he was making the biggest mistake of his by staying. There wasn't much common ground left between us after that.

Isabelle smiled sadly and reached up to touch my cheek. I abruptly tossed the cigarette to the ground; I didn't need it anymore now.

"Come on," I gestured with my head to the door. "Let's go inside."

"I'm pretty excited, actually," she informed me as I held the door open so she could step through. "I can't remember the last time we were here."

My heart knotted at the word *we,* but I shelved that for now.

"Would you believe me if I told you they have actually have pretty decent burgers here?" I laughed as I led her over to an empty table.

"I guess we were always here too late to ever take advantage of that, huh?"

Isabelle was already swaying to the music blaring from the speakers overhead when I pulled out a chair for her before sinking down into the one across from her.

"*You'll always be a part of me,*" she bopped her head a little as she sang along. "*I'm part of you indefinitely. Boy, don't you know you can't escape me, ooo darlin' 'cause you'll always be my baby...*"

I cocked an amused eyebrow at her, shifting my weight to dig my wallet out of my back pocket. Now she was leaning across from me as if we were simply gravitating toward each other from our respective chairs.

"I like this," she whispered just loudly enough to be heard above the music.

"What?"

"Being here like this, normal with you," she smiled. "I like it."

"Me too, Iz."

It seemed like we sat there like that for hours, eating our greasy bar burgers and fries, laughing and reminiscing about all the times we'd used to come here, but carefully overlooking who else we'd been here with. Even as the bar filled up, more people crowded the space, and the DJ made some announcements, I didn't think either of us really noticed.

When our server set two beers down in front of us, I leaned forward on my elbows with a frown, more than a little annoyed at the intrusion. "Hey, man, we didn't order these."

The server turned on his heel and pointed at the two figures waving at us from the opposite end of the room. "No, but your friends did."

"Holy shit!" Isabelle exclaimed, her eyes wide with surprise.

"Oh hell," I muttered under my breath.

Talk about shitty luck.

Of course Brandon Davis and some chick who only looked vaguely familiar would be here at this bar right at this moment. And now, they had their drinks in hand and were making their way right over to our table. Great.

"Who's that chick with him, Iz?"

"Jessica Torres," Isabelle whispered loudly. "She was on the cheer squad with me."

So much for having her all to myself tonight. I could already see how this was going to play out: Isabelle would get roped into conversation with her old cheerleading friend and they would sit reminiscing about 'old times' for the rest of the night while I'd be stuck with Davis.

"Hey guys!" Isabelle called over to them and pointed down at the beers in front of us. "Thanks for the drinks. You didn't have to do that."

"Not a problem," Davis laughed and I swallowed heavily as Isabelle slid off her chair to embrace her ex-boyfriend.

"It's good to see you," Isabelle was telling him now, quickly releasing Davis just as soon as her arms wrapped around his shoulders for a brief moment. "And Jess! It's been so long!"

Isabelle then proceeded to hug her friend, or at least she was acting like they'd been friends, and gestured to me. "Jess, you remember Caleb Sawyer, right?"

"Of course I do," Jess laughed with a grin. "Nice to see you again, Caleb. God, I don't think I've seen you since, what? Our graduation?"

And now I just felt like an even bigger asshole for having no real idea who this chick was. I vaguely remembered seeing her in the hallways of Claremont High in the same blue and white cheer skirt Isabelle used to wear. Of course, back then I'd spent most of my time pretending to look elsewhere whenever Isabelle pranced around in that skirt.

"So," Isabelle smiled brightly and gestured to Davis and Jess. "How are the kids?"

My eyes flew back to Isabelle. I'd had no idea those two were even together, let alone had any kids, and I was the one who still lived in town with them.

Now Davis held out his iPhone and pointed down at a picture of two little kids. "That's Emily. She's four, and that one's Alex. He just turned two a few days ago actually."

"Oh, wow," Isabelle squinted down at the phone to get a better look. "Alex looks just like you, Brandon. I saw that video you posted a few months ago of him singing in the bathtub...so cute!"

She shot me a quick wink and I had a hard time not rolling my eyes up to the ceiling. Right. Thank God for social media. How else would she know what her high school boyfriend and his wife were up to? Jesus.

Finally, I decided it was time to act civil.

"Hey, congratulations, man," I jutted out a hand for Davis to take. "You've got a great-looking family there."

"Thanks, Sawyer," Davis shook my hand with a grin, his eyes darting between me and Isabelle. "It's really good to see you guys."

"You too," I nodded back.

There would've been a moment of awkwardness had the DJ not rescued us with his latest announcement.

"Alright, alright," the DJ's voice rang out through the speakers. "I hope you all are enjoying Retro Night here at Graffiti's. We've got all the 80's and 90's classics you forgot were completely *awesome*. Now I wanna see all you fine ladies out on the dance floor with this next one and don't forget to tip your bartender!"

As the first beats of Michael Jackson's "Thriller" thumped from the speakers, Jess was already tugging on Isabelle's hand to lead her out onto the makeshift dance floor, even as she threw an apologetic glance over her shoulder at her husband.

Davis spread his arms out and gestured with his head toward the door. "I thought we were leaving now?"

"Come on, baby," Jess called out to him, still pulling Isabelle toward the dance floor with one hand and waving her husband off with the other. "You know this is the only night we get off from the kids. I wanna dance! Besides, me and Isabelle know all the moves. You know you're jealous!"

That got my attention and I lifted my eyebrows at Isabelle with an amused smirk even as Jess kept pulling her away from where I wanted her to be. "All the moves, huh?"

Isabelle laughed and just shrugged, calling back to me: "Well, you'd know that if you'd ever gone to a pep rally or a basketball game or a football game, you know."

There wasn't much I could do other than to just shake my head and lean back against my chair to watch.

"I'm really sorry about this," Brandon was muttering to me now as he sank down into the chair Isabelle had vacated. "I swear to God we were leaving."

"Nah. Don't worry about it," I gestured to our two girls with the neck of my beer. "I think we should just sit back and enjoy the show."

With a chuckle, Davis settled back just like I had suggested and we watched Isabelle and Jess re-enact the familiar dance moves, pretty impressively I had to admit.

"Damn," I muttered into my beer and shook my head. "Shoulda went to more pep rallies."

Davis laughed heartily at that. "Oh well. Lesson learned, right? Man, I forgot how good Jess used to be at all that shit. So," he gestured to Isabelle with his beer bottle, "you guys back together then?"

My lips pulled to one side of my face and I wished to God I had a different answer. "It's complicated."

"It didn't really look that way to me when you first got here," he just shrugged. "You guys pretty much looked like you were together."

Davis seemed to take my silence as answer enough and went on anyway. "You know, I was a real dick to her when she broke things off with us. I deserved that sucker-punch you laid into me right over there all those years ago."

"I think it might've been more than one," I threw back with a grin.

"Yeah, well, I shouldn't have said that shit about her mom, about you...that was just a complete asshole move and I didn't handle us ending for a second time as well as I should've. I've always wanted to tell her that, but tonight's probably not the night to rehash old shit from the past, huh?"

I glanced over to the dance floor, my eyes finding Isabelle almost immediately, and my heart twisted when she smiled at me, playfully waving to the dance floor in an exaggerated attempt to coax me out there with her as she sang along to "Summer of 69".

"Well," Davis laughed with a shake of his head. "I think it's safe to say she hasn't changed much."

"Yeah," I smiled, my eyes following Isabelle's every move.

"That's good to see, especially after everything you guys..." Davis trailed off and stared down at his bottle with a wince.

That was the thing about small towns. Even if you went out of your way to avoid 99 percent of the people in it, everyone still managed to know all your business and then some.

"How's her dad doing?"

"Ah, you know, he's still dying. Things are going downhill pretty quickly."

"Right," Davis nodded slowly. "I figured as much. I was really sorry to hear he was sick."

"I'll tell her you said that."

"Thanks, man," Davis pressed a grim smile on his face, but his expression lightened up as soon as he saw that his wife and Isabelle were making their way back to us. "Finally. Our babysitter's not gonna be real happy with us. Hey, I know this isn't any of my business, but I really hope you guys figure it out. I was pissed as shit when I first found out you guys were together back—what was it, like eight, nine years ago? But she deserves to be happy and from what I can tell, she looks pretty happy here with you. Just don't screw it up this time, alright?"

I didn't know how to respond, mainly because I didn't really want to discuss my personal life with someone I'd spent too much time loathing. Then again, the reason for said loathing was currently wrapping an arm around my neck as Brandon Davis left with his wife.

After some quick goodbyes, we settled back into our table, but this time, I pulled my chair right next to hers so I could drape my arm leisurely around her shoulders, which was really just another excuse to touch her. We sat there at the table like that for a little longer and I was perfectly happy with my arm around her, tucking her into my side, and listening to her sing slightly off-key to some Boston and Whitesnake classics I'd completely forgotten were awesome.

"Alright, guys," the DJ's voice rang out again through the speakers. "We're gonna slow it down a little with some Cyndi Lauper. Here's 'Time After Time'."

As the slow thump-thump of the song's opening beats streamed from the speakers, Isabelle lifted her head from my shoulder and gestured with her head towards the dance floor.

"Dance with me?"

There was no way I'd ever be able to say no to her, so I nodded and let her lead me out onto the dance floor. With the strains of the song and the words circling around us, I slid my hands around her waist to tuck her into my chest. Breathing in the soft scent of spicy vanilla and flowers in her hair and feeling her curl into me was more than I could've ever expected for this night. Swaying with her to the slow music, holding her close enough that I could feel her chest lightly rising and falling, everything else just slipped away.

If we could just hang on to this moment, when all that existed between us was the love I knew was still very much alive, maybe working through all the other shit wasn't going to be as wide a mountain to climb as I thought.

"Iz?" I murmured in her hair.

She lifted her head off my shoulder to look at me.

"Stay with me tonight," I leaned my forehead into hers and whispered, "I don't want you to leave."

Her lips parted and finally pressed together in a firm line. With pain and indecision flickering across her face, I was lucky she was still standing here like this and letting me touch her.

"Why?" Isabelle exhaled. "Why do you want me to stay?"

The rest of her question lingered in the air: *what exactly do you think is going to happen tonight?*

"I know what I'm asking here, okay? I know I'm overstepping—I just...I don't know. I guess I could say it's because I don't want either of us to have to be alone tonight. And I guess I could say it would just be easier for you to be with me tonight because then I know you'll be safe. But the truth is that I just need to be with you. This night has been one of the best nights of my life and I don't want it to end by going back to your dad's and sleeping on the couch. If I could just hold you all night, that would be enough. Please, Iz, just stay with me."

I watched her suck in a shaky breath and squeeze her eyes shut before she finally leaned into my shoulder again. The conflict written across her face made me flinch. Any other night of the year, I might be able to handle her rejection with some humility and leave it at that. Tonight, though, I wasn't so sure I'd survive without her.

Finally, she put me out of my misery, glanced up at me with watery eyes, and whispered: "Okay."

. . .

Isabelle

I fumbled with the T-shirt a little as I slipped it over my head and brought the material to my nose so I could inhale deeply. My eyes fluttered shut and I let myself get lost in his T-shirt for just a moment before pulling on the sweatpants he'd insisted I wear.

I just want you to be comfortable here, he'd told me, but what he was really saying was, *I want you to be comfortable here and clothed as much as humanly possible.*

Short of coming out of his bathroom decked out from head to toe in scuba gear, his T-shirt and sweatpants would have to do for tonight. He could handle it and I hoped I could, too.

I closed my eyes again as his words washed over me. *Please, Iz, just stay with me.* It was amazing how something so simple could be so complicated. I would've given anything to hear those words the day I left Claremont for good, but he let me leave instead. As much as every alarm bell in my head screamed, *Warning! Warning!*—as much as I wanted to hold out and ask him to drive me back to my dad's instead, one look, one kiss, one moment, and I was sunk.

Why did he make me feel so weak when all I wanted to be was strong?

I didn't really know what I just signed myself up for. Whether I stayed one night or any more after it, this would be a short-term stay. But when he looked at me with such vulnerability, such sincerity, such *love,* and finally saying the words I'd wanted to hear even if it was six years too late, any resolve I had to keep him at arm's length crumbled. And it just didn't feel all that wrong to be here with him right now, to want to be near him, to want to feel his arms around me.

So I shut out the rest of the noise and opened the bathroom door.

Caleb had his back to me as he rummaged around his tiny apartment, shoving some dishes in the sink, and turned on his heel to backpedal toward the bed, stopping only to straighten the comforter a little, none the wiser that I'd opened the door.

I took a few careful steps out of the bathroom and his head shot up at the movement. His lips curved and he rubbed the back of his neck anxiously as his eyes trailed up and down my body as if he wanted to memorize the way I looked right now in his T-shirt and sweatpants. I glanced down at my attire and tugged on my pant leg.

"They're a little big, huh?"

"Maybe just a little," he laughed lightly, still watching me as I bent down to roll up the sweatpants so I could move around easier.

I shuffled aimlessly deeper inside the apartment, so treacherously close to the bed, and fought the urge to wring my hands. Why the hell didn't he have any other furniture in here? I guess he didn't really need to considering the bed was just ten feet away from his TV, but right about now, I wished this apartment was just a little bit bigger so there could be just a little bit more space between us.

Screw it.

It was now or never.

I flopped down on Caleb's bed and mentally congratulated myself for only thinking about how many other women had been in this bed one time. That thought passed through the deep recesses of my mind and I rolled onto my back, testing the mattress a little with my elbow before folding my hands across my stomach.

Caleb hesitated. He stood at the foot of the bed, chewing on the inside of his cheek, scrubbed his face with both hands, and finally gave in, collapsing next to me, but careful to give me a good foot of much-needed space. I tried to stare up at the ceiling in peace until I felt his fingertips leave a light trail down the side of my neck, tracing the three stars underneath my ear.

"What does this mean, Iz?"

The truth wasn't something I wanted to admit out loud. I couldn't tell him I'd gotten it after one of the darkest days I'd ever had post-Claremont and post-Caleb. I couldn't tell him I'd cried in the chair and that my tears had nothing to do with the sting from the tattoo gun. And I definitely couldn't tell him the tattoo had been intended to form some sort of cosmic, ill-conceived connection with him in spite of all the distance between us.

My eyes fell to the upside-down compass on his left arm as he rested his forearm against his stomach where I had clear view of it, as if to taunt me into telling the truth, to admit that as much as I denied it until I was blue in the face, I knew as well as anybody that our connection had never faded away. And because I was either completely stupid or inherently strong, I couldn't give him that full truth.

"I was feeling lost," I whispered, my eyes still trained on the compass. "I guess I was just trying to find my way."

Caleb glanced down at the ink on his arm, the design I'd painstakingly created for him so long ago, and I knew he understood. Compasses and the stars: cosmic symbols of the literal and metaphorical search for direction. His fingertips continued their exploration, making me shiver with every inch of skin he grazed, until his thumb brushed my cheek.

I wanted to ask him if he still had my name inked right over his heart, but finding out for sure would require him to take his shirt off and I just wasn't mentally prepared for that tonight in light of everything else.

Instead, I reached out to let my fingers skim across those three letters written on the top of his left wrist.

"When did you get this?" I murmured.

"Awhile ago," he whispered hoarsely, echoing my vague answer from last night.

Tears stung my eyes. I'd put up a brave front all day, but I just didn't have the strength.

"How did we get here, Caleb?" I whispered.

He sighed heavily and his hand dropped back down to the mattress. "Shitty luck and even shittier decisions."

"Yeah," I laughed mirthlessly. "I guess that sounds about right. I mean, I know how it happened, but it still just doesn't make any sense. I just don't understand *why* it happened."

While on paper, my life was everything a well-adjusted, mature 30-year-old should want—professional success, stability, money, a tiny bit of fame, and a healed relationship with my dad—none of it felt real except for the part about my dad. The truth was I just wasn't all that well-adjusted. I just wasn't all that happy. And I probably wasn't as mature as I pretended to be either.

"I know what you mean," Caleb's thick voice called out to me. "I think about that everyday."

"Me too," I admitted.

Silence permeated the air between us before I finally found the words I wanted to say.

"I can't believe she'd be eight."

He winced and swallowed hard, rubbing his eyes with his hands. When his hand dropped back to the mattress again with his palm out to me, I knew what he was asking for. I slid my hand into his waiting palm and squeezed tight.

"You know," he murmured. "I always pictured her with your eyes. Your smile, too. She would've looked just like you. Would've driven me crazy, too, probably."

I smiled through my tears and finally wiped them away with the back of my free hand.

"Well, I always pictured her with *your* eyes. You know that crazy look you get sometimes when you're up to no good? She would've totally had that."

He laughed, but it was a pain-filled one, the kind of laugh that took as much as it gave.

"Sometimes when I take Coop for walks in the park, I purposefully avoid the playgrounds just because I can't handle seeing all the moms there with their kids. Part of me wants to scream at them because they don't know how lucky they are and part of me just wants to scream."

A strangled sound choked in his throat and he rubbed his mouth with his free hand, but I pressed on.

"I just never knew anything could *hurt* that much. The contractions felt like someone was stabbing me from the inside and I could feel it, Caleb. I could feel her leaving us. The doctor didn't even have to tell me because I already knew. And all the rest of it, seeing her, holding her, having to say goodbye to her..."

He shifted long enough to wrap his arm around my shoulders to pull me to his chest and I buried my face in his T-shirt.

"I've never felt so helpless in my entire life," he whispered in my hair.

"You were there," I told him. "That's what I needed."

His lips brushed against my forehead and I leaned into him, letting him envelope me as the memories of that day washed over us.

"I still feel like it's my fault," I exhaled, finally voicing what I'd never been able to say out loud before, not even in front of my therapist.

"Iz—"

"I felt those pains in my stomach for almost an hour before I did anything about it," I cut in abruptly. "I was too scared. I thought if maybe I pretended it wasn't happening then it would go away, but all that did was make it worse."

"You didn't do anything wrong," Caleb murmured. "And there wasn't anything we could do."

"I know that now," I nodded into his chest. "But I still keep thinking, *did I not take care of myself the way I was supposed to? Did I not eat enough? Sleep enough?*"

For some reason, feeling his arms around me finally gave me the strength to say the words that always lingered below the surface of my guilt and my heartbreak.

"I'm so scared," I whispered and he tilted my head back to look at me, his blue eyes watering with unshed tears. "What if it happens again, Caleb? I'd never survive it."

His thumb ran across my cheek to catch a stray tear and then he leaned down to brush his lips against mine. It was exactly what I needed and all of my fears didn't seem quite so momentous as long as he was holding me like this.

"That doctor told me it happens a lot," Caleb swallowed tightly, brushing some hair out of my eyes. "He said plenty of women go on to have babies after and I believe that, Iz. When we're...when *you're* ready, things'll play out in that hospital differently."

I smiled at the gesture. There was no way either of us could possibly know for sure that it would, but now hope trampled through all that lingering fear. And here we were, talking about this like we were almost a real couple, making plans and getting ready to make more babies. Bittersweet irony, especially today.

"Do you regret any of it?" he asked me now.

"What do you mean?"

He lifted a shoulder and sighed into my hair. "Do you wish you hadn't—"

"No, not for a second. I don't regret that we got to hold her, that we got to see her. I'll never regret that as long as I live."

Caleb nodded somberly and kissed me again.

"I guess sometimes I think maybe we should've done *something* to acknowledge that she was real."

"She was real," Caleb told me hoarsely. "You gave birth to her. We held her. She was real, Iz."

"I know," I smiled again through my tears. "I just wish we'd had some sort of service or something like that. I'm not even all that religious, but I think it would've been nice."

It would've been closure, too, but neither of us were really in the right mindset at the time for that.

"I didn't know you..." he shook his head. "I never even thought of that. I'm sorry, Iz. Everything just happened so fast, you know? I could barely keep my head on straight, let alone keep up."

"We crashed and burned pretty epically, didn't we?"

"Yeah," he laughed sadly. "We did."

"I think we were just too young to handle all that at once."

He nodded and blew out a deep breath. "I'm sorry I couldn't give you all the things I wanted to back then. I just couldn't balance everything in a way that would've gotten us a different ending. I guess it's like you said—I was too young and too stupid to know that I didn't know everything."

The problem was that somewhere, deep down, I still wanted him to give me all those things we'd wanted when we were young and naive and hopelessly, recklessly in love. I just didn't trust myself to reach for it.

I nuzzled his chest a little more, pressing myself against him, and he sucked in a hard breath.

"Maybe I should sleep on the couch in my office," he chuckled. "That might be safer."

"No," I shook my head, just burying my face even deeper in his chest. "I want you right here."

He stilled against me and swallowed tight. "Iz, I'm gonna tell you something right now and I don't want you to say anything, okay? I'll just hold you for the rest of the night."

I almost didn't want to know. I almost didn't want to let myself hear. But what else was I supposed to do?

He must've taken my silence as his answer because he leaned forward, pressed his lips to my forehead, and whispered: "I should've married you when I had the chance."

I let him wrap his arms around me even tighter, drawing me closer, pressing me in deeper, and I buried my face in his chest, finally allowing tears, grief, and heartbreak to rest for the night. Wrapped up in Caleb, surrounded by his warmth, enveloped in the safety I always felt in his arms, it was almost too good to be true. Too real not to be a dream.

And that was enough to carry me away until it was too good to be true, until I jerked awake in the middle of the night to the sound of breaking glass.

CHAPTER TWENTY-EIGHT
I Got You

Caleb

I shot up in bed, stiff and on high alert. Isabelle had already jerked out of my arms and stared back at me, wide-eyed and chest heaving. Everything seemed to rush around me in a blur—I leapt off my bed, dove underneath it for the handgun I kept hidden there for this very reason, and skidded over to the window overlooking the garage.

Four hooded figures stalked through my shop wielding crow bars and bats and with each step, another crash. Another blow. Another wave of destruction. Breaking glass, smashing metal—it all pounded through my ears, but my adrenaline had me taking a different course. There was no time to even consider an alternative because I had a one-track mind now.

I turned on my heel to sprint back to my bed, hauled Isabelle to her feet, and pushed her to the window on the opposite end of my apartment.

"We gotta get outta here, Iz," the words tumbled out of me in a rush. "We're going down the fire escape, okay? Stay with me."

She nodded as I shoved the window open and gripped her hips to steady her climb through. I followed her once both her feet were solid on the makeshift metal stairs, pushing her head down, and putting myself out in front to shield her as much as possible. Which was lucky, too, considering the second we passed the shop's first story window, a cacophony of gunshots and shattering glass rained down on us.

"Get down!" I pushed out roughly and jerked away from the window just in time to narrowly miss another bullet.

The side of my neck stung and burned white-hot, but that was the least of my concerns right now. I wasn't hit and neither was Isabelle and beyond getting inside my truck, that was all that mattered. We just had to get to my truck—

Another round of bullets blasted through the walls of my shop, obliterating everything in its wake. We had to move.

"Go, Iz!"

My hands found her back to shove her in front of me so my body was squarely between her and my shop. Even though my knee was already locking up on me, I pushed the stiffness away and powered through it, letting adrenaline take me the rest of the way.

We rounded the corner of the building and took off into a hard sprint, moving as fast as we could through the open parking lot. My heart thudded in my chest as another bullet zipped past my neck, but I just had to keep her moving. Another string of bullets screamed out from behind us and I hauled Isabelle down to the pavement, covering her body with mine as much as possible until we got an opening.

My right bicep stung, but adrenaline pushed me through it. And kept pushing. And kept pushing until I was the one pushing Isabelle headfirst into my truck on the driver's side. Sirens blared down the street, but I just kept pushing.

"Keep your head down, Iz," I grunted as I turned the ignition to get us the hell out of there.

The pain in my arm had morphed into a sharp throb when I twisted the steering wheel to peal out of my parking lot. As soon as I had us speeding down the street and away from my shop, my hand clenched her thigh to make sure she was still in one piece.

"You okay?"

She nodded, wide-eyed and terrified, and then her eyes settled on the stream of blood dripping down my arm.

"It's just a graze," I shook my head, but kept my eyes on the road. "I'm alright."

We flew past a trio of squad cars and Isabelle whipped around to watch them head right for my shop.

"Where are we going?"

"Anywhere but here," I told her and kept my hand firmly on her thigh just to remind myself she was really okay and that we'd really survived this.

I could deal with everything else later.

My shop and everything in it was replaceable, but the cargo sitting next to me in my truck was not.

. . .

About an hour later, and after I'd gotten the confirmation I needed from Saul, we pulled back into my shop's parking lot and I braced myself for the damage.

The parking lot was crammed full with trucks, motorcycles, and squad cars—I guess I shouldn't have been surprised. This was pandemonium, at least in Claremont terms. A break-in, a shooting, a hit, whatever this was, it wasn't something that happened here on a regular basis mainly because the Horsemen were smart enough to keep that off their turf as often as possible.

Cops and the club were the least of my problems right now. And as I surveyed the parking lot, some of the familiar faces surrounding me were exactly the ones I expected to see. Saul aside, I saw every single person I'd hired to work for me in the shop. They'd all shown up, faces etched in somber determination—this was their livelihood too and they needed it just as much as I did. Even Sam was here and I guessed that had more to do with the fact that Jared had been working his shift at their house tonight.

But I did not expect to see Dom and my mom standing off to the side, decked out in their familiar leather uniforms and trying to maintain a respectful distance.

I barely had time to nod their way because Chief Kelly and a few of his deputies had already descended.

For insurance purposes, this was exactly what needed to happen. I couldn't file any sort of claim without a police report, but at the same time, making this official could easily escalate this little situation faster than any of us could ever anticipate.

We gave our statements, each of us regurgitating the story exactly as Kelly needed to hear it for his report, and even when he warned me that his team was still taking pictures for evidence, I pushed right past him and headed straight for the garage, but I still skidded in my tracks when my feet crossed the threshold.

It was like someone had ripped my shop right off the ground and flipped it over on its side. Every project. Every work station. Every single piece of equipment. It was all destroyed. A fucking tornado might as well have torn through this place. There was broken glass, shards of metal, blown-out tires, overturned tables and chairs, dumped-out toolboxes and not a single square foot of concrete inside my shop had gone untouched.

Hands closed over my shoulders to keep me in place, but I wasn't with it enough to even know who was touching me.

All my blood, sweat, and tears...it was all gone. And with it, thousands and thousands of dollars-worth of damage.

The depth of my fury knew no bounds and all I could see was hot shards of red, splintering my vision and tearing through the little control I had left.

Finally, I gave in to all the emotions I knew Wallace wanted me to feel—rage, devastation, helplessness, hopelessness—they were all here for this sick, twisted party.

So I picked up the first stray, leftover crowbar I could find and finished the job. My only victim, a mangled Yamaha that was just in the wrong place at the wrong time, weathered the brunt of my fury as I heaved that crowbar down into it again and again and again until I finally tossed the crowbar to the ground and kicked over what was left of it.

I crouched down to the ground with my head in my hands and squeezed my eyes shut before finally screaming muffled obscenities into my hands. Everything I'd built, everything I'd done and every sacrifice I'd made...it was all for nothing. I didn't need an insurance appraiser to tell me the damage done tonight wouldn't just take months to repair.

It would be *years*. Fucking *years* before I worked myself out from underneath this shit. The equipment and this building were insured, but everything else? All the business I had booked solid through the end of the year and beyond? My shop's reputation?

It was all dead now.

And now I just couldn't handle this pity party. Didn't want to see the sympathy and the horror on all their faces because it just mirrored what I already felt. I couldn't take this shit anymore.

Soft hands skimmed over my shoulders and I felt her crouch down next to me as she wrapped her arms around my waist to hold me tight.

"Iz," I croaked and shut my eyes to the sight in front of me. "There's glass everywhere and you're not wearing any shoes. You gotta stay away from me right now."

Her touch lifted for just a moment and then her face pressed into my shoulder. She shook her head and seemed to move in even closer.

"You're not wearing any shoes either," she reminded me softly.

"Yeah, well, I don't really give a shit about my feet."

She smiled into my shoulder. "Just mine?"

"Something like that," I muttered and scrubbed both hands over my eyes.

Isabelle's hands ghosted over the sides of my face and I gave in to her touch for a moment, letting the softness I found there drown everything else out. Reprieve was fleeting. Comfort felt hollow. And even though part of me just wanted to fall into her arms and cry myself into a pathetic stupor, it wouldn't erase what happened tonight.

So I pushed up to my feet, missing the feel of her hands on me the second they slipped away, and faced the crowd behind me with my hands on my hips and my resolve steeled. Their faces were just as grim as they were before, not like I expected anything different, and when my mom stepped forward, I wavered.

Her hands reached out, something I hadn't seen in years, and they closed around my shoulders, pressing me in tight and giving me a little bit of that unconditional love I'd always thought I had.

"I'm so sorry," she whispered in my ear. "This is just...our shop doesn't look much better than yours."

My head jerked back and my eyes shot over to Dom, who just nodded grimly. There wasn't much time to ruminate on the way she said *our shop*, as if it was an ever-present, not-so-subtle way of reminding me of all the ways she thought I'd failed her.

"Maybe it's time you finally came back to the clubhouse," she pushed on, her eyes pleading and watery. "You can talk to Marcus, figure out a plan, and then everyone can get in front of this before it gets worse."

Of course, by saying *everyone* she was lumping me in with the club. As if she'd ever do anything else. As if I could forget she'd all but frozen me out of her life. And as if she could read my thoughts and sense where this was heading, my mom's dark gaze flitted to Dom, who'd already stepped forward to intervene.

"Caleb," he told me, his voice gravelly and thick with emotion. "She's right. I think you gotta come back now, even if it's just to talk out what the next step needs to be."

I shook my head immediately, acutely aware that Isabelle had slipped underneath my arm on one side and that Saul stood his ground on the other so that they flanked me on both sides in a show of solidarity.

"I'm not gonna do that," I shrugged as my mom's face crumbled in a predictable mixture of disappointment, animosity, and worry. "I'm sorry. I just can't. The second I step foot in the clubhouse is the second I throw away everything I've built here and I'm not giving that up."

My mom stepped forward again to make her point. "But, Caleb, this isn't gonna stop. *He's* not gonna stop. You're both lucky as shit to be in one piece."

"I can handle it," I shot back and Isabelle's arm tightened around my waist.

"You're tellin' me you don't care that Isabelle could've gotten hurt? That she could've gotten *shot*?"

"Of course I care," I growled and pulled Isabelle closer to me just to reiterate my point. Just the thought of how this night could've ended differently had my blood boiling, but acting on that wouldn't help either. "Going after Wallace now isn't gonna do anything but throw more gasoline on the fire. Besides, I don't have a place at that table anymore. I think we've all made that pretty clear."

Her black eyes narrowed dangerously and in a flash, softened when they darted over to Isabelle.

"It's good to see you two back together," she murmured. "At least one good thing came out of all this stupid shit."

I sidestepped that comment and moved on. "I appreciate you coming down here. I really do, but I got it from here. You have your mess to clean up and so do I. Let's just leave it at that."

My mom stared at me for a moment and after her eyes flicked back to Isabelle one more time, she nodded tightly before turning on her heel to head back to the parking lot. Dom shot me a quick, uneasy smile and followed suit, falling in line like a good soldier.

I didn't waste any time to get this moving and turned to the rest of the crowd still standing here in the wreckage—my guys from the shop, Saul, Sam, and finally, Isabelle—and gestured with my head to the exit.

"I think everybody just needs to head out for the night. It's late and there's nothing we can do right now. I'll touch base with you all in the morning, okay? Just...just go home."

Luckily, all my guys knew me well enough to know when to argue and now was not one of those times. They shuffled out of my shop one by one and headed off into the night.

I nodded to Jared, who was still standing there waiting for some more instructions. "Take Iz and Sam home, alright?"

Jared and Sam moved for the exit, but Isabelle stayed right where she was and I geared myself up for that stubborn streak to rear its ugly head.

"Iz—"

"I'm not leaving you tonight," she shook her head furiously and folded her arms across her chest. "And you can't stay here either. Please tell me you're not planning on staying here for the rest of the night."

I glanced wearily at Saul, who just nodded. "I'll crash at Saul's place tonight."

"Fine," she shrugged. "Then I'm coming with you."

"No, Iz," I sighed and rubbed a hand over my mouth. "You can't. Not after what happened tonight. It's not safe for you to be around me right now. Jared's gonna stay at the house tonight with you guys, Trent'll be there in the morning, and Dylan'll be there tomorrow night. That's just the way it's gotta be."

Her mouth opened and closed, but that was as far as she got. I could see the wheels in her head turning, trying to narrow in on the best, most logical argument, but coming up empty. She wasn't going to win this one.

"Caleb—"

"I'm not gonna argue with you," I lifted a shoulder and gently pushed her toward her dad. "You can't stay here, Iz, and I think we need to keep our distance for awhile."

As much as the idea of putting any space between us stung, when we'd finally just begun to gain some ground, my hands were tied. I wouldn't risk her safety again and if keeping her safe meant keeping her away from me, then so be it.

Her eyes clouded over, watery and filled with grim understanding. Finally, she nodded and let her dad take her by the elbow to lead her out of my shop and somewhere she'd actually be safe.

. . .

With one deep breath and a long exhale out, my eyes just about rolled into the back of my head as my body relaxed in a way only nicotine could provide. This light-headed buzz was probably the only thing clearing my head of all the dark thoughts bouncing around in there and I kept my pen moving against the paper as I leaned back against the building from my spot on the pavement.

Hey Iz,

I think I'm handling this shit a lot better than I would've in my past life. Back then, I probably would've gotten onto my bike, hauled ass to wherever Wallace was and went in with guns blazing without stopping to even think about what might happen next. Now I know better and I also know that's a pretty stupid way to get myself killed.

Everything I'm feeling right now, anger, frustration, desperation, those are all emotions Wallace wants me to feel, what I know the club feels too. If they want to retaliate, if they see the attacks on both our shops tonight as an act of war, that's their problem. No good can come from war, especially since the end result would just be a pile-up of blood, dead bodies, and more prison sentences.

All my work, all my plans, all my time, money, and energy spent on building a different kind of life—it couldn't have been for nothing. I won't let Wallace take it from me.

I just don't know where to go from here. How can I even begin to bounce back from this kind of destruction, Iz? I'm already hundreds of thousands in the red and that's even without whatever payout I'll get from my insurance. At this point, it makes more financial sense to just close the fucking place and start over, but then Wallace wins.

I can make it work. I just need to figure it out first.

A noise to my left shook me out of my revelry and my eyebrows flew into my forehead when I saw Saul holding the shop's back door open for Isabelle. For a second, I couldn't believe what I was seeing. Here I'd been, writing to her, conjuring her in my mind like she was sitting here listening to me, and now my eyes snapped to the cigarette in my hand. I immediately flung the burning cherry into the pavement, cursing under my breath. Isabelle catching me red-handed wasn't exactly on my to-do list today.

My next move was to snap my notebook closed as she slid down on the pavement next to me. Her eyebrows shot up at the movement, but she didn't press the issue. We had more important things to discuss right now.

"What're you doing here, Iz? I'm pretty sure I told you to stay away for awhile."

She just shrugged. "I didn't want to stay away."

I shot her an exasperated glance and shook my head. "Well, congratulations. Now I have to kill Trent for bringing you back here."

Her light laugh split through the night air and I found myself shifting closer to her, even though I knew I was supposed to be keeping my distance.

"Oh, he followed his orders 'til the very end. It didn't matter how much I begged and pleaded with him. He never backed down. He even chased me out of the house when the cab got there, so I'll happily take the blame."

Part of me really wanted to be angry, if not at least a little annoyed, that she'd blatantly disregarded her own safety in coming back. The other part of me, the part surging with disbelief and happiness that she wanted to be here with me, won out instead.

So I did the only thing I could and wrapped an arm around her shoulders to tuck her in even closer to me.

"The shop looks a million times better already," she mused quietly and leaned her head against my shoulder as she spoke.

I sighed and squeezed my eyes shut. Most of the destroyed projects and equipment had been covered and pushed to one side of the shop—out of sight, out of mind, right? The rest of the damage, the stray bullets, the shattered glass, crushed metal, and all the trash had been swept into various piles in the shop, but that still didn't change anything. The damage was still done and I was still screwed for the time being.

"You know," Isabelle's soft voice pressed on. "Those guys are pretty loyal to you, aren't they?"

"Yeah," I shrugged. "They are. I also pay them pretty well, so there's that. Or I guess, I *did* pay them pretty well."

Darkness clouded my vision for a short moment and she slid an arm around my waist.

"No, I think it's more than that. The way they all dropped everything to get here last night, all the work they did for you today just to help you any way they could, or even them even agreeing to babysit me and my dad in the first place...they love you, Caleb. That's why they're so loyal. And you now, when you think about it, you're kind of like a family, aren't you? The way you look out for each other?"

There were so many connections brewing underneath everything she said that I wasn't sure I liked. From her perspective, all I was missing now was a chair at the head of a certain table, a gavel, and a leather cut.

"It's not a bad thing," she told me like she'd just read my mind. "I think you just figured out a way to create what you were always missing with the club and you did it on your own terms."

"I never thought of it like that before," I laughed, but the truth of her words hit home in a way I hadn't expected.

My eyes shifted down to the pavement in thought and I blew out a rough breath. All that loyalty and now I bet they were all wishing they'd hitched their wagon to a different kind of horse. Namely, one that didn't have irreparable ties to outlaw organizations.

"Do you wanna talk about it?" Isabelle's quiet voice called out to me.

Glancing at her out of the corner of my eye, my lips lifted into a small smile at her words. Just having her here next to me while I worked all this shit out was enough, but I wasn't stupid enough to turn down this opportunity.

"Where to start, right?" I chuckled lamely, but she still smiled sympathetically back at me. "I've spent all this time working toward one thing—*one* fucking thing—and I feel like it all went up in flames last night."

"How bad is it?"

"I don't really know," I sighed and tilted my head up to look at the night sky before glancing back at her again. "I mean, I'll figure something out, but what I'm really worried about is how long it's gonna take. And now I can forget all those big plans I had for expanding. That's not even the half of it though. It's everything else—all the business I lost last night, all the customers who aren't going to trust me anymore, those are the things I might never be able to get back. Honestly, Iz, that scares the shit out of me."

Isabelle's eyes, soft and warm, seared right through me and when she leaned her head into my shoulder and slid both hands around my waist to give me what I needed right now, I could've thrown my head back and cried with relief.

"I'm so sorry, Caleb," she whispered.

"Thanks, Iz," I tilted my head to press a kiss into her forehead. "I just appreciate you being here like this. It's not like there's much you can do about it."

I trailed off when Isabelle's head suddenly shot off my shoulder. Her eyes were shining and she was practically beaming up at me, bursting with whatever it was that had suddenly come over her.

"I think I can help you a little bit."

I barked out a laugh. "What do you mean?"

She dug a hand into her purse and handed me some thick, folded papers without another word. I took them from her, frowning down at the papers in my hand, and when I skimmed the first page, I shook my head because my brain just couldn't catch up. It was all here in black and white and the contract was pretty cut and dry, too, from what I could tell, but it still just didn't compute.

"So," Isabelle laughed at my confusion, a gorgeous, happy smile playing on her lips. "How does it feel to be an owner of two point five percent of The Warehouse? You bought a house without telling me, helped my dad pay for his house without telling me, so I figured I was well within my rights to do *this* without telling you."

I'd stood here for the last hour trying to figure out how in the hell I was going to dig myself out of this mess and then Isabelle showed up, like a fucking angel, and just dropped this on my lap like it was no big deal. Like offering this to me was just all in a day's work. God, I loved her.

When I didn't immediately respond, she must have charged right into damage control mode. "I know it's not that much in the grand scheme of things and it's probably not even something you really want, but I just wanted to—"

"Iz."

Whether she heard me and chose to ignore me or was just too wrapped up in convincing me this was a good idea, she just kept right on going: "—do something to help you. The Warehouse has been doing really well the last couple of years and I know it won't make up for all the money you lost last night—"

"Iz," I tried again, tugging on her hands to get her attention with a grin.

"—but you have all the paperwork you need. It's got all my earnings detailed there from when I bought my five percent, and since I'm splitting it with you now..." she paused only when I kept playfully tugging on her hands to force her to stop talking. "What?"

My lips curved up into a smile now that I finally had her attention. But the next words that fell out of my mouth were not the ones I'd initially intended.

"I love you."

My eyes widened as my words caught up to my brain and Isabelle tensed, staring back up at me with a stunned expression written across her beautiful features. She should know that my feelings for her had never changed; in fact, they'd only gotten stronger. All that mattered now was that I'd finally said it and she'd finally heard it.

Whether or not she had the response I wanted to hear was up to her.

I could wait.

I *would* wait.

So when her eyes softened and she swallowed back whatever it was she might've said, I figured that might be as good as I was going to get right now. All I could do was tuck a stray piece of blonde hair back behind her ear and lean forward to press my lips into her softer ones.

What I hadn't expected was for her to respond the way she did. Her hands slid up from around my waist to wind around my neck with her thumbs brushing the stubble on my cheeks as my lips continued to move over hers. When she parted her lips just enough, I didn't hesitate to take the opportunity she was offering and slipped my tongue inside her sweet mouth, taking just as much as I was being given.

Not wanting to push her too far, I leaned back, but kept a hand on her face just for good measure.

"So," I murmured as my thumb brushed her cheek. "Tell me everything."

. . .

Isabelle

"Well," Saul mused as he flipped through the rest of the paperwork. "Seems like a fair deal, boss."

Caleb bumped my shoulder with his and cocked a grin at me. "Of course it is."

About three hours ago, I'd been pacing my dad's office under the watchful eyes of both Trent and my dog, driving myself and everyone else around me insane. Now, I found myself in the exact position I'd been trying to avoid in the first place: helplessly and hopelessly free-falling.

The moment of reality of Caleb's business problems sunk in was the moment I made a split-second decision to help. It was just like a reflex. Like it was just instinct to jump to help him. All his hard work, all his plans, all his sacrifices—he didn't deserve to forfeit them now.

"Whew," Saul whistled when he turned the next page. "You really weren't kidding. That's some yearly income you guys got there."

That got Caleb's attention and he leaned forward as Saul just held up the report my PR rep had sent me and pointed to a number he'd circled. Once the number registered and the shock wore off, his eyebrows shot up into his forehead.

"Holy shit," Caleb exhaled as he fell back against the desk. "I knew your gallery was doing well, but I didn't know it was doing *that* well."

"We've had a good couple of years," I shrugged as nonchalantly as I could. "It's not like splitting that with you will really help all that much, but I don't know. I just wanted to help somehow."

Now I felt a little stupid about the whole thing—whatever he decided to do with that tiny percentage of the gallery, it wouldn't be enough to even cover a fraction of the rebuilding he needed to do. There was just literally nothing else I had to offer and I'd offered it willing without a second thought.

"This'll help," Saul nodded to the papers. "From what I can tell, the gallery sponsors, what, at least one show a week?"

"Sometimes two on the weekend," I clarified.

"So," he nodded. "Caleb'll get a little commission from every show the gallery sponsors, just like you do, and from the looks of it, that will probably keep us afloat for now until that insurance check comes in."

"It won't make up for all the business you've already lost," I told them softly.

Saul glanced at Caleb out of the corner of his eye and shrugged. "Maybe this is just the old accountant in me talking, but I think you gotta take help anywhere you can get it right now. Sign the papers, boss."

I was still waiting for Caleb to refuse, to tear up the paperwork and tell me he wouldn't take my money or my contribution because he needed to earn his money on his own. Instead, he was still staring at me with such awe, such surprise, such *love.* While it was exactly the reaction I'd wanted, now that I had it, I didn't know what to do with it. And so I backpedalled.

"I don't want you to feel like you have to do this," I told him carefully and swallowed tight when he shifted on the desk to frown at me. "I mean, it's okay if you want to look into other options. I sort of sprung this on you and..."

I trailed off, unable to figure out what I really wanted to say or why I wanted to say it in the first place. Underneath everything else, I just didn't want to make him feel like less than because he was taking my help.

Saul's eyebrows shot up into his forehead and promptly shoved the papers back at Caleb as he turned to head back to the door. "I think I'll, uh, just give you two some time to talk this over."

When Saul shut the door behind him, a few long moments of silence passed between us before Caleb's quiet voice called out to me.

"Iz, I don't think you have any idea what this means to me. And I know it won't make up for everything I lost last night, probably not even close, but this, from *you*...Iz, I can't even begin to tell you, but is this really okay? I mean, are you gonna be okay money-wise if you just give this to me right now?"

"I wouldn't have offered it if I couldn't afford it. And think of it this way, whenever I have to sell the house," my throat tightened a little at the thought, "and when you sign your part of the house over to me, you can just think of it as paying me back."

He draped an arm around my shoulders to tuck me into his side and huffed out a laugh. "I guess I should've known you'd figure out how to pay me back for the house somehow."

"It's not about that. I wanted to help you and I guess the house is just an added bonus," I smiled up at him and lifted a shoulder. "I got you."

His lips twisted into that grin that made me forget my own name. "I really love you, you know that?"

The way he was looking at me, the feel of his fingertips curling around my shoulder, the way his body seemed to fit perfectly with mine...I almost gave in. I almost let those words slip right from my lips.

Instead, my eyes dropped to our feet and I shifted uncomfortably on the desk. It was hard to reconcile that we were here right now, just like this, with those words hanging in the air like they were the most natural things for him to say. Maybe they were, in a different time, in a different life, but now, I didn't know what to do with them.

"So, uh," Caleb coughed lightly into his fist to clear his throat. "How 'bout I sign those papers, huh?"

The second I nodded, Caleb didn't hesitate. As soon as those papers were back in his hand, he scribbled his name on the dotted line in those familiar chicken scratches before grinning down at me and pressing a quick kiss into my lips. It all happened so fast and once it was done, my head was still spinning.

When the pen was safely resting on top of the desk, Caleb thrust his hand out for me to shake.

"Hello, partner," he nodded to me, that grin still beaming back at me.

I just laughed and shook his hand. "Hi."

Caleb pushed off the desk and pulled me up with him. "C'mon, Iz. Let me take you back to your dad's, okay?"

Wait. That wasn't what I wanted. At least not yet. And I had a feeling he didn't exactly plan on staying there with me either. Tonight, I just didn't want to be anywhere he wasn't. Whatever that meant, I could sort it out later. I just needed to be with him.

"Where will you stay?"

He just lifted a shoulder. "I'll probably just crash at Saul's again. Trent said he's good staying at your dad's tonight to keep an eye on things."

"But—"

"Iz, we're not going there again. Maybe Wallace won't come after me again tonight, but I'm not going to put it past him and I'm not going to take the risk."

I stood up so we were standing toe to toe and rested both palms on his chest. "I'm pretty sure the only person I feel safest with is you. Nothing is going to happen to me as long as I'm with you, Caleb. And let's face it, if Wallace really wants to come after me, he will. Wouldn't you rather be close if that ever happens?"

His lips parted to respond and then immediately snapped shut just as quickly. He knew I was right; he just wasn't ready to admit it yet.

I was so tired of fighting it, so tired of denying what I knew was true. Maybe it was time to finally acknowledge that white flag and surrender. It's not like I ever really stood much of a chance anyway.

"Wherever you're staying tonight, Caleb, that's where I want to be, too. We could stay at Saul's, my dad's, or a freaking hotel for all I care. I just want to be with you."

The true implication of my words hit us both at the same time and the myriad of reactions that flickered across his face almost made me laugh out loud. First came the genuine confusion and then disbelief mixed with shock. Now a sly, wolfish grin curved his lips and it was clear any confusion between us was long gone.

"Let's get the hell outta here then," he murmured in my ear.

Suddenly, his hands were on my waist, playfully pushing me toward the door.

"Where are we going?" I laughed, letting myself get swept away by the butterflies floating down my body at his featherlight touch.

"I don't know," he leaned his forehead into my shoulder. "We can't stay here, Iz. I'd feel kinda weird about taking you to Saul's and I don't want to make your dad uncomfortable either."

Right, because if he was coming to my dad's with me, he was sleeping in my room. We both knew that was exactly how it would be. That really only left us with one option.

"Hotel?" I lifted a shoulder.

He chewed on the inside of his cheek, contemplating the pros and cons of actually doing something like that and at this point, I was too far gone to over-analyze.

"That's the only place we'll really be alone if we don't stay here," I reminded him.

That, apparently, was all the convincing he needed.

. . .

He really didn't waste any time.

We stood in front of a hotel room door after Caleb hustled us through the length of the hallway and he reached around my waist, fumbling with the keycard because he was moving too quickly and muffled his frustrated laughter in my shoulder. When he finally got the stupid keycard in and pushed the door open, he almost, literally, knocked me right off my feet he was moving so fast.

Biting down on my bottom lip to get myself under control, I shifted on my heel to face him and rested my hands on the tops of his shoulders to get *him* under control a little more too. He seemed to sense we needed to slow things down, that there was no need for the hurry anymore, and reached up to gently brush his thumb across my cheek. That was all I needed to send myself flying off the cliff.

I just hoped he would be there to catch me.

Letting go had never been easier and as I leaned forward to brush my lips against his, there was no hesitation. No second-guessing. All that was left was just this moment, the fact that we were here, surrendering to something we'd never really been able to fight off in the first place. This wasn't about need right now. This was just about the emotional connection we'd always had manifesting itself physically.

With that last thought propelling me forward, my fingertips slid up underneath his white T-shirt, relishing in each inch of taut skin under my touch, and slipped the shirt over his head, sending it drifting down to the carpet. Caleb remained motionless, allowing me to take control and letting me set the pace.

My gaze lingered hungrily on the sinewy display in front of me until my eyes locked on my name, inked directly over his heart. I reached out to trace the letters, flitting my eyes shut when his hands slid around my waist to pull me against his bare chest.

"Do you..." he murmured, trailing off to grasp hold of the words. "Do you still have it?"

He didn't need to elaborate. Of course it was still there. Just like my name was forever marked on him, his name was still written on me, a permanent reminder of what we'd had, of what we still had. Wanting to put him out of his misery, I obliged him by lifting my tank top over my head, standing before him now in just my bra and jeans, and turned so he could finally see what he'd been waiting for.

When his fingers brushed against the pair of angel wings on my lower back, he blew out the breath he must have been holding and then placed a gentle kiss on the top of my shoulder. Putting just enough pressure on my hips to tell me what he wanted me to do, we walked toward the bed with his lips working their up my shoulder until they stopped at my neck, sucking and moving on my skin until I thought I might crumble right under his hands just from that touch alone.

Desperate for a little more control, I whirled around to face him and playfully tugged on his belt to pull him closer so I could rid him of all these clothes he was still wearing. A roguish smirk played on his lips as I made quick work of unbuckling his belt and yanking his jeans down to his ankles. He did the rest of the work and kicked himself free of his jeans before reaching out to return the favor.

His entire body followed in the direction of his hands, lowering himself inch by inch as he lazily dragged my jeans down my legs, and pausing every few moments to kiss the newly exposed skin. My hands tangled themselves in his hair when his lips moved over my panties and I sucked in a haggard breath when he kissed me through the material.

Moments later, Caleb's rough fingertips slipped inside my panties, making me jump from the light, familiar touch, and then my hands were on the tops of his shoulders to somehow steady myself as he helped me step out of them.

Now I was almost completely exposed in front of him and he was kneeling in front of me, as if he was worshipping me at my feet. My eyes just about rolled back into my head at the heady sensation of feeling him so close and I nearly fell right out of my skin.

While I could've easily stood there, basking in his adulation for the next hour or so, this wasn't what I wanted right now. We could do this some other time when I didn't have this sudden sense of urgency attacking me.

"Caleb," I murmured desperately. I didn't want to wait anymore. We'd already been waiting for so long, even a few more minutes felt excruciating.

Luckily, he seemed to read my request in between everything I was too worked up to say and pivoted on his knees until he bounced back on the bed, spread out in all his glory. God, how had I survived so long without this? Without his touch? I'd been completely insane for thinking I could somehow live a full life without having him this way, without letting him love me this way.

He was already sprawled out on the bed with his hands folded behind him on the pillow, grinning back at me as I crawled up the length of him before finally settling myself down.

There was no going back now and I didn't want to.

Caleb met me the rest of the way and his mouth closed over mine before I even had a second to react. There was really only one way we could possibly get any closer. He sat up, pulling me with him, so that I was straddling his lap and I wrapped my arms around his neck. When I angled my hips down, pushing him inside me, tears sprung into my eyes at the sensation.

Finally.

Now that we were finally connected the way we needed to be, there was no reason to hurry. There was no reason to rush the feel of his chest pressing into mine, or the sweet, torturous pressure building between us, or the way he couldn't seem to get enough of me, or the way his teeth nipped at my bottom lip, or the way his eyes seemed to sear right through me, or the way we both clung to each other, holding on for dear life.

This was what I'd been missing.

Everything else just fell by the wayside. Wave after wave of ecstasy washed over me and then I was clinging to the back of his head to try to somehow bring him closer. My head fell back as my breath grew rougher as I struggled to keep up with the rest of my body, and the precipice was right there, beckoning to let myself go. Then, with one more rock of my hips down into that sweet spot, I came apart on top of him completely.

My entire body shivered against his chest and I cried out with relief, desperately clinging to the tremors and pricks of pleasure that coursed all the way down to my toes. A moment later, Caleb groaned into my ear, tightening his forearms around my back as he tensed underneath me and buried his face into my chest.

We stayed like that, with our chests heaving, wrapped around each other's body, with me straddling his lap in this embrace, until he sighed into my neck and pressed a gentle kiss into my collarbone.

"I love you, Iz," Caleb murmured against my skin.

My eyes flitted shut at those words and now my heart thundered in my chest for a different reason.

"I know," I whispered back and buried my face into his neck. "I know."

CHAPTER TWENTY-NINE
Push-Back

Caleb

The sunlight peeked through the cracks in the blinds and I groaned into my pillow at the intrusion, pulling Isabelle closer to my chest. Just the feel of her bare skin resting so easily against mine, almost like she was melting into me, was enough to shake the sleep right out of me. Right about now, I could think of a lot things I'd rather be doing in bed with her instead of sleeping.

I brushed some soft wisps of blonde hair off her neck and pressed my lips there, lazily dragging them up and down her sweet, smooth skin until she stirred in my arms.

A slow, sleepy smile curved up the side of her lips and I shifted my lips there, tasting as much as I could as quickly as I could get it. Isabelle murmured something against my lips and one muffled laugh later, my lips were still glued to hers as I shifted myself until I was resting comfortably in between her thighs. Finally right back where I wanted to be, I didn't feel like wasting any time, even if we technically had all morning.

I just couldn't shake this feeling that if I made one wrong move or said one wrong word, Isabelle would disappear from my arms and from my life. Now that that I had her back exactly the way I wanted her, I suddenly felt like I was running on borrowed time.

All those thoughts about needing to keep my distance disappeared the moment she handed me those papers yesterday. So because she was here, in this bed, in my arms, I knew I needed to hang on to these moments for as long as they lasted. It was that thought that propelled me right where I needed to be and I buried myself inside her.

"Wow," Isabelle laughed in my ear as I found that easy rhythm again we'd had last night. "Good morning to you, too."

"Couldn't wait, babe," I murmured back.

My lips caught her muffled response, pressing myself even deeper into her. It was fucking amazing—all this time and our bodies still seemed to fit perfectly. The time I'd taken to memorize her body when we were first together had totally paid off; there were no awkward, clumsy encounters here. This just all instinct.

Everything last night had absolutely needed to be on her terms and her pace, but now, there was no reason to hesitate. The feeling of her smooth skin slipping and sliding along my body...there was nothing better than this. Absolutely nothing. If this was as far as I got today, if this was all I did, I could just roll over, call it a day, and be completely satisfied with my accomplishments.

How had I survived this long without her? How had I survived for eight fucking years without feeling this? The answer was simple: I hadn't survived. What I'd experienced hadn't been real living. It was just existing.

So I wasn't entirely willing to let her slide out of bed when it looked like she had that very idea. Winding an arm around her waist, I playfully yanked her back against my chest and held her there.

"Ah!" Isabelle laughed as she pretended to struggle against me. "Caleb, stop! I have to get up, you know."

"No," I told her, rolling us until I was on my back and held her firmly against my stomach. "You don't."

"Yes, I do," Isabelle laughed breathlessly, turning her face just enough so we were cheek to cheek. "I have to get back to my dad's. You know that."

I sighed, knowing I was fighting a losing battle anyway and begrudgingly loosened my grip around her waist. "Alright, alright."

"Besides," Isabelle shot me a smirk as she shimmied back into her jeans. "It's not like we can stay in bed all day."

"Oh really?" I cocked an eyebrow at her as my gaze hungrily trailed up and down her beautiful curves despite the fact that she was covering them up now. "I have a lot of ideas of what we could do in bed all day, Iz, and I think you'd love every one of them."

"I don't doubt that for a second," Isabelle laughed and tossed my long-forgotten T-shirt at me. "But I still have to get back to my dad's before the hospice nurse gets there."

It was kind of difficult to justify cracking jokes about keeping her in bed all day when she had real, serious reasons to get out of bed. At some point, I needed to head back into the shop, too. It wouldn't clean itself and I had an insurance appraiser coming later.

Besides, this way, we could let some anticipation build throughout the day until I could get her back in bed again. Yeah, that was the way I needed to look at this.

So when we sat in her dad's driveway with only the sound of my truck idling to cut through the silence, I didn't know where to go from here. And in the end, I let Isabelle call the shots.

"I, um," Isabelle whispered into the silence, rubbing her hands on her jeans as she spoke. "I should probably head inside."

"Okay," I shrugged, reaching out to slide a hand over her shoulder to tell her everything really was okay. "I can bring some lunch back to your dad's after I'm done with the insurance guy if you want."

"You don't have to do that," Isabelle paused for a moment to gauge my reaction. "It's more important for you to be at the shop now more than anything, right?"

No, it wasn't. Not if being at the shop meant being away from her, but I knew what she was doing right now. She needed some space; that much was clear, but she wasn't completely pulling away from me either. She wasn't running and she wasn't telling me to leave her alone. Well, she wasn't really telling me much of anything, but I had to choose my battles with her carefully.

"Okay," I shrugged again, willing to play this game if that was what she needed. "That's cool. I'll just swing by your dad's after I'm done at the shop for the day, alright?"

Her lips curved up into a beautiful, almost shy smile and that just reinforced how much I needed to give her the time and space she needed. We were on fragile ground, despite what had happened last night, and if she'd been cagey before, she had to feel even more so now.

And when I leaned over, pretty much invading her space, she met me halfway and let me kiss her goodbye. My mouth lingered over hers and she smiled into my lips, giving me one more kiss before sliding out of my truck.

The rest of the day seemed to go off without a hitch. The appraiser came and went and clean-up duties went on as planned. I walked around my dismantled shop, despite the fact that it wouldn't be up and running again anytime soon, almost feeling like things had finally fallen back into place.

Of course, that was right up until Saul called me.

. . .

Isabelle

"Aw, shit," I murmured under my breath and threw all my cards down. Beat again. Go figure.

"It's alright," Saul called out from across the table. "Happens to the best of us."

"Well," my dad chimed in from his place at the table. "It's probably a good thing we're not playing with actual money, otherwise you'd be SOL, Isabelle."

I rolled my eyes and shook my head, glancing down exasperatedly at Cooper, who dutifully kept watch at my feet. "Wow. Thanks, Dad."

"Just you watch," Saul nodded to my dad like they were old pals. "When Caleb gets here, things'll take a turn. I've taught that kid everything I know, but no matter what I did or how hard I tried, he just never really got the hang of poker. He always had a good poker face. Still does, to be honest. He just never had any patience. Always wanted to go all in before all the cards were dealt."

"Sounds about right," I muttered under my breath.

Saul just shot me a wide, toothy grin as he shuffled the deck again and dealt out another hand.

"So," my dad started and the effort seemed to make him a little out of breath. "What are the sleeping arrangements going to be tonight?"

I sucked in a harsh breath and shifted uneasily in my chair. Up until now, I'd managed to curtail the fact that he saw me wearing Caleb's clothes yesterday.

"Honestly, Dad, I don't know. We haven't really talked about it yet."

We.

I didn't know how I felt about referring to us in those kind of absolute terms.

Oh my God. I just did it again.

My dad's eyes lingered on me for a little too long before nodding. "Alright. Just let me know if you'll be home tonight."

My breath hitched at the word *home.* I wasn't even sure how to define the idea anymore. Home used to be mean where I felt the safest, the most loved, the most accepted, the most at peace. This house had always felt like home and in a way, it still was. After leaving town for good, the idea of home became more tangible, more concrete. An actual place rather than an abstract ideal. After spending two nights in a row in Caleb's arms, I didn't know what to think anymore.

Luckily for me, the conversation shifted to the latest episode of *American Pickers* my dad and Saul had just watched before we sat down at the table and at this point, I would've been happy even if they wanted to talk about football or anything else I didn't care about.

Any more discussion of Caleb and I would've had to leave the table.

I'd made a split-second decision yesterday, two of them actually, and I still hadn't caught up. All I knew was that helping him, sleeping with him, wanting to be with him, feeling a little crazy because he wasn't here right now...it was as natural as breathing.

And just like that, the tiny wave of panic I'd been holding at bay since this morning finally burst right through the dam.

That was also the moment my dad stood up from the table on shaky legs, shuffled a few paces, and crumbled to the floor.

. . .

The emergency room was exactly the way I remembered. Frenetic. Sterile. Terrifying. Sad. In my past experience, all places like emergency rooms could do was prep you for the inevitable, make you comfortable, and then send you on your way when there was nothing more they could do for you. This time, just like last time, really wasn't much different.

I sat almost catatonically in a chair next to my dad's hospital bed, listening to the monotone beeps from the machines attached to him, and stared at my feet. There wasn't much more I could do. There wasn't anything anyone could do and I'd always known that. Always known this day would come where he'd turn a corner and it'd be all downhill from there.

Some movement at the window caught my attention and Caleb was there, extending a hand to Saul with his chest heaving like he'd sprinted all the way here. They lowered their heads together for a moment, murmuring lowly to one another, and then the door opened so Saul could poke his head through.

"I'm gonna head out now," Saul told us and my dad lifted a hand to shoot him a weak goodbye as Caleb stepped through the door.

He shoved his hands deep into his front pockets and glanced at me out of the corner of his eye to make sure I was okay. I wasn't.

His hand ghosted over my shoulder and then he pressed a kiss into my forehead. I leaned into his chest, basking in this little reprieve from all the darkness swirling around me, and I felt like I could finally breathe again. Part of me could've stayed like this for hours, letting him hold me, letting him comfort me, letting him love me, but the other part, the shell-shocked part, pulled away.

Even as I leaned away from him to put some space between us, Caleb's hand stayed right where it was on my shoulder as if to remind me he wasn't going anywhere.

"How you feeling, Sam?" he called out softly to my dad.

My dad just lifted a shoulder from his hospital bed. "I'm dying, but I guess things could always be worse."

I huffed out a laugh and shook my head. Of course he'd joke now. Try to play it off like everything was fine. Like the doctors hadn't just given us the news I'd been dreading for months.

"Yeah, I guess," Caleb grinned at him, but the smile was wistful, like he already knew without either of us having to tell him.

Now, my dad leveled his gaze at me. "When are you busting me out of here?"

I sighed and rubbed my face with my hands. "Dad—"

"I meant what I said, Isabelle," he told me, his voice firm despite the fact that it barely carried over to my chair. "I'm not being admitted. I want to die in my own home and in my own bed."

A fresh set of tears stung my eyes and I had to squeeze them shut. Caleb's eyes had widened the size of baseballs and he shot me a worried glance, willing me to explain what was going on here. When I couldn't find the strength to say it out loud, my dad filled in the blanks.

"Apparently, a blood vessel burst in my stomach tonight," he told Caleb in such a calm, easy voice I almost got up and left right there. "I guess that's just one of the many complications from having liver cancer, but there you have it. My stomach filled up with fluid, or so the doctors said, and all signs point to my kidneys and just about every other organ in my body getting ready to give out on me. They said I've got a few weeks if I'm lucky and I've never really been all that lucky, at least not where it counts."

"They want to keep an eye on his vitals and help keep him comfortable," I murmured and squeezed my eyes shut.

Caleb blew out a slow breath and nodded tightly, squeezing my shoulder in an effort to give me that little bit of comfort I needed. It wasn't enough. I didn't want to face it, didn't want to accept that my time with my dad had a real, tangible expiration limit and that he was racing toward the expiration limit at breakneck speed.

"Isabelle," my dad called out to me again. "I just want to go home. There's nothing they can really do for me here anyway."

He was right. I knew that. I just didn't want to believe it. And as my eyes found my dad, sitting on his hospital bed with tubes and machines attached to him, looking so miserable, so weary, and so, so unhappy here, the choice was simple. It had never really been my choice to begin with.

"Alright, Dad," I relented with a heavy sigh. "Let's get you home."

After that, the process was fairly easy. Some paperwork and forms to sign. Prescriptions for higher doses of pain meds to fill. A few instructions from the ER doctors in case we needed to come back anytime soon. The whole time, Caleb stood by my side, giving me that quiet strength I needed to get through this and through it all, I found myself inching further and further away from him.

Every time I stepped away, he moved closer. Every time I leaned back, he leaned forward. As if he could sense me pulling away, as if he could feel those walls sliding back into place. He never faltered. He never backed away. He just stayed right next to me with his hand on my shoulder, forcing me to acknowledge his presence.

It wasn't until we got back to the house, settled my dad into his bed, and shut the door behind us that I finally felt myself slipping. Panic was inevitable. Fear had me by the throat and it wasn't just because my dad was sleeping in his bed waiting to die. My eyes flitted shut as those familiar sensations flooded through me, shooting all the way down to my toes. My fingertips tingled. My throat felt like sandpaper. My chest cranked tighter and tighter, winding up into an air-tight vice.

"Iz," Caleb murmured as he pivoted in front of me, approaching me slowly with his hands out almost like he would a caged animal. Maybe that's exactly what I was.

He could feel it. Sense the anxiousness and the alarm probably flying off me in waves. I'd finally reached my breaking point and now the inevitable crash was upon us.

"Maybe you should just sit down or something. Take it easy for awhile."

"I'm fine," I shot back a little too harshly. "Just give me some space, okay?"

His eyes widened at my clipped tone and he swallowed hard, but he still didn't move. I couldn't take it anymore and side-stepped around him so I could hustle down the stairs to put more physical distance between us and he was hot on my heels, just like I expected. And so, I whirled around at the bottom of the stairs and set out to help that inevitable crash along.

"I really appreciate you being here tonight, Caleb," I told him tightly. "I think I've got it from here. Just—I don't know, go home, okay? I don't need you here anymore."

His sapphire eyes darkened at my words, but still, I couldn't stop myself from pressing on.

"I mean it. Just go home."

His eyes flashed one more time and then he was advancing on me, stepping into the space I'd tried so hard to shape, and wrapped an arm around my waist to tug me even closer.

"I get it, Iz," he murmured. "You're scared. I get what you're scared of too. I really do. Just don't push me away. Not after—"

"Don't say it," I whispered, my voice trembling at his closeness. I wanted to be even closer. And I didn't. That was the problem.

He cocked an eyebrow at me. "What? Not after we slept together last night or not after your dad ended up in the hospital today? Which one is it?"

"Both."

"That's what I thought," he nodded at my honesty and leaned back just enough to give me a little more space. "Let's talk about that, Iz."

I shook my head abruptly and pivoted away from him, but he caught my arm to pull me back again.

"There's nothing to say. Let's not make this a bigger deal than it has to be."

"What are you talking about? This," he gestured in between us, "is a big deal, Iz. And it doesn't have to be this way. All you need to do is talk to me so we can work through it."

I jerked out of his grip and skidded into the kitchen, desperate for some relief I knew I'd never find, not as long as Caleb was still in this house, forcing me to face things I hadn't even been able to admit to my therapist.

Cooper had followed our voices, padding down from my dad's room and didn't stop until he'd positioned himself directly in front of me, careful to keep himself in between Caleb and me. I leaned down to kiss the top of his head and scratched his ears, looking for another distraction that wouldn't last.

"Look, Caleb, I just got caught up in the moment. Both of us did. It didn't really mean anything and it doesn't really matter because when I have this house ready to sell, I'm just going back to New York and you're just going to stay here."

All the color seemed to drain from his face and suddenly, without a moment's notice, everything changed on a dime. It was like all the air had been sucked right out of the room and now, Caleb's features had contorted into a dark, furious mask.

"It doesn't matter?" he snapped. "The fact that I told you I loved you yesterday doesn't matter? The fact that I've *always* loved you doesn't matter? What happened last night doesn't matter? That's bullshit, Iz, and you know it."

"It doesn't matter," I whispered, shaking my head furiously. "We might as well just quit now while we're—"

He advanced on me, groping for my hands to bring me closer to him and force me to stay put. "Look me in the eye, Isabelle, and tell me you don't love me."

There was no escape from this. No way I could lie right to his face. He was daring me to tell the truth, daring me to come to terms with everything I'd spent years pushing away. And so, I gave him that as I shoved out of his grip.

"Of course I still love you, you asshole."

Triumph flickered across his face for a brief moment and, for reasons I wasn't quite ready to admit, I sought to squash it.

"I wish I didn't," I whispered hoarsely, watching all the light fade from his eyes with every word. "Everything would be so much easier if I just didn't."

Still, he wasn't deterred and reached for me again. "Iz, listen to me. I know we have a mountain of shit to work through, but that doesn't mean we can't do it."

Shrugging myself free of him, I sidestepped around the island in the kitchen to put more space between us. "Just stop, Caleb. We both know how this ends. We both know this whole mess with Wallace and the club isn't over. And when it starts to get worse than it already is, when *you* decide it's too dangerous, you'll push me away again because you'll just be trying to keep me safe. Because you'll just be trying to protect me from you and the club and everything else that goes along with it even though you're supposedly done with all that now. And then I'll just be abandoned and left behind again to pick up the pieces, just like the last time."

He flinched as if he'd been physically struck by my words and he shuffled backward in a vain attempt to regain his bearings.

Somewhere, deep down, I knew exactly what I was doing. I wanted it to hurt, I wanted it to sting, and in the end, I wanted him gone. I'd already had so much loss in my life...it was better to just cut him off now before he got even closer, before I got even deeper, and before he could hurt me even more than he had before.

Then I just let it fly.

"I don't know what I was thinking last night," I shook my head bitterly.

"Going to a hotel with you? Sleeping with you? I just didn't think about it. I just did it. And I really wish I hadn't. We didn't even use protection. How stupid is that?"

He folded his arms across his chest, staring me down and keeping that hard, impassive mask carefully in place. "What're you saying, Iz?"

"You know exactly what I'm saying," I laughed bitterly. "It's not like I expected you to be celibate. I know I wasn't. And I guess who you've been messing around with wasn't any of my business until last night."

On the inside, I was screaming. Just the thought of him with another woman sent a wave of crazy possessiveness tingling my entire body. Even as I said the words, I knew how wrong they were, how hurtful they were...to throw his past in his face like that, to even suggest that he'd fallen back into old habits when there was absolutely no evidence that was true. It was just a bitchy, low blow and I hated myself for it.

Caleb's face twisted darkly and from the looks of it, I'd hit every bullseye without even trying that hard.

With his face an impassive mask of stone, his jawline rippling with anger, and his fists clenched tightly against the edge of the island, Caleb struck a menacing figure. If I hadn't known better, I might've been a little scared of him.

He exhaled tightly and leaned across the island. "There are a lot of things we need to talk about, Iz, and a lot of things I have to say to you, but I think we should start with what you just said. You know the part about me not being celibate? Let's start there."

Now all I could do was backpedal. "I shouldn't have said that."

"Yeah?" his eyes glowed with frustration. "Well, you did. I can barely count on one hand the number of other women I've been with since you and you wanna know why? Because I don't wanna be with anyone *but* you. And you wanna know something else? I'm not the guy who thinks he can just screw his way through his problems anymore. I've been done with all that shit for a long time and that's because of you. And I don't wanna hear about anyone else you've been with since you left town because just thinking about it makes me sick."

Even if I had the ability to speak right now, I wouldn't have had the balls to tell him that the number of men I'd actually been with since him were few and far between. I hadn't been celibate, just like I said, but that also didn't mean I was happy about it. Not like I'd ever admit that out loud.

"I've never really wanted to be with anyone but you," Caleb went on, his voice rough with determination. "And I'm sorry I waited this long because I didn't want to push you, Iz, but there're so many things we have to talk about. So many things I gotta say."

"It's too late, Caleb," I sighed. "We can't just pick up where we left off and act like everything will be fine. It doesn't work like that."

His face twisted with grief and he tilted his head to the side, like he was in physical pain, as he ventured a cautious step around the island. "The biggest mistake of my life was not listening to you about that goddamn run. You have no idea how much I wish I could take everything back, that I hadn't been such a stubborn, stupid asshole, how much I wish I'd just talked to you about all that money shit instead of trying to figure it out on my own...so many things would've been different for us. There's not a day that goes by that I don't live with that regret, that I don't wish I could do something, *anything*, to take it all back, but I can't."

"You're right," I shrugged nonchalantly despite the tornado of emotions rolling through me. "You can't."

He stalked around the island, refusing to take that as my answer, determined to prove me wrong, and took my face in his hands. "I still love you, Iz. And you still love me, too. We can't just walk away when we can get it right this time."

"Caleb, stop—"

His mouth closed over mine, swallowing my words and some of my resolve in the process, and every movement of his lips burned. Maybe that was what he wanted. Maybe he wanted it to burn, to remind me of what I'd be missing if I really walked away.

"I love you, Isabelle," he murmured against my lips.

I pushed roughly against his chest, needing to get away from him, and stumbled backward as I readied to deliver the blow.

"I don't believe you."

Even as the words left my mouth, I hadn't realized just how true they were until they were finally out in the open. That lingering doubt, that mounting panic hadn't been there for no reason. It festered and rotted away at me for years and now that I'd finally spoken my darkest fear out loud, it didn't make me feel any better. I just felt worse.

Stunned and bewildered, Caleb reached for me wide-eyed. "You don't really mean that, Iz."

"Then why did you let me leave?" I shot back, finally asking the burning question that always haunted me. "If you love me so much then why didn't you ask me to stay? Why didn't you ever come to New York?"

His mouth opened and closed on its hinges as he struggled to find the words to answer me. Still, he staggered toward me, reaching for me again and refusing to allow me to put any more distance between us.

"Would it have mattered?" he demanded now.

That was a fair question. Would I have still decided to leave? What really would've happened if he'd shown up in New York to tell me he'd decided to leave the club? I didn't know how to even begin to answer those questions and I wasn't sure if they really mattered anymore.

"You never called," I whispered as the dam opened and all the emotions I'd kept at bay, all the dark thoughts I'd kept bottled up were finally exposed out in the open for better or worse. "You never even texted to make sure I was okay. You just...you just let me leave and then that was it. Like you were glad it was over. Like you were glad to finally be rid of me."

Caleb sucked in a harsh breath, his entire face drained of all color.

"Iz—" he started, reaching out in desperation, but I just batted his hand away, backpedalling until we were a more comfortable distance apart.

"No," I shook my head furiously. "You don't get to suddenly start acting like you care just because I came back to town. You had no problem just writing me off before you went to prison and after you got out, it was the same thing. The second I told you I was taking that internship, that was it. You never even *tried* and I'm supposed to just believe you still love me because you say you do?"

Caleb shook his head, his face etched with pain and his eyes glassy with unshed tears. His jaw clenched as he fought for control and reached for me again. This time, Cooper's low growl penetrated the silence and my head snapped to my dog, whose teeth were already bared right at Caleb in a snarl.

"It's alright, Coop," I reassured him from around the island. "I'm okay."

That was really just for Cooper's benefit. I wasn't okay and I had a feeling I wouldn't be for a long time after tonight.

"Iz," Caleb's soft, grief-stricken voice called to me. "I left you alone because I thought that was what you wanted."

"That doesn't change the fact that you fucking abandoned me *twice*," I shot back, pushing down the sobs that threatened to cut through those words.

Caleb's face twisted in agony. "I'm so sorry, Iz. I told you not to wait for me and you had every right to leave when you did. I wasn't going to force you to stay or force myself into your life if that wasn't what you wanted. When you left, I thought we were done and I wanted to respect—"

"Bullshit," I spat back and shoved his hands away from me before he could reach out again. "You have no idea how many nights I cried myself to sleep over you, how many fucking panic attacks I've had just from *thinking* about you, how many hours of therapy I've been spent trying to wipe you and everything that happened to us out of my head, how many times I've walked around the city looking for you, hoping you'd..."

I trailed off, unable to find the words to tell him that even now, how many years later, when I knew he wasn't coming, when I knew I wouldn't see him anywhere, I still looked for him every single day.

"And you know the worst thing about it all was that when you went to prison," I pushed through my tears, "I had to deal with all of it on my own. The baby...losing her and losing you at the same time, I don't know how I survived it. I needed you, even if it meant just seeing you once a week. You were my best friend, Caleb, and I fucking *needed* you. But you didn't really want to hear any of that, did you?"

"Yeah," he nodded tightly and swallowed hard. "I did. I needed to hear that."

"It doesn't matter," I shook my head as more tears streamed down my cheeks. "Sometimes I wish it did, but it just doesn't."

We could play the what if game for the rest of the night and that still wouldn't change the fact that there was just too much tormented history between us for this to go further. When there was so much pain leftover from years of bitterness, anger, disappointment, and heartache, where could we possibly go from here?

"You should leave now," I whispered, my eyes falling on Cooper, who was still seated stoically at my feet with his eyes focused on Caleb, waiting to pounce at a moment's notice. "If you really think someone needs to be here tonight, it's fine if you want to send Saul or anyone else, but I really don't want you here right now."

"Iz," he pleaded, gripping my hands and refusing to let go when I tried to struggle free of him. "Don't shut me out now. We can figure this out. Please, Iz. Just let me try."

"It's too late," I lifted my shoulders in defeat and stared down at the tiled floor.

"No, it's not," Caleb told me firmly, resolve creeping into his voice. "I know I've screwed up more than I can even wrap my head around right now, but I'm never gonna make those mistakes again. Whatever you need, however long you need, I'll wait. I'm never gonna abandon you again."

"I wish I could believe you," I whispered and stared down at our hands. "But the fact is I just don't trust you anymore. I mean, yeah, I'd trust you with my life if push came to shove, but everything else? I've worked so hard to try to find some sort of normalcy again and I just can't risk it. Everything in our history is telling me this isn't going to work. It didn't work the first time and it's not going to work now. I don't think I'd survive having to go through all that again...I can't."

His jaw clenched tightly and he squeezed my hands one time before letting them go with a sharp nod. Before I had a chance to respond, his hands closed around my face to press a hard kiss into my lips.

"I gave up on us once before," Caleb told me as that resolve, that confidence I knew so well bursting through all the pain and heartache I'd just caused both of us. "I didn't fight for you like I should've and I honestly didn't think I deserved to keep you in my life. But that was a long time ago, Iz, and I'm not gonna make the same mistakes twice. Do whatever you need to do, but I'm not giving up."

He leaned forward to press one more hard kiss onto my lips, filled with all the promises he'd just made.

"I love you," he murmured against my lips and leaned back to look me square in the eye. "And I know you love me too."

Then he stalked toward the front door, pulled it open as he threw me that confident, almost cocky, crooked grin that had haunted both my dreams and my nightmares over his shoulder. And then he stepped through the threshold and closed the door behind him, leaving me stunned, motionless, and completely speechless in his wake.

CHAPTER THIRTY
Okay

Isabelle

When I got up in the morning, I just went about my normal routine as usual. As far as I was concerned, I had bigger issues right now, like making my dad breakfast and picking up his new meds from the pharmacy. His ER doctors sent us home with slightly adjusted prescriptions to help manage his pain and keep him comfortable, so getting that taken care of was right on the top of my list today.

I wouldn't spend any time playing what happened with Caleb over and over again in my mind, which was exactly what I did all night. Tossing and turning, sketching on any paper surface I could find in my room like a madwoman, pacing the floor—it was a little scary. No panic attacks though, so I guess there had to be a silver lining somewhere.

Just as I was in the middle of piling some eggs onto both my dad's and Trent's plates, I jumped at the doorbell. My heart just about leapt out of my chest. He wouldn't really be that stupid, would he? What part of *go away* did he not understand?

When Trent showed up last night about 20 minutes after Caleb left, I'd been suspicious. Not necessarily that he'd sent someone to keep an eye on the house. Even I knew that was still a necessity for the time being, but it was *who* he'd sent that waved some red flags.

Trent was a little rough around the edges, but polite, quiet, and dutifully did the job Caleb asked him to do. He just wasn't Saul. I'd fully expected Caleb's right-hand man to show up last night and when he didn't, when Trent parked in the driveway instead, I knew there had to be some sort of ulterior motive. Some sort of plan that would just piss me off even more.

"Ah," Trent mumbled through his mouthful of eggs. "That's gotta be my replacement for the day."

"Oh," I smiled back innocently. "Are you coming back later tonight?"

He shifted in his chair, his lips pulling apart in an awkward wince, and finally rubbed his free hand on his jeans, telling me pretty much everything I needed to know.

"Uh," he stammered a little, as if I didn't already know the answer. "That's not the plan, as far as I know."

"So what *is* the plan, Trent?"

He winced a little and rubbed the back of his neck. "Don't you, uh, think you should open the door?"

Oh hell, why did I even bother? This was the same guy who'd chased me through the yard to try to stop me from getting into that cab two days ago. Even if he hadn't been sworn to silence, his loyalty to Caleb pretty much solidified it.

I unceremoniously plopped the pan down on the table and stalked toward the front door with Cooper right behind me.

Low and behold, Saul stood at the door with a broad, if not slightly sheepish, grin on his face. My eyes flew to the shoebox in his hands with a pile of notebooks resting on top of it and my stomach dropped down at least 10 stories. Somewhere, deep down, I knew exactly what this meant without Saul needing to even utter a word.

He did anyway.

"Hey, Isabelle," Saul started easily. "I'm here to take over for Trent, but I guess you probably already figured that, huh?"

I nodded numbly and when he held the shoebox and all those notebooks out to me, reflex had my arms moving forward to take them from him. My gaze stood frozen on the box in my hands and I hardly even looked up when Saul pulled an envelope with just the word *Iz* scribbled on it from his back pocket.

"He said you're supposed to read that first," he nodded to the envelope as he set it on top of the pile, "and then you can read the rest of it in any order you want. When you're ready."

When you're ready.

Right.

Well, Caleb was nothing if not resourceful.

I blew out a deep sigh and stiffly moved aside so Saul could walk through the doorway. He never bothered to turn back to check on me as he ambled into the kitchen. I lingered by the front door, swaying a little from the emotional weight of what was in my hands.

When I heard Saul say, "Hey, breakfast looks pretty good," and my dad's muffled voice telling him to have a seat, I turned on my heel and slowly, painstakingly climbed the stairs until I pushed through my old bedroom door. I set the bundle in my hands down on my bed carefully, as if his letters and notebooks were fragile, as if they were precious somehow, and I guess that's exactly what they were.

I stared at them, my chest heaving in and out with my hands on my hips before I lunged forward and snatched the letter off the top. My fingers traced my name and I could almost see him hunched over, scribbling my name on the envelope in those familiar chicken scratches. Before I could stop myself, my thumb slid underneath the seal, tearing through it without even a second thought.

Then I hit the brakes.

I just wasn't ready.

Not yet, a quiet voice whispered.

The half-opened envelope floated back down to the pile of notebooks and a half-second later, I backpedalled out of my room, practically flying down the stairs to put as much space between myself and that pile on my bed as possible.

I found my dad and Saul sitting at the table, happily eating their eggs and chatting about the logistics of some football play from a game last night. They paused when I stood in front of the table with my shaky hands clenched around my purse. Cooper, who'd been especially attentive to my dad ever since we came home from the hospital last night, lifted his head from my dad's thigh to cast me a wary glance.

"I, uh, just remembered I need to get to the pharmacy to pick up those new prescriptions," I told Saul breathlessly. He'd have to be my escort, of course, because going anywhere by myself wasn't a good idea for too many reasons right now.

I just needed to get out of this house and more importantly, away from that shoebox of letters and pile of notebooks. The walls were closing in on me here and the sooner I could get out, the sooner I could finally breathe again. So, as soon as the fresh morning air hit my lungs, I inhaled deeply, finally feeling a little more in control. Saul met me at his truck just a few moments later and then we were off down the street toward the pharmacy.

"Thanks for driving me," I murmured quietly from the passenger seat.

Saul just lifted a shoulder. "Ah, it's no big deal. Didn't have anything else going on today, you know?"

"Sure," I cast him a sideways glance out of the corner of my eye. "I have to say, though, I kinda expected someone else at the door this morning."

I had a sinking feeling he'd misinterpreted because he shot me a wide, knowing grin that was starting to look a little too familiar.

"I think the boss is just tryin' to give you some space right now."

I blew out a deep breath and turned my head to stare out the window. *Right now. When you're ready. Not yet...*

"Hey," Saul called out to me again. "Did Caleb ever tell you why I was in prison?"

My head snapped to turn to him. Well, *that* wasn't what I'd expected him to say and all I could really do was shake my head.

"Hm," he nodded. "That's what I thought. I figured he'd keep that to himself. Vehicular manslaughter."

"What?" It just slipped out before I could stop myself.

He smiled sadly and turned his eyes back to the road. "I was in for 10 years."

I had nothing.

"A long time ago, back when you were probably just a little girl, I used to go out every night to any bar I could find, it didn't matter where it was or if anyone was with, I still went. Now that I look back on the whole thing, it's so stupid, you know? I was stressed from work, which, I have to admit was pretty damn stressful when you're working 60 hours weeks for someone else and not all that happy doing it. If you're wondering, I used to be an accountant for an IT firm in Raleigh. Anyway, the point is, the reasons why I drank as much as I did were stupid and unnecessary and weak and reckless. All I knew was that for a little bit, I felt better and that was all that really mattered."

He sucked in a hard breath and I knew we were coming to the part of the story he'd have to power through to tell.

"One night, I had a few too many drinks, got into my car anyway, and T-boned another car with a family in it. The kids were okay, I broke my leg, the dad broke his collarbone and an arm, but the mom didn't make it. Killed on impact. That's what they said at the scene. So I went to prison. And every day since, not a day goes by that I don't think about that family, that I don't think about that husband who has to raise his kids and live his life without his wife, those kids who have to grow up without a mother—I stole that from them. Ten years is a drop in the hat compared to the deficit I caused in their lives. Nothing can ever get that back for them either...that's the thing about life, you know? Every beat is precious, but we don't see it that way until it's too late. We should hold on to every moment we get, but we piss it away drinking, complaining, working a job we hate, living a life we hate, and just being all around miserable because we're too scared to find another path..."

He trailed off like he was gathering his thoughts, trying to figure out the best way to articulate his message.

"Anyway, I spent the first eight years of my sentence trying to figure out the best way to die and when I wasn't doing that, I spent the rest of my time wishing I was already dead. I tried to start some fights, but all that did was send my ass to the infirmary and made me even more miserable. I tried to hang myself twice. The first time I couldn't go through with it and the second time, the piss-poor rope I bought off a guy a few cells down from me broke."

Those words hung in the air and tears stung my eyes as Saul shot me a crooked grin that didn't quite reach his dark eyes. He ran a hand over his hair, smoothing the short salt and pepper edges before glancing at me out of the corner of his eye.

"Caleb doesn't know about that last part," he confided quietly. "Don't tell him, okay?"

It was right on the tip of my tongue to ask him why in the world he was telling me all this, especially if Caleb didn't even know, and somewhere, deep down, I knew where this was all headed. So, I gave Saul what he needed and nodded.

"There's just no escaping it," he went on, his voice thick and gravelly. "It eats you alive. Follows you around. Stabs you in the back. I think it must be what drowning feels like—there's no life preserver and you're flailing, just swallowing seawater until you sink deeper and deeper, until everything goes black. Your lungs just keep filling up with water over and over again, sucking the life out of you, and all you can do is let your misery pull you under."

My eyes watered, tears threatening to slip down my cheeks, and I still couldn't move.

"When you take the life of another person, the guilt swallows you whole. You wish you could trade places with them, but that's too easy. Nothing is ever that easy. So you start to retrace your every move, your every step, your every decision, trying to pinpoint that one wrong turn that got you where you are, where you deserve to be, but there's no undo button for life. So when I first met Caleb, I guess you could say I wasn't in a good place. I had my job in the library and that was pretty much the only distraction I had."

He laughed suddenly, shocking me right out of the deep melancholy I'd sunk into.

"I still remember that day. He saunters in the library with all that swagger, all pissed off with that huge chip on his shoulder, leans up against the desk, and goes, 'Hey, uh, can I get some help here?'"

I laughed in spite of everything and shook my head. "Yeah, that sounds like something he'd say."

"He really was a punk, wasn't he? What the hell did you ever see in him back then? Never mind, don't answer that. Anyway, let's just say that if I hadn't been lookin' for something to do that day, I might've told him to stick it where the sun don't shine. But I was bored, so I grabbed a few books for him, thinking I'd probably never see them again, and a week later, he was back. And then he came back again. And again until we finally got to talking about what he was really doing in that library and why."

Saul paused, gauging my reaction and trying to see if I knew.

"I think he might've written to you about that," he went on with a small smile and a not-so-subtle nudge, "I guess his counselor told him he needed to find a way to use his time productively instead of getting into fights and getting his ass killed. He got into a pretty nasty one within the first couple of months he was there—pissed off the wrong Aryan brother was what I heard—but I guess that's one of the hazards of being in an MC and being in prison at the same time."

My breath hitched in my throat at the thought of Caleb getting into fights, of putting himself in danger like that without even caring about what might happen to him, and I closed my eyes to force myself to wipe those images from my mind.

"I used to think it was just because he was mad at the world," Saul added. "And then one day, *I* was the one having a shit day. It was just one of those days where it was all I could to just get out of bed. I needed some absolution and a priest and I guess I got Caleb instead. And when he came in that day looking for another Stephen King book, asked me what was up my ass, it all came pouring out. Jesus, we must've talked for hours that day. I told him things I'd never told anyone before—all those deep, dark feelings of hate and self-loathing just fell out and then it was like the dam broke. We traded stories and I got it then. I got why I always managed to set aside his shit attitude and why he kept coming back: we saw something in each other we recognized. We just didn't know what it was until that day."

I sighed heavily and stared down at my toes. When he first started talking, I'd known this wasn't going to be easy to hear, but now that we'd come to this part of the story, I wasn't sure if I'd be able to handle hearing it.

"I've never seen anyone carry that kind of guilt, that kind of self-loathing —he completely owned everything too, all the missteps, all the piss-poor decisions, he knew none of that fell on anyone's shoulders but his. He just looked like every word, every move took something out of him and I felt like I was looking in a mirror. After that, things started to get a little better for both of us, I think. When he started workin' on that degree, it gave both of us a purpose, something to hope for, something to live for even if I was just sort of living vicariously through him with it. And when he came to see me a month after he got out and told me his plan to leave the club and that I'd have a job as soon as I got out, I believed him. He came to see me every week until he picked me up the day I got out and I've never looked back."

By this point, we were already sitting in the pharmacy's parking lot, but I couldn't move if I tried.

"The only time I ever saw any light in him, I mean *real* light," Saul glanced at me with a wistful smile, "was when he talked about you. I've never seen anyone so devoted to a woman...definitely never felt anything close to that for either of my wives, that's for sure. If he wasn't in the library reading or studying with me, he was telling me stories about you or he was writing to you. That's pretty much how he spent his time in prison."

I narrowed my eyes at him. "I appreciate you telling me all this, but how he spent his time in prison doesn't change our history."

Saul sighed and nodded sadly. "He'll probably try to murder me in my sleep for telling you this, but I'm gonna do it anyway. The last night he spent in that house he bought for you, he spent it in that third bedroom, the one that was supposed to be your nursery. I only know that 'cuz I saw the half-finished mural you painted in there and because the stupid son of a bitch left his pillow and blanket on the floor when I came to help him move. I'm not just telling you all this because I love that kid like he's my own son, Isabelle, I'm telling you all this because I figured you should know."

My chest heaved in and out, but I still couldn't find any words.

Saul cocked an eyebrow at me. "You wanna know what I think?"

I meant to shake my head, but found myself nodding numbly instead.

"I think life has a way of working itself out. Now, maybe you don't get there the way you thought you would and maybe you don't even end up where you expected, but you always get there at the right place and the right time because that's exactly where you're supposed to be."

The words hung in the air, heavy and almost suffocating. I couldn't breathe and the truck just seemed to grow smaller and smaller the longer I sat in here.

"I, um," I rubbed my hands on my jeans anxiously and sucked in a deep breath. "I should go inside."

Saul probably nodded, but I didn't stick around long enough to see. I got out of that truck as fast as my feet could carry me.

. . .

The next morning, I just couldn't pull myself out of bed. I normally set an alarm for seven at the earliest just so I had plenty of time to check my emails, get some coffee going, and shower before my dad needed his meds and his breakfast. For reasons I wasn't ready to acknowledge, my body just wouldn't cooperate today.

Maybe part of it was because I knew Saul was still here, crashing on the couch, and that I had a little backup in case something happened. Maybe part of it, too, was because my body had finally succumbed to the stress, the pain, and the heartache. Maybe I just didn't want to face whatever waited for me today. Whatever it was, I probably wasn't going to like it.

And then I heard it.

That unmistakable roar of a lawn mower screamed through my window and I shot up in bed. It wasn't the roar I'd been expecting—from the sounds of it, there were no motorcycles around—but that wasn't my dad out there in the yard.

All my sleepiness shook out at that stupid sound and I leapt out of bed to skid down the stairs to the window right next to the front door. My eyes tore around the yard to take inventory of anything out of the ordinary. Saul's truck was long gone and my dad's BMW sat in its place. This wasn't a good sign. Finally, my gaze found what I'd been looking for and dreading at the same time. There, driving around the riding lawn mower like he owned the place, was the bane of my existence.

Some rustling to my left had me jumping practically two feet in the air.

"I guess he decided to get an early start, huh?"

My head snapped to my dad, who peered out of the window next to me.

"What?"

He just lifted a shoulder. "He called me this morning to see what needed to be done around the house. I gave him a whole list of things I've been meaning to get done for a long time, but for some reason, I just haven't gotten around to it, you know?"

There was a slight mischievous twinkle in his eye I hadn't seen in a long time and I might've cried, or at the very least, thrown my arms around him, if he wasn't such a backstabber.

But because my mind was still playing catch-up, I played along.

"Like what?"

"Oh, you know," he told me a little too easily. "Pretty much all the yard work, there's that old ATV in the shed. You remember that thing? He's gonna fix it up so you can get some money for it. The faucet in the upstairs bathroom is still leaky, all those boxes in my office need to go somewhere, the basement needs to be cleared out...there're a ton of things that need to be done before you can sell this place."

"Dad, we can *pay* someone to do all those things for us."

"Sure," he shrugged and gestured to the window. "But why spend your money when he's just going to do it for free? Besides, I don't see you doing any of it."

I narrowed my eyes. "What's that supposed to mean?"

He was on pretty shaky ground with me right now and when he held his hands up in defense, he seemed to know it, too.

"Hey, *someone* has to do it. And you shouldn't have to, not with everything else you have on your plate right now. You're spending all your time and energy taking care of me, but who's taking care of you?"

And there it was.

"Dad," I huffed exasperatedly. "I love you, but I really don't like you right now."

He just lifted a shoulder, like all of this really wasn't a big deal, like Caleb being here was just a foregone conclusion. "Oh well. Hey, you want any coffee?"

I gaped at him. Then he just turned on his heel and headed back into the kitchen. No big deal. Nothing out of the ordinary happening here.

My eyes snapped back to the window to find Caleb spinning the lawn mower around some landscaping in the middle of the yard. He looked into the window at the exact right moment, or maybe the exact *wrong* moment, and shot me a cocky, shit-eating grin as he waved at me. Finally, something just snapped.

"Oh, hell no," I muttered to myself as I threw open the door and stalked across the yard to stand my ground right in the lawn mower's path.

Caleb shut off the mower just as quickly and leaned forward on the steering wheel, amusement quirking his lips. "Morning, Iz. I like the PJs."

My eyes shot down to my attire: a tiny pair of sleep shorts and a barely-there tank top. Right about now, I was really glad I'd thrown on a yoga bra last night. He didn't move from his perch on the lawn mower, his eyes trailing up and down my body, taking in every inch of bare skin I'd unwittingly put on display.

Who the hell did he think he was just barging into my life like this? Did he really think he could just show up uninvited, do some chores around the house and then, *poof,* I'd just forget everything?

It shouldn't have even started in the first place because the man in front of me was a weakness. As much as I wanted to attribute everything that had gone wrong in my life to Caleb, the only one really to blame was me. My choices had brought me to this. I never should've invited him out to the swing-set with me. Never should've kissed him. Never should've agreed to spend the night with him. Everything just escalated from there and spun completely out of control.

Well, it was time to grab hold of that control and put my foot down.

I charged right for him, smirking at the way Caleb's eyebrows danced up his forehead in surprise. He didn't get to come and go from my life whenever he felt like it and he didn't get to suddenly decide to give a shit just because I'd pulled the plug on whatever it was we'd been doing the last couple of days.

"Hey," I called out sharply. "What do you think you're doing?"

That lazy, unbelievably sexy, crooked grin curved his lips and I was somewhere in between grabbing him by the collar to jump him and punching him in the face.

"What does it look like?" Caleb shot back easily and rocked back on in the chair as he gestured to the yard with his head. "I'm mowing the lawn."

"No, you're not."

"Oh, yes I am."

I blew out a shaky breath, balling my fists up at my thighs. This route clearly wasn't the way to go. We weren't kids anymore and we could handle this like the mature adults we were, couldn't we?

"Caleb," I tried again, slowly and a little gentler this time. "I appreciate what you're trying to do, but I don't need you doing all this stuff here at the house. You've got more important things to worry about right now like getting your shop back in order. I can pay someone to do all this. Just go home, okay?"

The hard shift in his cerulean eyes told me I'd probably just made things worse.

"I'm not going anywhere, Iz," Caleb informed me pointedly. "At least not anywhere you're not."

"Come on," I tried again, flailing my arms out in front of my in a weak attempt to keep him at bay. "Nobody likes having to do all this kinda stuff, especially if you don't have to."

"I may not necessarily like mowing the lawn or anything else like that," Caleb shot back with an easy shrug. "But I sure do like you. In fact, I *love* you. I'm pretty sure I'll survive."

"Can we not do this?"

He just smirked and lifted a shoulder. "You started it."

So it was going to be like that. Fine.

"Do you want me to hate you? Is that what you want? Because if it is, you're doing a really good job of making that happen."

At least that seemed to get the reaction I was looking for because his features softened and his eyes shone with remorse. But when he jumped off the lawn mower and took a hesitant step toward me, I instinctively moved to put more distance between us. At this point I just needed to use my head and protect what was left of my heart.

"I'm sorry, Iz," Caleb murmured, his voice hoarse and thick. "That's not what I want. I *know* you don't feel that way, but I'm not doing this to make your life harder. You need someone here with you and you can't take all this on by yourself. I'm not gonna let you do it anymore."

"You know what really pisses me off?" I didn't wait for a response and charged ahead, gesturing toward the house. "I need to be in there right now with him for as long as I can because I don't have that much time left. And instead of doing that, I'm out here, arguing with you and wasting that time."

"I hear you," he nodded tersely and when his fingers brushed my forearm to pull me in closer, my body just wouldn't move. I wanted to bolt and sprint inside, leaving him and everything else behind, but my body stood frozen to the grass because my brain short-circuited the moment his fingers touched my skin.

"Look, Iz," Caleb went on softly, his blue eyes imploring and impassioned. "I've spent the better part of these last six years trying to figure out how to earn the right to have you in my life and all I had to do was pick up the damn phone. I've made so many mistakes with you I lost count—I never should've pushed you away, I should've got down on my hands and knees and begged you to take me back after I got out of prison, I should've come to see you in New York the second I decided to leave the club, but I'm done with that, Iz. I know you don't trust me right now, but all I'm asking is that you give me a chance to earn it back."

When my lips parted to protest, Caleb closed both calloused hands around my cheeks and kissed me with an ardent, whirlwind force that threatened to buckle my knees. By the end of it, I would've been a puddle on the grass if his hands hadn't been keeping me upright. When he finally tore his lips away, he leaned his forehead into mine, his chest heaving and I shivered at the feel of his breath brushing against my lips.

He lifted his forehead so he could look me right in the eye and the determination I found there was almost enough to topple my resolve completely.

"I want the life we're supposed to have together," Caleb whispered, his eyes never leaving mine as he spoke. "I want you to be my wife. I want you to be the mother of my children. I want to love you until the day I die, Iz, because there's no other way I can spend my life. I don't care what I have to do or how long I have to wait to do it. Wherever you are, that's where I'm gonna be."

His words enveloped me, warming my insides and squeezing me tight. At this point, it was difficult to tell where he ended and I began. There was too much in everything he'd just said to focus on all at once and so, in a vain attempt at self-preservation, I pulled away completely.

"You can't make promises you can't keep, Caleb, even if you want to," I sighed and scrubbed a hand over my face. "Too much has happened. I just don't know if I'll ever be able to forget and playing these games now isn't fair to either of us."

"This isn't a game to me," his eyes blazed with each word. "You're it for me, Isabelle. It's *always* been you and it always will be. There's a reason we've just gravitated toward each other since you came back. There's a reason we're standing here right now. You can deny it until you're blue in the face, but at the end of the day, you know it's true."

There was also a reason why I hadn't had a panic attack during or after the break-in two nights ago.

I wasn't stupid. I was in denial. And that was perfectly fine.

"Caleb," I tried again, desperate to resolve this once and for all, desperate for him to just give me some space. "I don't want you to think this is going to end any other way than me back in New York and you still here in Claremont. I don't want to give you false hope and—"

"Isabelle," Caleb cut me off sharply. "Sooner or later, you're just going to have to realize that you're stuck with me. I'm not going away. And I'm not going to let you deal with all this by yourself anymore. It's just not happening. You need me here with you, Iz. You just can't admit it yet."

"Caleb, I—"

"Iz," both of his hands closed around my face to force me to look at him, to force me to see, "I could give you everything you need, be everything you want. I feel like we've both been stuck in limbo, but we don't have to put our lives on hold anymore. We could have everything, Iz. You just have to give me a chance to prove it to you."

My lips parted and before I even had a chance to consider responding, he leaned forward and pressed a hard, penetrating kiss on my lips. When his hands finally slipped away from my face, I stumbled backward a few paces, desperate for some breathing room. My brain felt foggy and heavy with everything he'd just laid on me and for the life of me, I couldn't find the words to respond.

And now, with my chest heaving and my pulse thundering through my veins, the only word I wanted to say was "okay". The problem was I wasn't so sure what I'd exactly be agreeing to, so I just sucked in a deep breath, shifted on my heel, and headed back inside the house.

I took the stairs two-by-two to get back inside my room and shut the door behind me. Against my better judgment, I found myself edging closer to the window when the lawn mower screamed back to life.

My heart flip flopped in my stomach as my eyes found him, perched on the seat again with his phone in his hand. About two seconds later, my phone buzzed next to my nightstand and Caleb lifted his head up to my window. He waved to me with a bright, reassuring grin spread across his handsome face. It was really everything I needed to see, but couldn't at the same time. My lips quivered and I had to bite down on my bottom lip just to keep myself from bursting into quiet sobs.

When I dared another glance out the window, I found Caleb winding around to finish a lap around the front yard. A beat later, his ocean-blue gaze flicked up to meet mine and his mouth curved up into a smile that breathed understanding, devotion, and the unconditional love I'd always seen in him. Then my hands closed around my phone and I swiped across my screen to read the text:

Just let me know when you're ready to let me in. I'll be out here. Love you.

My eyes landed on that old shoebox and the pile of notebooks sitting just a few feet away from my bed and I blew out a deep breath before finally murmuring the only real response I could give, the same one that sparked so much fear and need in me at the same time:

"Okay."

CHAPTER THIRTY-ONE
Finally

Isabelle

For the rest of the day, I had a tiny bit of peace, mainly because Caleb kept his distance and stayed outside. He must've decided it was a good day to get all the yard work done in one shot because he only came in the house twice—once to use the bathroom and once to wash his hands after pulling some weeds in the landscaping. Unfortunately, it was dinner time now and my dad was already halfway out the door to invite him inside for dinner.

And then a terrible thing happened.

I literally *ran* upstairs and shut my bedroom door behind me. I scampered around, digging through a few piles of clothes until I found something a little more acceptable than yoga pants and a ratty T-shirt. Once I'd settled on a pair of snug skinny jeans, an over-sized, slightly transparent white shirt tucked into the front of my jeans, and a long pendant necklace, I kept right on going and headed for the bathroom. It wasn't to hide. It wasn't even to use the bathroom. No. I had much bigger problems now. Because now, I stood in front of my mirror with a tube of Diorshow mascara in one hand and a can of hairspray in the other.

I was sick. And pathetic. And in denial.

But I got to work anyway because this mess needed a lot of fixing.

I spritzed on a tiny bit of perfume just for good measure, happily feigning ignorance at the real reasons why I was even doing this in the first place, and went back down the stairs. At least now I felt a little more like myself with all the necessary armor and masks in place to hide everything I couldn't lay bare.

Caleb was already leaning against the island on his elbows, laughing at something my dad said, and my breath hitched in my throat at the sight of the two of them standing there like that so easily. I took a few hesitant steps inside the kitchen and even though his back was almost completely turned to me, Caleb seemed to be hyper-aware of my presence. His head immediately turned to me and his lips spread into a wide, welcoming smile that warmed me a little too much.

"Hey, Iz. Dinner smells pretty good," he called out easily, his lips curling in a self-satisfied smirk as his eyes trailed up and down. "You look nice."

I narrowed my eyes at him, ignored that last comment, and carefully stepped around the island to pat my dog on the head and to check on the lasagna I'd put in there about an hour ago. But when I set the dish on top of the stove to cool for a while, Caleb's eyebrows shot up into his forehead when he got a good look at the pan of oozing cheese and meat sauce.

"Holy shit," he exhaled and licked his lips. "*You* made that? Really*?*"

"No," I rolled my eyes. "I have Rachel Ray on speed dial."

Caleb smirked at me and then leaned forward to sniff the air. "Nice work, Iz. Maybe there's hope for you yet."

"You wanna give it a taste test?" I shot back. "Maybe I poisoned it."

"You wouldn't do that."

"Try it and find out."

"Okay," he sunk a little deeper into the counter, his eyes dancing with mischief. "Where'd you get the poison?"

"From the poison store," I could feel my lips curling in annoyance. "Where else would I get it?"

Caleb just grinned as my dad chuckled on the other side of him. "Alright. Maybe I just think you like me too much to poison me."

My eyebrows lifted in defiance and the best I could come up with was: "Don't you have something better to do than piss me off?"

He shook his head and lifted a shoulder. "Nope. Can't think of anywhere else I'd rather be."

"What about the shop? You've kinda got your hands full for awhile."

"Well," Caleb smiled at me. "Saul's got everything under control while I'm here. And thanks to you, I've still got some money coming in to keep my staff and pay some bills. So I figure this is as good a time as any to take a little time off and help you guys out here."

My dad nodded in agreement and my eyes practically shot fire at him. He blinked back at me for a second, realized his error, that he was supposed to be on *my* side, and held his hands up in defense.

"Sorry," my dad winced a little at my withering expression. "I can't help how entertaining you two are. I'm serious. This is way better than anything on the History channel."

I lifted my eyes to the ceiling and shook my head. Then I shot my glare right where it belonged.

"You know, I'm really starting to regret ever helping you."

He didn't miss a beat. "No, you're not."

I glanced around the island at Cooper, who happily sat in between us on the floor with his tail wagging.

"Coop," I pointed at Caleb. "Sic 'em."

Cooper's eyes shifted to Caleb, then back to me, then back to Caleb again. Finally, he took his sweet time getting up to his feet and trotted the short distance over to Caleb, who shot me a cocky grin as he ruffled Cooper's dark fur.

"Hey, buddy," Caleb murmured to my dog.

"Traitor," I muttered under my breath as I put a Texas-sized portion of lasagna on a plate for my dad.

He took the plate from me as he eyed the portion skeptically. There was no way he'd ever be able to finish that much food, not with all the meds he was on now, but I wanted to treat him like he was sick as little as humanly possible.

"I think Cooper just knows he's not a threat," my dad told me with a sly grin. "He's smart like that."

"Sure," I huffed and glared daggers at my dog, the same one who wasn't even paying attention to me because he was too busy enjoying Caleb's ministrations.

I really shouldn't have been surprised when Caleb praised my lasagna like nobody's business or when he insisted on helping with the dishes or when he plopped down on the couch next to my dad to watch the *Vikings* marathon on the History channel or when my dad was ready to head upstairs for bed, he didn't hesitate to grip my dad's arm to help him off the couch.

And when my dad started his slow, awkward shuffle up the stairs, he didn't put up his usual fight. Instead, he actually let both Caleb and me to take an arm and help him up the stairs without so much as a protest. We got him up to his door and I kissed his cheek, he waved goodnight, and then Caleb and I were standing there alone in the hallway.

He smiled at me a little shyly and shoved his hands deep into his front pockets, a gesture I'd seen a million times, but for whatever reason, *this* time my heart tugged a little more than I remembered.

"I take it you're planning on crashing here tonight?"

He rocked back on his heels and the grin on his face just widened. "Yep."

"Alright," I sighed. What was the point in arguing? "Just sleep on the couch, okay?"

The guest bedroom was right next to mine and I just didn't want to go there tonight. Exhaustion, frustration, and just about everything in between had sucked what little energy I had left and I didn't want to waste it fighting with him.

Caleb nodded tightly, the smile slipping down just a little, but it still never left his face. One of his hands unearthed from his pocket and he reached out to tuck some hair behind my ear.

"Okay," he whispered. "Night, Iz."

I blew out a deep breath. "Night, Caleb."

And when I shut my bedroom door behind me, my eyes flew right to that shoebox of letters and piles of notebooks. I just couldn't help it.

. . .

For the next week, this was pretty much how it went: Caleb did some odd jobs around the house, whether it was cleaning up my dad's office, sorting through the garage, emptying the dishwasher, doing a few loads of laundry, or taking care of the lawn, and I spent the days with my dad. We managed two walks, one dinner at his favorite restaurant in town, which Caleb dutifully drove us to and waited in the parking lot while we ate, and the rest of the time we looked at photo albums, watched a few old home movies, and at night, Caleb would join us for dinner and some TV.

There was a little whispering between the two of them about the Horsemen's retaliation against the Warlords. Apparently, they'd hijacked one of the Warlords' 'shipments' en route and redirected it to one of their warehouses. From the little I heard, Caleb fully expected this move to backfire, and I supposed I did too given the way things were headed, but that was all I heard of it.

For the most part, we all just tried to pretend like everything was normal.

It wasn't. He was getting ready to die. I knew it. Caleb knew it. Cooper knew it. Now it was just a matter of when.

When I woke up this morning, I could feel it. Something was about to change. Like turning the last page in a good book or turning left instead of right—sometimes the simplest changes are the hardest ones to accept. It was in the air, crackling with electricity and a little bit of hope. The weight of whatever waited for me today was so heavy I almost couldn't drag myself out of bed. And then I heard my dad shuffle into the bathroom, close the door behind him, and a loud thud about three seconds later.

As the sounds of Cooper's clipped, anxious barking bounced off the walls,

I shot out of bed, practically tripping over the covers I was moving so fast, and sprinted toward the bathroom, throwing the door open as soon as my hands found the knob. My dad was sprawled out face-down on the floor with his right leg twitching a little as he struggled to sit upright.

"Dad!"

I crouched down by him as he grumbled out a moan. He tried to push himself up with his palms, but slumped back down to the floor just as quickly. Caleb appeared in the doorway a moment later and he scrambled around to the other side of my dad, gripping him by the shoulders to turn him over.

"It's alright," my dad batted a hand at us.

"Dad—"

He never gave me a chance to finish. "I just slipped a little and lost my balance. It's not a big deal."

"Maybe we should—" I tried again, but he vehemently shook his head.

"I'm not going to the ER again," he told me tightly.

My desperate eyes found Caleb and I silently pleaded to him for some backup. Just a little reassurance, a little support, and he nodded sadly. Both of us knew it wouldn't really make much difference, but I had to try and I needed Caleb to have my back. Besides, my dad might actually listen to him.

"Maybe it's a good idea just to go in and see your normal doctor, Sam," Caleb told him in a calm, even voice I barely recognized. "We could wait a little bit and see if you're—"

"It's not worth it," my dad cut in and shot Caleb a hard glare. "And just so you know, I expected better from you."

Caleb just blew out a deep breath and shook his head. "Come on, let's get you up, okay?"

At least my dad agreed to that and he nodded numbly as Caleb gripped him around the shoulders to heave him up to his feet. Once Caleb had him up high enough, I ducked underneath my dad's shoulder to help carry some of his weight. The three of us shuffled out of the bathroom and into the hallway, just long enough for my dad to get his bearings back and shrug away from us.

"I'm good," he waved us off, even as Caleb refused to loosen his grip. "I'm just gonna go sit out on the porch for awhile and get some air."

Caleb's expression mirrored mine and we both gaped back at my dad like he'd just said he wanted to run a marathon today. I'd expected him to want to lay down for awhile, but then again, nothing about this morning was normal.

"Hey Isabelle," my dad turned back to face us at the top of the stairs.

"Why don't you come out and sit with me when you're ready."

When you're ready.

We watched, helpless and shit out of luck, as my dad ambled down the stairs, only slipping once and catching himself just as quickly with Cooper right on his heels. I didn't know which was worse: knowing how much effort he needed just to take the stairs inch by inch or knowing that in a few days or maybe even a few weeks if I was lucky, I wouldn't be able to watch it anymore.

My shoulders started heaving and then it was all downhill from there. I could feel those tell-tale signs pricking up and down my body—clammy palms, thundering heart, and a tightening throat. The fact that it had taken *this* long was probably a miracle in itself.

A fresh wave of tears worked their way down my cheeks, but Caleb's thumbs caught them before they got very far.

"It's okay, Iz," he murmured. "I got you."

I squeezed my eyes shut, searching for some of the strength I needed to get through today and whatever it held. I found it in him the moment my cheek rested on his shoulder. His hand worked its way through my hair and then my hands reached out until my fingers gripped the front of his T-shirt to pull him in. My lips sought him out, needing to feel him against me, needing to feel the love, understanding, and devotion that he'd never backed down from showing me. I just needed *him.*

Our lips collided, our first real kiss since our fight over a week ago, and moved together with a practiced familiarity and an intimacy I hadn't realized how much I'd missed.

Finally, we both seemed to remember where we were and I quickly pulled away from him, laughing a little as I awkwardly tugged my hair back into place. The problem was that I didn't really know where we went from here. Now that I was on the edge of *something,* I just didn't know which way to turn.

Right now, what I needed was just a little bit of space. A little more time.

His hands closed over my shoulders, warming me and making me just want to sink into him again, but I stepped away to put some space between us.

"I think I should, um, maybe take a shower and get some coffee going," I rubbed my palms anxiously on the front of my sleep shorts. "Do you want any?"

Thankfully, Caleb always seemed to know exactly when to push and when to pull. He ran a hand over the top of his head and shot me a quick smile.

"Don't worry about it, Iz. I'm gonna work on the ATV most of the day, so I'll just grab a cup on my way out to the garage."

His thumb brushed away one last stray tear before his lips curled up again as he headed back down the stairs. I swallowed heavily and finally resigned myself to the mercy of this day.

. . .

I handed my dad a cup of steaming coffee as I sank down into the chair next to him on our porch. He slid it out of my hand with slightly trembling fingertips and shot me a weak smile. Cooper lifted his head out of my dad's lap and went back to guard dog duty as soon as I settled into the chair.

"Nice morning," he murmured and squinted up at the clear, brilliant blue sky.

"Yeah, it is."

My eyes fell on Cooper, who hadn't moved from his post, and I felt my heart sink a little deeper into the pit of my stomach. It was coming. I could feel it in this warm, breezy North Carolina air, floating and tightening around me like a vice.

"We're getting to the end," he told me quietly. "I can feel myself heading for that finish line and I don't think it'll be long now. I'm ready to be with your mom again."

My breath hitched in my throat and tears stung my eyes. I couldn't do this. I couldn't sit here and have this conversation, not when he was acting so nonchalant about dying. But I also knew I wasn't going anywhere either.

I swallowed hard and managed to find my voice. "Are you scared?"

He smiled, but it didn't quite reach his eyes. "I used to be. Mostly, I was scared of leaving you and I still am. But now, I don't know. I think you'll be okay," he shifted his eyes to the garage, where Caleb had the ATV all but torn apart in an effort to put it back together again, "I'm not happy about all the things I'm gonna miss though. Watching you become filthy rich and famous, holding my grandchildren and watching them grow, watching you be a mother—you're gonna be a great one, you know that?"

Because I couldn't find the words, my lips just lifted into a pained smile.

"You've got so much of your mom in you. When she died, I couldn't stand that about you. I hate myself for that. I should've held you closer just *because* of that and I shut you out instead."

"Dad—"

"No, just listen," his voice was firm with resolve now and I didn't argue any further. "Everything that was good in your mom, her kindness, her compassion, her light, her ability to love unconditionally—that's in you, too. I'm so damn proud of you, Isabelle. Everything I ever wanted for you, everything I ever hoped for you, you've realized all of it in a way I never could've imagined."

I sucked in a harsh breath and my eyes flitted shut. "Dad..."

He smiled at me again and it still didn't reach his eyes. "I have so many regrets, sweetheart, but most of all I wish I'd been able to be there for you after your mom died and I wish I'd cherished the time I had with your mom while I had it...I can't even explain it to you. One minute you're 20 and have the whole world at your feet and the next, you're 55 and you've got nothing to show for it. I spent too many years wallowing at the bottom of a bottle when I should've been trying to figure out how to find some happiness again."

His words hung in the air, heavy with all the ways he could've found a second act in life, but chose to remain buried in his grief instead.

"Life is fleeting, Isabelle," my dad told me, looking me square in the eye. "You can't waste the little time you have being miserable, especially not when the key to your happiness is sitting right in the garage."

All the air left my lungs. My body felt heavy and frozen to the chair. I still sat there even when my dad stood up on shaky legs and leaned down to kiss my cheek.

"I'm gonna lay down for a little while."

I just nodded, watching numbly as my dad shuffled back into the house with Cooper right behind him. But instead of following him inside like I probably should have, I sat there with my eyes glued on the driveway with a torrent of thoughts racing through my mind. I couldn't have pinned down one coherent thought if I tried and suddenly, I was back inside the house, taking the stairs two by two until I shut my bedroom door behind me.

My hands, trembling with the weight of what I was about to do, closed around that half-opened letter and I traced my name scribbled on the front. Then, with a quick inhale for strength, I ripped it open the rest of the way and tore the paper from the envelope, my heart racing as I read the first words, *Hey Iz.*

My lips lifted into a grin and I bit down on my bottom lip.

If you're reading this, I must've finally done something right. Or maybe I finally wore you down and you're just reading this to humor me. I don't care as long as you keep reading. I know you think I let you leave all those years ago and never gave you a second thought, but I've written to you almost every day since the day you pulled out of the driveway. I just never sent you the letters because I figured you wouldn't read them, so instead, I wrote in the notebooks Saul gave you.

I've never stopped thinking about you. I've never stopped wanting you. I've never stopped loving you. Everything's in those notebooks and in that shoebox, Iz. You just need to read it all, okay? Come find me when you're done.

Love you always,

Caleb

I sucked in a deep breath and swallowed back the lump in my throat. And before I really understood what I was doing, I gently set aside the notebooks for now and took the lid off the shoebox to lift out the first letter my fingers touched.

Hey Iz,

Today's Christmas. It's weird being in here with all these guys who are feeling the exact same thing I am right now. We all miss somebody. We all wish we were somewhere else. We all wish we'd done something different so we wouldn't be in this place. We've been watching Rudolph and I wish someone would turn on Elf because I know you like that movie better...

The next one was more of the same.

I was talking to this guy in the library today about you. I told him I used to have a girl who streaked through the campus at Duke and he didn't believe me. Then I realized I said 'used to' and I had to walk away. I thought I was going to break down right in front of that guy...

And then there was this one:

I dreamed last night we were in our bed. I was holding you and some crying woke us up. I told you to stay in bed and went into that third bedroom. There was this little tiny baby in a blue crib and I picked the baby up and sat in the rocking chair until he went to sleep again. Is it weird I dreamed we had a boy? I know that's what I thought I wanted awhile ago, but now I just keep thinking about little girls: fluffy princess dresses or whatever little girls wear, playing with Barbies or My Little Pony, glitter, and all that pink. I probably sound like a pedophile or something to anyone else who reads this, but I know you get it...

And this one:

I've been dreading today. I knew it was coming and that there was nothing I could do to stop it, but now that it's here, I don't know how I even got out of bed. She'd be a year old today and every time I close my eyes, I'm right back in that hospital, holding your hand

and trying to keep it together. I wish I had that memory box they gave us. It would make me cry and crying is the last thing you should do in here, but seeing it might help a little. I hope you're not alone. Maybe you're with your dad or my mom? I don't want you to be alone today...

Each one was more devastating than the last and each one showed me yet another facet to Caleb I hadn't known before. Everything he did in prison, every fear, every thought, every single one of Skyler's painful visits, every time he wished I would visit or take his calls, it was all documented in his letters. And at the end of each letter was the same closing: *Love you always, Caleb.*

His letters were exactly what I'd always known they would be: testaments to his guilt, his self-loathing, his unwavering love for me and most of all, the spark that would've sent me right back into his arms.

Now as I sat here with every letter he'd ever written to me in prison scattered around me, I found myself wondering what really would've happened if I'd read them when I first got them, but then I remembered Saul's words last week: *life has a way of working itself out.*

And so I pulled the first notebook off the top of the pile and flipped it open. The first entry was dated almost a week after I first left Claremont six years ago and my eyes immediately fell to the words he'd scribbled there.

Hey Iz,

This is all I've got. I know you're never going to read this and that's okay. I earned you walking away from me. I earned you never wanting to see me again. I earned having to sit here alone in our empty house. I just don't know what to do anymore. I can't be a part of the club, but I still have to work out the details. I wish you were here, Iz. You'd tell me what to do, which way to go, and everything would be okay...

So not even a week after I left, he knew he was going to leave the club. That particular knowledge wasn't necessarily comforting because he'd had every opportunity to reach out, but he never did. Somewhere, buried underneath my own bitterness, I was beginning to understand why.

Then I started turning the pages, devouring each notebook one by one and picturing him hunched over scribbling on the page like he was sitting right here next to me, starting and ending each entry the exact same way.

Hey Iz,

I did it. I really left. I couldn't write to you yesterday because I was too nervous and I didn't want to say too much before I actually went through with it. The hardest part was walking into the clubhouse with my cut in my hand. I just kept thinking about my dad, about what he would say if he knew what I was doing and why. I don't know, the more I think about it, the more I think he might've at least understood.

Everything after that needed to happen. The second Marcus opened his mouth, it was just over. I can't even tell you what he said because it's just going to piss me off again and I might put my fist through the wall. But I'm done with the club now. I have to be. I won't stay alive if I let myself go back there. I guess it took losing you to realize how much I wanted to live, how much I wanted to have a better life. At the same time, it just doesn't mean as much without you...

My heart crept up to my throat and tightened there, holding me in place, forcing me to move on to the next pages.

The loan got approved. I figured it would since I had an airtight business plan (at least I think it was). Now the real work begins. Now I have to start buying equipment, hiring staff, figuring out marketing, and everything else that goes with it. Saul can only get me so far with all the financial stuff. I'm on my own for everything else and that's okay...

I'm sitting here in our third bedroom and I know I should get to sleep, but I just can't. Everytime I look up, I see that half-finished mural you painted on the wall and I just want to curl up into a ball on the floor and cry. This is my last night in our house, Iz. You have no idea how hard I tried to keep it, but there's no way I can pay for our house <u>and</u> the building for the shop at the same time. I guess it's just for the best. Living here is like walking around a museum. I feel like I can't touch anything because it might break or disappear and then that memory will be gone. I think I'm going to sleep in here tonight. Torture myself a little more. Wish things were different one more time...

Things are going good, Iz. I don't know how, but the shop is actually making money. Everything I've been working for is finally starting to happen...

I saw all those pictures online from your show last night. You looked beautiful. I bet it sold out in an hour. I wanted to buy one, but I wasn't sure if you could see who all the buyers were and I didn't know how you'd feel about it. You deserve everything, Iz. All this success, all this recognition, I knew you'd find it there. I'm so proud of you I can barely see straight...

Even as I tore through the most recent notebooks, each entry wasn't that different from the last. I'd never been far from his thoughts and he'd never gone a day without wishing things were different.

Your dad came to see me today. I don't really know what happened with the house, but if he needs money, if he needs some help, I wasn't going to turn him away. I know you'll shit a brick when you find out, but your dad just nailed it on the head. He told me I wouldn't say no because I love you. He was right. There was no way I wasn't giving him that money if it meant making things easier for you down the road (I know you won't see it that way) and if it means sparing you some pain right now, I'm good with you being pissed at me later...

So your dad keeps showing up at my shop. I think he's checking on me. Yesterday he asked if I wanted to get some food with him and you'll never believe this, but I actually went and it was actually okay. I never thought I'd ever say that, let alone go anywhere with him willingly...

Finally, I got to the entry he'd written the night before I came back to Claremont and I knew that after this entry, I'd be ready to stop reading.

Hey Iz,

Tomorrow is the day I've been waiting for. I always knew you'd come back eventually. I just didn't know when and I didn't know it would be for something like this. I'm so sorry, Iz. I wish there was something I could do to make this better for you, but I know it doesn't work that way. I don't know when I'll see you and I don't know how you'll react to me when you do, but I can wait a little bit longer. Maybe this place will finally start to feel like home again when you're back. I don't know. I think anywhere would be just fine as long as I was with you. I know I shouldn't hope for anything because it's been too long and so many things have changed, but I'm still going to hope anyway.

Love you always,

Caleb

I swallowed hard as I shut the notebook and stared at the mess of paper and envelopes covering my floor. Tears pricked my eyes and my chest tightened, but there would be no frantic scrambling to get away as fast as I could and hide in the bathroom. I'd just done exactly what I always said I'd never do and a rush of calm flowed through me, easing my tears and softening the blow of everything I'd missed, everything I hadn't wanted to see, and everything I'd lost.

Then I pushed up to my knees so I could scoop up the letters and put them back inside the shoebox. Once I had everything in order again, I picked up the shoebox filled with his letters and the pile of notebooks filled with his words and headed back down the stairs. I passed my dad, who'd perched himself back on the porch sometime during my refuge in my room, and he smiled softly. Cooper just lifted his head off my dad's lap again to acknowledge I was there and then he went back to ignoring me.

When I finally made my way over to the driveway, I found Caleb hunched over the ATV's engine with his back to me, covered almost all the way up to his elbows in grease and grime. With both hands working tirelessly, cranking and turning something inside the engine, he was too engrossed in his work to hear me approach.

I cleared my throat. That moment I'd known was coming this morning? It was here.

"Hey, Caleb?"

He turned abruptly, his face lined with a confused frown. But then his eyes dropped to the box and the notebooks in my hands and he blinked back at me in surprise as I stepped forward. His Adam's apple bobbed up and down and his eyes never left me as I gingerly held the box out to him. A second later, he wiped his hands to take the box from me and his lips parted, but I cut him off before he had a chance to say anything.

"I think I'm just gonna take a little walk, okay?" I murmured and jumped to squash any attempt he might make at coming along. "I need to clear my head. I'll be right back."

His forehead was still lined with a frown, but he nodded anyway. "Okay. Take Coop with you though."

Right. Safety first. If Caleb wasn't coming with me, Cooper was the next best option. And when we were on the sidewalk with some distance between us and the house, I knew this was exactly what I needed. I just needed a little more time, a little more space and then what? Maybe that was the problem. I knew what was coming next. It was just the coming-to-terms-with-it part that had me dragging my feet.

I glanced over my shoulder to find Caleb sinking down into the chair next to my dad on the patio and couldn't help the smile that tugged at my lips. I knew he'd do just about anything for me, even if it meant hurting himself.

In the time leading up to my return to Claremont, I'd managed to convince myself that Caleb hadn't wanted me. That he hadn't wanted to deal with the aftershocks of everything we'd suffered, hadn't wanted to shoulder the responsibility of helping me heal and the radio silence on his end was nothing but ammunition for my despair. At times, my feelings for him had wavered between pathetic longing and desperate hatred, but I'd never been able to convince myself that all the other feelings, the ones buried underneath the shattered pieces of my heart, had ever disappeared.

And even though the distance between us had been very intentional on Caleb's part, his motivations for cutting our ties were more defined now in a way I could finally wrap my head around.

He'd honestly believed he was doing the right thing by letting me walk away. In the process, he'd also willing put himself in a self-inflicted purgatory of despair and loneliness. Like he was paying penance for the role he'd played in what had happened to us. Like his guilt was so all-consuming that he'd honestly believed he didn't deserve me.

In the end, what more did I really want from him at the time? He'd done what he thought I wanted and all I'd done was say one thing but really mean something else like a typical girl. And all my accusations, all my pouting about him not reaching out when I'd basically told him not to by leaving wasn't fair and it definitely wasn't very mature. I wasn't completely innocent here either.

And I think I understood the root of all my anxiety better now too—aside from my decisions involving school and my internship, I'd had almost zero say in any major aspect of our relationship. From our house all the way to his arrest, Caleb had called all the shots while I'd helplessly and passively flailed out of control with nothing to do but stand by and watch my life fall apart.

But now, I couldn't help but feel that time and clarity had finally put us on an even playing field.

As I rounded the corner of our block, my steps slowed, subconsciously giving myself just a few more minutes.

I loved Caleb Sawyer. I wanted the family and the life we were supposed to have together. I wanted *him*. I wanted to spend every day and every moment with him for as long as I could.

What it all came down to now was a matter of trust. Walking up the driveway, stepping onto the porch, and taking my place next to Caleb would mean I would have to choose to trust him. There was nothing he could really say or do to prove he would never push me away or take me for granted again.

If I did this, I'd have to proceed on trust, faith, and love.

Life had broken us and the pieces scattered around the highway from Claremont all the way to New York, but I didn't want to be broken anymore.

I wanted to come home.

I dropped Cooper's leash when we got into the yard and smiled when Caleb hopped down from the porch to meet me halfway. I gripped the front of his shirt when he was close enough and then leaned forward to press my lips into his mouth. His thumb grazed my cheek and his arms wrapped around my waist to pull me in even closer. My lips moved over his, wanting to taste him, and wanting to show him everything I still hadn't said.

Finally, I pulled away and leaned my forehead against his with one hand still grazing his cheek. Our eyes locked and the soft lift in his smile told me everything I needed to know.

"I love you," I whispered.

Caleb's eyes squeezed shut for just a moment and when they opened again, they gleamed back at me with the unconditional love I'd always found there.

"I love you, too," he whispered back.

He tilted his chin just enough to brush his lips against mine again. The finality and the inevitability of it all left me feeling exactly the way I knew I would: calm, peaceful, elated, and blissfully happy.

"So I guess this means you want me to stay?" Caleb asked me now, a light, knowing smile curving his mouth.

I bit back a laugh and grinned. "Yeah, I want you to stay."

Caleb's smile just widened as his fingers trailed down my cheek and he leaned in to murmur, "Okay, Iz."

CHAPTER THIRTY-TWO
i fear no fate

Caleb

Light slipped in through the blinds and I tugged Isabelle closer to me so I could bury my face in her hair. Her alarm would probably go off soon, but I needed to hold on a little bit longer. All that mattered was her skin and her warmth pressed against me. She hummed a little, turning around so she could press her face into my chest and I slipped my fingertips underneath her tank top.

"I have to get up soon," Isabelle murmured into my chest.

"That's alright. We've got plenty of time."

She laughed and I could feel her smiling against my skin. "Always thinking with one part of your body, huh?"

I just shrugged. Couldn't really argue with that. Now that I had her back, now that nothing was standing in our way, some part of me always had to be touching her. It wasn't easy to hold back, especially since when we weren't in her bed, we didn't have any other real alone time—the kind that we'd missed out on for so long. On the other hand, we couldn't exactly rip each other's clothes off in her dad's house either.

It wasn't perfect, but that was okay. We still had some issues to work through, some hills we'd have to climb, and that was okay, too. Just as long as she was still here.

My lips had just found the side of her neck when her phone alarm blared from the nightstand. She reached for it, but I pulled her wrist behind her back, ignoring her playful yelp as I swiped her phone and hit snooze.

"Caleb!" her muffled laugh echoed in my ears and I couldn't stop my lips from starting a trail down her neck. She squirmed a little, but I didn't let go. There was no way I was letting go.

"I have to get up," she swatted me on the shoulder. "Seriously."

"No, you don't. Ten minutes, babe. That's all I need."

Her eyes lifted up to the ceiling, but her beautiful lips still curved into a smile. "Ten minutes, huh? Where have I heard that before?"

"Okay, fine. Fifteen minutes, babe. That's all I need."

Isabelle's sweet laugh filled my ears again and I grinned down at her as she leaned into my shoulder. I took that opportunity and skimmed a hand up her back in a vain attempt at getting that tank top over her head. It didn't work because she just batted away my hands and playfully pulled out of my arms.

I slumped back on her pillow, still reaching out for her as she slipped out of bed and shimmied on a pair of those tiny sleep shorts she knew drove me up the wall.

"Ugh," I groaned. "You're gonna kill me, you know."

"I know," she laughed and leaned down to kiss my cheek before she scampered off, leaving me no opportunities to yank her back down into bed.

When she closed the door behind her, I figured I might as well get my lazy ass up and be helpful. Coffee would probably be appreciated and since my list of things to do around the house were dwindling every day, this was something I could do. But when I padded out of Isabelle's bedroom, I stopped short in front of the bathroom. I could hear her rustling around in there, probably getting ready to hop in the shower, and that gave me an amazing idea.

We might not have had a ton of time to ourselves these last few days, but I wasn't about to miss an opportunity when a golden one presented itself. Unfortunately for me, the second my hand found the bathroom doorknob was also the second the door across the hall opened.

I froze and squeezed my eyes shut.

Shit. Caught red-handed.

I could already feel my face turning red and ran a hand over my head awkwardly. Sam just cocked an eyebrow at me as if to say, *Yeah, I know what you were just about to do to my daughter, you asshole.*

His daughter might be mine, but this was still his house.

"I was just, uh," my lips pulled apart sheepishly and that was about as far as I got. There was no easy way to explain why I'd wanted to be in the bathroom at the same time as his daughter.

"It's not like I've got my head buried in the sand. I'm well aware you two lived together, you know," he called out to me and I didn't know what made me wince more: the embarrassment or the fact that his voice seemed even weaker than when I saw him the night before.

His weary eyes, so faded now they were more grey than blue, scrutinized me sharply and it took me a moment to realize just what held his focus.

"I didn't know you had that," he lifted his chin and pointed at my chest.

I glanced down and ran a hand over my bare chest, right where Isabelle's full name was inked on my skin. That tattoo had always been a badge of honor, a source of pride, and up until just a few days ago, a pain-filled reminder of what I might never have again. Now I had half a mind to walk around shirtless everyday for the rest of my life just to show it off.

"I've had it for a long time," I told him from across the hall.

A weak smile pulled at his lips and at this point, I figured, what the hell? I hadn't necessarily planned on doing this today, but I didn't want to waste any more time. So I just went for it instead.

"Hey, Sam? I've been meaning to talk to you about something," I motioned with my head to the stairs. "Do you think we could...?"

Why was I suddenly nervous? My palms got a little sweaty, my heart galloped a little in my chest, but this wasn't the kind of thing I needed to be scared of. It's not like I didn't know what either of them would say.

"Probably a good idea to do it now while she's preoccupied," he gestured toward the bathroom door as he spoke. "She'll be in there for a while."

I huffed out a laugh. Yeah. We had at least a good half hour. Probably more.

So after I skidded back into Isabelle's bedroom to grab what I needed and I had a pot of coffee going in the kitchen, I leaned up against the island as he sank down onto a stool. I smiled wistfully at Cooper, who sat next to Sam with his head in his lap. The dog had barely left his side ever since we brought him back from the emergency room, but I couldn't dwell on that now. We had some important business to take care of.

With that thought, I dug into my pocket and set the tiny velvet box down on the island. His eyebrows lifted into his forehead as he reached out to snap it open. He nodded to me when he shut the box and set it back down on the counter.

About eight years ago, I never would've pictured this moment as even a possibility, let alone a reality. Never could've imagined I'd ever get here with this man, who, at one point, I'd definitely threatened to throw into an unmarked grave.

"So," I grinned at him. "I'd like to marry your daughter. I just need your permission first."

He laughed heartily and his gaze fell to the counter, right back on that velvet box. "I was wondering when you were going to talk to me about that. It's about time."

"Right," I shook my head and leaned back on the counter. "I guess I just never thought I'd ever be in a position again where I'd get to actually ask you and where she might actually say yes."

"Ah," he just batted a hand at me. "I was never too worried about that. She's a stubborn little thing—gets that from her mom. Let me tell you, her mom just got more stubborn with age, so I guess you have that to look forward to."

And it will be a pleasure, I thought with a smile.

"And," he went on, "I have to say I'm still not convinced anyone's good enough for her, but you come pretty close. I trust you, Caleb. I hope you know that. And while I might be leaving the house to Isabelle, I'm leaving her to you. That's not something I'm doing lightly."

I swallowed hard. "I know that, Sam."

"Whatever she needs, whatever she wants, you have to make sure she gets it, okay?"

My eyes stung and I had to bit down on my bottom lip just to keep it from trembling. This wasn't how this conversation was supposed to go, but somewhere along the way, he and I had gotten to this point. Built out of necessity, at first, but it had slowly morphed into a mutual respect I'd never expected. I couldn't have been more grateful for it.

"I will," I murmured hoarsely. "I promise."

He smiled and from the looks of it, his own eyes were already misting with unshed tears. He held out a hand and I took it, clasping his hand firmly.

"You're not going to start calling me Dad, are you?"

I choked out a rough laugh and shook my head. "No. Hadn't planned on it."

"Well," he told me, his voice hitching a little as he spoke. "I'm proud to call you my son-in-law. You're a good man, Caleb. You're smart, you're loyal, and you're strong. You love my daughter. You'll take care of her and all my future grandkids. I couldn't have asked for anything more for her."

I smiled through my blurry vision and swallowed back the lump in my throat. "I won't let you down, Sam."

"I know," he nodded. "I just have one condition though."

He went on to detail his request and I found myself nodding in agreement before he even finished. It was simple enough to pull off and at the end of the day, I couldn't think of anything better. In fact, it was *exactly* the way it was supposed to be.

Now all I needed was to put that ring back where it belonged.

. . .

"Oh hell," Saul tsked and shook his head, gesturing for me to move a little closer. He made quick work of straightening my tie and patted my shoulder when he was finished. "There. You're all set now."

I tugged at my collar a little—definitely wasn't used to wearing stiff clothes like this—and winced. My gaze dropped down to my simple white button-down, black dress pants, and dress shoes that were about a half size too small. "I look okay, right?"

He huffed out a laugh, but that proud grin never left his face. "Yeah, boss. You look just fine."

I blew out a deep breath and glanced at the clock right over our heads in the hallway. We still had a little time before it was our turn, so Isabelle had run into the bathroom to check her makeup and freshen up, but my nerves were starting to get to me the longer I stood here without her next to me.

By the time I'd resorted to pacing the small waiting area for lack of anything better to do, I heard a low, familiar chuckle from the bench a few feet away from me. My eyes shot to my mom, who just shook her head at such an unnecessary display, and my lips lifted in a soft smile. I still couldn't believe she was really here, not necessarily that she wouldn't have come, but that in spite of everything, all the hurt feelings, disappointment, bitterness, and distance, we might actually be able to get to the other side of it.

"Hey, Mom," I'd told her yesterday when she answered the phone. The surprise in her voice wasn't lost on me.

"Caleb? Is everything okay? What's—"

"Everything's good," I'd laughed. *"I just wanted to tell you that me and Iz are getting married tomorrow at City Hall. Her dad wants to give her away, so that's what we're doing. Anyway, I don't know what you're doing or if you're busy, but if you wanted to come, I—"*

That was about as far as I'd gotten.

"Of course!" she'd yelled so loud I had to pull the phone away from my ear. *"Oh my God, of course I'll be there! You just tell me when and I'll be there."*

Everything about this day had to be perfect, or at least as perfect as I could make it. We wanted to do this right, which was why we'd scrambled to make it happen as soon as possible, why Isabelle was putting a little bit of distance between us right now—after all, I really wasn't supposed to see her before the wedding—and why my mom needed to be here, too. Just like it wouldn't be right to do this without Sam here to give her away, it wouldn't be right without my mom either, regardless of history.

My eyes flew to the clock yet again and I bit down on my bottom lip. Just a few more minutes and we'd be able to get inside that room. Just a few more minutes and she would finally be my wife. My heart swelled at that thought, so much that I thought it might burst, and Isabelle stepped around the corner a moment later, sending all my anxieties flying right out the door.

She smoothed down the sides of her soft pink dress as she walked toward me, a warm smile playing on her lips, and she tugged at the material on her elbow a little. The dress was just another thing that helped make this day a little closer to perfect. I'd made the mistake of suggesting she wear the dress she'd originally planned on the wearing the first time we were supposed to come here and she'd quietly reminded me that had been a maternity dress. After that, I'd wanted to punch myself a few times in the face.

Instead, she'd pulled one of her mom's old cocktail dresses from the back of her closet, ones she'd saved a long time ago. It didn't fit perfectly, but with its rouched material that hit her just above the knee and curved neckline that dipped just low enough, it was just one more piece to the day, one more way to pay tribute. Her hair fell in soft waves just above her shoulders and her makeup was simple, but pretty. She'd never looked more beautiful to me.

Isabelle closed the short distance between us and slid her hand into my waiting palm. Maybe, in normal circumstances, we would've waited a little longer, but I'd been patient enough already and it was time to finally make this woman my wife.

As we took those first steps towards the room where the Justice of the Peace waited for us, my mind flashed back to the day before:

Isabelle sat on a stool by the island, the same one her dad had vacated just a few minutes before to give us some space, quietly eating the toast I'd put in front of her and none the wiser. I watched her for a few moments, my heart racing and my stomach flip-flopping, and then I reached inside my pocket to pull out that velvet box and set it in front of her on the counter.

She froze mid-chew, her eyes locked on that familiar velvet box, and she swallowed hard as her eyes darted back up to me.

My lips lifted up and I took a deep breath. This was it. I hadn't really planned on giving it back to her just yet, but it felt right.

"It's yours, Iz," I told her hoarsely, my voice cracking a little. "I think it's time you

started wearing it again."

Her lips parted, curving up into a soft smile, and she snapped the box open to reveal the round diamond ring with smaller diamonds circling the band, the same one I'd given her eight years ago, before I went to prison, before we lost the baby, before everything crashed around us.

Isabelle pulled the ring out of the box without any hesitation and slipped it back onto the fourth finger of her left hand, right where it belonged. I stepped around the island, reaching for her and took her face in my hands.

"You still wanna marry me?"

She smiled back at me with tears in her eyes and nodded into my hands. "Yeah, I still do."

Now, as we pushed through the double doors in the courthouse, I brushed my lips against her knuckles. All five of us took our places as directed, I stood to the right of the judge with Saul on my left, and my mom stepped over to the other side as we waited for Isabelle and Sam, who were standing at the bottom of the makeshift aisle on the opposite side of the room. He murmured something in her ear, kissed her cheek, and then reached up to wipe away a tear underneath her eye.

Then he jutted out his elbow and she slipped her arm through it as they started their slow walk toward us. He managed to get her all the way to the front of the small podium where the rest of us waited until I took my cue and stepped forward.

Sam extended his hand to me with watery eyes and nodded firmly when I shook it. He glanced at Isabelle, who'd watched the exchange between us through a smile and tears, and then he stepped away so I could take my place next to her.

I grinned at her, wanting to commit every detail of this moment to memory. The curve of her lips, the light in her eyes, the way her hair kissed her collarbone, the way she squeezed my hand, the way I didn't think I could possibly love her more than I did right now, right at this moment. I'd never forget any of it.

The Justice of the Peace cut right to the chase, asked us if we were both here of our own free will, and then he jumped into the rest of it, prompting me with my vows.

I swallowed back the lump in my throat, took a deep breath, and my eyes locked on the only person who made my life worth anything.

"I, Caleb Sawyer," my voice was hoarser than I expected and I inhaled shakily, "take you, Isabelle Martin, to be my lawful wedded wife to have and to hold, for better or worse, for richer or poorer, in sickness and health, to love and to cherish till death do us part."

I didn't know how I managed to get through it all with my voice only breaking once. Those simple words felt heavy as I said them—I hadn't expected to feel that weight settle over me, the finality of it all, and the fact that despite their simplicity, I'd never said anything truer or more heartfelt. I'd carry those words with me for the rest of my life.

As Isabelle squeezed my hands and repeated her vows with tears in her beautiful blue eyes, I blinked back my own tears. This wasn't really the time for crying, but given the weight of everything we'd been through to get here, those tears stung my eyes all the same.

When it was time, we exchanged the wedding bands we'd purchased late last night after getting all our paperwork in order and I brought her hand up to my lips so I could brush my mouth against her knuckles.

From now until the day I died, my life had one clear trajectory: to spend every day and every moment possible loving this woman, taking care of this woman, and protecting this woman. She'd been part of my life since we were kids, but I'd never gotten it right until now. I'd had so many opportunities, even when we were in high school, to take what was always supposed to be mine and I'd mangled every single one of them. Until now.

I took her face in my hands and kissed her as the Justice of the Peace pronounced us husband and wife and our witnesses clapped and whooped around us. Isabelle leaned into my chest, letting me wrap my arms around her to pull her in even closer, and I murmured in her hair, "I fear no fate for you are my fate...my wife."

Isabelle laughed against my chest and wiped away a stray tear with her free hand. "Aw, you remembered!"

"How could I forget?" I grinned down at her. "I'm pretty sure I swiped that from some book in some bookstore a long time ago."

She laughed again, this time against my lips when she pressed them there a moment later. Then she pulled away so our wedding party could congratulate us. Saul pulled me into a hug, my new father-in-law shook my hand with more tears in his eyes, and my mom clung to Isabelle like her life depended on it.

And when it was time to leave the room to make way for the next people waiting, that was it. Short, sweet, and right to the point. Just me, Isabelle, our vows, and the people we wanted here with us. Just like it would've been if we'd made it here the first time.

"So what should we do now?" Isabelle asked me from underneath my arm.

Saul and Sam exchanged glances and then Sam shrugged at me.

"I think Saul and I are going to grab a bite to eat, you know? Maybe we'll see a movie or something too. Should be gone for a few hours."

In light of the day's events, it took me a second to catch up. Then a slow smile crept up my face and I practically hauled my wife over my shoulder to hightail out of the courthouse and back to the house as soon as possible.

"We'll, uh," I called out behind me as I pushed Isabelle toward the main exit. "We'll catch you guys later. You said a few hours, right?"

Saul's laugh just echoed down the hallway.

. . .

Isabelle kicked off her heels and bit down on her bottom lip as she turned back to me with a smile. I loosened my tie and closed the distance between us, gripping her hips to pull her forward.

"Hey there, wife," I grinned down at her.

"Hello, husband."

My thumbs grazed her cheeks and I brushed my mouth against her lips, savoring the way she responded and the sweet taste of our new life together. She hummed a little as the kiss deepened and as we edged closer to the bed. My fingers fumbled with the zipper on the back of her dress, but they found their course and that dress slid easily off her shoulders so it could float down to the carpet.

I drank her in, my eyes roaming up and down her beautiful curves and all I could think was, *Mine.*

"I love you," she murmured and closed her eyes as my lips started a trail down the base of her neck.

"I love you, too," I smiled into her skin. "I'm never leaving you again."

"I know."

I believed her, too. I believed this was forever. That my life hadn't really started until now. That the future had never felt so tangible or so bright. That my happiness was forever intertwined with hers.

The worst was behind us and now the rest was easy.

My hands skimmed along her sides, squeezing and lifting her up so she could wrap her legs around my waist. We collapsed on the bed, the same bed we'd spent the last few nights in together, but this time was different. I planted my hands on both sides of her shoulders and propped myself up, eager to savor this moment for as long as I could stand it.

"You okay, Caleb?"

I grinned down at my wife with her hair fanned out on the comforter and her legs wrapped around my waist, pulling me in and tugging at my belt.

"Trust me, Iz," I whispered hoarsely. "I've never been better."

Maybe I didn't completely deserve to have her in my life. All the things I'd done, the things I'd tried and failed to forget, some of them were bad enough to justify a lifetime of pain and loneliness and regret, but the way she looked at me, the way she trusted me, the way she *loved* me, it was enough to wash away everything ugly in my past. It was enough to give me a clean slate.

The moment I finally found what I'd always been looking for the day I decided to leave the club was finally here. I'd finally found the better life I never thought I'd get to have.

And hell, I was going to take it.

CHAPTER THIRTY-THREE
Best Laid Plans

Isabelle

My dad died on a Thursday.

We found him, warm in his bed, a few days after the wedding and that was it. He was gone.

All this time I'd had to prepare and it just didn't matter. Nothing can ever prepare you for the death of a parent and all the emotions surrounding it hit me like a tidal wave. They were all there: relief that his suffering was finally over, devastation from the blow, happiness that he was with my mom again, heartache at the thought of never hearing him laugh again. Each emotion hit me harder than the one before it and sometimes they hit me all once, suffocating what little control I had.

Every time that happened, though, Caleb was there. Calling our hospice nurse, filling out all the necessary paperwork, watching him get wheeled away, the funeral and all the arrangements that went with it, every time I broke down...Caleb was right next to me, lifting me up and helping me through it. I never would've survived an hour without him.

With each day that passed since the funeral, it got a little easier. Of course, it helped that we had a lot of work in front of us between the house and the shop and I was all about distractions right now.

"Hey, Iz?" Caleb's soft voice jerked me out of my thoughts and I jumped a little in my chair.

He shifted next to me on the desk and the worried lines that seemed to be ever-present these last few days crossed his face yet again.

"We can take a break," he gestured down to the paperwork scattered across his desk and then glanced back over to me with uncertainty creeping into his eyes. "We don't have to look at all this right now anyway."

I just batted a hand his way and lifted the mortgage paperwork for my dad's house off the desk. In an effort to get me out of the house, he'd gathered up all the business that had piled up at our feet since our wedding and brought me to his office in the shop instead. A change of scenery, he'd said, but it was also more neutral territory for us now, especially since we were currently discussing when and how to sell my dad's house.

"We don't have to sell it right away, you know," Caleb murmured to my right. "We could just keep making payments like I've already been doing. There's no rush, Iz."

My eyes drifted to the numbers and figures littered on the desk and shrugged. At this point, hanging onto the house didn't really matter. I had a feeling the house, at least as far as my dad was concerned, had already served its purpose. Sooner or later, I would've found that contract he and Caleb had signed eventually—he hadn't exactly made it difficult to find either.

"He wanted us to sell it," I sighed and let the mortgage papers fall back down. "I don't think he really wanted us to live there, you know? I think he wanted us to just take the money and run. Besides, we need our own place, our own life. The sooner we can move on, the better."

There was another issue we needed to talk about, too, and since we were already on the topic, I figured now was as good a time as any.

"What about my brownstone in New York?" I asked quietly and chewed on my bottom lip.

"What about it?" he frowned back at me.

I could see exactly how this was going to go because neither of us wanted to be the one to say it first. It probably would've been a good idea to have this conversation *before* we got married, but it was a little late for that now.

"Ugh," I groaned into my hands and rubbed my eyes as Caleb's fingers found the back of my neck. "We kinda rushed into all this, didn't we?"

Caleb blew out a deep breath and his hand dropped to my shoulder. "Don't worry about it, okay?"

Worrying about where we were going to live, how that would impact both my career and his business, and ultimately, how that would impact our married life didn't seem too irrational. In fact, it sounded pretty practical to me. Now my head was spinning. My career was in New York, but his shop was here. How were we going to make that work?

His lips just dipped downward like he could read my thoughts and just as his mouth opened, most likely to reassure me once again that *everything was going to be okay*, my phone buzzed in my purse.

I slipped my phone out of my purse and froze when I got a good look at the caller ID.

"What's up, Iz?"

"It's my PR rep," I told him quietly. This call was a long time coming and to be honest, I was sort of surprised she hadn't called sooner.

Caleb nodded, his forehead still furrowed in a deep line as I swiped across my screen to answer.

"Hey, Jen."

"Isabelle!" my ever-cheerful gallery-assigned PR rep chirped into the phone and I felt my teeth grinding already. I loved this girl, I really did—she was helpful, knowledgeable, efficient, and damn good at her job, but the peppiness had gotten old fast. "It's so good to hear from you!"

"Yeah, you too," I rolled my eyes a little at Caleb and he gestured to the door with his head, letting me know he was going to step outside. In light of all the conflicting thoughts roaming around right now, a little space while I had this inevitable conversation seemed like a good idea. I waved to him as he made his way out of the office with Cooper right on his heels.

I blew out a deep breath and nodded into the phone as I listened to the invevitable. "Okay. I think I can manage that. Can you give me until the end of the week?"

When I swiped across my screen again to end the call, I sat back in my chair, tilted my head up to the ceiling, and squeezed my eyes shut. Reality had finally reared its ugly head, as if it hadn't before. My eyes fell to some of the papers strewn around the desk and flipped open the folder marked, *Expansion and Marketing*. All the plans were lined out in painstaking detail, point for point, on the exact areas Caleb wanted to expand the shop, specifically staffing, a new addition on the building, and newer, more state-of-the-art equipment that would allow the shop to take on bigger and possibly more high-profile projects.

The dotted line, of course, was money. His insurance check from the break-in would only cover what he'd lost and would need to rebuild, not what he wanted to add. Who knew how long that would take?

Now, as I thought about all the sacrifices he'd made and how hard he'd scraped and fought to build this place from the ground up, I had to swallow back tears.

He needed the shop and I wanted him to have it.

I just didn't know what that meant for me in the long run. We'd stay here, buy another house, and I could work from home and send my paintings to the gallery for shows. Sure, I'd have to travel a few times a month for meetings and promotion, but what other options did we really have? I could really work anywhere...Caleb, not so much. His shop was here, so we needed to be here, too.

I swallowed hard at the thought of losing New York—the bustle of the city, the acceptance of my talent I'd found there, walking through Central Park with Cooper, vibrant, earthy fall colors and all that snow, the food—oh my God, the *food*—my cozy brownstone, the complete unpredictability of each day there, and I squeezed my eyes shut. I had a good life there, but it was an incomplete one without him.

My head jerked up when the door opened again and I smiled when I saw he had two Mountain Dews in his hand. He threw me that sexy, crooked grin he knew could make me do just about anything he asked as he set a can in front of me and leaned up against the desk.

"Everything okay?"

"Yeah," I sighed. "They're just a little anxious to get my next show scheduled."

"That's great, Iz," Caleb grinned and then that grin slipped away, probably because he saw the dejection on my face. "Isn't it?"

"No, it is," I leaned forward in the chair and rubbed my face with both hands. "It's just that I'm probably going to have to be ready in about three months just to keep them happy and I have nothing done. Nothing new I can actually *show* and thinking about getting ready for that...I don't even want to think about it right now."

"So don't," he shrugged and I just huffed out a laugh.

"Come on, Caleb," I shook my head at him and cracked open the can just for good measure. "It's not that easy. They've been pretty patient with me the way it is and that's money in our pocket, you know? It's stupid to push it any longer just because of that alone."

He nodded quietly and folded his arms across his chest. Reality was apparently setting in for him now too. I took a deep breath and decided to just dive right in. We had to talk about this sooner or later and it was better late than never.

"I can work here, but I'm going to have to go back to New York at some point to prep for the show...ugh. There's so much to do here at the shop and then we still have to—"

"Iz."

"—pack up the house and figure out what we should keep. I don't even know where to put everything and then we have to figure out where we're going to live. I mean, we can't live in your apartment here. That's just not going to work—"

He grabbed my left hand to get my attention and brought it up to his lips. "Iz, stop talking."

My mouth opened to protest, but the glimmer in his eyes stopped me short.

"I was going to wait a little while to talk to you about this because I figured you'd want to get the house straightened out first," Caleb told me, rubbing my knuckles as he spoke and straightened my wedding ring a little. "I've been doing some thinking and I think maybe we should reopen the shop in New York."

My mouth dropped open, but I couldn't find the words I needed. That must've been the opening he was looking for because he swooped in to take it.

"I figure I'm already getting enough insurance money to cover everything I already have to replace and I can either sell the building or rent it out. Either one would still open me up to getting a new building where you are."

I inhaled sharply as the true meaning of his 'idea' washed over me: *where you are.*

"What about your staff?" I protested quietly as my mind screamed. This wasn't what I wanted. I didn't need him to give this up for me. "They're like family to you and what about everything else? Can you really just pick everything up and start over? There's marketing and word of mouth and everything else that goes with it."

His lips curled up and his fingers twirled my wedding band around my finger again. "I have to pretty much start from scratch again anyway. There's no way business will ever be the same again after what happened and a fresh start somewhere else is probably the best thing I could do for the shop at this point. I did it once before and I can do it again. It's not easy and it's work, but I can do it. And my guys...I'll miss them, sure. Maybe I'll even be able to talk a few of them into coming with me, but Iz, none of that matters because it just doesn't make any sense for us to live here in Claremont when your life's New York."

"What about—"

He cut me off again, but this time he leaned forward to catch my words with his lips. I didn't let him get away with that distraction tactic for too long and pulled away as soon as I had my bearings again.

"Wait a minute," I jabbed a finger in his chest. "You can't just make a decision like this without talking to me about it first. This is huge, Caleb and I can't ask you to give up everything you've built here."

"First of all," he grinned back at me and all that did was just piss me off even more—he knew it too. "I *am* talking to you about it first. I haven't made any moves to get my shop to New York yet."

Shit. He was right. He *had* said something about that before I flew off the handle. And he grinned broadly, like he knew he had the advantage now.

"The only thing I did ahead of time was run it by Saul," he went on and held his hands up in defense. "Just the financial part, nothing else."

I cocked an eyebrow at him. "And what did Saul say?"

"He said it wouldn't be easy, but that it wasn't completely financially irresponsible either, considering the money I'm getting from my insurance," Caleb shrugged.

Of course that was what Saul would say, not like I was all that surprised. I blew out a deep breath and before I knew it, my hands were wringing together in front of me.

"And I'm not giving anything up because the reality is if we stayed here, *you* would be the one having to make all the sacrifices and I'm not just talking about traveling back and forth from New York. Let's face it, if things had worked out for us the first time, you would've been lucky to even finish school, let alone actually have a career doing what you love to do. You would've ended up working at the desk in the club's shop and taking care of our family and both of us would've been stuck—me in the club and you here in town. And all that talent you've got, Iz, it would've been wasted here. I would've let it happen then because I was an idiot, but I'm not letting it happen now."

He leaned forward to brush his thumb over my cheek and I squeezed my eyes shut. I didn't know how to argue. I didn't know if I *wanted* to argue.

"You need to be in New York, Iz," Caleb told me, his eyes glittering with love and excitement. "That's where your career is and it wouldn't be the same if we stayed here. There's no good reason to stay anyway and nothing really keeping us here anymore. Besides, the rest of it doesn't matter. The shop is just a building, Iz. I can do all the rest of it anywhere. But you...you're home to me. Wherever you are, that's where I need to be."

Tears stung my eyes and he caught them with his thumbs as he leaned in to press his lips to mine.

"Are you sure?" I whispered. The last thing I wanted was for him to make a decision like this because this was what he thought I wanted—this had to be the right decision for *both* of us, not just one of us.

"Compromise, Iz," he murmured into my lips. "That's what marriage is supposed to be about, right?"

"Yeah," I laughed. "I guess."

"So I think we should move to New York when you need to go back for your show. Until that insurance money comes through I can't do much anyway besides scout locations and start looking into a new staff. And hey, you know what? Maybe we can use this time off to work on something else too..."

He waggled his eyebrows and his fingers skimmed down my shoulder, playing with the strap of my tank top a little until I batted his hand away.

"I think we may be getting a little ahead of ourselves here," I laughed.

"What?" he frowned. "Is it so wrong that I want to see you knocked up with my kid like yesterday?"

"No," I grinned, shaking my head as I had to bat his hands away yet again. "It's not. But how about this? Let's get to New York, get through my next show, get the house ready to sell, and figure out how you're going to reopen the shop, okay? Besides, we need to go on a honeymoon somewhere in between all that and I don't know about you, but I *really* want a honeymoon."

His eyes glimmered with mischief. "You don't have to tell me twice."

"And once we've done all that," I smiled back at him and brought a hand to his face. "I think we should revisit this conversation."

"Maybe *during* our honeymoon?" he cocked an eyebrow at me.

"Maybe," I shot him a hard look and shoved him away, but I didn't struggle too hard when he pulled me right back to him again.

. . .

A few hours later, Saul pulled into my dad's driveway and I shot him a quick, grateful smile. He wasn't necessarily going out of his way by driving me back, but I still appreciated his kindness nonetheless. Now that the plan to move to New York was underway, Caleb threw himself into research, touching on just about everything from buildings within a 30-mile radius of my brownstone to how in the world he was ever going to get rid of the building he had now.

The actual building itself wasn't the problem—it was what had happened there that might be an issue to any future renter or buyer. Getting over that hurdle might mean we'd lose some money, he'd told me, and we might have to take out another loan to expand in the new location the way he wanted to, but

I already had an idea about how we could make that happen. In fact, it was already shaping up to be a pretty good business plan, at least with the little knowledge about business I had.

And because he'd been so engrossed in the details, I finally had to call in a ride to get back to the house. After all, I had some serious work to do too.

"Thanks for this, Saul," I told him as I let Cooper out of the backseat. "I really appreciate it."

"Oh, no problem," he just waved a hand. "Didn't have anything else going on tonight, that's for sure."

"Well, I'm sure Caleb wants you to hang around until he gets back, but you're welcome to stay for dinner," I grinned back at him as we stepped up to the porch. "So, I heard Caleb talked to you a little bit about moving the shop to New York?"

"Yep."

"And you think it's a good idea?"

"Well," Saul shrugged a little too easily. "It's not the *worst* idea he's ever had. Besides, family comes first, you know?"

"Yeah, I know," I smiled and bumped his shoulder. "That includes you, too. You're coming with us, right?"

He shot me a wide grin and I already had my answer. "Well, I figured I would. What else would I do? It's not like I wouldn't follow that kid into hell and back if he asked me to...which is pretty sad now that I think about it. But hey, I didn't want to impose. A guy likes to be asked now and then, you know?"

"You're not imposing on anything," I laughed. "I fully expect you to live right down the street from us if not next-door..."

I trailed off when I felt my phone buzzing in my purse. When I slipped it out and glanced at the caller ID, my lips dipped into a frown as I swiped across the screen to answer.

"Skyler?"

"Isabelle!" her frantic voice rang out in my ears and everything else faded around me. "Thank God! I've been trying to call Caleb and he isn't answering, but you're okay. Thank God, you're okay."

"He's working at the shop," I told her, my frown only deepening as I put my key in the lock. "What's going on?"

"The Warlords attacked the clubhouse tonight. Drove right up and let bullets fly through the whole place. Marcus got hit in the shoulder and Tiny's in an ambulance right now. I just...I don't know what's gonna happen now. Where are you?"

"I'm at my dad's with Saul," I whispered and glanced at him, who'd been hanging onto every word with grave intensity.

"Good. Just stay there until you get a hold of Caleb. And please, *please,* tell him he needs to call me or Dom or *someone,* okay?"

The desperation and the fear in her voice sent ice through my veins and I shivered a little from the impact.

"Okay, Sky," I whispered again. "I will. I promise."

"Okay, sweetie. Just be safe. I'll see you soon."

I swiped across my screen to end the call as we pushed through the front door and immediately called Caleb. There were a lot of reasons why he might've chosen to ignore his mom's calls, but I prayed he wasn't too caught up in work to notice who was calling him now.

Thankfully, he picked up on the third ring and I blew out a quick sigh of relief.

"Hey, Iz. What's up?"

"Caleb—"

I skidded to a stop with Saul and Cooper right behind me as I rounded the corner and got a good look inside the kitchen. There, sitting calmly at the table with a gun in his hand, was Theo Wallace.

"Iz? Is everything—"

"He's here. He has a gun," I fired off as fast as I could because now, Wallace sprang up from the table, pointed the gun directly at my head, and held his hand out for the phone.

"Iz?" Caleb called to me through the phone, but I couldn't answer.

"One move," Wallace murmured evenly, his eyes shifting to Saul as he spoke. "And I'll shoot her, got it?"

Saul's hands immediately flew up in the air and he nodded tightly. Now, Wallace's gaze settled on me and he motioned for the phone again. My breath was already coming in haggard gasps as I slid the phone into his hand, immediately jerking back to put some more space between me and the gun, as if that would matter, as if that would somehow save me.

Wallace brought the phone up to his ear. "Hey, Sawyer. Look, I'm sorry it has to be this way, but all you and your club had to do was cooperate. You didn't do that and now I don't have a choice."

He listened impassively and nodded into the phone a few times at whatever Caleb was telling him, probably more like pleading with him, and Wallace just shrugged.

"It's too late for that. Now this is happening."

With that, he swerved the gun right at Saul's thigh and fired one near-soundless shot.

I didn't even realize I was screaming until the sound of my own voice vibrated and crashed in my ears. Blood splattered the tile floor with wet, scarlet splashes. My hand clutched my stomach as the other moved to cover my mouth and I was vaguely aware that Cooper was barking. All I could do was stumble backward into the hallway because now that gun was leveled right on me again.

The attachment on the gun stared me right in the face. Nobody would hear if he shot me right now. Caleb was probably already speeding through the streets to get to me, but Wallace had plenty of time to do what he'd come here to do.

Wallace didn't miss a beat and despite the yelling I heard coming from my phone, he tossed it onto the table and stalked toward us.

"I'm sorry," he told Saul pointedly. "You weren't the one I was expecting to be with her."

Saul groaned on the floor, gripping his wounded thigh, and despite everything, he somehow managed to crouch onto all fours in a fruitless effort at getting in between me and my would-be assailant.

"Come on," Saul pushed out through gritted teeth. "You don't have to do this. You just turn around right now and get out of here. That's all you have to do."

Wallace studied Saul for a moment and then glanced at Cooper, who'd moved to stand protectively in front of me with all the hairs on his back standing on end. A low growl rumbled from my dog when Wallace dared a step closer.

"It's too late for that," he told Saul quietly, his voice still calm and chillingly even. "I'm sorry."

He raised his arm once more and fired again, this time right into Saul's other leg. More crimson blood splattered across the tile as Saul howled in agony and curled up into a tight ball on the floor. Every instinct in me screamed to go to him, to help him somehow, to protect him somehow, but now, Wallace had turned the gun to me and strode toward me with a menace I couldn't begin to comprehend.

"Caleb is on his way," I whispered, my voice shaking.

He blew out a deep breath and nodded. "It doesn't matter. I'm really sorry about this, you know. I'd always hoped it wouldn't have to come to this. He told me he would take your place, but it's just too late for that."

Something in his voice opened a door and new hope flared in me. My mind raced through all the survival tactics I'd ever been taught. He hadn't moved to physically hurt me yet, so there was still a chance I could get away or, at the very least, disarm him somehow. The way he kept apologizing, the way he seemed to be hesitating...if he really wanted to shoot me, wouldn't he have done it already? He might be a man with nothing to lose, but he also didn't look like a man who really wanted to hurt me.

What did I have on me that I could use? I had my keys, pepper spray, and my pocket knife, but that wouldn't really do me much good against a gun. Then, I remembered something my self-defense trainer had told our class. It seemed so insignificant then, but now there was nothing more important to my survival: *above all costs, do whatever you have to do, say whatever you have to say, but force him to understand that hurting you hurts him too.*

When Wallace ventured another step in my direction and Cooper crouched in front of me, ready to pounce with a low snarl, the words tumbled out before I could really think them through:

"Please don't hurt me," I whispered as I dipped my hands into my purse, groping for the first thing I could find. "I'm pregnant."

The lie rolled off my lips easily and it was worth it because Wallace skidded right in his tracks, his eyes widening as all the blood drained from his face.

"I just found out," I kept going, playing on what I hoped was a weakness. "I know you don't really want to hurt me and you have to see that you just *can't.* Please...please don't hurt me."

He squeezed his eyes shut and that was enough time for me to pull my keys out and fist them in my knuckles. Wallace blew out a breath, the internal battle raging within him, and when he opened his eyes again, his decision froze me in place. He was going to do it anyway.

My instructor's voice rang in my head: *hurt or be hurt.*

Three things happened all at once. Wallace took another step forward with the gun still in his hand and I slashed him right across the face with my keys as Cooper pounced, clamping his jaws down on Wallace's arm. He roared as he struggled with my dog, who never gave an inch, growling and snarling as he attacked. The gun clattered to the floor and I stumbled to reach for Saul, but he shook his head furiously.

"Run," he whispered.

I scrambled back to my feet just in time to see Wallace hurl my dog to the floor, sending him sliding into the wall in a crumbled heap. There was no time to react, no time to run because even though he didn't have a gun anymore, he advanced on me all the same. The murderous rage in his eyes seeped through the room, drenching me with fear and then I felt his hands crash around my waist.

Survival was the only thought running through my mind and I stomped on his right foot as hard as I could. He grunted, giving me an opening to stomp on his left foot with just as much force as before. His hold loosened for just a split second, but that was enough time for me to jerk my elbow out of his grip and rear it behind me, catching him in the cheek.

I spun away from his reach and kicked, aiming for anything and everything I could connect with. My foot slammed into his knee and he jerked from the impact, stumbling backward and giving me the opening I desperately needed. I ran for the hallway as fast as my feet could carry me, slipping only once on the blood pooling on the floor, and I almost made it too. I was almost there...so close to the front door I could almost touch it. Almost.

Hard muscle slammed into me from behind, tackling me to the floor and pinning me there, powerless and helpless to stop this from happening. I had no way out and no one that could really help me because Wallace's body had me nailed down and his hands clamped around my throat.

My hands scratched and clawed at his grip, trying and failing to maneuver out from under him, but as light-headedness began to overpower me, there was no use in fighting it. From the corner of my eye, I could see Cooper limping toward us and Saul army-crawling for the gun inch by inch, but they would both be too late.

Wallace's face, red with violent fury and streaked with blood, blurred and white spots danced across my eyes as I gasped and wrenched for air.

This was it. This was how I was going to die.

Wave after wave of images flashed through my head as my awareness dwindled and slipped away into a fog. Flickers of blue swept over my vision and my mom's beautiful, smiling face appeared. She was laughing and reaching for me and then my dad wrapped his arms around her, smiling into her hair, happy and healthy again. And then I saw Caleb. Desperately handsome and shooting me that crooked grin, pulling me in closer, sliding a ring on my finger, hovering above me, loving me.

My parents and Ava were waiting, but I wasn't ready yet.

God, Caleb. This was going to destroy him...

And then the pressure around my throat disappeared.

Air filled my lungs and I gasped, sputtering and heaving. My hands flew to my throat as I rolled onto my side, coughing and disoriented, and my eyes watered with tears. Caleb was here. He had to be. But when the haziness lifted, it wasn't Caleb I saw.

It was Theo Wallace.

Staggering backward with his chest heaving, his eyes flying alternately between his hands and my stomach as he mumbled something I couldn't hear. Horror filled his pale face and he shook his head at me, as if he couldn't believe he was standing here in this kitchen, scattered with blood and bodies at his feet.

He stumbled over Saul, finally seeming to grasp his surroundings and his current predicament, and he fumbled for his gun, still just out of Saul's reach, and tucked it behind his back. Then, he shot me one last look with torture in his dark eyes, murmuring, "I'm sorry."

A moment later, he disappeared through the back door of the kitchen and was gone.

Even though the cloudiness still hovered around me, I was still able to grasp the finality here: he may have won the physical battle, but I won the mental war.

Somehow, I managed to pull myself to my feet, sputtering through the pain in my throat and my head, and shuffled over to where Saul laid on the floor with wobbly legs to grab my phone.

CHAPTER THIRTY-FOUR
Death Rattle

Caleb

When the house finally came into view, my adrenaline spiked, raging furiously and coiling as my fears took on a more tangible shape. Dread and lethal fury raged through me for control, but neither one was an option for me right now. I had no idea what I was going to find in the house, but it didn't matter. If Isabelle was in there, I was going in there too.

I leapt out of my truck, sprinting up the walkway as I untucked my Glock from behind my jeans, and gently nudged the door open. If Wallace was still in there with them, startling him would only make things worse. I'd purposely taken my truck so he wouldn't hear me as easily when I pulled in the driveway, so bursting in here now would destroy any leverage I'd just gained.

Tilting my head to get a better angle, I peered down the hallway and found nothing. It was just too damn quiet. Cold panic spiked in my chest, tightening and choking me, but I had to push through it.

And then I heard it.

It was faint and barely above a whisper, but I still heard it: "It's okay, Saul. They're on their way. Just hang on, okay? I know it hurts."

My steps quickened into a frantic stumble toward the kitchen and I skidded into the tile at the sight of Isabelle hovering over Saul as she pressed two bloodied towels into both of his thighs. I almost couldn't believe what I was seeing. That dark, terrified part of me had fully expected to find two dead bodies and blood covering the kitchen. The fact that my worst fear *hadn't* come true, that she was living and breathing and still in one fucking piece...my knees buckled and I fell to the floor next to Isabelle, exhausted with relief.

Her face was streaked with tears, but she was still here. Thank God she was still here. I jerked her into my arms, clinging to her out of sheer desperation. And here I'd thought all my feelings of powerlessness and helplessness were behind me. All I'd been able to do was listen and scream into the phone, knowing full well I might not get there in time. Now the best I could do was hold her with everything I had.

"Iz," I murmured in her hair. "Just tell me you're okay."

"I'm okay," she nodded into my chest with a cracked voice and gripped the front of my shirt to pull me in even closer. "He left, Caleb. He just walked away."

I didn't understand what that meant and right now, I just didn't care. We could sort through the details later. My fingers found her chin and I brushed away her tears with my thumb. I needed to really *see* her, so I could really see for myself that everything was still intact and that my mistakes hadn't once again risen from the ashes to torment us.

And then I got a good look at the purple splotches smattered across her throat. My blood ran cold and for the life of me, I couldn't tear my eyes away from the bruising I found there. The pieces of what happened here began to click together and I clenched my hands around her face, willing myself to stay in control.

All I could see was red. Violent, murderous red. My lips curled into a snarl and my nostrils flared with rage. That motherfucker put his hands on her—almost fucking *killed* her. I couldn't even see straight. Slashes of black and red dotted my vision and I had to squeeze my eyes shut just to find a little bit of control. My right hand squeezed the gun in my palm, itching to pull the trigger, itching to chase after that sorry bastard, but then Isabelle's hands pressed against my chest to get my attention.

"Caleb," she whispered with wide eyes darting to me and the gun. "I called 911. You can't have that. If they find you with a gun, they can arrest you, can't they?"

Of course. A bitter laugh shook from my throat and I shook my head. Ex-cons weren't supposed to have firearms, regardless of how long they'd been out and what they'd been in for. And of course, Isabelle was thinking of me without giving any thought to herself and her own well-being. From what I could tell, she needed that ambulance almost as much as Saul did.

Oh shit, Saul.

My gaze jerked down to find him already watching me. Underneath the absolute agony was clear understanding as if he could read every single one of my thoughts. He nodded from the floor and waved to me with a bloody hand.

"Hey," he grunted. "What took you so long?"

I huffed out a laugh and reached down to grip his shoulder. "You okay? You look like you just got shot."

Saul jerked his middle finger up at me, wincing a little from the effort, and I just squeezed his shoulder.

"Thank you," my eyes drifted down to the two soiled towels covering his wounds and I swallowed tightly. "Whatever you did tonight, thank you."

"I didn't do shit," he hissed through clenched teeth, jerking his head toward Isabelle. "Your wife handled it."

My eyes flew to Isabelle, but she just shook her head and shocked the hell out of me when she gestured for the gun in my hand.

"You can't have that," she whispered again. "They'll be here any minute. Please, Caleb. Just give it to me."

I stared back at her for a moment before snapping out of it and flipped the safety on so I could hand it over. She slipped it from my hand and stood up on shaky legs, stumbling a little when she finally got her bearings.

"Take it easy, Iz," I told her, leaping up to support some of her weight.

"Just stay with Saul. They said to keep pressure on his legs," she threw over her shoulder as she shuffled down the hallway.

I swallowed hard watching her disappear up the stairs. Now, more than ever, I just wanted to be close to her. I just needed to touch her to remind myself she'd really survived this. Somehow, some way, she'd managed to survive. It was nothing short of a goddamn miracle. Saul's labored breathing yanked me out of my thoughts and I finally turned my attention back to him, taking Isabelle's place and putting as much pressure on those towels as he could handle.

"What happened?"

Saul chuckled a little and then grimaced in pain. "She told Wallace she was pregnant."

My eyes just about fell out of my head. "What?"

"Yeah," he laughed again. "You shoulda seen the look on his face. Looked a little like yours right now, too."

Now my head was swimming as I tried to pin down one coherent, logical explanation for everything that happened tonight. I knew she'd lied, but that still didn't explain the bruising on her throat.

"But what about—"

"He walked away, didn't he?" Saul shook his head. "That's all that matters. There aren't many men out there who'll knowingly kill a pregnant woman and I guess Wallace isn't one of them. He must've realized what he was doing before it was too late."

My hands clenched around the towels. That didn't mean shit. That didn't mean I wouldn't find him and make him bleed, make him feel every second of the pain and fear he'd caused her. Theo Wallace needed to die for what he'd done to her.

"Don't do anything stupid, you hear me?" Saul's quiet, pained voice called out to me even as the ambulance sirens roared from outside. "You keep your head and you take care of your wife."

I didn't have time to respond because Isabelle was already letting in the paramedics and gesturing toward the kitchen. How she was even able to move around, let alone talk, was beyond me.

The EMTs moved me aside and it was just as well because two squad cars had already parked out in the lawn. I pulled Isabelle to me and wrapped my arms around her, breathing her in and squeezing my eyes shut for just a moment as the battle raged inside me. I needed to hold her, but I needed to hunt Wallace down and beat him to bloody pulp just as much. I needed to stay calm and level-headed, but every time I looked at her, every time I saw those purple, finger-shaped bruises on her throat, the more what little control I had slipped away and fell into oblivion.

"I put it in my dad's room," she told me. "If anyone finds it, we can just say we didn't know it was there."

I nodded tightly, my eyes darting to the front door to make sure the cops approaching us were still out of earshot. "Tell the cops you didn't see him. Tell them he was wearing a mask or something, but you never saw his face."

Her lips parted in surprise, but that quickly gave way to the reaction I was expecting: disbelief and fear. She saw it in an instant—all the ways I wanted to mutilate Wallace's body, all the blood I wanted to drain from him, all the violence I always knew I was capable of. I could feel it bubbling up and rising to the surface, just begging to be untethered. All I needed was this lie.

"What are you going to do?" she whispered and I felt her tremble in my arms.

"Let me worry about that. Just do it, okay?"

Isabelle's lips curled into a deep frown and her worried eyes never left mine even as the cops approached us with their questions. Given the circumstances, I probably shouldn't have been surprised by what happened next.

She shook her head at me and murmured, "I'm telling them the truth. Deal with it."

All I could do was hold her. All I could do was kiss her hair as the EMTs wheeled Saul out of the house on a gurney. All I could do was listen as she gave the cops her statement, slow and hoarse from the attack she'd suffered, and I felt myself wither and coil at the same time with every word. I stood stiffly next to her, hanging onto every word as she described what happened in my absence—how Wallace was waiting for them, how he pointed a gun at them, how she tried to reason with him, how she fought back, how he almost killed her just five minutes before I got there, and finally, how he simply stood up and walked away.

I should've been there. I never should've let her leave the shop without me tonight. Better yet, I never should've let her leave at all. But then again, I knew Wallace still would've been waiting for us and I knew the outcome would've been very, very different.

In the end, there was no way I was leaving her just yet. Instead, I lifted her into an ambulance and slid in right next to her, never leaving her side as an EMT inspected her injuries all the way to the hospital.

When it was all said and done, after the ER doctor felt good about sending Isabelle home and after Saul safely made it through surgery, I finally pulled out my phone and called my mom.

We traded information and as each new piece of the puzzle slipped into place, my heart plummeted deeper and deeper into my stomach. God, I never imagined it would ever come to this and now, I was torn apart from the inside yet again. Nothing would ever make this right. Nothing would ever erase what happened. And with every passing moment, that low boil on my blood turned up to a simmer.

I shoved my phone in my back pocket and closed my hands over her shoulders.

"Iz," I told her hoarsely. "Lex was attacked tonight too. Two of them broke into the house and took turns beating her up. My mom said Chloe saw the whole thing."

Isabelle's hand flew up to cover her mouth and her eyes watered with fresh tears. She squeezed her eyes shut, sending a new trail of tears streaming down her face and I wiped them away as best as I could.

"Is she—"

I shook my head tightly. "She won't come to the hospital. Doc's been patching her up."

Those words hung in the air for a few long moments before I took a deep breath. What I had to tell her was something I never thought I'd ever say again, something I never thought I'd ever *want* again, but here we were.

My grip tightened on her shoulders for strength to finally say the words: "I think we need to go to the clubhouse."

. . .

My hands curled around the steering wheel and I blew out a deep breath, my eyes darting to the building that loomed just a few yards in front of my truck. The last time I'd been on this property I'd thrown my patch down on the table and walked away for good. At least, at the time I'd thought it was for good. Being here right now was just a means to an end because I didn't exactly have the manpower behind me to go after Wallace on my own.

Every time I thought that name, every time I glanced at Isabelle's throat, I wanted to just leap out of my truck and run. Wherever Wallace was hiding, like the fucking coward he was, I would find him even if I had to track him down on foot so I could wrap my hands around his neck and squeeze until all the life drained out of him.

"Are we going in or what?"

I almost laughed, but then the sound of her rough, cracked words rang in my ears. Just one more reminder of what he'd done to her. The way he'd hurt her. Hearing her voice only made my hands clench around the steering wheel tighter.

"Maybe you should stay in the truck," I thought out loud. "You should be resting for fuck's sake, not going inside the last place on earth I want to be right now."

Her pained, uneven voice called out to me anyway. "You don't have to go in there either. Maybe we should just go back to my dad's and decide what to do in the morning."

She was good. Real good. Seeing as how she knew me better than I probably knew myself, she probably figured stalling and giving me as many outs as humanly possible would somehow derail the inevitable. It wouldn't work.

"We can't go back there right now even if we wanted to. It's a crime scene, remember?"

Not to mention the fact that Saul's blood, and what I assumed was also Wallace's blood, was all over the kitchen.

Isabelle flinched at the reminder and I pushed out a heavy sigh, reaching for her shoulder. I knew I should be grateful she didn't push me away, she wasn't screaming at me—if she was able to scream—she wasn't threatening to pack up her shit right now and jump on the first plane to New York to put as much distance between herself and this mess as possible.

Something nagged at my mind with that last thought. The last thing I wanted was to be separated from her. If I went inside the clubhouse, if I gave in to all the dark thoughts firing through my mind, that's exactly what I'd be doing.

Then I glanced at my wife, at the finger-shaped marks circling her throat, and I opened the door.

The evidence of the drive-by was mostly cleaned up by now. Shards of glass and some stray bullets still littered the pavement, but it wasn't like those little pieces of scenery were exactly out of place here. I wrapped an arm around Isabelle's waist to pull her in closer and it was just as much for my benefit as it was hers. She leaned into me and pressed her face against my shoulder as I pushed through the double doors.

I couldn't hesitate. If I took a breath, if I thought about it too much, I'd back down, and I couldn't let that happen. Something tugged at my mind, something just below the surface, and I had to shove it back down again because now, Isabelle and I were standing inside the clubhouse and everyone inside was staring at us.

It wasn't like I'd expected anyone to roll out the red carpet, but in light of what had happened to Isabelle tonight, a little empathy would've been nice. And fucking human too. Instead, Marcus, with his shoulder wrapped up in a bloody bandage, curled his lips into a snarl and turned away from us completely. That seemed to be the litmus test everyone else needed because one by one, they all fell in line and followed suit.

Everyone, of course, except for my mom, who rushed at Isabelle like a bat out of hell and practically threw herself at her, wrapping her in all the motherly warmth I would've expected from her.

Some of their gazes were locked right on Isabelle's neck—Casey, in particular, looked especially stricken at the sight—but none of them moved any closer. None of them stepped up to even ask if she was okay or if Saul was okay and my steps skidded to a halt. I sucked in a harsh breath as I surveyed this room. There were so many memories here, good and bad. So much of my life had been spent here. So much of my life had been *wasted* here.

This was completely insane. And stupid. And reckless. And fucking dangerous to even be standing in this place right now.

And then my eyes fell to Isabelle, who was staring up at me with watery devastation swimming in her blue eyes. She wasn't afraid of our surroundings, though. She was afraid for me. Terrified of what I wanted to do and the hell that would follow. That coiled rage just waiting to spring loose started to slip away even before Dom stepped around the hallway and stalked toward us.

"Brother," he nodded to me and shifted his gaze to Isabelle, wincing when he got a good look at her throat. "You're okay, right?"

She nodded as the man I used to consider family pulled her into a tight bear hug and murmured something in her ear.

"Lex is my dorm," Dom informed her in a tight voice. "You can go see her if you want."

Isabelle hesitated and I could see the indecision written all over her pale, exhausted face. She wanted to see for herself that Lex was really okay, or at least, as okay as she could be, but she didn't want to leave my side either. It was all there in those eyes: the fear of what I might agree to if she left for even a second.

"I will," she promised, but shook her head. "Just not yet, okay?"

Now I stood in front of the men who I'd grown up with, and who'd also written me off without a second thought, with my anchor at my side.

I didn't know which way I wanted to be pulled.

"What's the plan?" I asked Dom. He was the only one I really wanted to talk to and the only one who had just as much stake in this as I did.

"We're going after them," he told me curtly as if it were already a foregone conclusion.

"You know Iz told the cops Wallace was the one who attacked her, right?"

Dom's demeanor shifted on a dime. His face hardened into a stony mask and any lingering concern he might've had for Isabelle evaporated. A switch flipped and it was all gone now. His cold, menacing glare shifted to Isabelle and he had the balls to actually take an aggressive step toward her.

And that was it.

That last string keeping us tethered together finally unraveled.

"Whoa, Dom," I gritted my teeth and shot my hands out to keep myself in between them. "You get any closer to her like that and we're gonna have some problems. Don't you think she's been through enough already tonight?"

Dom blinked at me and he heaved out a long, tortured sigh. I got it. I really did. I wanted to burn Wallace's body to a crisp and bury the ashes just as much as he did, but wanting to do it and actually doing it were two very different things. I hadn't let myself really think about why Isabelle had stubbornly refused to lie to the cops tonight, but it made sense now. It was the same reason she'd hidden my gun in her dad's room, too.

"I'm sorry, Isabelle," he whispered as he shuffled backward to give us some space. "I didn't mean to—"

I just shook my head. We never should've stepped foot in this place tonight. God, what was I doing?

"She gave them a statement, Dom. Told them everything. They're gonna be looking for him just as much as you are. Maybe you should—"

"I don't give a shit about the cops," Dom snapped. "It doesn't matter anyway. We'll find Wallace long before they ever catch a whiff of him."

"And how are you planning on doing that?"

He threw a look over his shoulder. "Eli's on it."

Right. Of course. Stealth tracking and all that shit. Eli's specialty.

Now that tugging and nagging at my conscience was starting to get the better of me. I didn't even need to hear Dom's plan to know it was a bad one. Given the hard stares leveled our way, I knew I probably wouldn't get too many more details as long as Isabelle was in the room.

To them, she wasn't someone who could be trusted. She was someone who'd run to the cops and potentially blown their one and only chance to put Wallace and the Warlords into the ground. And because of that, my arm just tightened around her waist.

"Look, brother," Dom's voice dropped lower and he shot another quick look over his shoulder before pressing on. "We're gonna be moving on Wallace soon and you're welcome to come with us. You have just as much a right to go as I do," he threw a pointed look Isabelle's way before looking to me again. "You *should* come with us."

About five minutes ago, I was all in. Ready to pounce with guns blazing and ready to unleash the blood-soaked, rage-fueled vengeance Wallace deserved. Now I wasn't so sure. Now I swallowed hard and turned to my wife, whose swimming eyes had never left me, who I'd promised I would never leave again. It all washed over me: the new life we were about to have together, the fresh start I'd always wanted, the family right on the horizon, and then I heard Saul's voice in my head. He was always full of sage advice and I'd brushed this one off nearly two months ago without a second thought. Now they were the only words in my head.

It's not in the stars to hold our destiny, but in ourselves.

There was no other choice but her. No other fate but her. No other life but with her.

This was the third time being with Isabelle would save my life and it wasn't just getting myself out of the club either. The night of the break-in, if I'd been alone, if she hadn't agreed to stay with me, I probably would've ran down the stairs with my gun in my hand and gotten my stupid ass shot. And if I went with the club, if I gave in, I wouldn't survive the night.

I just shook my head. It was both the easiest and the hardest thing I've ever had to do.

"I can't," I murmured hoarsely. Dom's eyes widened and I heard a strangled sound from Isabelle next to me.

I wanted to. I wanted to hop on my bike, race to wherever Eli had tracked Wallace down with Dom, and drive a knife right into Wallace's heart. I just couldn't.

"What do you mean *you can't*?" he demanded.

I lifted a shoulder and closed my eyes so I wouldn't have to see the betrayal and the disappointment on his face. I didn't know if I could stand it.

"I need to get Iz out of here," I stated softly despite the murmurs echoing from around the room at my admission. "It's not safe for either of us right now, so we're getting on a plane and we're going to New York."

I peered over Dom's shoulder to find my mom watching this scene play out with tears in her eyes and a hand covering her mouth.

"Mom," I called out to her. "You should come with us."

She gaped at us, her dark eyes darting from me to Isabelle and back to me again before she shook her head.

"I have to stay with Marcus."

Right. What other choice did she have? Not her son and only *real* family, of course. By now, Dom had had enough waiting and he unleashed.

"What the hell is wrong with you?" he bellowed in my face and all I saw was pure desperation and disbelief.

I got that, too. I knew that desperation. Knew what it felt like to listen to a gunshot through the phone and hear my wife scream. Knew how helpless I'd felt running to my truck, knowing I might not make it time, knowing that offering myself up to Wallace's mercy in Isabelle's place hadn't been enough, and knowing that if she died, it would've been because of me. I just couldn't let it own me anymore.

"He walked away," I pointed out and swallowed hard when Dom's expression contorted into barely-contained fury. "So I'm walking away too."

Dom just shook his head, as if he couldn't make sense of what he was hearing.

"We both know going after him isn't going to undo what happened to Iz and Lex. Hell, it won't make either of us feel better because we'll just end up in the back of a squad car or in a body bag. You've always been smarter than this and it's just not worth it."

Taking Theo Wallace's life wasn't worth losing either of ours. Dom had to see the truth there. Maybe he just wasn't ready to accept it yet.

"So I should just walk away too, huh? That's what you're saying?" Dom sputtered, shaking his head in fractured disbelief and ran a hand through his hair as he laughed bitterly. "How am I supposed to explain that to my wife? How am I supposed to explain to my daughter that I just let the men who beat her mother up in front of her get away with it?"

"You let the cops handle it like I'm going to. Even if that means a trial and everything that goes with it, it's better than the alternative. They're not getting away with anything."

Dom shot me a hard glare. "Isabelle giving Wallace's name tonight doesn't help Lex."

He was right. I couldn't argue against that one and all I could do was nod.

Dom jabbed a finger in my chest with all the animosity I'd never seen in him before and growled, "If you walk out that door, we're done. You might as well be dead to me if you're willing to just pretend what happened to my wife and what happened to *your* wife doesn't matter."

"If you really think I don't care about Lex, if you really think looking at Iz's throat right now doesn't make me want to tear Wallace apart..." I trailed off for a moment and sucked in deep breath. Here it was. The death rattle. "Then I guess you never really knew me that well after all. Good luck, Dom."

I didn't wait for a response.

Instead, I steered Isabelle out through the clubhouse's main doors, helped her into my truck, and drove away.

CHAPTER THIRTY-FIVE
Carry You Home

Isabelle

The Raleigh-Durham International Airport was pretty dead at this hour and it was just as well. I'd gotten us the first flight to New York I could find and if it meant taking off at two in the morning, we could live with that as long as it meant we were as far away from Claremont as possible. The craziest part about it all was that I felt safer here in this near-empty airport with strangers than I'd ever felt inside the clubhouse.

Making the arrangements was the easiest part. We'd booked the tickets, checked in on Saul one last time at the hospital, and had been able to get inside my dad's house long enough to pack a bag and get Cooper.

Now we just had to get through the hard part: actually boarding the plane.

I glanced at Caleb out of the corner of my eye. He was still hunched over in the chair next to me with his elbows on his knees and his head in his hands, just like he'd been the last time I glanced his way. At first, he'd tried to play it off like he was just nervous about flying. This was a first for him, he'd said. I knew better.

Guilt and almost manic fury ate away at him like acid, burning and singeing the very foundation of this new life we were about to embark on.

I could see all of it even though his hands covered most of his face. The deep lines on his forehead, the way his eyes crinkled and clamped shut, the pain radiating from his body. Walking away from Dom and any chance of getting to confront Wallace tonight sent him plummeting down that deep, dark rabbit hole. Part of me was just waiting for the moment he'd turn to me and tell me he couldn't come to New York, that he couldn't let Dom deal with Wallace on his own, that he couldn't walk away without putting Wallace in a shallow grave.

Those familiar pinpricks of panic spiked from my neck all the way down to my toes. This was totally irrational, right? No way was Caleb going to bail on me now. Not after everything we'd been through. Not after all the promises he'd made.

Yeah, a snide voice whispered in my head, *he's done it before.*

I blew out a shaky breath and bit down on my bottom lip.

It's not too good to be true, I mentally chanted. *He's with you all the way. You know he is.*

I wished that worked. I wished that stopped my fingertips from going numb. I wished that stopped my already burning throat from catching fire. I wished that stopped my chest from tightening like a vice.

As if he could sense the inevitable meltdown, Caleb shifted his gaze away from the floor and glanced at me with a deep frown.

"You okay?"

I blew out a jagged breath. Lying had already saved me once tonight. It was worth a second shot, wasn't it?

"Yeah. I'm just worried about Coop all by himself right now," I attempted a weak smile, but it must've looked monstrous and mangled because his lips just dipped down even more.

"We'll get him to the vet as soon as the clinic opens, Iz," he nodded and his Adam's apple bobbed one too many times as he made me yet another promise I was worried he wouldn't keep. "He'll be alright until we get there."

Right, that dark voice whispered. *We just have to get there first.*

Focusing on my dog wounded and all alone in the cargo hold of a plane wasn't exactly doing my panic any favors. The floodgates were open. The dam had burst. And I leapt up from the seat before I could stop myself. If there was even a possibility he was going to abandon me again, I didn't know if I could stick around long enough to see it.

"Iz?" he called after me.

"I just need to use the bathroom," I threw over my shoulder. God, I couldn't even look at him right now.

It would just hurt too much.

What I needed was to have this meltdown in peace. I didn't need him hovering. I didn't need him feeling any more guilty than he already did. Riding out this unnecessary panic in the sanctuary of the women's bathroom was the only option I had. But when I finally got inside a stall and shut the door behind me, my long-lost tormentor hadn't released its grip on my throat. Which sucked, considering what my throat had already been through tonight.

I sank down on the edge of the toilet with my head in my hands and willed myself to breathe.

In and out. One at a time. Just breathe.

Easier said than done.

This was so unfair. Caleb didn't deserve this. *I* didn't deserve this.

Instead I was huddled in an airport bathroom, fighting back a panic attack through gritted teeth and holding on to the end of my rope with both hands, struggling and gasping for air.

We were so close to getting on that plane and leaving this place forever. So close to finally having the life we were always supposed to have. That was what had terror rippling down my spine. That was why I was here now.

This could all get ripped away at a moment's notice. I knew that better than anyone.

. . .

Dom glanced at Casey, who sat in the driver's seat motionlessly. All he needed to do was say the word and this would start. It had taken some work and some time, but they found him and now he'd pay.

That was all that mattered.

In all his years with the club and the time he'd spent seated to the left of Marcus as his VP, he'd always been the level-headed one. The quietest one in the room. And most times, the smartest one in the room, too. It was the role he was most comfortable with and the one he'd prided himself on fulfilling.

Tonight, however, there was no room for caution. Tonight was a night for vengeance. Tonight was a night for retribution.

All he could see was Lexie's battered, bruised, and bloodied face and any sense of integrity vanished. He didn't care about himself; he didn't care about the repercussions; he only cared about how much longer he had to wait. How much more time the man responsible for his wife's brutal beating had to make his escape.

"You ready, brother?" Marcus's fiercely calm voice called out from the back seat of the van.

Dom pulled his hood over his head, readying himself for what he had to do. "Ready as I'll ever be."

Hot fury glazed his vision as his wife's terrified face flashed in his mind and his daughter's frantic wails echoed in his ears. Wallace needed to answer for what he'd done and he planned on swallowing those answers through the barrel of his Glock. He simply nodded behind him to his president, who, even though he had a hole in his shoulder, had still pulled it together long enough to come along for the ride. Unlike someone else he knew.

Dom closed his eyes and pushed all those distracting thoughts away. The Caleb he'd grown up with, the Caleb he'd once trusted more than any other man in the clubhouse, would've never cut and run. Would've never walked away. That man was long gone now.

"Let's go," he jerked his head toward the back entrance of Ringers, probably the dive bar to end all dive bars in Memphis and one of the Warlords' frequent pit-stops in between runs, and then opened the passenger door.

If Wallace thought holing up in a public place would save him somehow, he was stupider than Dom gave him credit for.

One by one, they all filed out of the two black vans they'd hopped in the moment Eli tracked a few of the Warlords' members here to this bar on the outskirts of Memphis. Even if Wallace wasn't here and all they found was a few Warlord cuts, they weren't leaving until someone talked. Whatever he had to do, whatever methods he had to use, it was just a means to an end if it meant seeing Wallace swimming in a pool of his own blood.

Even as they stalked toward the back entrance, something nagged at his mind. There really wasn't a plan other than to go inside and gun Wallace down. After that, making a clean getaway wasn't really on the table yet. Each man approaching the bar had a reason to want Wallace and all the Warlords dead—starting from the way the Warlords had manhandled their business associates to the break-in at Sawyer Auto Repair, the drive-by attack on the clubhouse, and finally, the attack on the VP's family in his own home.

In the outlaw world, this was the only justice Dom knew. The only justice that made sense and it had been a long time coming. And so, he buried that nagging feeling deep into the recesses of his mind and moved forward.

The back entrance was locked, but Casey took care of that in under a minute as he jimmied the lock with well-honed skills to let them in. Dom went in first—this was first and foremost his operation—with Marcus right behind him. Casey, Doc, ZZ, and Eli followed suit, filing in right behind him as they snuck down the dark hallway where vengeance waited.

With his gun drawn and his heart thundering in his throat, Dom edged around the corner, stepping lightly on the grimy tiled floor, as the bar finally came into view. It was almost too good to be true because, seated on a bar stool with a beer in his hand and deep, red slashes across his face, was Theo Wallace. To his left sat Rubin Lloyd, Wallace's VP, and to his right, Antone Jeffreys, the Sergeant-At-Arms. Scattered all around the bar were a multitude of Warlord cuts.

Wallace shifted in his seat and his face dropped in a frantic mixture of disbelief, panic, and shock. He clearly hadn't been expecting any visitors tonight. Oh well.

Just as Lloyd and Jeffreys turned in their seats to see what was going on, Wallace held up a desperate hand. All sense and reason left the building the moment Wallace began to speak.

"Now listen, Fletcher, I didn't—"

Dom didn't need to hear anything else. Instead, he raised the gun in his hand and fired.

. . .

Isabelle

I splashed some water on my face and squeezed my eyes shut. That icy shock helped a little bit, but it wasn't quite enough to do the job. What I really needed was warmth. What I really needed was my husband's strong arms wrapped around me.

Ugh. This was so stupid. What was I doing in here anyway? Our flight would start boarding in less than ten minutes and here I was, swallowing back a panic attack with about as much luck as if I'd attempted it in front of an oncoming train.

This had to be the end of it. I couldn't sit in this bathroom anymore and wallow. Caleb wasn't leaving. Caleb wasn't leaving. Caleb wasn't leaving.

Maybe if I just thought it over and over again in my head it might actually be true.

We were leaving. We were leaving. We were leaving.

I blew out a deep, tortured exhale, wiped my face with a paper towel, and wrapped my thick scarf around my neck again to hide the purple bruises there. At this point, Caleb was probably pacing a hole in front of the bathroom. Probably tearing through the short hair on his head and rubbing his scratchy goatee anxiously. I smiled a little at the thought of him waiting for me, worried for me—what was I still doing in this bathroom?

Everything was going to be fine.

That delusion carried me all the way out of the bathroom where I skidded to a stop.

Our seats were empty.

Caleb was gone.

I sucked in a breath, my eyes scanning the boarding area frantically for some evidence that he was still here, but all I could find was our two bags on the floor, right where we'd left them. Tears stung my eyes and all the air left my lungs in one fell swoop.

That panic I'd worked so hard to bat down washed over me once again and I swallowed back an agonized scream. All I wanted to do was curl up into a ball and wail. Or maybe just run until all this disappeared. It just didn't make sense. How could he—

"Iz?"

I whirled around at the sound and my lips parted as I flailed for words. Caleb stood just 15 feet away from me with a Mountain Dew in one hand and a bag of pretzels in the other. Everything rushed over me all at once in waves: he was still here, he hadn't left me, I wasn't alone, and he was staring at me now with one eyebrow cocked like he was trying to make sense of all this himself.

My lungs finally revolted and gasped for air as one hand braced the rest of my body against the wall behind me. God, I was so stupid. How could I have ever doubted him?

"Iz?" Caleb tried again, this time venturing a few slow steps toward me. "What's wrong?"

"Nothing," I lied. The smile I pressed on my face wouldn't have fooled anyone. And it certainly didn't fool my husband. "Hey, don't you know you're not supposed to leave your luggage just sitting out like that?"

He glanced over his shoulder before shooting me a wolfish grin. "What? And make all these people nervous?"

Fair enough. There were literally no people around to make nervous, let alone even notice us. That, I supposed, was one of the few benefits of red-eye flights.

"Where, um, where did you go?"

His eyes narrowed ever so slightly as he finally closed the small space between us.

"I thought you might need to take one of those pills before we got on the plane, so I got you this," he held up the bottle of soda in his left hand, "and then I wasn't sure if you should take one on an empty stomach, so I got you these," he held up the pretzels in his right hand and my cheeks flushed with embarrassed heat.

Shit. I'd been having a meltdown and on the verge of sprinting for the nearest exit to look for him when all he'd been doing was taking care of me. Again. Maybe I really did need to take one of those anti-anxiety pills before we got on the plane.

I tried nonchalance on for size, but it didn't quite stick. "Thanks. That was really sweet of you."

He shifted his weight from his bad knee to his good one and lifted an eyebrow. "You're not okay, Iz. Why?"

As if I could ever keep anything from him.

I blew out a shaky breath and let it fly: "I thought you left."

He frowned and he glanced around like he was trying to figure out just where I thought he'd gone off to. "What do you mean?"

As soon as those words left his lips, his eyes widened with sharp awareness. It was right on the tip of my tongue to reassure him, but what was I supposed to say? *Sorry, honey. I thought you deserted me again. My bad.*

Suddenly, his hands were shoving the soda and the pretzels inside my huge purse. A moment later, his strong arms enveloped my shoulders and crushed me to his chest. His lips were in my hair, on my forehead, brushing my cheek, and finally my lips before I even had a moment to catch my breath. That was all the reassurance I needed.

Our heads jerked up at the announcement over the intercom: "Now boarding United Airlines flight 1311 to New York City."

Caleb's eyes found mine and his lips curled up. He leaned down to kiss me and murmured against my lips, "Let's go."

All I could do was follow his lead. He grabbed my hand and led me over to the waiting area so we could get our carry-ons. The rest of it seemed to happen in slow motion: the attendant scanned our tickets, we walked through the gate, stepped onto the plane, and found our seats. It was really that easy.

It wasn't until the plane hit the runway that I felt Caleb squeeze my hand from the seat next to me. My eyes immediately snapped to find his head pushed back against the seat with his eyes closed as the plane's engine roared to life.

"Iz," he mumbled above the sounds of the plane gearing up for take-off. "Tell me it's okay."

My lips parted and it took me a second to grasp the full weight of what he was asking me. He needed permission to leave. He needed reassurance that he'd made the right choice. And he needed it from me.

I leaned to my right until my head rested against his shoulder so he could hear me clearly. He'd been so strong up until now and I needed to carry him home.

"It's okay," I whispered as the plane shuddered, lifting us into the air and sending us soaring into the night sky.

Caleb finally opened his eyes and I gestured to the window. There wasn't much to see just yet, but even in the darkness, the entire landscape seemed to fade away. The trees, the highways, the houses, the open parking lots, all of it dimmed as we finally left North Carolina behind until only the city lights blinked up at us.

"Hey," I hummed into his shoulder. "I've been thinking and I think we should take the money we get from my dad's house and put it into the shop."

His head snapped to the side, eyes wide with surprise. "What?"

"You heard me," I laughed.

Caleb's eyebrows lifted high into his forehead. "That's an awfully big decision to make without talking to me about it first, don't you think?"

"What do you mean? We *are* talking."

His lips quirked in amusement and he kissed my forehead. "You sure?"

"I think it's a pretty good investment—my dad would agree. Besides, it's your money too, Caleb. Compromise, right?"

"Right," he smiled into my hair.

We watched the North Carolina landscape drift further and further away until I heard Caleb singing softly and completely off-key.

"*Start spreading the news...I'm leaving today.*"

A laugh erupted from my throat and I ran a hand over my face.

"Oh God," I muttered. "Not this again."

He just lifted a shoulder and waggled his eyebrows at me. "*I want to be a part of it, New York, New York.*"

"Stop," I laughed. "Seriously. You're embarrassing me."

Caleb's eyes flashed evilly. "*These vagabond shoes...*" he bumped my shoulder, "come on, Iz, you know the words."

"Shut it."

Now he rocked a little to the music in his head. "*I want to wake up in a city that doesn't sleep.*"

"I swear to God I'm going to smother you with a pillow when we get home."

His lips brushed my forehead and he laughed against my skin. I just couldn't help myself. I leaned into him, letting my chin rest on his shoulder and smiling as he kept right on singing softly in my ear.

"*These little town blues are melting away...*"

. . .

Wallace slumped to the floor in a bloody heap and hell followed.

There was no time to react, no time for Dom to even raise his Glock to Wallace's VP because the barrel of another gun leveled right at him. An explosion rang in his ears and heat shot through his right shoulder. He crumbled to the sticky floor, already wet with Wallace's blood, and he closed his eyes to the cacophony of roaring gun blasts, shattering glass, and screaming bouncing off the bar's walls.

Air whooshed around him as a body collapsed just inches away from him. Dom turned to find Marcus's lifeless black eyes staring back at him, blood gaping from the hole in his head. Shock and horror stunned his limbs, kept him locked in place on the floor as the bullets whizzed through the room. More shouts. More cries for help. More blood splatter. More limbs and bodies falling to the floor.

Finally, Dom managed to roll onto his side, where he came face-to-face with the man he'd just murdered in cold blood. Doc dropped to his knees, covering the pooling wound in his chest until he fell face-down at Dom's feet. Another Warlord cut fell to the floor. Dom turned his head as the sound of sirens blaring echoed from the front door and just grew louder with every thundering beat of his heart.

He somehow crouched onto all fours just in time to witness Eli and another Warlord cut trade bullets to the stomach. His wet fingers groped for a gun, any gun, and when he finally found one, he snapped it to his right, firing aimlessly into the abyss of bullets and blood. Smoke fogged the space above him, but he continued to fire until the gun clicked, empty and useless.

Dom tossed the gun aside and grabbed the first bar stool he could find for cover, but he was too late. Fire exploded in his foot, his side, and his left shoulder. Agony split his body in two as he tumbled back down to the floor, slipping and sliding around the glass and puddles of crimson.

Somewhere above him, there was shouting. More gunfire. More explosions.

ZZ's body lay slumped over a table, right next to the Warlord he'd just killed. Casey crawled toward the front door with one arm—the rest of him covered in blood from the waist down. His bleary eyes scanned the room for any Horsemen cuts, but all he could see was red. All he could hear was screaming.

Was that his voice? Was it someone else's?

Suddenly, light poured in through the front door and shouts echoed from the back hallway.

"Hands up!" a voice boomed from behind him. "Weapons down or we'll fire!"

What was the point? Was anyone else even alive?

Hands groped his neck to check for a pulse and he choked, mumbling incoherently and numb with agony. It was too much. Too much blood. Too many bullets.

Suddenly he was suspended in the air, settling back on something soft and cool, a stark contrast from all this heat.

Then consciousness reared its ugly head. All he could think was, as he was rolled out into the parking lot on a gurney and lifted into an ambulance, that this was the last time he'd ever see the sky as a free man.

It was a really shitty night, too. The city air clouded the sky, hiding all the stars he desperately wanted to see one last time.

As the ambulance doors shut, all he could see was Lexie. Chloe. *This* was the consequence. *This* was the price.

Everyone was gone now. The life he'd known. The family he'd tried and failed to protect, to avenge. Everything that mattered had been taken from him in a fiery string of bullets.

He'd done this.

He'd brought this on himself.

There was no comfort here. No absolution. Now that it was over, he wished he could go back to the moment where he'd had a choice so he could make a different one.

But now, that moment was gone too.

. . .

Isabelle

I opened the cab door and slid out, finally putting my feet on solid ground, finally in front of my brownstone. With its rows of polished windows, high planes and arches, and age-washed brick, it really was a sight for sore eyes. I'd forgotten how much I'd missed this place and how much I loved it until it was right in front of me again.

The cab door slammed behind me as Cooper hobbled around the side and limped up the steps, waiting for us at the top as if to say, *Come on, guys. You're literally killing me here.*

A low chuckle echoed around me and I turned to find Caleb with his head ducked under the passenger side window as he handed the driver some bills. Nerves shook through me as Caleb slung his bag over his shoulder with one hand and gripped the handle of Cooper's empty crate with the other. His eyes lifted to my building and they widened, awestruck at the sight before him.

His lips parted and his chest heaved.

I knew what he was thinking. It was written all over his handsome face, the same face I'd get to wake up to every morning and fall asleep with every night.

Nothing about our lives together had played out the way we'd planned—not even this move to New York—and that was okay. We still made it. Finally.

I wasn't so sure I believed in things like destiny and fate, but I felt the weight of them now as the inevitable enveloped me and held me close. This was where I was always supposed to be. Right here, with this man, in this city.

I climbed a few steps, ready to reach for the rest of my life.

"Hey," I smiled at him from over my shoulder and gestured with my head to the front door. "You wanna do this or what?"

Caleb's lips curved up into that crooked grin I knew so well and nodded. Then he jumped up the stairs and followed me inside.

EPILOGUE

Three Years Later

Caleb

I glanced at the stack of paperwork from over my laptop and sighed. Well, I could stay a little bit longer and finish going through the damn things or I could say screw it, go home, and take care of it on Monday. I blew out a deep breath, mentally ticking through all the work I still needed to do: ordering supplies, finishing up payroll for the month, tweaking next week's schedule, and calling the buyer for some new equipment I had my eye on. My eyes darted to the wall right next to my desk and my lips lifted at the sight.

Bright, vivid colors splashed the wall as the images came into clearer focus. I dragged my gaze from one to the next: a few round circles with dog ears scribbled with black crayon, some green trees, a few that were just colorful scribbles, a yellow sun shooting out rays, three stick figures, then another one with four stick figures.

Screw it.

I was going home.

Getting ready to leave didn't take long—I shut my laptop, filed the few forms I'd managed to finish today, grabbed my coat, and locked my office behind me.

"Finally heading out, huh?"

I glanced over my shoulder and shrugged. It was getting easier and easier to leave early and I didn't feel guilty about it at all.

"Don't worry, boss," Saul laughed and clapped me on the shoulder. "I'll hold down the fort for the rest of the day."

"Aw, come on," I shook my head, rolling my eyes up to the ceiling. "I'm leaving an hour early. Not a big deal."

He shifted his weight a little and shuffled toward the front office of the shop with that familiar double-limp hobble. After two surgeries and months of physical therapy, Saul wasn't exactly back to his old self, at least not physically, but everything was still a work in progress. Just like the shop.

Now Saul practically pushed me out the door and laughed in my face.

"Go on now," he half-ordered, half-chuckled. "Get outta here. I mean it. I don't want to see your face in here all weekend, you hear?"

I mock-saluted him as I shrugged on my coat. "Got it."

A few of my guys threw a wave my way, some of the others called out to me to enjoy my time off, and the rest were too busy finishing up their projects for the day to notice me sneaking out early—just the way I liked it.

Heading outside, I zipped up my coat and shoved my hands in my pockets to keep warm just in time to catch myself from slipping and falling right on my ass.

"Shit," I muttered under my breath and pounded out a quick, frustrated text to Saul to let him know somebody needed to get out here with a shovel and some salt before someone hurt themselves.

Once I had my bearings again, I set off down the street to start my four-block trek home with fat snowflakes floating down from the sky and coating my shoulders. It had been pretty damn cold here earlier this week, but today, the cold was tolerable. That was probably the biggest adjustment for me: the bitter, snowy New York winters.

The first time I ever saw a foot of snow piled outside our door, I just about shit my pants. Not to mention the fact that even though I had a truck for the shop, driving in snow and walking around in snow were two very different things. Or the fact that I could only ride my bike about six months out of the year if I was lucky...yet another adjustment.

New York might as well have been a foreign country, but I was a fast learner and I had the best teacher. Once I got the hang of the city's flow, I relished life here. There was always something new, always some restaurant to check out, always some band playing somewhere we could see, always some new adventure in the park, always something moving and changing and it didn't take me long to fall in love with it.

After 30 years stuck in a town where nothing ever happened, the city was a welcome change.

Luckily enough, I'd managed to catch a building right at the perfect time about four months after we moved here. It wasn't exactly the size I'd been hoping to find and it'd needed more than a little spit-shine to get it ready for business, but the location was what sold me. This way, I was always close by and at the end of the day, that was what really mattered.

Finally, I turned down our street and took the steps two by two to get inside faster. The snow was really starting to come down now and I had to stomp my feet a few times to get all the build-up off my boots as I unlocked our front door. When I shut the door behind me, I waited. Depending on the day, my welcome could vary. Sometimes I had so many arms wrapped around me I could barely move. Sometimes I was treated a little indifferently if I was interrupting. Sometimes I just heard their voices calling out to welcome me home.

I didn't find any of those welcomes now. The whole place was dead silent, which was particularly disconcerting considering Cooper usually barked his ass off when I came through the door.

It was just too damn quiet.

My heart pounded as I slipped off my snow-covered boots and coat. Swallowing back some irrational panic didn't really help either. There was probably a logical explanation for why I still stood here by myself.

And I didn't wait to find out either.

I swiveled around to the kitchen, only to find some leftover drawings of motorcycles and crayons sitting on the table. Okay, next option. I took our stairs two-by-two, ignoring the stiffness in my knee, and headed right for the nursery, sticking my head in the doorway and finding it empty yet again. My lips curved up a little—this room always managed to calm my nerves.

Pale yellow walls cocooned the room with a crib against one side of the wall and a comfy love seat on the other. Gender neutral, Isabelle had called the paint color, and as always, her foresight was spot-on. Books were piled high on a bookshelf right next to the rocking chair, which was exactly where I'd half-expected to find them. That was still his favorite hang-out even if this wasn't really his room anymore.

I slapped my hand on the door frame in frustration and let my eyes drift over the delicate, winding mural of two intertwined trees with their branches reaching out above the crib. That sight would never get old.

There was one more place I needed to try before I could really let the panic set in and I tip-toed down the hallway until I could push our bedroom door open ever-so-slightly. My breath left my lungs in one long sigh of relief.

Of course they were still here. Where else would they be?

Isabelle was nestled into her pillow, her hair fanned out around her like something out of a dream. Beautiful. Peaceful. Mine. And there, curled into her arms was the reason I couldn't love her more. He shifted a little in her arms and blinked back at me as I padded closer.

"Hi, Daddy."

I smiled down at him and reached out to push some blonde hair away from his forehead. "Hey, Connor."

He shot me a wide, gap-toothed grin even as I moved my attention to his mother, whose eyes, the same eyes I saw mirrored in our son, watched this interaction with a softness I was seeing a lot of these days.

"Hey, Iz," I murmured as my lips found her skin and she smiled into my kiss.

By now, Cooper finally remembered he had a job to do and leapt off the bed, huffing and puffing a measly bark until I ruffled the fur on top of his head.

"You're home early," she mused, staying right where she was, all cuddled in the warm blankets and pillows even as Connor reached out for me to pick him up.

"Just wanted to get out of there and get home, I guess," I grinned as Connor wrapped his arms around my neck.

"What did you guys do today?" I asked him.

"Mommy tired," he informed me in that sweet little voice I'd never get enough of.

I glanced at Isabelle, who just shrugged against the pillows like this was really nothing new, which in retrospect, really wasn't, and I turned my attention back to Connor. "Yeah, but you remember why, right?"

He nodded, reaching out to tug the scruff on my chin. I laughed and gently pried his fingers away.

"What else did you do?"

"Play with Tooper. Read book. Legos," he rattled off easily and reached for my goatee again even when I batted his hand away. "Ice cream!"

I laughed and glanced at Isabelle. "Ice cream? Today?"

"I know," she just rolled her eyes at me, but that soft look in her eye bounced right back when her gaze shifted to Connor. "Mommy had hot chocolate instead."

She tossed the comforter back, but that was about as far as she got. I shifted Connor to my hip a little more and pulled her up until she slid out of bed carefully, and a little stiffly too, I noticed. As soon as she had two feet on the ground, my arm slid up her hip and I smiled when her swollen stomach pressed into my side.

"You feeling okay?"

She nodded, her face flushed just enough to let me know this exhaustion was nothing but normal. Nothing to be worried about. I leaned down, brushing my thumb across her cheek, and kissed her before Connor tugged on my chin again.

"Potty, Daddy," he whispered in my ear.

"Okay, buddy," I whispered back. "Thanks for telling me this time."

He just nodded shyly. There was no need to rehash the epic potty training fail we'd had the night before that ended with me covered in piss from the waist down and Isabelle laughing her ass off.

"Well, I think this is as good a time as any to get dinner going," Isabelle reached out to scratch Connor's belly. "Hey, Con-man, tell Daddy what we're making for dinner."

He didn't hesitate.

"Pizza!"

My shoulders shook with laughter and I smiled as Isabelle and Connor exchanged kisses before she started out of the bedroom with Cooper right on her heels.

"Pizza *and* ice cream all in one day?" I told him, cocking an eyebrow at him. "You must've been really nice to Mommy, huh?"

He nodded slowly with a faux-innocence that had me wondering if maybe there was a little more to their day than what they both let on.

"Oh hey, Caleb," Isabelle called over her shoulder, her voice catching as her hand rested on the doorframe. "You got some mail today."

Judging by the way that softness in her voice dropped into something more sober, I had a pretty good idea what mail waited for me in the kitchen.

"Dom?"

She just nodded, shooting me a weak, supportive smile, and disappeared down the stairs. I blew out a deep breath and squeezed my arms around my son, reminding myself once again that I was a lucky son of a bitch to be here right now.

Dom's letters had started about six months into his sentence, right after he'd gotten released from the medical ward, and right after my first visit with him. From what I could tell, and the little he gave away in his letters, I was pretty much the only one he had any regular contact with outside of his lawyer. Lex had visited regularly when he was still in the hospital, but once you get a 25-to-life sentence with little hope of parole, your marriage doesn't really have a leg to stand on.

His letters were disorganized, muddled with random musings about everything from prison politics to prison food most of the time and other times, he wanted details about my family and my business, but regardless of topic, they kept coming. That was what I needed to focus on.

They didn't come often, but when they did, I made sure to get my reply in the mail the next day. I guessed it had less to do with what was left of our friendship and more to do with the sharp reminder of what could've been, of what our lives could've been like if we'd made different choices that night, and neither of us wanted to forget that.

But, for now, I'd have to shelf that letter until after we put Connor to bed. Reading Dom's letters was better done when I could take a few moments to myself and read them in solitude where my family couldn't see the emotions that came with reading them.

"Daddy," Connor tugged on my chin to get my attention. "Havta go *potty*."

"Okay, okay. Sorry."

Once we were in the bathroom, we went about our normal routine. Connor didn't really want much help from us at this point, but since he wasn't completely ready to be in the bathroom by himself yet, I leaned up against the door, trying to give him as much space as possible. I stared at the tiled floor and swallowed hard, thoughts of prison, orange jumpsuits, and losing life as you knew it flashed across my mind. It wasn't exactly easy to get down there, but I tried to make the trip a few times a year. It looked like I was going to have to make that trip again sometime in the near future.

"Daddy?"

I glanced up and grinned at Connor, who was sitting on his little potty chair and staring up at me in furrowed concentration. "Yeah?"

"I get kitty soon?"

A hard laugh escaped my throat and I shook my head. Persistent little shit.

"You know what Mommy said and she said we have to wait until after your sister gets here. Just a couple more months, buddy. You remember what I told you?"

He grumbled a little under his breath and shifted on the seat a little as he shot me his patent stink eye. I crouched down to get a better look at him.

"We always do what Mommy says because Mommy's always right."

Isabelle also had a theory that once the baby was here in a few months, Connor would completely forget about wanting a cat. She was probably right about that, too.

Connor's head tilted to the side and he giggled, shooting me that toothy, adorably dimpled grin that made me melt into a puddle at his feet.

"And hey, you know what?" I went on, pushing off the door and crouching down to his level. "Guess who you're gonna see tomorrow?"

Connor hesitated for a second, contemplating what was happening tomorrow that he needed to remember and then his blue eyes flashed with excitement. "Grandma!"

"That's right," I laughed and helped him pull his pants back up. "Grandma's gonna come over and play with you while Mommy gets some work done."

At first, my mom was too swallowed in grief to do much besides cry and drink herself into a coma, but the second we found out Isabelle was pregnant, she changed her tune pretty quickly. Just a few weeks later, I was helping her move into an apartment a few miles away from our brownstone.

Since then, my mom and Isabelle had found an easy rhythm, falling back into the routine they'd had years ago when they worked together, and shared a schedule that worked for everyone: Isabelle stayed home with Connor every other day of the week and my mom babysat on the odd days Isabelle went to her studio a few blocks away to work.

I wasn't completely sold on this happy-family act my mom played at every time she was here, but if she wanted to have a relationship with my son, I wasn't going to be the one to stop her.

"Still want kitty, Daddy."

Nothing if not stubborn and persistent—the best and worst of both his parents, I supposed. With a sigh, I lifted him up to the sink so he could wash his hands and I wondered how many times I'd have to have this conversation. Not necessarily *this* conversation, but given that he was only two, I had a feeling the advice I was about to give him was the same advice I'd be handing out for years to come.

I sat him down on the sink to face me so I knew I had his attention.

"I'm gonna tell you something really important, okay, Con?"

He nodded seriously, his eyes wider than the rest of his head, and I had to bite back a smile.

"Everything worth having in life comes with patience. You have to work for it and you have to wait until the time's right."

Connor studied me carefully, like he was actually processing what I'd told him, but I knew most of it flew right over his head.

"You wanna go help Mommy make pizza now?"

He nodded furiously, reaching up to me so I could lift him off the sink. He took off, skidding right for the stairs and I thought my heart just about leapt out of my throat.

"Slow down, buddy!" I called after him.

Connor glanced over his shoulder, shooting me a look I was all too familiar with, and slowed down just enough to keep from tumbling down the stairs and hitting every step on the way down. My eyes closed and I scrubbed both hands over my face before I followed in his wake.

I rounded the corner to the kitchen, stopping short and leaning against the threshold to give myself a moment to take it all in. My wife lifted our son up onto a stool so he could hover over the counter. She kissed the top of his head and he patted her pregnant stomach with a wide grin. Then they got to work, pushing the pizza dough around the pan with their palms, their heads leaning in with twin expressions of determination.

Sooner or later, I'd have to get over this lingering feeling that my past would blow up in my face again and something would happen to them because of it.

The past would always stay right where it was—in the past.

Everything I'd ever wanted was here in this kitchen. I had the love of my life, a beautiful, healthy son, and a daughter on the way. What more could a man like me possibly hope for?

Nothing, I thought as I pushed off the wall to join my family. *Absolutely nothing.*

About the Author

K. Ryan is a former English teacher, who graduated from the University of Wisconsin-Stevens Point in 2009. When not writing, she's either binge-watching something on Netflix, running, reading, or cheering on the Packers. She lives in the Green Bay area with her crazy-supportive boyfriend and the best decision of her adult life, a not-so-stray cat named Oliver.

Follow her on Twitter, Instagram, and Facebook or visit her website, authorkryan.com, for updates and news.

Check out the bonus materials section on her website for two short prequels about Caleb and Isabelle in high school.

Also by K. Ryan

Finding Emma

The Carry Your Heart Duo

Carry Your Heart

Carry You Home

Acknowledgements

First of all, I think a book is really only as good as its cover, so I owe a huge thank you to Christa at Paper and Sage. Not only did you create something that was vibrant, full of life, and beautifully eye-catching, but you also managed to improve on the original. Thank you so much for your patience and your diligence.

I know I mentioned my first readers in my dedication, but I'm going to do it again here. Without your constant support through these last few years, Caleb and Isabelle really wouldn't be here. I don't really want to think about where I'd be either.

To all the bloggers who read and reviewed *Carry Your Heart*—thank you so much for taking a chance on a rookie author and helping my book find its audience.

To Missy—thank you so much for your patience. I went back recently and re-read that four-in-the-morning, rambling mess of an email I sent you and I thought to myself, 'Wow, I can't believe she even replied to me'. You gave me the kick in the butt I needed to finish this and finish it right. I'll always be grateful to you for that.

To Morgan—thank you for your ever-present enthusiasm. You've always been one of my loudest supporters and I've appreciated it every day since. Your love for Caleb and Isabelle (and the way you rooted for them all this time) lets me know I might have done something right.

To Ally—thank you for your willingness to work around your schedule for me. Your constant feedback really made a huge difference in the way I looked at my own writing. I don't know how long we've been exchanging documents—a few years, maybe??—but I think this is a good habit. Thank you so much for being my writing buddy.

To my mom—I know this genre isn't exactly your thing and I know you'd probably prefer if I wrote different 'types' of books, but thank you for never telling me not to and for analyzing and discussing this with me like we were in a book club ;) Thank you for supporting this crazy undertaking of turning two books into one.

To Michael—I know this one was really stressful for both of us. December buried us alive and it sort of felt like it was never going to be over, didn't it? Thank you for wanting me to do this just as much I've wanted to and pushing me to continue. Thank you for working so I could write.

www.ingramcontent.com/pod-product-compliance
Lightning Source LLC
Chambersburg PA
CBHW030617250626
47154CB00006B/1821

9780692634479